T0370441

# The
# TRACKER

## WILLIAM WRIGHT

authorHOUSE®

*AuthorHouse™*
*1663 Liberty Drive*
*Bloomington, IN 47403*
*www.authorhouse.com*
*Phone: 833-262-8899*

*Published by AuthorHouse 05/21/2024*

*ISBN: 979-8-8230-2607-9 (sc)*
*ISBN: 979-8-8230-2605-5 (e)*

*Library of Congress Control Number: 2024908547*

*Print information available on the last page.*

*Any people depicted in stock imagery provided by Getty Images are models,*
*and such images are being used for illustrative purposes only.*
*Certain stock imagery © Getty Images.*

*This book is printed on acid-free paper.*

# DEDICATION

I would like to dedicate this book to God, without him i wouldn't be where i am now. God has got me threw som very hard times recently. My two children Miranda and Alexander who helped me both financially and emotionally. Patterson and Gimlin for the footage they took popularizing Big Foot in pop culture. last but certainly not least is my mother, who left us to early. I wish you could have met your grandchilden and gotten to see how far i have come. I love you mom!

William

# ACKNOWLEDGMENT

I would like to thank God and Jesus Christ for giving me a new path in my life to walk. To my son Alexander who gave me money and time to help write this book and keep me moving in the right direction. Thank you son! My daughter who gave me support and love to keep me moving forward. My brother Glen who was a inserperation for the Tracker. Thank you all, I love you withh all my hart! To Jenny R. for the wonderful job on the book cover, thank you Jenny! Thank you Essential Ghostwriters for the contributions to my book the make it easier to read. thank you Author House Publishing for the help with making this all possible. To all my friends Daniela, Valeria, Claire and Jane who in their own way helped me get through some of the tuff times writing and keeping me on track with this book. Thank you to my Mother who i wish could see me now. She would be so proud of her grandchildren. To my friends who are no longer with me but are on a journey of their own, maybe one day we could come together again 'miss you guys' Tony and Tracy' God Bless you all.

William Wright

# CONTENTS

# ABOUT THE AUTHOR

My name is William I was born in Ohio Jun 1959. I was adopted by my uncle in 1962, i was never good in school with writing and spelling. When i graduated i started working as a custodian for thirty three years. While working there i learned how to work hard and was looked up to not only the other custodians but other staff at the school district. I retired from that job because of a back injury and other heath issues. I was married for twenty six years now I'm devorced. I lost not only my childhood home but my children's childhood home bceause of the devorce. Me and my children moved to a new house together with my daughter eventually moving out on her own. I'm trying to make a new life writing this book and working on a one hundred year old house. I thank God for this opportunity for a start for a new life. Thank you all for reading my book! God bless you all.

William

# CHAPTER 1

+ + + + + +

## HOW I CAME TO BE

**T**HIS IS THE STORY OF how I became a Tracker, and it's what made me the man I am today. Across every terrain, I've marked my steps. From the scorching heat of deserts where each grain of sand seems to tell a story to dense rainforests with trees older than time, from mountains that seem to pierce the sky to open plains that stretch beyond sight. In each place, my purpose remains unwavering: to protect people who only wish for a day's peace.

Each assignment I take on has its own challenges. Sometimes, it's tracking down a rogue individual; other times, it's a creature from legends. Regardless of the adversary, I'm there, ensuring the safety of every innocent individual. Whether it's in my own land or in distant territories, when people face threats too big for them to tackle—be it from those with malicious intent or sinister creatures of the unknown—that's when I step in. Some refer to me as "The Tracker" because of my relentless pursuit, while others have named me "The Executioner" because, when we meet, I will execute you, as ordered by the courts, and the death warrant. You might try to run, but that will only postpone the inevitable. You'll only die tired, for I will not stop until you are dead.

In over a hundred countries, I've worked discreetly, helping not just the common folks but also their governments. Sometimes, they're unequipped to handle the danger; sometimes, they're hesitant, fearing for the safety of their citizens. But with me on their side, they find the courage to push through, knowing that I'm there, ever vigilant, ensuring that peace and security prevail.

Across the globe, there are stories the world isn't meant to hear. These tales often echo the missteps of governments too proud to admit their mistakes. "We've messed up," they'd murmur behind closed doors, too afraid of the backlash. So, they'd reach out to their trustworthy ally, the United States, asking in hushed tones, "Can you lend us your Tracker? Can you help us out of this mess?" That's where I come in.

The weight of these covert missions rested heavily on my shoulders. "We need your expertise," whispered a representative from a country seeking help, his voice tinged with desperation. "It's a delicate matter."

I'd nod, understanding the gravity of the situation. While some governments dread their shortcomings becoming public knowledge, they're hesitant to deploy their own forces, be it police or military. Their fear isn't unfounded; their own might turn against them, or worse, the truth might get out. That's why specialists from their own ranks can't always resolve these situations.

So I step in, working "silently and discreetly," acting as a shadow on the wall. The mission? To eliminate the looming threat, no matter its size or form, and ensure the secrecy of the operation. The United States sends me not only to its allies but occasionally even to those labeled as 'enemies.' An unexpected move, some would say, but aiding an 'enemy' often garners favorable PR.

However, it's not all smooth sailing. The higher-ups of these 'enemy' territories often bear a deep-seated animosity towards me. "It's him," I'd overhear in hushed conversations, the intent clear in their eyes. More than once, I've found myself in situations where they've tried to eliminate me. But the local people, they are happy to see me, and they have a different story to tell.

A lot of innocent people become trapped in situations their governments don't want anyone hearing about. Situations that scream, "The government messed up." It's then they turn to the United States, pleading, asking if I could help them out of their mess. Wherever I'm needed, that's where I go, responding to the cries of entire nations, whether it's a whisper or a shout.

Some governments operate in the shadows, concealing mistakes and mishaps. They don't want it to get out that they had a hand in whatever went wrong. They don't call in their police or their military; they want the situation to vanish without a trace. Many specialized forces struggle with the complexity of these tasks, so they call on me, the one who can clean up their mess. My approach? Silent, discreet, and methodical. I eliminate the problem at all costs, leaving no trace behind.

The United States has sent me to both allies and sometimes even enemies to resolve these intricate, often dangerous issues. It might seem like a mere gesture of goodwill, but I know what lurks behind the political curtains. While the governments might resent my presence, often going as far as attempting to eliminate me, the locals see things differently. Their eyes light up when I show up because they know I'm there to help. The people are who I connect with when I come to these countries; they're the reason I keep going.

In the desert nations, where the sun beats down with unforgiving intensity, or the dense jungles, where every step is a battle with nature itself, my mission remains the same. Be it a small village tucked away in the mountains or a bustling city overwhelmed by its own complexity, the faces I meet and the lives I touch are what drive me.

I've felt the tension in the air and cut through it with the same determination that guides my every move. I've seen the fear in people's eyes replaced with hope, knowing that someone cares enough to help them. The challenges are endless, but so is my resolve. In every corner of the world, from the most peaceful countryside to the chaotic urban landscapes, my purpose rings clear: to help those who cannot help themselves, to bring justice where it's needed most, and to be the silent guardian that never wavers.

Through it all, I've discovered not just the complexity of the world but also the simple joys of human connection. The smile of a child once terrorized by fear, the gratitude in the eyes of a mother whose family is safe once more, the firm handshake of a village elder who recognizes the value of peace—these are the moments that fuel me, that make the dangers, the betrayals, and the endless pursuit all worthwhile.

Whenever I step foot in these countries, the government shadows linger, watching my every move. Their surveillance, however intense or covert, is no match for my skills. Inevitably, I slip through their grasp. Their feeble attempts? Simply laughable, making me think, 'losers'!

The horrors I've witnessed and the chilling tales I've heard reflect a dark side of humanity that most can't fathom. The depths to which some descend, treating their fellow humans with such malevolence and disdain, shake my core. The ways in which people, driven by their twisted desires or guided by corrupt governments, can inflict suffering on their own kind, treating them even worse than animals, are beyond comprehension. The pain, the torment, the sheer brutality unleashed upon the defenseless—it's a grim reminder of the depravity some can reach.

It's during these times that I step in, tracing the steps of those monsters who, despite appearing human, have lost every shred of humanity. My targets aren't limited to just these human beasts. I've chased down cryptids, entities of folklore, and beings that seem straight out of a horror story— entities that seem to relish in human fear.

The scale of devastation and chaos these forces can create in a mere blink is staggering. Innocent lives had been snuffed out or traded as mere commodities, all for the allure of power or wealth. Often, it's the bipedal monsters—humans who've strayed far from morality—that are the most terrifying.

Governments, in a bid to salvage their public image, call upon me to clear the mess and extinguish the flames they often had a hand in igniting. If only the masses knew the actual narrative and the grim realities painted behind the curtains of political theater. The world, already teeming with its share of malevolence, doesn't need more darkness. Yet, it's this very darkness that I'm drawn to and that I'm committed to eradicating.

My superiors often remind me, with a mix of admiration and caution, that I am a force unto myself: "You send pure evil to kill pure evil." They aren't wrong. My mission, my very essence, revolves around this principle. In the battle against unrelenting wickedness, I stand as the executioner, ensuring that pure evil meets its end at my hands.

A bit about me: At the tender age of 13, I was forced into a life on the run, seeking refuge from the brutal tyranny of my father, whose psychological and physical abuse became unbearable after the death of my mother. She succumbed to cancer when she was just 50, and her absence only amplified the hellish nightmare at home.

In my desperation to distance myself from that haunting past, I found myself entangled in the gritty labyrinth of the Vietnam War. It wasn't just Vietnam; the fires of war and unrest had spread across various nations, and I found myself in the thick of it all—Cambodia, Laos, Thailand, Japan, Vietnam, and even China. The Far East became both my battleground and my classroom, where I honed my skills and perfected my craft. From taking down menacing drug lords to facing off with infamous warlords and their gangs, the challenges seemed endless. Along the way, friendships were forged in the furnace of combat. Yet many of those bonds were tragically cut short, leaving me with memories of comrades from lands afar.

To this day, I cherish the memories of those I've helped and worked alongside. Friendships in the line of duty are like no other—deep, trusting, and often short-lived. It's the pain of losing these friends, coupled with the countless adversities I've faced, that eventually brought me closer to God. He's been my unyielding pillar, especially in times of solitude. This journey has also taught me the importance of candidness. I've always believed in confronting people with the truth, whether it's sweet or bitter.

Regarding the adversaries I've faced? They are often wealthy, possessing not just immense wealth in cash, gold, and silver but also hoarding priceless works of art in the unlikeliest of places—deep within jungles. Their arrogance, perhaps. While I never understood their penchant for displaying opulence amidst the wilderness, I made sure to return stolen treasures to their rightful owners. My survival often depended on using a portion of these ill-gotten riches, and over time, this became my financial backbone, as the U.S. government never paid me a dime. Being an underage operative in a war zone? That's a PR disaster waiting to happen, one the U.S. government would dread.

Ironically, there have been instances when the very government I served tried to eliminate me, thinking I was a liability. Their attempts were futile. Once, in a grim act of defiance, I returned their dispatched assassin in pieces—a chilling message that undoubtedly grabbed their attention.

They seemed fine with me carving my own path, probably wishing I'd just vanish. The skills I picked up came from all over, from the alleyways of Europe to the hidden mountains of Asia. Even when I made my way back to the USA, it felt like they'd rather I hadn't. They'd ring me up, always staying in the shadows, letting me deal with the mess.

But among all the chaos, Japan offered a surprising pause. In a quiet corner of a busy Tokyo street, with the hum of the city around and the soft glow of lanterns lighting the dusk, I met her. She had a way of looking past all the rough edges and seeing something in me that even I sometimes doubted was there. For six months, between the hush of night and the break of dawn, we'd find moments just for us. Every smile, every shared meal, told me she was special. She didn't probe or question; she just... was there.

One evening, with the gentle hum of the city as our backdrop, I asked if she'd be with me forever. Her eyes sparkled, a hint of tears and a lot of joy, and she nodded. But first, a nod to tradition: I had to ask her father.

With a mix of hope and anxiety, I met him. After a long, pondering look, he agreed—but with a twist. "Find a steady job," he said, his voice firm but kind. A father's love, wanting stability for his daughter, and just like that, a new chapter awaited us.

Under the canopy of a dimly lit restaurant nestled in a private corner, we spent three and a half hours lost in conversation. Every word, every shared memory, sealed our bond even further. His eyes, glistening with tears of joy, met mine, and I could see her mother, radiant in her happiness, mirroring the same emotions. We tied the knot not long after, and like a cherry on the cake, our lives were blessed with a beautiful baby girl a year later.

"Darling," I'd say to her each time I left, "there are things about my work I can't share, places I go that I can't name. Just know, everything I do, I do for us." My job remained shrouded in mystery, its details locked away. Only a handful knew the details, and even they would only provide cryptic instructions. Every mission was a puzzle; its location was unknown, and its time unspecified. They'd tell me where to be, and I'd have to decipher the rest, finding my way in, then out, always against the clock.

I took every precaution, every measure to ensure the safety of my precious family. But the cloak of secrecy, the walls I built to protect them, crumbled one fateful day. The news that they had been taken from me shattered my world. Every waking hour since then, for the next 38 agonizing years, has been dedicated to finding them.

Seeing my anguish and unyielding determination, they sent me support. An advocate, a beacon in my darkest times. She was more than just a messenger; she became my anchor. "Focus," she'd often tell me, her voice gentle but firm, updating me with necessary intel. Whenever injuries plagued me, she'd ensure I received care. If hunger gnawed at my insides, she'd be there with sustenance. She preempted my every need, ensuring I was always mission-ready. She wasn't just a colleague; she became a confidant.

Then, three decades later, they paired me with Max, a diminutive figure whose purpose I couldn't fathom. "Why him?" I'd wonder aloud.

Every time Max walked into the room, a wave of tension followed. "I can't stand him," I'd often think to myself, the very sight of him igniting a spark of frustration. While I'd mastered the art of working alone in some of the world's most treacherous environments, dealing with his arrogance was a challenge I hadn't prepared for. His snarky comments and blatant rudeness grated on my last nerve. His unwillingness to heed advice or listen to reason only made things worse.

I found myself repeatedly circumventing his roadblocks, sneaking around to get the supplies I needed. Each covert mission to secure equipment at my own expense reminded me how much I loathed being paired with him. I'd often vent, "I truly despise this guy," to my ever-patient advocate.

She, understanding the explosive nature of our relationship, often played referee. With a stern gaze and firm voice, she'd reel Max in, fully aware of my boiling point. She knew the depths of my frustration, and she was all too aware that if pushed, I wouldn't hesitate to remove him permanently from the equation.

Setting aside my issues with Max, my assignments often required immense resilience. The solitude that came with tracking down individuals, elusive creatures, or cryptids was something I had come to cherish. The loneliness, sometimes lasting for months, taught me patience and self-reliance. Oddly enough, the cryptids and creatures weren't the main challenge—it was the basic needs: food, water, and medicine. My advocate, the true backbone of my operations, would usually ensure I had what I needed. But during times when she couldn't be by my side, I'd have to rely on my own skills and the allies I'd cultivated during my extensive career.

In truth, I preferred working solo. My journey had taken me across numerous terrains, introducing me to myriad cultures and people. And in those travels, I forged silent alliances. These friends, sprinkled across different countries, were invaluable. They'd assist silently, never uttering a word about our dealings. Collaborating with most other operatives was a nuisance. "I'm not here to babysit," I'd grumble, knowing that adding more people often complicates matters more than it helped.

In the calm embrace of solitude, I find my true self. When I'm alone, every rustle in the underbrush and every shadow cast speaks to me. It's a dance I've grown accustomed to—an intimate pas de deux between me and my environment. That's how I prefer it. Simple. Predictable. Safe.

But sometimes, the weight of a mission necessitates extra hands. That's when I'm paired with a team. The positive side? These individuals are top-notch. Highly trained, razor-sharp skills and dedication that rivals my own. Their eyes gleam with determination, and I can respect that.

Yet, every coin has two sides. The flip side of this team is their overconfidence. They often waltz into situations, believing they've seen it all. But this world—our world—has a way of surprising even the most seasoned veterans.

"With a team this size, stay close," I'd often warn, looking each one in the eyes. "In this terrain, it's too easy to lose someone."

And that was the rub of it. The larger the team, the harder it became to keep everyone together. The vast forests, the treacherous trails—they'd easily swallow an unsuspecting soul. If someone goes missing, our entire mission grinds to a halt. The once-clear objective shifts to search and rescue.

"That's our priority," I'd reinforce, "Keeping everyone alive. Remember, out here, we're all we've got."

Now, when is it just me? The waters are clearer. Decisions are faster. But throw in a group, and the dynamics shift. Suddenly, I'm not just the hunter; I'm a guardian. The lives of every single person rest on my shoulders. It's a responsibility I never asked for, but one I won't shirk from.

And then there's Max.

Just when we're gearing up, mentally preparing for the task ahead, he struts in like a rooster in a henhouse. Each time he shows up, I can't help but sigh. Max loves to play the leader, puffing out his chest and barking orders. His voice booms, full of instructions he probably read in a manual somewhere.

"Listen up! This is how it's done!" he'd proclaim, pointing and gesturing dramatically.

I'd often catch the eyes of my team members rolling in shared exasperation. We all knew the drill. We'd nod and let Max have his moment, and when he'd retreat, I'd gather everyone.

"Forget the theatrics," I'd tell them. "Stay close, trust in your training, and trust in me. We'll get through this together."

The wilderness was no place for ego. And with every mission, it became clear: while Max was busy flexing, I was focused on keeping my team alive.

When it comes to steering the treacherous paths and unpredictable elements of the field, there's a level of intuition that can't be taught. It's an unspoken language between man and nature. I've often told my team, "I'll tell you where we need to be and how we'll get there." And I mean it every time. It's never easy, but that's the essence of our job. But every task, every mission, has its challenges. And for me, one of those challenges wears a name tag that reads 'Max.'

"Little man Max," I'd think to myself, "is the epitome of cluelessness." The guy couldn't find his way out of a wet paper bag, let alone navigate the wilderness. Yet there he was, trying to run the show with his misplaced bravado. To me, he's always seemed like someone more keen on collecting accolades and basking in the glory than genuinely understanding the ground realities. He dreams of political power, of a world where his name rings out. I once told him, "Good luck with that ambition, but count me out of your grand designs."

In no uncertain terms, I'd made my feelings clear to Max. "Stay out of my way," I warned, "and keep your bureaucratic nonsense to yourself." In my eyes, he was nothing more than a liability—a distraction from the real work at hand.

It was frustrating. Here I was, a man shaped by the crucible of war. My time as a sniper in Vietnam sharpened my instincts. The rhythm of the jungle, the silence before the storm—it's a melody I'd learned to dance to. After the war, my journey took me to the rigorous training grounds of the Navy Seals and the U.S. Army Rangers. Those almost two years transformed me, forging my body and mind into a weapon.

And when I thought I'd seen it all, my path led me to Israel. There, I learned the brutal efficiency of house-to-house combat, witnessing firsthand the ferocity with which the Israelis defended their homes. The lessons I learned there—the tactics and strategies, became an invaluable part of my arsenal.

Yet, with all these experiences and the weight of my training and missions, I had to deal with the likes of Max. It was almost comical if it weren't so maddening. But in this line of work, patience is as crucial as skill, and I had an abundance of both.

They assigned a seasoned colonel to guide me through the intricacies of the desert culture. This wasn't just about language; it was about the heartbeat of a society so different from mine, the rhythmic dance of desert winds and shifting sands. House-to-house combat in such terrain is an entirely different beast. It's intimate, raw, and each decision carries a weight that can mean life or death, not just for me but for my comrades or even an unsuspecting bystander.

In the tight corners of urban warfare, there's no margin for error. Each step echoes in the narrow alleyways; every shadow could be a friend or foe, and every silence is charged with anticipation. The gravity of a split-second decision could be a matter of life or death. One miscalculated move, one momentary lapse, and it might be over for you, a comrade, or an innocent soul caught in the crossfire.

Recognizing the enormity of this responsibility, the British didn't leave my training to chance. Another colonel, this time from Her Majesty's Land, was dispatched to equip me with the prowess of the British special forces. After intensive training, they sent me to the venerable Scotland Yard to familiarize myself with the workings of MI6. While their techniques were polished and unique, they also saw the value in the expertise I brought. This exchange wasn't just about me learning; it was mutual. I soaked up their tactics while they gleaned from my field-hardened insights.

Training with Britain's elite and the formidable Israeli army wasn't just about combat; it was about blending in, understanding the nuances of their societies, and absorbing the very essence of their cultures. Such depth in training was pivotal. While I imparted to them modern strategies, they grounded me in the traditions and tactics honed over centuries.

It's often said that iron sharpens iron. In this cauldron of knowledge exchange, we all emerged sharper and more focused. I've always taken pride in being the best, but it's also a privilege to be trained by the best. And whenever they needed a hand, they knew they could count on me.

Of the myriad adventures that marked my journey, there's one that stands out, not for its success but for the lessons it taught me.

The weight of my past casts a long, haunting shadow over my days. While I've learned to move with purpose and precision, the exhaustion of a lifetime in the field is catching up. My bones creak, and my heart longs for the calm embrace of retirement. A time to take off the boots, lay down the weapons, and bask in the peace of a life away from conflict. But those aspirations are marred by memories. Memories of her—my wife and our daughter. Their laughter, their love, snuffed out in an instant.

The cold, biting realization that they were taken from me by someone from the inside has always lingered. Someone thought they could rattle me by targeting my family, but they should've known better. When they come after me, they don't last long. For those responsible for my family's demise, their reckoning awaits. I've always been good at lurking in the unseen, becoming an unseen phantom, a whisper of death in their ear. And when their end comes, it'll be swift and silent. I'll be their worst nightmare and their final thought.

A mantra echoes in my mind, "When you seek revenge, dig two graves." I'm well aware of its implications. If avenging them costs me my life, then that's a price I'm willing to pay. Let fate have its way. But until then, every breath I take, every step I take is in pursuit of justice. May the heavens be my witness.

Just as I thought I was nearing the end, a cryptic message pulled me back in. Why was my advocate, my trusted ally, summoning me to an isolated ranger station somewhere in the vast expanse of the United States? The details remain shrouded in secrecy—"top secret," "classified" labels I've grown indifferent to. All I know is that there's a target: a being of pure malevolence, whether human, cryptid, or something even more sinister. Its reckless carnage points to a creature out of legends, perhaps even aided by others of its kind.

Would this be my final mission before I find solace in retirement? Only time will tell. One thing was certain, though: I'd stop this threat, whatever it took, ensuring it never took another innocent life again.

In the cold, crisp air of the ranger station, the scene was almost surreal.

The trees, swaying softly in the background, were beginning to shed their leaves in preparation for the winter. The atmosphere was thick with tension. My protector, Sue, whom I've begun to affectionately refer to by my daughter's name, was there waiting. The weight of the mission ahead was evident in her eyes. Just behind her stood Max, that pesky little man, now flanked by two imposing bodyguards.

"Why the bodyguards, Max?" I asked sarcastically, my voice dripping with disdain. "Scared I'll come for you?"

Max shot me a dirty look, clearing his throat. "Just a precaution," he retorted smugly, puffing out his chest.

Rolling my eyes, I looked at Sue, "If he ever crosses the line, believe me, those bodyguards won't make a difference."

Sue tried to play mediator. "Let's focus on the task at hand," she interjected, handing me a folder.

As I skimmed through its contents, I could feel the weight of the challenge ahead. "A cannibal? That targets children?" I muttered, disbelief evident in my voice. "Now I see why they brought me in for this. Not the usual hit."

The deep sigh escaping Sue's lips told me this wasn't an ordinary mission for her either. "The last known location was the mountains," she added. "And with winter approaching, the park will be deserted."

I nodded, taking in the information. "I suppose that's the only good news," I commented. "Fewer potential victims."

The atmosphere turned soft when Sue hesitantly said, "Look, once you're done with this, would you... would you consider spending Christmas with me? It's been lonely, and you know, we've grown close."

The offer caught me off guard, but the warmth it provided was undeniable. "I'd love that, Sue. Truly. I'll do everything in my power to make sure I'm back by then," I replied with a hint of a smile.

She smiled back, her eyes shimmering. "I know we have to keep things professional, but... well, it would be nice."

Taking a deep breath, I looked at Sue. "I'd really like to spend Christmas with you," I began, my voice sincere and soft. "Honestly, I don't have anyone else in the world that knows me like you do. And I don't have any places to go. Being with someone I care about, someone like you... that'd mean the world to me."

Sue's eyes sparkled as she replied, "We do have a special bond, don't we? It's been hard keeping it from the higher-ups." She sighed, a touch of sadness in her voice. "Meeting secretly, always watching our backs. It's risky but worth it."

I nodded in agreement. "The bosses are getting too close, aren't they?" My voice was low, hinting at the danger we were both all too aware of. "This is something we can't let them know."

Before Sue could reply, the unmistakable presence of the general loomed nearby. He was the man at the top, the one I reported to, and he answered only to a select few in the echelons of power.

As he whispered something in Max's ear, I saw the little man's face contort in anger. An emotion I frankly didn't care for. Max's fleeting temper was always a source of entertainment.

Drawing nearer, the general's face was stern, almost foreboding. Preparing myself for a reprimand or some piece of bad news, I was taken aback when he extended his hand in a rare gesture of camaraderie.

"General," I greeted, shaking his hand firmly. "I'm holding up. Something on your mind?"

He didn't beat around the bush. "This operation has to be swift and silent," he stated matter-of-factly.

"Sir, I don't need backup. I can handle this on my own," I asserted, hoping he would trust my expertise.

The general's gaze was unwavering. "I know you can. Just make sure it's done right."

The general approached with a sense of urgency in his step. "When you catch this creature and end its terror, I need tangible proof of its death. There are countless missing reports from those mountain trails, and even some towns nearby are affected. The situation is graver than we've dealt with in a while."

Meeting his gaze, I assured him, "I'll head out right away, General."

As he shook my hand, there was gratitude mixed with the weight of responsibility in his eyes. "Thank you. I trust you with this more than anyone else. I'll await your return."

Sue approached me after the General left, a look of concern etched across her face. "I've never seen the general so worried," she whispered.

I tried to comfort her, laying a reassuring hand on her shoulder.

13

"This creature, whatever it is, hasn't met me yet. They don't call me the 'Executioner' for nothing. It'll be handled, Sue."

Before I could gather my gear, the imposing silhouettes of the two men who guarded Max ambled into my periphery. The first, Steve, stood a bit taller than the other, with a broad, muscular frame and tanned skin bearing several tattoos of intricate designs. Short-cropped jet-black hair adorned his head, contrasting sharply with piercing blue eyes that seemed to observe everything keenly. He smirked, revealing the glint of a silver tooth. "You must be the infamous one," he rumbled in a voice like gravel on asphalt, "The one who's got a special hatred for Max, just like us."

Beside Steve, Chuck, though slightly shorter, was no less intimidating. A dense beard covered much of his chiseled face, and his green eyes held a mischievous gleam. With an athletic build, one could sense that he was more of the agile type, the perfect counterpart to Steve's brute strength. The sleeves of his leather jacket were pushed up, showing more than a few battle scars.

Chuck added, eyebrow raised, "Heard a lot about you. Especially about how, if given a chance, you'd end Max. Truth to that?"

Without mincing words, I nodded, "Absolutely. And given the way he treats even those who guard him, I'm surprised you two haven't thought the same."

They exchanged amused looks. Chuck leaned in, lowering his voice. "Truth be told, if it's you doing the job, we'd be relieved. Just... make sure he doesn't come back to bother any of us."

Steve chuckled, nudging his partner. The weighty jingle of weaponry accompanied his movement, revealing more about his own personal arsenal. "Isn't he the one who's said to carry an arsenal with him? What was it, five guns, a couple of swords, and two axes?"

I grinned, the hint of mirth not reaching my eyes. I shifted my stance, causing the tailored hem of my long, weathered coat to sway. Under it, the faint outlines of compact pistols secured in chest and thigh holsters became evident. Twin blades, their hilts ornately decorated and suggestive of a long history, rested securely at my sides, their lengths concealed by the coat. Nestled against my back, easily reachable over my shoulders, were the axes. They weren't just any axes. Forged from fine steel, their dual-purpose design—one side a sharp, gleaming edge and the other a brutal, blunt force—promised a quick end for any unlucky recipient. I adjusted one of the guns, a custom-made piece with a pearl handle and engravings, to be slightly hidden beneath my coat. "Six guns, actually. But who's keeping track?"

Our banter was cut short by Max's shrill voice piercing the air. "You two oafs! Move it! I'm starving, and the last thing I need is you two overshadowing me wherever I go. If you dare to follow me to wherever I'm dining, you'll be jobless before you can protest."

Steve and Chuck rolled their eyes in synchronized annoyance. Chuck whispered, "If and when you decide to... handle our shared problem, just give us a heads up."

Nodding in understanding, I assured them, "Will do. And trust me, if it comes to that, it'll be a service to all of us."

# CHAPTER 2

❖❖❖❖❖

**C**HUCK WALKED AWAY, HIS FOOTSTEPS fading into the distance. With the weight of our previous conversation still lingering in the air, I turned to Sue, her face awash with concern.

"I'm heading to my place to pack up some more gear," I said, the thought of the looming journey ahead weighing on my mind. "The drive alone will take me about three days to reach the foothills."

Sue's eyes darted towards the horizon, a silent acknowledgment of the dangerous path I was about to tread. Once at my house, the real preparation would begin. Stocking up on all kinds of supplies, from food and ammunition to essential survival equipment. After that, I'd need to find a concealed spot to leave the truck hidden from prying eyes and the elements. The next leg would be on foot; hiking through the treacherous terrain might take me two or three weeks to find the target. The weather, always a wildcard, would play a significant role in my progress.

She hesitated for a moment before speaking, "Let me know where you're parking the truck. The general wants to keep an eye on it. If necessary, he might have to relocate it for safekeeping."

Understanding her worry, I nodded. "I'll let you know. If I end up injured out there, it's good to know the general has my back." It was a sobering thought, but reality was ever-present. The dangers of the mission meant injuries weren't just possible; they were probable. However, capturing or neutralizing the target was the ultimate goal. Risks were part of the job, and I'd encountered my fair share in the past. Bad things, unfortunately, do happen to good people, but my determination to finish the mission remained unshaken.

As I began to depart, the towering figures of Steve and Chuck, Max's bodyguards, approached. "Good luck," they said in unison, their deep voices echoing sincerity.

Max, on the other hand, remained silent, a sneer playing on his lips. I couldn't help but think he had been poisoning their minds against me. But I knew better; despite Max's assumptions, the two bodyguards had shown they respected me. As for Max, well, settling the score with him was a task for another day. One I suspected I might regret, but a necessary one nonetheless.

Lost in thought, I whispered to myself. "I can't stand him," I muttered under my breath.

From a short distance away, Max's voice cut through the growing dusk, sarcastic and jeering, "Hey! I hope you don't get hurt... much!" He punctuated his statement with a mocking laugh, the sound grating on my already frayed nerves as he sauntered off.

"You know," I whispered to the soft hum of the engine before cranking it to life, "sometimes you don't have to write a book to let out what's on your mind." I shifted the truck into gear, each motion deliberate and practiced. The destination was clear in my mind, but the resolve? That wavered just a touch, clouded by exhaustion and a deep-seated longing for comfort.

As I drove, memories of comfort food beckoned. Those 24/7 diners dotting highways with their neon signs promising a hot meal at all hours. The sort of hearty, unpretentious food that had been a staple during my many missions. "Been too long since I treated myself to a proper diner meal," I reflected. The road ahead stretched infinitely, the horizon blurred by hours of driving. Nine hours, maybe more.

Spying a quaint town up ahead, a glimmer of hope surged. It looked like the perfect place to rest weary bones. "Just a simple meal, a hot shower, and a warm bed," I yearned aloud. The very thought of sinking into a comfortable bed after a hot meal was nearly intoxicating.

Spotting a roadside café with its windows fogged from cooking, I decided to stop. Little did I know that this seemingly innocuous decision would thrust me into a new whirlwind of challenges.

As the saying goes, "The best-laid plans of mice and men often go awry." And as I was about to learn, this quiet town was far from the haven

I'd imagined. It seemed my bad luck wasn't quite done with me yet. Instead of peace, I was about to delve into another chapter of chaos in a town that promised nothing but trouble.

I stopped here, drawn to this town by the serene backdrop it presented, framed by a landscape that gently kissed the horizon. The cool breeze caressed my face, invoking a strong sense of nostalgia. Memories of the past and simpler times raced through my mind. It was that old-school cafe, with its exterior radiating vibes of the 1950s, that beckoned me. What had seemed like an inviting memory capsule turned out to be anything but that. My sense of foreboding grew stronger, but I had already parked and decided to give it a shot.

The café, with its neon lights blinking feebly, was a beacon of the past. The paint was chipping, but there was a certain charm about it that harked back to the golden days. With every step I took, the grave path crunched under my boots. The surrounding woods emitted a fresh, earthy scent, which, for a moment, distracted me from the increasing tension.

I paused for a second, took a deep breath, and pushed open the glass door. The soft bell above the door announced my entry. Four men sat huddled at a table against the wall, their laughter echoing, their eyes darting around, sizing up every patron. At the counter, two uniformed officers quietly conversed over coffee. Their presence should've been reassuring, but a prickling sensation at the back of my neck hinted otherwise.

I've always held a strong belief in God. Given my line of work, that faith was imperative. There were moments when I'd wonder about the paths God sets before us and why I had been guided here.

The waitress, a young woman with a ponytail, looked my way. I could sense her apprehension. "Find a seat anywhere," she said, her voice slightly shaky. She cast a nervous glance towards the table of men, their boisterous laughter now taking on a sinister tone.

"Go on," she added, her eyes betraying a hint of fear. "Take a seat."

I chose a booth with a clear view of the entire diner, especially that table of rowdy patrons. "Can I have a menu, please?" I asked, my senses on high alert. The feeling in the pit of my stomach told me this meal might come with more than I'd bargained for.

Taking a deep breath, I gave the waitress a once-over. Despite her efforts to maintain composure, her emotions were as clear as day. "Could you make a double cheeseburger with egg and bacon, a side of onion rings, and a Coke, please?" I asked, my voice gentle, trying to alleviate the palpable tension.

She hesitated, her gaze darting back to the table of the boisterous men. Concerned, I pressed, "Is everything okay?"

With a slightly quivering voice and a hesitant nod, she replied, "Yes, everything's fine."

Seeing her discomfort, I assured, "Don't worry about them. Everything will be okay."

She gave me a weak smile, gratitude evident in her eyes. "Okay, we'll make the burger for you."

As I waited for my food, my gaze wandered to the window. The picturesque view outside was a stark contrast to the brewing storm within. The lush greenery, the golden hues of the setting sun, and the distant mountains painted a serene picture. But my peace was short-lived. Turning to the waitress, I inquired, "Do you have any homemade pie?"

She hesitated, her attention again pulled towards the men by the door. My senses heightened. The two cops at the counter seemed oblivious, engrossed in their own world. I noted two other patrons in the back, trying to discern if they were potential threats. Every fiber of my being was on alert.

My attention was abruptly drawn to a hulking figure rising from the noisy table. With a smirk plastered on his face, he sneered, "Aren't you supposed to be leaving now, boy?"

His cronies were on their feet now, their intent as clear as day. Drawing in a slow breath, I calmly replied, "I'll eat, and then I'll leave, but not a minute before."

He glared menacingly at the waitress and snarled, "He's not eating here today. Get him a to-go bag. And if he decides to stay, maybe fetch him a body bag instead." His companions erupted in malicious laughter, their intent evident.

**I fixed him with a steely gaze, "Go back to the table where you were sitting and take your pet monkeys with you."**

He sized me up with a sneer. "You have some nerve on you, boy."

"Cut the 'boy' crap, redneck," I warned, "or you'll find out the real meaning of 'take out.'"

He glanced smugly at his crew and taunted, "Looks like we're gonna have to teach this bum some manners, boys."

Leaning forward slightly, my voice low and even, I responded, "Go sit down. Because if I stand up, there's no way all four of you dimwits are walking out of here. Some of you will be leaving in ambulances, and others... well, they might not be leaving at all."

My eyes swept over each of their faces, noting the bravado mixed with uncertainty. "And given how you lot look, you are probably gonna need a damn good plastic surgeon, too. Though, from the looks of it, even a world-class surgeon or a magician would struggle to make you presentable."

"Enough talk," I continued. "Go sit down before this gets far worse. And trust me, I have no qualms about how bad it can get."

The big guy seemed momentarily taken aback but held his ground, trying to keep the upper hand. The waitress, her voice tinged with anxiety, pleaded, "Please, don't start anything in here."

Without hesitation, the big guy barked at her, "Shut up!"

I immediately shot up from my seat, the chair scraping loudly against the floor. "Apologize to the lady. Now."

He hesitated for a moment, glancing at his buddies for support. Their once cocky demeanor was now laced with doubt. Taking a deep breath, he started advancing toward me, a mix of anger and challenge in his eyes.

As he lunged at me, attempting a roundhouse punch, I quickly parried, blocking his strike. Swiftly, I countered with a sharp jab to his face, followed by a gut punch. As he doubled over in pain, I seized his head, forcing it downward, and introduced it to my knee—not once, not twice, but three times. Holding on to him, I then propelled him to my right, sending him sprawling over a table and crashing onto the hard floor beneath.

Almost immediately, his second accomplice lunged at me, his wild right hand aiming for my face. But I was ready. With a quick reflex, I blocked his punch with my left forearm, capturing his head and forcefully driving it into the tabletop, repeating the action three times. He was dazed but not out. I shoved him into the big guy, who was just struggling to his feet. The force sent them both hurtling over another table.

The third redneck tried his luck, rushing at me. With precision, I landed a solid right on his jaw, and before he could recover, I gripped his shirt, pulling him downward to introduce his face to my knee. The impact sent him toppling over a table.

The second thug, not deterred by the defeat of his comrades, lunged at me again. In a swift motion, I grabbed his left arm, applying just the right amount of force to snap it. He shrieked in pain. "I hate that sound," I muttered under my breath, and with no hesitation, I landed a punch squarely in his face. He crumbled, landing flat on his back.

Suddenly, the sheriff stood up, his badge shining in the dim light. "That's enough!" he bellowed. "You're under arrest for public fighting and disorderly conduct. Now put your hands behind your back!"

As he marched confidently towards me, I took advantage of his momentum, delivering a swift punch to his midsection. He gasped, folding in pain. Seizing the moment, I hoisted him up and thrust him into the path of the third goon, who was attempting to regroup. The collision sent them both crashing over two tables, with the clatter of falling cutlery echoing around the room.

The massive thug, despite the blows, wasn't giving up so easily. From his position on the ground, he made a desperate move, lunging for my right ankle in an attempt to destabilize me. Swiftly, I repositioned my left foot, thrusting it hard into the side of his head. He was sent sprawling back, colliding with the very table he had toppled earlier. Like a defeated giant, he crumpled to the floor; his fall softened by the sheriff's prone body.

Out of the corner of my eye, I noticed the second man attempting to draw his weapon. My adrenaline-fueled instincts took over. I lunged, seizing his arm, just as the sheriff, having momentarily recovered, aimed his gun at me. Thinking quickly, I yanked the gun-wielding thug in front of me as a makeshift shield. The sheriff's bullet found its mark, piercing the man's chest. As the man's body began to sag from the impact, I withdrew my .38 magnum and, with unwavering precision, fired a shot into the sheriff's forehead. Both men dropped simultaneously, victims of their twisted fates.

The sound of a heartbreaking scream broke my focus. The big guy, fueled by blind rage and pain, was staggering to his feet. With a glare that was both accusatory and vengeful, he shouted at the waitress. "This is your fault!" he bellowed, starting to menacingly advance on her.

Without hesitation, I sprang into action. Approaching him from behind, I wrapped my right arm tightly around his neck, locking his head securely into the crook of my elbow. With a swift and decisive twist, I ended his reign of terror once and for all. His lifeless body dropped heavily to the floor, adding to the grim tableau that the café had become.

I turned my attention to the visibly shaken waitress. "Is my food ready?" I asked, attempting to bring a semblance of normalcy to the chaotic scene. "Could you please bring my double cheeseburger with egg and bacon, an order of onion rings, and a Coke to another table?"

Seeing the hesitation in her eyes, I added, "Don't worry. I'll handle this mess. Everything's going to be alright."

I settled into a seat beside the vast window, allowing a brief moment of respite. The outside world seemed distant, almost surreal, compared to the havoc inside. But that fleeting tranquility was interrupted by the sight of three cars pulling up. My heart sank as I recognized the occupants: Max, the always-troublesome; Sue, with her impeccable timing; and the General, the last person I'd hoped to see. Adding to the impending storm were their two looming bodyguards.

The door creaked open, revealing Sue and the General. Their simultaneous, surprised exclamation rang out, "What happened here?" Their eyes darted between the chaos and me, and without waiting for an invitation, they both sat next to me, a mix of concern and disbelief painting their faces.

Before I could even respond, the aroma of grilled meat and fried onions wafted in as the waitress, visibly trying to regain her composure, placed my meal in front of me. "It's a long story," I sighed, looking at the delectable burger before me. "I'll fill you in some other time."

Their expressions deepened, a shade of sorrow creeping in. But any further conversation was interrupted by Max's boisterous entrance. "What the hell did you do?" He bellowed, his voice echoing throughout the room. His bodyguards trailed in his wake, their expressions unreadable as they scanned the room. Silently, they took a seat nearby.

The General, ever the peacemaker, tried to quell the rising tension. "We asked the same thing. Now sit down and grab a bite, Max."

But Max wasn't to be placated. "So you're just going to let this slide? He's trashed the place!" Max exclaimed, gesticulating wildly at the surrounding chaos. "These fine folks didn't deserve this," he continued, shooting me a glare.

His voice escalated, each word dripping with accusation. "You're a magnet for death! You bring chaos wherever you go! You need therapy, man! You're a menace to everyone on this planet!"

Suppressing the bubbling anger inside me, I snapped back, "Shut up, Max! You have no idea what went down here."

With a fluid motion, I approached the fallen sheriff, knelt beside him, and removed his badge, feeling its cold metal weight in my hand. I also picked up his gun, which lay eerily silent beside him. Then, turning my gaze to the remaining deputy, who had witnessed the entire ordeal from his corner, I made my way towards him.

I faced the deputy, his eyes wide with both surprise and fear and declared, "You are the new sheriff."

He stammered, "But it's an elected position."

I met his gaze, my voice steady and determined. "Make them see you are the new sheriff. Let the townsfolk feel safe again. Restore peace. If you show them your unwavering commitment to justice and the law, they will rally behind you, and they will put you in the sheriff's position. I believe you have the potential to be a great leader for this town."

Max, ever the critic, couldn't resist his caustic commentary. "Oh, great advice coming from a man who leaves a trail of death wherever he goes!"

I turned my gaze to him, a sardonic smile playing on my lips. "I haven't killed you, have I?"

His two bodyguards shifted uneasily, their expressions hard to read. With a playful grin, I added, "Yet." I couldn't resist a chuckle, even in the tense atmosphere.

As I finally took a moment to enjoy my meal, I glanced over at Sue; her presence always a comfort, even in the most trying times. "Seems trouble shadows me wherever I tread," I remarked.

She offered a mischievous smile in return and playfully stole one of my onion rings.

Addressing the General, I asked, "Will you help clean up this mess?"

With a resigned sigh, he responded, "I always do, don't I? But there are more pressing matters you should be concerned about."

I arched an eyebrow, curious. "And what new challenge awaits?"

He looked around, ensuring no one was eavesdropping. "You have another issue to address. Remember, your duty is to protect those in need."

"I'll do whatever it takes," I replied, resolve in my voice.

The General nodded approvingly. "I will assist them. Together, we'll restore order to this town."

The new sheriff, now more composed, along with the cook and waitress, began recounting the events that had transpired in the town to both Sue and Max. Sue listened intently, her face etched with concern, while Max, ever dismissive, barely paid attention.

When they finished, Max, his voice dripping with disdain, said, "No matter what you do, to me, you'll always be an animal. Perhaps even less."

I took a deep breath, choosing my battles. Today had been long enough already.

The new sheriff approached our table, his expression grave. Everyone was settled in their seats except Max, who had stormed off, his temper evident. Taking a deep breath, the sheriff began, "We've got a severe drug problem in this town, and I simply don't have the manpower to address it. Can you lend some assistance?"

The general and I exchanged a knowing glance. "We'll send the DEA to back you up," I assured him.

Max, who had returned, scoffed, "This isn't our problem!"

With a stern gaze, the general retorted, "Max, stay out of it. Better yet, go back outside."

To my surprise, the general reached over and swiped my onion rings, giving me a cheeky grin. I shot the waitress a pleading look.

With a playful roll of her eyes, she said, "Another order of onion rings, please?"

She winked, adding, "I'll be right back with those."

True to her word, she returned shortly with a fresh batch of onion rings. However, no sooner had she set them down, Max swooped in and grabbed a handful, leaving the waitress chuckling.

Shaking her head in amusement, she told me, "Hold on. I'll fetch another round."

Once she brought the third plate, I guarded it closely. "For heaven's sake! What's with you lot? These are mine!" I exclaimed, motioning to the onion rings.

They all exchanged amused glances. "You couldn't possibly finish all of them anyway," someone teased.

The waitress burst into laughter, her eyes twinkling with mischief. Shaking my head, I dug into my burger, the jovial atmosphere a stark contrast to the earlier tension.

When it was time to leave, the general expressed his desire to speak privately with the new sheriff. "I'll stay and help clean up this mess," he offered, a faint smile gracing his lips.

Feeling a pang of guilt, I turned to Sue. "Could you arrange for a generous check for the cook and the waitress? For the damages?"

Max, never one to hold his tongue, interjected, "They've got insurance, don't they?"

"I think they could use some support, Max," I countered, trying to reason with him.

He scoffed, "It's not our problem, dumbass!"

I shot him a steely glance, noting the two bodyguards' dismissive eye rolls. With a resigned sigh, I finished my burger. "I'll catch up with you later, Sue. I need to head out."

With that, I ambled to my truck, the weight of the day settling on my shoulders. A long drive stretched out ahead of me, and I could already feel the creeping tendrils of fatigue. The highway, with its endless stretches of asphalt, often felt like a vast, desolate expanse. But it was also a sanctuary where one could find solitude and even commune with God. If you listened closely, beyond the hum of the engine and the roar of the wind, you could almost hear His reassuring whispers.

As I drove, the occasional truck and car zipped past, their headlights momentarily illuminating my path. Spotting a secluded parking lot off to the side, I decided it was as good a place as any for a brief respite. The area seemed quiet and slightly removed from the main road—just the way I preferred it.

Pulling in, I made myself comfortable in the driver's seat. The night was picturesque, with the horizon hinting at the impending rain. The scent, fresh and earthy, wafted in through my half-open window. I've always found solace in the gentle patter of raindrops, and tonight, they played a lullaby on the roof of my truck, lulling me into a short but deep slumber.

A bright light rudely interrupted my dreams. Squinting against its glare, I found myself looking up at two police officers. One of them, with the flashlight in hand, inquired, "What're you doing here?"

Rubbing my eyes and trying to orient myself, I asked, "What time is it?"

The first officer checked his watch. "About 1:30 AM."

Reaching into my pocket, I produced my badge. Their brows furrowed in confusion. "Federal Marshall?" one of them questioned.

I nodded, "Yeah. I deal with life and death situations, often crossing borders to assist other nations with their issues."

The officers exchanged skeptical glances. "You're pulling our leg," the elder one remarked, disbelief evident in his voice.

I met his gaze squarely. "I handle threats, often supernatural ones. Creatures and cryptids that need to be dealt with discreetly. It's crucial to maintain public calm."

A tense silence stretched between us. The younger officer, curiosity evident in his eyes, finally broke it. "How does one land a job like yours?"

I studied the young officer's eager face and began slowly, "To be qualified for this, you need military training, specifically from special forces. Moreover, you'd need a decade or more in law enforcement. Beyond those credentials, we gauge the strength of one's mental fortitude. It's essential to possess a keen survival instinct."

I paused to let it sink in, then continued with emphasis, "Bravery is non-negotiable. The situations you'd face are dire, dangerous, and often life-threatening. A single misstep, a moment of overconfidence, and it could be your end—or worse, result in innocent lives lost."

Leaning forward, my voice dropped to a whisper as I shared a personal tale, "I've been severely injured in the line of duty, alone with no backup. I had to fend for myself, endure the pain, and navigate my way out. Can you imagine that weight, that crushing responsibility? If you can, then maybe there's hope for you."

I held up a finger, adding another stipulation, "Also, being married is off the table. Remember, it's a government policy, not mine."

Seeing the young cop about to interject, I continued, "We'll be thorough with background checks. We can't have any liabilities out there in the field. If there's even a slight blemish on your record, it could compromise an entire mission."

I saw him gulping, taking it all in, so I softened my tone, "There are benefits, of course. The pay is substantial if you excel and maintain safety protocols. Quick thinking is crucial because, trust me, complications arise out of nowhere."

I gestured expansively, indicating the vast world beyond, "The challenges are global. Be it rainforests, mountains, or urban environments, you could be stationed anywhere. The world is vast, but in this job, the risks are even vaster."

Drawing a deep breath, I continued with a solemn note, "There are no second chances in this line of work. Mistakes are often fatal. Consider this. In this job, your mortality is always at the forefront. Think hard about whether this path is truly for you."

I fixed the young officer with a stern gaze, "There are no ifs, ands, or buts about this line of work. Mull it over. It's a life or death job, and it may not be a good fit for you."

Drawing a deep breath and feeling the weight of my years, I added, "I'm getting too old for this. If you're serious, I can mentor you and teach you everything. But heed this warning—once you're in, there's no turning back."

The older cop, looking somewhat incredulous, asked, "But you're thinking of leaving, aren't you?"

I nodded, "I've been at this for over four decades. My body's about reached its breaking point."

He arched an eyebrow, "Is this the life for you?"

The younger officer cleared his throat, "Sir, I meant no disrespect earlier."

I waved his apology away, "None taken. Go on."

He hesitated, his gaze drifting, "I'm married, and I doubt she'd be thrilled with this kind of career change. So, thank you, but I'll have to decline."

I reached into my pocket, retrieving a card, "If you ever change your mind, call this number. Speak with my advocate. She'll fill you in on the specifics."

The younger officer took the card, studying it briefly, "Thanks. I'll consider it."

With the conversation wrapped up, I turned to leave, realizing the pressing urge of nature. Damn age. I knew I'd need to find a rest stop soon. Once back on the highway, the rain continued its gentle descent. The droplets felt soothing—the kind of rain you'd appreciate from the cozy confines of a bed. I planned on driving another five or six hours before stopping. Unbeknownst to me, the road ahead held a surprise that would soon jolt me from my contemplative mood.

# CHAPTER 3

＋＋＋◆◆＋＋

**A**S THE MILES UNFURLED BEFORE me, the diner's dim lighting and the warmth of the conversation faded in the rearview mirror, replaced by the vast expanse of the highway, occasionally punctuated by the glow of passing headlights. The rhythm of the wipers synchronized with my heartbeat, creating a soothing ambiance.

However, the persistent drizzle outside painted a different picture. It was the kind of rain that made a warm blanket and a cup of cocoa the most desirable things in the world. Yet, here I was, planning to power through another 5–6 hours on the road. The journey was long, but the road had its own stories to tell, and today, it seemed, it had a twist in store for me.

The glimmering sign of a truck stop emerged ahead. Gratefully, I pulled in, my body already relaxing in anticipation of the relief. Once done, the idea of hot coffee from the truck stop was too tempting to resist. The aroma of freshly brewed coffee surrounded me, a small comfort in the midst of a long journey.

Refreshed, I returned to the road. The rhythmic thrum of the tires on wet asphalt and the gentle cadence of the rain created a hypnotic melody.

After another eight relentless hours on the road, fatigue began to claim me, blurring the edges of my concentration. Recognizing the dangers of driving in such a state, I found a secluded parking spot to rest. The rhythmic flash of the car's hazards provided a muted light show in the enveloping darkness. From the car's radio, Elton John's unmistakable voice filled the space. *"...So turn 'em on, turn 'em on. Turn on those sad songs when all hope is gone. Why don't you tune in and turn them on..."* The poignant lyrics of "Sad Songs Say So Much" seemed almost a reflection of my state of mind. Succumbing to its melancholy pull, I felt myself drift off, giving way to the embrace of sleep.

Suddenly, I was enveloped in the dream realm. It was as if the past had flung open its doors, thrusting me back into a dense, damp forest. The familiar anxiety of the hunt pressed on me. My target was not just any man; he was a shadow, an embodiment of malevolence. Every step I took was crucial, for he was as cunning as he was ruthless.

The memories of those two days tracking him played vividly. As the second day wore on, twilight began its descent, casting the forest in hues of deep blues and purples. A light drizzle, almost like nature's lullaby, tapped a gentle rhythm on the broad leaves overhead. Taking it as a sign, I set up camp beneath the dense canopy. Earlier that day, I had managed to down a deer, and as the dream continued, I found myself carving into the game, ready to sate the hunger that had grown with the pursuit. The forest around bathed in an eerie calm, watched me in silent anticipation.

As I began to carve into the meat, a flicker of movement caught my eye. Gazing into the depths of the woods, the dimming firelight reflected off two pairs of watchful eyes. The sight sent a chill down my spine—I wasn't alone.

The darkness was thick around me, but the faint glow of my campfire revealed the danger that lurked just beyond its reach. The growling started softly at first, almost imperceptible, like a gentle whisper of the wind. But then it grew louder and more ominous. Each step the creature took was evident in the increasing volume of the growl.

I tried to maintain my calm, steadying my breath and stilling the tremor in my hands. Without making any sudden movements, my fingers found the cold grip of my .38 Magnum. The weight of the gun provided some reassurance, a tiny anchor in the growing sea of unease.

Then, the firelight caught their eyes—two pairs, gleaming with an unsettling mix of curiosity and hunger. The wolves were massive, their sleek fur shimmering in the dim light. They approached, their gaze fixed not on me but on the remnants of the deer that I had caught earlier.

Taking this as an opportunity, I slowly stood up, using the drag of the deer's carcass as a distraction. With every ounce of strength, I pulled the deer to a neutral spot, hoping the offering would satisfy them. All the while, I maintained a cautious distance, my eyes never leaving those of the wolves.

To my relief, the rain ceased, amplifying the sounds of the forest around us. The fire crackled, sending sparks into the night and briefly illuminating the scene. The wolves, without hesitation, began feasting on the deer. But even in their indulgence, they remained acutely aware of my presence, their eyes periodically flicking towards me, a clear reminder of the wild unpredictability of nature.

After what seemed like hours but was only minutes, the larger of the two wolves, its fur dark and thick, raised its head. It began to move towards me, its nose twitching as it sniffed the air. The beast approached with a caution that was almost respectful, yet every step was a potent reminder of the power it held. Its eyes, deep pools of amber, never left mine. And then, only a few feet away, it halted. It lowered its head slightly, emitting a low, rumbling growl, a sound filled with curiosity rather than menace. We stood there, man and wolf, two creatures of the wild, each evaluating the other, each wondering what the next move would be.

Though I felt no immediate threat, caution tinged the air. The wolf, with a sense of silent curiosity, sniffed my boots, his eyes piercing, never leaving mine. Every muscle, every movement was deliberate. As the minutes dragged on, the tension ebbed slightly. Sensing this, the second wolf—a female, as I later discerned—approached cautiously, positioning herself to his left.

Both wolves radiated an undercurrent of fatigue; the female, in particular, was panting with a noticeable thirst. With slow and deliberate movements, I fetched some water and poured it into a nearby bucket. Their gratitude was palpable as they lapped up the water, their tongues creating gentle splashes that broke the forest's silence. That night, as the moon crept higher, casting a silver glow over the forest canopy, it felt as though a bond had been forged. The wolves chose to stay, settling near my campsite. Their presence, rather than instilling fear, brought a semblance of companionship.

Exhausted from the day's events, sleep overcame me quickly, and by the looks of it, the wolves, too, sought refuge in rest.

Dawn painted the forest in soft hues of gold and blue. As I began to clean up my campsite, a closer inspection of my newfound companions revealed a troubling sight. Both wolves bore scars and fresh bite marks, telltale signs of a recent skirmish. The realization dawned upon me: they had likely been driven out of their pack after a confrontation.

Approaching the female with extreme caution, I noticed her slight tremble but sensed no aggression. Over the next half-hour, I tended to her wounds, all while the male watched, his eyes sharp and alert. When it was his turn, he seemed reluctant, his body taut. Yet, as I moved closer, he relented. Every touch and every clean swipe of cloth over their injuries seemed to further strengthen the unspoken bond between us. Their gaze once filled with caution, now held a glimmer of trust.

I must admit, there was an unanticipated comfort in having the wolves by my side. Their very presence, with their raw power and instincts, provided a semblance of security in the vast wilderness. Having tended to their wounds, a bond of trust seemed to form between us. After dismantling the camp, they devoured the remnants of the deer from the previous night, their efficient nature evident in every bite.

As I shouldered my pack and made to continue my journey, I was pleasantly surprised to find them flanking me, their steady pace matching mine. Hours seemed to meld into one another, the rhythm of our feet on the forest floor being the only indication of time passing. After what must've been seven or eight hours, we reached a fork in our path.

To my left, a narrow cliffside trail presented itself, barely two feet wide, hugging the mountainous terrain with a perilous drop to one side. On the right, a more inviting, verdant pathway led further into the depths of the forest, promising the embrace of ancient trees and the songs of hidden birds.

It was there that our paths diverged. With little ceremony, the wolves chose their own route. They darted forward, their agile bodies a blur against the forest backdrop. I paused, watching them disappear, a pang of loss tugging at me. "I guess this is where our journey together ends," I muttered to myself. Their beauty, their majesty in motion, was a sight to behold. They were creatures of the wild, bound by no man, and I felt privileged to have shared a moment in time with them.

Opting for the cliffside route, I began the precarious trek along the narrow path. Pausing a moment to catch my breath, I was struck by the grandeur spread out before me: the sprawling expanse of the forest, the undulating hills, and the dappled sunlight filtering through the canopy. The scene was breathtaking, and for a fleeting moment, I lost myself in nature's splendor.

But then reality snapped me back. There was a purpose to my journey—a target to track down. And however much the forest might offer solace and distraction, my mission remained unchanged: I had to find him and end his reign of terror.

In all honesty, the vista I found myself gazing upon was more than just breathtaking—it was unsettling. A sheer drop of over eight hundred feet, punctuated by jagged rocks, stretched out beneath me. The scale of it, the sheer raw nature of it, was enough to make anyone's heart race. But more than the vertigo-inducing height, it was the silence that unnerved me. There was an eerie stillness devoid of even the faintest chirping of birds or rustling of leaves. It felt as though the world had paused, waiting with bated breath for something.

Moving forward, my steps grew cautious, acutely aware of every foot placement. I was so engrossed in my own thoughts that it took me a moment to realize the path ended abruptly ahead, presenting a precipitous corner of the cliff with the promised drop to the rock-strewn abyss below. The narrow stretch I stood on was no more than two feet wide, hemmed in by the towering cliff face. Above, another path beckoned, but it lay a daunting ten feet above me.

The gentle caress of a southern breeze ruffled my hair, breaking the oppressive silence. Weighed down by my backpack, I realized that its bulk might jeopardize my balance on this treacherous path. Reluctantly, I slid it off my shoulders, intending to retrieve it once I had scoped out the path ahead.

As I ventured on, the minutes seemed to elongate. Each step was deliberate and measured, knowing the stakes at hand. But nothing could've prepared me for the sight around the next sharp bend. A towering figure, easily nine feet tall, with broad shoulders and a dense covering of fur, stood in my path. Our eyes met, and for a moment, time itself seemed to suspend. This was no ordinary creature. This was Bigfoot. And we stood there, two beings from different worlds, locked in a mutual gaze of astonishment and wonder.

The look on his face mirrored my own: raw astonishment. Here we were, two creatures of myth and legend in each other's eyes, standing face to face. Our mutual surprise was palpable, hanging in the air like a thick fog. We stood, transfixed, neither making a move nor uttering a sound, save for the rhythmic heartbeat of nature itself.

Then, in a cruel twist of fate, the very ground beneath our feet began to tremble, sending tiny pebbles cascading over the edge. A deafening crack echoed, and a heart-stopping realization dawned: the cliff was giving way.

Instincts kicked in, and survival mode was activated. Amid the falling debris and the panic, I caught sight of a thick root jutting out from the cliffside. In one swift motion, I grabbed it, the rough texture biting into my palms. As the world tilted, my other hand reached out instinctively and latched onto the Bigfoot's muscular arm. The sheer weight of the creature was an agonizing force, and I heard a harrowing sound, a grotesque mix of tearing and grinding, emanating from my shoulders. It felt as if they were being wrenched from their sockets. Every second felt like an eternity, and the strain was immense. This beast, though in a perilous situation, must've weighed as much as a small car.

To my utter disbelief, I heard a sound from the creature—a deep, rumbling laughter. Even in this dire situation, the Bigfoot seemed to find humor. It swung from left to right, intensifying the pain and making it increasingly difficult to hold on. Desperate for it to understand, I nudged it on the head with my foot. The creature paused and turned its gaze toward me. Its deep-set eyes locked onto mine, now filled with confusion and a hint of hurt. The message was clear in my frantic eyes: "Help us!"

The Bigfoot seemed to understand the gravity of the situation. It looked around for a brief moment, then, demonstrating surprising agility, began to use me as a ladder. Muscular arms reached for purchase on the cliff, massive hands finding crevices and ledges. The creature's ascent, though beneficial for it, intensified the pain in my shoulders. But the thought of us both plummeting to our doom was enough motivation for me to endure.

The throbbing pain in my shoulders was excruciating, but it was soon overshadowed by an overpowering stench. The smell hit me like a brick wall—a rancid concoction of damp dog fur and the rank odor of sun-ripened fish left to decay. I gagged, choking back the bile that rose to my throat. And just when I thought the assault on my senses couldn't get any worse, a more potent stench wafted up from the Bigfoot.

As the creature clambered upwards, using my body as a makeshift ladder, its armpits were exposed, releasing an odor that defied description. It was as if the worst body odor known to man had been magnified a hundredfold. My eyes watered, blurring my vision, and it felt like an invisible hand was squeezing my throat. If not for our precarious situation, I might've let go just to escape that nose-wrenching miasma.

And then, to my growing horror, I realized there was yet another olfactory onslaught waiting in the wings. As the beast's massive foot neared my face, I was introduced to a smell so vile, so putrid that it made everything previously seem almost bearable. The stench was an affront, an all-out attack on my senses. I would've given anything at that moment to erase that fetid aroma from my memory, praying I'd never have to endure it again.

The overwhelming smell, combined with the fear and pain, had me teetering on the brink of consciousness. I desperately tried to hold onto my senses, knowing that succumbing to unconsciousness would mean a deadly fall. The will to survive can pull humans through the most intense ordeals, and it was that primal urge that kept me hanging on, even as every fiber of my being screamed in agony.

The stench was so potent, so unforgettable, that it seemed as though it was etched into every fiber of my being. It felt like the odor had driven away every creature in the vicinity. Not a fly buzzed or a mosquito bit. The world seemed devoid of life, save for the two of us on the cliff's edge. My consciousness was slipping, the world blurring at the periphery of my vision, but the creature's movements kept me tethered to the present, if only barely.

He maneuvered his massive arm upward, finding the thick root that had been my lifeline. With surprising agility, he pulled himself up, using my head as a stepping stone. The weight was immense, and a fleeting, absurd thought flitted through my mind, "Well, at least I won't have to worry about lice now." Yet the pressure caused something in my neck to give way with a sharp, ominous crack.

As the seconds seemed to stretch, I could hear the sound of the creature's heavy footsteps retreating, moving away from the precipice.

Darkness edged my vision, and I felt like I was on the brink of oblivion. Despite what I'd always been advised about not looking down in such moments, a morbid curiosity compelled me. I opened my eyes.

Rushing toward me was not the ground but rather an enormous tree, its thick bark and gnarled branches looking more like the textured surface of some behemoth than a plant. It was eerily reminiscent of a scene from an old cartoon where Wile E. Coyote meets his comical fate. Only this wasn't a cartoon. The impact was jarring. My chest compressed painfully, the sensation of snapping ribs echoing in my ears as I tumbled backward, collapsing on the unforgiving ground below.

Through the haze of agony, the sounds of laughter reached my ears. The beast, along with what seemed like a few others of its kind, was guffawing at my plight. It was the ultimate humiliation, the icing on the cake of my harrowing ordeal.

In my pain-addled state, I couldn't help but ruefully reflect, "Why did I ever have to ask if things could get worse?" The universe, it seemed, had a cruel sense of humor and was always ready to answer such questions.

Propped against the tree trunk, my senses dimmed, and the world around me oscillated between focus and haze. There were moments when I could only hear muffled sounds, like I was submerged deep underwater. And then, in sharp contrast, there were those moments when everything was painfully clear.

The female, towering above me, appeared to be directing the male, her voice unintelligible and filled with guttural sounds and strange intonations. The exchange between them seemed tense, and it was evident she was commanding him to do something he was resisting. When her patience ran thin, she delivered a swift, powerful blow to the back of his head—a force that would have unquestionably been fatal to any human. Yet it only seemed to anger and annoy him, causing him to stomp away with all the petulance of a toddler denied a treat.

My consciousness wavered again, but I was jolted back to reality by an unexpected movement. The female had taken a thick branch and, to my horror, thrust it between my teeth to prevent me from biting down. With grim determination, she positioned her massive fist under my dislocated shoulder and, with a sharp pull, wrenched it back into place. The pain was blinding—an agonizing surge that raced through my entire body. My vision dimmed, and once more, I succumbed to unconsciousness.

I was roused from my pain-induced stupor by a sudden weight on my chest. The male had returned, offering what he must have considered a token of peace or perhaps an odd gesture of care: a squirrel. It lay on my chest, its small heart racing, its eyes wide with terror. It was alive.

My mind raced. I wasn't about to consume a live creature, but it seemed the Bigfoot expected me to. As the realization dawned on him that I wasn't going to partake, he made a move to reclaim the squirrel. In my weakened state, spurred by adrenaline and compassion, I shoved the tiny creature into the inner pocket of my vest, offering it some temporary protection from the colossal beings before me.

His eyes, dark pools that seemed to sink into the depths of an ancient world, locked onto mine. Their look was not one of anger but rather a combination of confusion and disdain. Without warning, the female dealt him another powerful blow to the head, her exasperation with him evident. Emitting a deep, annoyed grunt, he turned and trudged off into the dense foliage, leaving me once again in the company of the towering female.

As the world around me faded, I briefly regained consciousness to find my backpack, a familiar yet distant sight, a few yards to my right. The two wolves, who had been my companions earlier, lay silently nearby, their alert eyes following the movements of the two giant creatures. They looked unharmed, and their presence was oddly comforting.

The interactions between the two Bigfoot creatures seemed to revolve around the same recurring conflict. The female's authority was evident, and she communicated with the male in a series of vocalizations that I couldn't decipher.

"Raka! Nigh'tar toomsha!" She'd bark at him, her voice a deep rumble echoing through the forest. *(Translation: "Listen! Do as I command!")*

He'd respond, almost pleadingly, "Ghar mei'loo. Droon'sha." *(Translation: "It's not safe. We should wait.")*

Despite not understanding their language, the tone made their dynamic clear. Each time, the male's defiance was met with her impatience. He'd stand there, his immense form exuding reluctance, until the inevitable display of her dominance—that signature, forceful smack to the back of his head. The strength behind her blows never ceased to astound me; any human would've been long dead from such treatment.

When I next blinked my eyes open, the scenario had changed drastically. I was no longer lying on the forest floor but found myself tossed over the male's broad shoulder. His massive frame barely registered my weight. Despite being 250 to 260 pounds of solid muscle, to him, I was as light as a feather. My body swayed with every step he took; each jolt sending waves of pain through my battered form. The forest around us became a blur of greens and browns as we moved swiftly through it. The journey had begun, and I had no clue where we were headed.

The unfamiliar forest's rustling faded into the background as my consciousness dipped in and out. The sensation of movement persisted even as I faded away. At times, when clarity briefly returned, I tried to gauge time. It felt like we'd been traveling for 8 to 10 hours, yet the beast carrying me showed no signs of fatigue. It was astounding, even surreal, to feel the ease with which he carried my weight. But every brief moment of consciousness was also tainted with that inescapable, nauseating stench.

Behind us, slightly distanced by a few paces, I heard the rustle of leaves and the occasional snap of a twig. On one of my few lucid intervals, I glimpsed a female Bigfoot. She was carrying my backpack, and to the left of her, almost like shadowy sentinels, were the wolves. They seemed to guard our flank, blending seamlessly into the forest like phantom figures, only their eyes occasionally catching and reflecting the dim light.

When my eyes fluttered open again, I was greeted by a jarring but familiar sight: my truck! It was a beacon of normality in a situation so wildly bizarre. I watched, almost in a daze, as the male Bigfoot handled the vehicle with unexpected gentleness. With each careful move, he seemed so aware, so considerate. The female observed intently, her sharp eyes taking in every detail as he settled me into the driver's seat. My backpack was delicately placed in the back.

The wolves lingered cautiously at the forest's edge, their keen eyes alert and wary. They blended into the environment but kept a watchful eye on the proceedings.

Suddenly, the crisp crunch of gravel echoed in the distance. I heard it, and so did Bigfoot. Urgency laced my voice as I whispered, "Hide! Get into the woods!" There was a moment's hesitation before the creatures retreated.

A dilapidated old truck made its way down the path. As it came closer, my heart sank. Of all the things I could encounter now, it had to be two rednecks in this beat-up vehicle. They drew nearer, and I braced myself for what would come next.

Blinking away the haze that clouded my vision, I found myself staring into the faces of the two rednecks. They wore expressions of half-concern and half-mischief. The first man parked their beat-up truck by the side of the road, using a nearby tree for some makeshift shade. His companion lumbered towards me, curiosity evident in his gaze.

The sight made me internally groan. "Just my luck. Rednecks," I thought bitterly.

His blue eyes, surrounded by a web of wrinkles and sunburn, bore into mine. He then cast a fleeting, assessing glance at my truck's interior. My consciousness was like a faulty light bulb, flickering on and off. I caught him leaning closer.

"Well, ain't this a sight?" He drawled, a smirk playing on his lips. "Boy, you look like you've been dragged through the woods and back. What'd ya get yourself into?"

Before I could muster any response, darkness consumed my vision again. Through the haze, I faintly heard his chuckling observation. "Damn, you're more messed up than I thought."

A sharp pain jolted me back to awareness as he struck me, and the taste of blood was immediate and metallic in my mouth. My head reeled, but before I could process the situation further, a bone-chilling, resonating sound echoed through the surroundings. It was a primal roar, raw and filled with warning, vibrating through our very bones.

In its wake, another scream, just as haunting and visceral, rang out. A cold dread enveloped me; I'd recognized that sound. The memories associated with it sent shivers down my spine.

The driver's face, visible from where I lay, had lost all its prior bravado. His complexion was now a shade paler, and his eyes were wide with genuine fear. Desperation apparent in his voice, he hollered at his friend, "We need to get the hell outta here, NOW!"

The palpable fear in the air was almost suffocating. The second man, the one who'd tried to rob me just moments ago, stood paralyzed for a brief second, caught between the urge to jump into his truck and the primal need to flee from the impending threat. His panicked gaze darted around, seemingly weighing his odds.

His companion, the driver, had already made the snap decision to run. Each step he took was clumsy, fueled by sheer terror, but he didn't get far. His eyes widened to an almost comical extent, reflecting the monstrous sight barreling toward him.

Emerging from the thick treeline was the male Bigfoot, the very definition of fury incarnate. His large strides covered the distance in mere seconds. With an effortless scoop of his arm, he seized the fleeing man, lifting him as one would a ragdoll. The deafening crunch that followed was stomach-turning as the man was brutally slammed into their truck. The force of the impact was so great that the truck buckled, molding into a grotesque 'U' shape around the tree it was parked next to. I could hear the agonized screams of the driver inside, cut short as the massive creature pressed further, sealing the poor man's fate.

The other redneck, trapped between the warped metal and the unstoppable force that was Bigfoot, met a similarly grim end. The echoing thud of his demise reverberated through the silent woods.

When the gruesome deed was done, the Bigfoot let out a victorious roar that rattled the trees and sent birds flapping into the sky. As the echoes of his victory faded, he slowly turned to face me. Those deep-set eyes, now softer than before, settled on mine.

Taking deliberate, almost gentle steps, he approached me, his massive hand reaching out. The touch on my face was surprisingly tender, a stark contrast to the brutality I'd just witnessed. There was something in that gaze—a fleeting hint of sadness—as if he understood the horrors of the day and silently apologized for them.

Slightly disoriented and weak, I managed to croak out, "I'm all right." With great effort, I motioned for the hulking creature to leave, wanting to protect him from being seen. As he began to retreat into the shadows of the forest, I called out, "Thank you." His deep-set eyes met mine for a brief second, acknowledging the gratitude.

Not long after the creature disappeared, the hum of an approaching vehicle caught my attention. It was a police truck, its lights piercing through the growing dusk. Two officers stepped out, and I braced myself, hoping for understanding but expecting more trouble. I couldn't help but sarcastically think, *Great, more 'rednecks.'*

"Well," the first officer drawled as he surveyed the wrecked trucks, "Looks like we got ourselves a truck accident here."

His partner, scratching his head, nodded in agreement. "Yup, and from the looks of it, our friend here," he gestured towards me with a smirk, "has had a bit too much to drink. Looks like you're inebriated, son."

I tried to protest, but my vision blurred, and the world spun. The pain from my shoulder shot through me, and darkness beckoned. As I slipped back into unconsciousness, I could hear snippets of their conversation.

"... handcuffs ... back of the police truck ... shoulder ... need an ambulance ..."

When I came to, I was met with the harsh cold of the road beneath me. One of the officers was still talking. "We'll charge him later. Drunk driving, manslaughter, whatever sticks."

Confusion clouded my mind. "Those guys... are they dead?" I managed to ask, but my voice was hoarse and weak.

The second cop gave a nod, his expression unreadable. "Yes, they're both dead."

Pain gnawed at me, but through sheer determination, I managed to free my hand. I stretched, reaching into my back right pocket. My fingers brushed against the familiar metal of the tracker beacon. Every ounce of me screamed in protest, but I pushed through, activating the device. It was my last shot at getting help from those who understood my situation.

The world dimmed, and when I next awoke, it was to the sterile scent of a hospital room. Dim light filtered in, revealing unpainted walls and a room that seemed caught in the middle of a renovation. The rough chafing on my wrists told me I had been handcuffed, though the restraints were now gone.

Days passed in a haze of pain and sporadic consciousness. Memories of surgeries and the echo of medical instruments became blurry. The weight on my shoulders and neck felt as if I were forever bearing an invisible yoke.

One day, clarity returned as I found Sue standing by my bed, her silhouette framed by the soft glow from the window. Her eyes, filled with a mix of relief and concern, met mine.

"How do you feel?" she inquired gently.

Summoning the little strength I had, I replied, "Like I've been run over repeatedly. Everything hurts, especially my shoulders."

A glance down confirmed that the handcuffs were off. As exhaustion began to pull me under again, I was briefly comforted by the sight of Sue, immersed in a book by my bedside.

My eyes fluttered open sometime later. Sue's familiar voice reached my ears. "How are you doing now?"

"Where's the general?" I managed to rasp it out, a knot of anxiety forming in my stomach.

"He's attending to some matters. He'll be here later," she replied, her eyes searching mine, perhaps for signs of how lucid I was.

I tried to sit up, my gaze darting around the room. "What's with this place? Why does it look like a construction site?"

She pointedly directed her gaze to a corner of the room. "Look there and tell me what you see."

Following her indication, my eyes widened in recognition. There, resting with an air of calm assurance, were two majestic wolves. Their presence brought a flurry of questions to my mind, but for the moment, I just watched them, entranced.

"The wolves," Sue began, her voice tinged with amusement, "haven't left your side since they found you here. In fact, they've managed to keep the local sheriff at bay. The man's terrified of them."

I tried to process what she was saying, but my mind struggled to keep up. The thought of two wild wolves wandering around a hospital was surreal, to say the least.

Sue continued with a glint of mirth in her eyes, "They've had quite the adventure, roaming the hospital freely. At one point, they found their way to the children's ward. Can you imagine the surprise on the kids' faces? But the little ones adored them. The wolves seemed to sense the children's innocence and shared a few tender moments with them."

"They're magnificent creatures," I whispered, filled with a sense of awe. The bond I had unknowingly developed with these wild beings filled me with a warmth that momentarily pushed aside the pain.

As if on cue, Sue pointed to another unexpected visitor, "And then there's your little squirrel friend, currently eyeing you from his cage. He's made several daring escapes, but each time, he ends up snuggling atop your chest and drifting into sleep. It's as if he's keeping watch over you."

I followed her gaze to the corner where the tiny creature sat perched, its beady eyes fixed on me. A smile played on my lips at the bizarre but endearing tableau.

"You're probably wondering about this odd room," Sue said, her tone shifting to a more serious note. "They're renovating parts of the hospital. With your... unique entourage, the administration thought it best to place you here, away from the regular patient wards. This way, you and your animal friends won't be disturbed."

Nodding slowly, I took in my surroundings once more. The unfinished walls, the makeshift furnishings—it all made sense now.

Sue leaned in, her voice softening, "And just so you know, everyone's been incredibly supportive. The nursing staff even gave the wolves a much-needed bath and tended to their injuries. They've been feeding them, ensuring they have fresh water, and even taking them out for walks. They're in good hands, just like you."

Sue hesitated for a moment, her gaze softening. "While you were out," she began, "The General took matters into his own hands. He had the sheriff and that deputy arrested. They're being charged for harassing a federal agent and providing false statements."

I exhaled a breath I didn't realize I was holding. "Good. Once I'm on my feet, I want to see them face to face," I muttered, the weight of past confrontations pulling at my energy.

Recognizing my exhaustion, Sue laid a gentle hand on mine. "You should rest now. We can talk more when you wake up."

"Thanks, Sue," I whispered, my eyes heavy. "I'm just so tired." And as I drifted into the welcoming arms of sleep, my mind transported me to a time when life was infinitely more treacherous.

I was back to being a 13-year-old boy, with fear as my constant companion. Every day was an agonizing dance to dodge the cruel hands and words of my father. His physical and mental abuse was relentless, driving me to make the desperate decision to flee. I ran as far away as possible, all the way to Vietnam. Safety, I believed, would come from enlisting and from becoming invisible in the chaos of war.

Though I wasn't part of the official army, I became an indispensable aide, running errands for any captain or sergeant who needed assistance. But the fire of determination inside me wanted more. I was driven to prove myself and to rise above the life I had left behind. And so, with hard work, dedication, and an innate talent, I transformed from a mere errand boy to a formidable marksman and soldier.

As my skills in tracking both men and beasts sharpened, I grew in rank and respect. The higher-ups quickly took notice of my unique abilities. My small stature, which once was a disadvantage, became my greatest asset. I was nimble, swift, virtually invisible – the perfect assassin.

They began assigning me tasks that most deemed arduous, ones that would typically span two to three days. But with my exceptional prowess and swiftness, I would complete them in half the time. It wasn't long before my age became a matter of concern. Discovering I was underage caused an uproar among the higher-ups. The war might've been over, but the revelation of an underage soldier would have cast a dark shadow on the entire operation—a PR disaster waiting to explode.

"What do we do with him?" they whispered amongst themselves. Their solution was to reassign me to the ominous-sounding "Death Squad."

There, my targets expanded beyond mere enemy combatants. I was sent to neutralize those who posed a threat: individuals who attempted to kill others, the influential drug and warlords, and anyone else deemed a menace. To the leaders of the north, I was the embodiment of terror. Those who dared to oppose the military or were flagged as threats to U.S. interests found themselves in my crosshairs.

It was then that an idea took root in my mind. There was a lucrative business in doing covert assassination work for the government. Not just the U.S. government but others, too. They never officially paid me; my existence was off the books. This anonymity meant they never had to justify or explain my actions. However, I had lines I wouldn't cross. Personal vendettas of generals, politicians, majors, or colonels were off-limits. I was not their pawn for personal scores.

My resolve was firm. If there were secrets or ulterior motives behind a task, I would delve deep, seeking clarity. I wouldn't act unless I knew the reasons. When it came to drug dealers, warlords, or those threatening innocent lives, my convictions were unyielding. They needed to be stopped, and I was the one to do it.

These influential figures, awash with wealth, ranged from your typical politicians to military personnel. Many amassed fortunes through covert and illegal means. Their methods, though concealed in the shadows, were invariably illicit. They exploited, they deceived, and they lined their pockets with the spoils of their wrongdoing.

It was against this murky backdrop that I found my purpose. My mission was simple: eliminate these individuals. In doing so, I would seize their ill-gotten wealth. However, this bounty wasn't just for my own enrichment. Contrary to what one might believe, my heart harbored no greed. Locals often lamented, "If not for the corrupt, we'd be penniless!" Their very livelihoods were intertwined with the very individuals who oppressed them.

So, in my own way, I tried to restore balance. After completing a mission, I would take half the procured wealth and distribute it among the local populace. This allowed them to rebuild and start afresh, free from the shadows of the corrupt. I took immense satisfaction in these acts, not just for the material aid they provided to the downtrodden but for the hope and relief evident in their eyes. As for the nefarious figures I targeted, they were bestowed with a flurry of challenges and threats from my end.

However, my path wasn't without peril. On more than one occasion, I found myself in the throes of intense firefights, moments where death seemed an imminent outcome. Yet, by some divine grace or sheer willpower, I always emerged, if not unscathed, then alive.

But there's one memory, sharp and unyielding, that's etched into the forefront of my mind. We had set up camp near the Cambodian border. The tranquility was punctured by the unsettling scream of one of our soldiers. He claimed the source was just beyond the adjacent hill. This particular encounter stands out not just because of the combat that ensued but also due to its timing—it commenced as dusk began to cast its somber hues upon the land.

As night draped its velvety cloak around the clearing, the sound of small arms fire first pierced the silence. The sporadic gunshots rapidly escalated into a cacophonous symphony of battle. Straining our eyes against the darkness, we discerned the silhouettes of the most unlikely combatants: creatures resembling apes yet unlike any we'd ever seen. Standing approximately six feet tall and weighing around four hundred pounds, their agility was astonishing. They deftly navigated the dense canopy, leaping from tree to tree with the grace of seasoned acrobats.

The surreal combat persisted till dawn, with neither side relenting. The relentless cries and gunfire from the North Vietnamese finally started to wane around mid-morning. The aftermath was horrifying: the once-verdant jungle was now an abattoir, strewn with mangled corpses and splattered with blood. The North Vietnamese soldiers and their allies had been decimated, their lifeless forms serving as a grim testament to the creatures' might.

"Everyone, lower your weapons! If we show aggression, they'll turn on us," I urgently instructed my unit.

Sergeant retorted defiantly, "I don't take orders from you!"

In that charged moment, survival instincts took over. Swiftly drawing my weapon, I pressed it to the Sergeant's forehead. "This time, you will," I declared coldly, my voice filled with steel. "Your recklessness won't be our end."

Once the immediate threat had passed and the distant sounds of conflict finally quieted, we ventured cautiously towards the opposite side of the forest. The sheer scale of the devastation was sobering. Body parts littered the landscape, creating a grotesque tapestry of death and destruction. Incredibly, amidst the carnage, a few of the creatures were still alive, albeit gravely injured.

I turned to our medic, eyes pleading. "Can you do anything for them?"

He hesitated, clearly out of his depth. "I don't know, but I'll certainly try," he replied, compassion evident in his tone.

The medic's deft and gentle hands worked on the creatures with genuine care. As we rendered aid to the injured, a palpable tension hung in the air, each of our movements closely monitored by the creatures' kin. Their eyes, filled with a mixture of suspicion and gratitude, followed our every action. The largest among them, an imposing male who exuded authority, observed us particularly intently. I could feel the weight of his scrutiny as if he were evaluating our intentions.

Having done all we could, we started packing up our supplies, readying ourselves to depart. As I shouldered my pack and began to move out with the rest of the unit, I cast a glance back. My eyes met the leader's intense gaze. As a gesture of peace, I raised my hand and waved.

He simply watched, offering no reciprocal gesture, but I felt an unspoken understanding pass between us.

In the days that followed, whenever our missions led us through their territory, I couldn't shake the feeling of being watched. It was as if unseen eyes tracked my every move. Remembering the profound connection I'd felt with the leader, I began leaving little offerings—sweets and other treats—hoping to foster goodwill. After all, in this unpredictable landscape, I've always believed it was better to cultivate allies than enemies.

By the time we reached our main base, I was mentally and physically drained. To my surprise, I was summoned to the colonel's headquarters almost immediately. I entered to find the sergeant in the middle of a heated tirade. The colonel's stern voice cut through the tension, ordering the sergeant to depart in no uncertain terms.

Once the room was devoid of the sergeant's hostile presence, the colonel turned to me, his demeanor more businesslike. "I've got a mission for you," he began, detailing a covert operation that would require me to navigate delicate diplomatic channels at the Thailand-Vietnam border. "Your target? Two high-profile drug dealers who've been causing considerable problems in both countries."

Negotiating with both countries was an exercise of patience, requiring tact and diplomacy in equal measure.

"Agent, you comprehend the weight of this operation, don't you?" The ambassador from Thailand began with a tone of both concern and caution evident in his voice.

"I do, sir," I responded firmly. "I'm completely aware of the sensitivities. My main objective, beyond apprehending the dealer, is ensuring that both nations' interests are respected."

The Vietnamese representative leaned in, "This isn't merely about capturing a criminal. This is about acting discreetly without leading to any diplomatic tensions."

"I've operated under the radar many times before," I assured. "I'll make certain that my actions won't compromise the relationship between our countries."

The back and forth continued, and it wasn't until a senior intelligence officer passed me a sealed envelope that the atmosphere palpably shifted.

"Inside, you'll find the coordinates of a potential hideout," he said, his voice grave.

I met his gaze, "This will significantly aid in wrapping up the mission."

The Thai ambassador added, "It's not just the mission. It's about trust. It's about maintaining harmony between our nations. We trust you'll act wisely."

With official clearance finally in hand, I ventured into the dense wilderness that straddled the border. Weeks turned into a relentless hunt, shadowing every potential lead. One day, while discreetly observing a remote village, a face familiar from the many dossiers I'd studied appeared—the first of the drug dealers. What followed was a heart-pounding chase, with bullets flying through the air thick with tension. Our paths crossed and diverged over rugged terrain, spanning a grueling three days and thirty-five miles. "Tough guys? Hardly," I muttered under my breath when I finally cornered him, exasperated by his refusal to surrender without a prolonged chase.

With one target neutralized, my focus shifted to the second dealer. Word on the ground was that he'd been tipped off and had vacated his recent hideout. A few of his loyal men remained, some choosing to flee at our approach while others stood their ground defiantly. Their loyalty, while commendable, was their undoing.

As the sun set one evening, a local informant whispered of a secluded valley rumored to be the dealer's latest refuge. With hope renewed, my team and I trekked towards the valley, each step a silent promise to see the mission through. Using the topographical advantage, we laid out a meticulous plan, ensuring he wouldn't escape our dragnet this time.

Our suspicions proved correct when we caught sight of him trying to stealthily navigate the treacherous trails leading out of the valley. It wasn't long before our paths converged again, this time on the Vietnamese side. The tension was palpable as I approached him, knowing the game of cat and mouse had reached its climax.

Navigating the dense jungle terrain, I was aware that he aimed to reach the Thai border, where he had connections and safe houses. The border wasn't far, and with his group of loyal henchmen, it wouldn't take him long. I decided to try a more diplomatic approach first.

"Hey, Bridg," I called out, trying to keep my voice firm yet non-threatening. "Can we talk?"

He halted briefly, his eyes darting around, gauging the distance to his camp. "Why should I? I'm nearly safe," he responded, a hint of mockery in his tone.

Knowing I had to play this right, I pressed on, "Consider it a last offer. Stop your trade in Vietnam, Thailand, Japan, and Hong Kong, and I promise, I'll let you walk."

For a moment, there was silence, just the rhythmic chirping of the jungle critters. He looked thoughtful. "Alright," he finally said, his eyes never leaving mine, "I accept."

Though I had my reservations about his sincerity, a deal was struck. I knew Bridg's word was shaky at best, and it was highly probable our paths would cross again, especially with whispers of his operations reaching the USA.

The return journey required me to pass through the mysterious creatures' territory, a region that always gave me an uncanny feeling. As the familiar sensation of being watched enveloped me, I wasn't surprised when I spotted them—those enigmatic beings. Their human-like eyes studied me intently, and among them, the towering figure of their leader stood out. He must've been about 6'6, weighing somewhere between 390 to 420 lbs. His powerful frame suggested strength beyond anything I'd ever encountered.

As he stepped closer, halting about 25 feet from me, his deep-set eyes bore into mine, exuding a mix of curiosity and disdain. He took a moment to sniff the air as if testing it for truth or lies. The tension was palpable, but after what felt like hours, his stern expression gradually softened.

Recognition flashed in his gaze. It was clear they remembered me. Perhaps it was my previous act of kindness or merely our past encounters that influenced his response. Regardless, I was once again reminded that even in the heart of the wild, relationships matter.

Recognizing me, they didn't seem threatened or aggressive. Instead, they joined us on our journey, maintaining a respectful distance. A couple of them, curious or perhaps protective, paced beside me about twenty feet away. Their presence was oddly comforting; a silent camaraderie formed between us as we trudged through the dense underbrush. For days, they accompanied us, their silent footsteps in stark contrast to the bustling jungle sounds.

One morning, as the sun painted the sky with hues of gold and amber, they vanished. Their sudden absence was as mysterious as their sudden appearance. They had returned to their homeland, somewhere beyond the familiar boundaries of the Vietnamese border.

Their silent companionship taught me a valuable lesson. In the heart of chaos, when the noise of conflict drowns everything else out, taking a moment to breathe, to assess, and to let the dust settle often leads to the right decision. Even when gripped by fear and uncertain of the outcome, there's a chance for reconciliation and understanding. It might swing either way, good or bad, but hoping for the best outcome and acting right often tips the balance.

Their memory of how we once aided them served as a protective shield. Our earlier act of kindness—tending to their wounded with our medic—had solidified a bond of trust. These creatures, enigmatic and wild, had chosen peace over conflict. I'd like to believe there was mutual respect, perhaps even a semblance of fondness.

Upon my return from Vietnam, I briefed my superior on the situation. "The drug lord, Bridg, won't be an issue—at least I believe so," I reported, leaning against the worn-out table. "But if he surfaces again, give me a call. I'll ensure he's dealt with, Colonel."

The colonel's tacit approval was all I needed—a small reward for a task done well. With a weary sigh, I retired to my quarters, laying my gear down methodically, each piece telling a story of a different mission or a different danger faced. Exhaustion washed over me, and I allowed myself a few moments of reprieve, sinking into a short, dreamless nap.

Awakening with a start, the feeling of grogginess still lingering, I decided to freshen up. As the cool water from the shower cascaded down, rinsing away the sweat and grime, I felt a semblance of normalcy returning. But that feeling was short-lived.

Outside, the camp had come alive. A group of unfamiliar faces had arrived, and as quickly as they appeared, they seemed to disappear, leaving a trail of whispered conversations and curious glances. My attention, however, was captured by one man in particular, a stern figure who exuded authority. Our eyes met, and in that fleeting moment, he offered what might have been a smile, though it barely touched his lips. I came to know him as the 'general.'

We exchanged a silent acknowledgment. He continued his discussion with the others while I returned to my bunk, the weight of the day finally pulling me into a deep slumber.

Awakening hours later, the camp was buzzing with news: our time in Vietnam was drawing to a close. Word had spread quickly—we were to leave and not say a word about the mysterious creatures we'd encountered. Though I felt relief, a pang of nostalgia hit me. The war was over, but its memories would stay.

Seeking respite, Japan seemed like an appealing destination. A place where I could blend in, rejuvenate, and perhaps even find a semblance of normalcy. With my connections, hitching a ride on an army plane wouldn't be too hard.

On that plane, amidst the noise of engines and the chatter of soldiers, a singular figure caught my eye. She was statuesque, her posture elegant, and her smile? Radiant. As our gazes met, I couldn't help but wonder, "Could this chance encounter be the start of a new chapter?"

The sprawling cityscape of Tokyo, a mosaic of neon lights, historic temples, and ultra-modern skyscrapers, offered a semblance of solace after the harsh realities of my profession. One evening, amidst this bustling backdrop, I found myself stepping into a lavish banquet hall, welcomed by the familiar face of Tokyo's police chief. He had always been gracious, a beacon of old-world honor in a rapidly changing world. Over the years, our professional paths had intertwined many times.

"Ah, it's good to see you," the chief greeted, a warm smile creasing his age-weathered face. "You've been away, doing what you do best. Tokyo feels safer with men like you around."

The dinner was in full swing, a melting pot of people who'd worked with the chief over the years. Between the clinking of glasses and the soft hum of conversation, a silhouette captivated my attention. Standing poised near the cherry blossom centerpiece was a woman whose grace seemed to eclipse everything around her.

The chief, catching the direction of my gaze, chuckled softly. "That is Lily," he introduced, leading me towards her. "She's my niece, recently returned from studying abroad."

Lily's raven-black hair cascaded down her back, and when our eyes met, it felt like the world had momentarily paused. Her name, gentle and delicate, was a stark contrast to the harsh realities I had grown accustomed to.

Our conversations over the following days blossomed into late-night phone calls and stolen moments. Tokyo, with its vibrant streets and tranquil gardens, became the backdrop of our clandestine romance. But my role as a fixer for the US and other Far East governments meant that our time together was interspersed with my disappearances, often for days on end.

The drug trafficking in the region, a festering sore, had been my mission for years. And each day, a new name and a new face would add to the ever-growing list of those that threatened the stability of the region. Every mission meant potential danger, and every return meant another stolen moment with Lily.

Our relationship, initially a secret whispered amidst the alleys of Tokyo, evolved into something deeper and more real. Deciding to embrace this unexpected gift of love, we soon found ourselves exchanging vows and settling in a quaint house on the outskirts of Tokyo. The gentle hum of nature replaced the city's bustle, and the proximity to her parents meant that her laughter, often punctuated by their visits, filled our home.

As the Tokyo sunset bathed the horizon in shades of orange and pink, my phone rang with urgency. Memories of Vietnam and Thailand, always lurking in the background of my mind, came rushing forward. Someone there needed to see me, and another mission awaited.

As the Tokyo sunset faded behind me, I made my way toward the border between Vietnam and Thailand, guided by the whispers of villagers and the rustling of palm leaves. The dense vegetation of the region made it challenging, but that's precisely why Bridg thought he could operate with impunity here.

The officials I met with were clear about their expectations. "He's a menace," one of them began, his voice thick with concern. "The lands he's seized, the lives he's taken, and the opium fields he's planted—it's all tearing our countries apart."

I nodded, remembering our last encounter. "I'm familiar with Bridg."

The official's eyes darkened. "You might have heard that he's also escalated things. It's no longer just his usual operations. He's ignited a full-blown war with another drug lord. The crossfire has cost many innocent lives."

"That's why I'm here," I replied, my tone even. "He once promised me something, and he failed to deliver. Now, it's my turn to keep my end of the bargain."

Deep in the treacherous terrain, two weeks of relentless tracking led me to a clearing surrounded by thick, sinewy vines and tall trees whose canopy seemed to merge with the sky. There, Bridg and his cronies were encamped, their laughter and conversation a stark contrast to the silent, watchful forest around them.

The moment I stepped into the clearing, everything changed. An armed guard, his fingers twitching near the trigger of his rifle, caught my movement from the corner of his eye. Without a second's delay, a storm of bullets was unleashed in my direction. They whizzed past, tearing through the air and leaving a trail of sonic booms in their wake. One grazed my arm, and another embedded itself into a tree trunk just inches from my face, splintering the bark.

The forest floor was a battleground; every step was treacherous. Branches snapped underfoot, their sharp edges threatening to trip me up. From all sides, shouts echoed, some in surprise, others in an attempt to coordinate their attack against me. I could hear the thumping of boots, the frantic reloading of weapons, and the metallic clinks of ammunition.

In the midst of this chaos, I maneuvered with precision, evading bullets, taking cover behind trees, and using the element of surprise to my advantage. I was outnumbered, with at least ten-to-one odds, but I had something they didn't: a deep knowledge of the terrain and a lifetime of training.

Drawing a breath and pausing just for a moment behind the massive trunk of an age-old banyan tree, I yelled, piercing through the gunfire and chaos, "Remember me, Bridg? You never believed I'd come for you. But here I am!"

A sudden silence fell. I could see the recognition, then the fear, flit across Bridg's face. His cronies looked to him for direction, their bravado replaced by uncertainty. In that moment of hesitation, I knew I had the upper hand.

"You can't touch me!" he shouted back defiantly.

"I kept my word, and now it's time you face the consequences of breaking yours," I retorted, advancing with determination. Cornered and desperate, Bridg retreated towards his camp.

Deep within the dense foliage of the jungle, the distinct sound of gunfire shattered the otherwise tranquil setting. It took a grueling three and a half hours of relentless combat, with bullets flying from all directions, sweat dripping, and heartbeats resonating louder than the cacophony of gunfire.

Cornering Bridg against the gnarled trunk of a tree, its bark marred by bullet wounds and the ongoing skirmish, I glared at him, my voice cold and steady. "You broke your promise, Bridg. You told me there'd be no more shipments. But you got greedy, didn't you?"

His defiant eyes met mine, searching for a shred of mercy but finding none. "It was business," he rasped, attempting to justify himself. But his voice faltered, betraying his fear.

A sardonic laugh escaped my lips. "You lied, Bridg. And now, you'll pay the price."

A profound sense of accomplishment washed over me as I ended the tyranny of Bridg, one of the Orient's most notorious drug dealers. Governments showered their gratitude upon me, lauding my efforts and the risks I undertook. But to me, this was simply a job. A task. A duty.

"People say Bridg is dead," an official murmured in a hushed tone during a debriefing. "Our men confirmed it. They took care of his body."

I glanced at him sharply, skepticism evident in my eyes. "I'll believe Bridg is dead when I see his body for myself. And if he's not, I'll hunt him and his men down. Every last one of them."

The official shifted uncomfortably, but I continued, the weight of my determination evident. "If you value your lives, don't play games with me. If I return and find this unfinished, the consequences will be dire."

I let my words hang in the air, ensuring they'd be etched into their minds long after our conversation ended. "Understood?"

A murmur of agreement rippled through the room.

Satisfied, I began planning my departure, eager to leave the jungles of Thailand behind. But as the saying goes, 'Always expect the unexpected.'

As I stepped out of the meeting, a small group of distressed locals approached me hesitantly. Their wary eyes scanned me, and I realized that somehow they knew who I was.

"Are you the one they say can help?" A tall woman, evidently their spokesperson, asked in a tone that bore a mixture of hope and desperation.

Behind her, murmurs of agreement rippled through the crowd. They recounted tales of a tyrant warlord who executed those unwilling to toil in his opium fields. "The government?" she scoffed bitterly, her voice laced with resentment. "They're in his pockets. He's bought the police and even some of the army's high command."

I weighed their words; the weight of their predicament was heavy on my shoulders. It wasn't just about a warlord; it was about corrupt systems and a cycle of terror that needed to be broken. "We have good soldiers in Vietnam and Thailand, people who genuinely want change," I told her. "Together, we can pinpoint this menace in the thickets of the jungle."

Tears welled up in the eyes of a few, and a gentle murmur of gratitude swept through the crowd. One elderly man, his hands wrinkled with age, stepped forward, "How much do you charge for such a service?"

I met his gaze and, after a brief pause, replied, "I don't charge those who truly need help, especially when they're facing such dire circumstances." I could see the relief on their faces, and it fueled my determination even more.

The group led me away, some eager to share more, others apprehensive yet hopeful. With a mix of local intelligence and the commitment of the honorable soldiers from Vietnam and Thailand, I was ready to embark on another mission to rid the land of yet another peril.

Upon joining forces, the group of citizens, Vietnamese and Thai soldiers, became a formidable unit. Their shared purpose was to hunt down the warlord and dismantle his reign of terror. We had local informants who knew the warlord's movements. Their intelligence indicated his troops were on the move and heading towards a known location. We reached there ahead of them, the dense foliage providing the perfect cover for an ambush.

I could hear the soft murmur of prayers from some of the citizens, the rhythmic click of ammunition checks from the soldiers, and the barely audible footfalls of the approaching enemy.

The ambush was triggered by a loud cry, "Now!" The battle that ensued was fierce; the air was punctuated with the staccato of gunfire and the anguished cries of the wounded. After what seemed like an eternity but was, in fact, about two hours, the dust settled. Our enemies lay defeated.

But victory came at a cost. Some of our own—brave villagers and gallant soldiers from Vietnam and Thailand—had paid the ultimate price. Their sacrifice was felt deeply. "Sometimes," I mused aloud, "the cost of freedom is unbearably high."

We cautiously approached the warlord's stronghold, an imposing fortress made of cold gray stone surrounded by a moat of still, dark water. The fortress, nestled in the heart of the dense jungle, stood in stark contrast to its surroundings, an ode to the power and brutality of its occupant. High walls, dotted with archer loops, hinted at the battles this fortress had seen and the ones it was designed to withstand.

The battle to penetrate this fortress was fierce. Explosions echoed, and the scent of gunpowder and sweat pervaded the air. The cries of combatants, the clash of weapons, and the piercing whistles of bullets created a symphony of chaos. But with unwavering determination, we overpowered the warlord's guards, cutting through their ranks and finally stepping into the heart of the stronghold.

Inside, we discovered an opulent chamber filled with the warlord's illicit treasures. Gold coins, jewels, and artifacts shimmered under the dim light, casting glimmers across the walls and ceiling. Opulent Persian rugs lay underfoot, and intricate tapestries depicting tales of conquest adorned the walls. At the room's center stood an ornate chest, its lid slightly ajar, revealing heaps of gleaming gemstones and stacks of currency from different nations.

The sheer magnitude of the plundered wealth was staggering. For a moment, everyone present was rendered speechless, their gazes locked on the vast expanse of riches that lay before them. The silence was almost reverent, a quiet tribute to the countless lives affected by the warlord's greed.

A robust man from the villagers, sweat, and grime on his face, broke the silence, "What do we do with all this?"

"We split it," I declared, "equally. Everyone played a part in this mission. And while no amount can replace the lives we've lost, this can help rebuild lives and communities."

The agreement was unanimous.

With my portion secured, I felt the weight of the mission and its consequences slowly lift. Before heading home, I made a detour to the Vietnamese capital. The president, already briefed on my involvement, welcomed me with a firm handshake. With gratitude reflected in his eyes, he said, "What you've done for our people... it's immeasurable. Thank you."

Navigating the bustling streets of Hong Kong, I made my way towards the government building. The city's towering skyscrapers loomed overhead, each a symbol of progress and change, their gleaming facades reflecting the sun's golden rays. The scent of street food wafted through the air, mingling with the distant hum of traffic and the chatter of passersby.

Once inside the official building, I was ushered into a spacious office adorned with traditional Chinese art. The mayor, a distinguished gentleman with graying hair, greeted me with a firm handshake. His eyes, a testament to years of leadership, showed both gratitude and concern.

"I've heard of your endeavors," he began, gesturing for me to sit. "And for that, we're truly grateful. But as you've pointed out, the drug trade's roots run deep."

I nodded, understanding the weight of the situation. "It's a complex web. But every step counts."

After updating the officials and sharing a few more insights, I caught a flight back to Japan. Tokyo's skyline, familiar and comforting, welcomed me. But it wasn't just the city that beckoned—it was Lily.

Finding a quiet moment, I gazed into her eyes, the gentle glow of the city lights illuminating her features. "Lily," I began, hesitating for a moment, "Would you... would you like to marry me?"

Her eyes widened in surprise, then softened with warmth. "Yes," she whispered, her voice quivering with emotion.

The tradition of seeking a blessing from her father was something I deeply respected. As I approached him, the weight of the moment pressing down on me, he graciously gave his consent. Our wedding, though quiet and intimate, resonated with love and shared history. Her family, kind and welcoming, embraced me wholeheartedly.

While I had reservations about a full traditional ceremony, we incorporated elements that held significance to Lily and her lineage. The rituals, imbued with centuries of meaning, brought us closer, forging an unbreakable bond.

After the ceremonies, we found a quaint house on the outskirts of Tokyo. Together, we transformed it brick by brick, painting walls and choosing decor, each choice reflecting our shared journey.

Tucked away amidst the serene outskirts of Tokyo, our house was my sanctuary. A secret known only to those I truly trusted. It was an embodiment of my unwavering need to protect Lily, especially with the thought of our family growing. My heart craved the peace this space provided, even though my life was often filled with chaos and danger.

The local police and I shared an understanding—a silent agreement. It was a unique relationship, one forged from a mix of respect and trepidation. Their eyes often held an evident wariness when our paths crossed, but it was interspersed with the acknowledgment of the mutual benefit our interactions provided. They were aware of the stakes. My family's safety was paramount, and any lapse on their part would have consequences.

Lily, my anchor in a tumultuous world, had to bear the brunt of my absences. My missions, shrouded in confidentiality, took me across continents, from the dense jungles of South America to the bustling streets of Europe and the expansive deserts of the Far East. I'd even find myself in the vast landscapes of America on occasion. Every assignment, pulling me further from home, leaving an ever-present pang of longing in my chest.

The day I returned after a particularly grueling two-month-long operation, I found Lily, her face glowing with a mix of joy and apprehension. The reunion was always bittersweet. The weight of my choices and their implications were heavy on our minds, but we tried to focus on the love we shared.

"I have news," Lily whispered, her fingers interlocking with mine.

I sensed a mixture of excitement and trepidation in her voice, "What is it?"

"I'm pregnant," she shared, her eyes shimmering with tears of happiness.

A wave of emotion washed over me—a blend of elation and sudden anxiety. The thought of being a father was both exhilarating and daunting. Our world, once just the two of us, was expanding, bringing with it new joys and challenges.

"The baby... our baby," I murmured, embracing her tightly.

The stakes had never been higher. The realization that I couldn't be omnipresent, protecting every facet of their lives, weighed on me. But one promise was clear in my mind: I would be by Lily's side when our child entered the world.

The days leading up to the delivery were a whirlwind of emotions and preparations. Lily and I attended prenatal classes, trying to grasp the magnitude of what awaited us. Late nights were spent decorating the nursery, painting it in soft pastels, and assembling furniture that seemed to come with an impossibly vast number of pieces. Every detail, no matter how minor, was given careful attention, from choosing the softest baby blankets to selecting lullabies that would soothe our little one.

The air was thick with anticipation, and our home seemed to hum with a kind of electric energy. Friends and family frequently checked in, offering their advice, love, and support. Every kick and every movement from our unborn child brought both of us immeasurable joy. Conversations often veer towards imagining our child's future, the kind of person she would become, and the dreams she might chase.

And then the day came.

The sharpness of Lily's labor pains cut through the early morning quiet. We rushed to the hospital, our practiced plans and packed bags finally serving their purpose. As the hours in the delivery room drew on, every passing minute was a test of patience, resilience, and unwavering hope.

Finally, as the first rays of dawn painted the sky, the culmination of our anticipation and love manifested. The joyous cries of our newborn daughter echoed through the room, harmonizing with Lily's soft laughter. As I watched the delicate bond between mother and child take form, the weight of the world seemed to lift. There, under the soft glow of the room's lights, with Lily cradling our baby girl, I felt a rebirth of purpose.

A gentle tear rolled down Lily's cheek, mirroring the emotions swirling within me. My once indomitable spirit forged and hardened through countless missions and battles now felt tender and raw, reshaped by the purest form of love.

Holding them close, I whispered, "It's time. Time for me to leave the shadows and embrace the light with you both."

Days later, I found myself in the imposing office of General Nakamura, the man I'd reported to for years. His stern face, always marked by experience and the weight of command softened a bit upon seeing me.

I took a deep breath, steeling myself before addressing the general. "I've decided to retire," I firmly stated.

The general raised an eyebrow, genuine surprise etched on his face. "Why?" he inquired, leaning back in his plush leather chair.

I paused, collecting my thoughts. "Personal reasons," I began, "I'm tired of this life, this... endless cycle. I want to be there for my family."

He chuckled lightly, the sound echoing in the spacious office. "I suppose everyone reaches the end of their career at some point. So, what's next for you?"

"I've secured enough to ensure I don't have to lift a finger again," I replied confidently.

The general nodded with a knowing smile. "You've made me quite wealthy as well, thanks to our... ventures. Perhaps it's time I considered retiring, too."

I leaned forward, my tone insistent. "Do what you need to. I want out. And I want it done swiftly. I have other responsibilities now."

He steepled his fingers, his gaze unwavering. "I'm well aware of your new life. Your wife, your newborn..."

A surge of anger welled up in me. In a flash, I was out of my seat, pinning him against the wall with one hand around his throat. "If even a whisper about my family reaches anyone," I hissed, my eyes blazing with fury, "I will end you. I won't hesitate to bring down everyone in my path."

He struggled to speak, his face turning a shade redder. "Calm down," he choked out. "Everything's classified. Only one other person aside from me is in the loop."

My grip tightened, "Who?"

"He's the director of our program," the general managed, his voice strained. "And I assure you, he's as discreet as they come."

"You better hope so," I snarled. "Because if anything happens to my family, you'll be the first I come for."

He nodded frantically. "Understood. Just... let me go."

"I just want a chance at happiness," I said, my voice low and desperate. "I want out. Now."

The general, running a hand through his graying hair, let out a heavy sigh. "You're right," he admitted, "I'd feel the same if I were in your shoes."

His gaze met mine, holding genuine remorse. "I apologize for what I said. It's between us. No one else will ever know."

The transition to life outside wasn't instantaneous. It took an agonizing six years for everything to fall into place. Every year, I undertook missions that further anchored me to this perilous life. A particularly grueling assignment whisked me away to Europe for half a year. When I finally returned, battered and weary, the sight that greeted me was unexpected.

The general, usually composed and detached, awaited me at the airport. His face was painted with an emotion I couldn't quite place. Alarm bells rang in my head.

He ushered me into a secluded room, away from prying eyes. There was an eerie silence before he finally spoke, his voice trembling slightly. "I have news," he began, pausing as if gathering strength to continue. "It's about your wife and daughter." My heart raced, sensing the gravity of his words.

"They've been... murdered," he whispered, his eyes brimming with sadness.

Time seemed to stop. The weight of his words crashed down on me, shattering my world.

The general's face was tight, and his eyes were wary. "Do you need anything?" he began, attempting to offer some comfort.

"NO!" The word burst out of me, full of anguish and rage.

He hesitated for a moment, then quietly said, "We're taking you to your house." As we approached the remains of what used to be my home, tendrils of smoke still spiraled up into the gray sky. A gut-wrenching sight of smoldering ruins and charred memories greeted me. The undeniable truth hit me hard—my wife and child were gone.

Tears of anger welled up in my eyes as I turned to face the general. "How? How did this happen?" I demanded, my voice shaking with emotion.

He swallowed hard, choosing his words carefully. "We believe there's an informant, a mole," he said hesitantly.

My mind raced, processing the ruin before me and the general's words. The dreams, the plans for the future—everything had been snuffed out in an instant. The general's entourage, sensing the rising tension, tensed visibly. Twelve of them stood alert, hands on their weapons, eyes trained on me. They knew my reputation and my capabilities and were prepared for any sudden move.

"You knew the stakes," I whispered, every word dripping with bitterness. "I warned you what would happen if my family was harmed. Both you and the other man."

Grief threatened to overcome me, intertwining with the rage that surged inside. My fingers itched for the knife concealed within my coat. For a brief moment, I envisioned exacting my revenge right then and there. But a shred of rationality held me back. Taking a deep breath to steady myself, I locked eyes with the general. "Tell me, in clear terms, what the hell transpired here," I demanded, my voice quivering with suppressed fury.

"We're still piecing it together," the general responded, his voice cautious. "But all evidence points to a mole within our ranks. We never imagined... I never imagined they'd go this far."

I cut him off, my voice rising in volume and intensity. "That's it? That's all you've got? My family is gone because of someone's treachery, and all you can say is, 'We think there's a mole?'" I was shaking, desperate for answers, for some semblance of clarity amid the chaos.

In a mix of agony and fury, I shouted, "Well, when I find this traitor, they won't have a place to hide! Everyone associated, even remotely, will pay the price." I was beyond reasoning. The thought of my family's killers walking freely consumed me. "There's no force on this earth that can hold me back now!"

The general raised his hands, trying to defuse the situation. "Please calm yourself. We need to talk rationally."

But rationality was a distant memory. My hand instinctively moved to my gun, a habit born from years of distrust and danger. The soldiers flanking the general noticed and shifted uneasily, their fingers poised near their triggers.

"We had no hand in this," the general pleaded, his eyes earnest. "Neither did the police. This atrocity originated from outside. Someone has been leaking information, compromising our operations."

"Information?" I spat, my voice dripping with venom. "I don't give a damn about your 'information' or who's selling 'secrets.' Whoever did this, I'll ensure they'll meet the devil personally."

With a reluctant sigh, I released my grip on the gun. It seemed so meaningless now. Without my family, the world was a vast void of emptiness. Turning back to face the remnants of my once-happy home, I was dimly aware of the general's soft-spoken order, "Give him a moment. It'll be alright, men. Just... give him some space."

The general might have been my superior, but over the years, our bond had evolved beyond the professional. He was the closest thing I had to a friend in this dark world of ours. And right now, he was the only tether keeping me grounded.

Tears welled up in my eyes, a sensation I had not felt in years. It was as if a dam had broken inside me, unleashing a torrent of sorrow, anguish, and despair. I was adrift in a tempest of emotions, with every wave threatening to pull me under.

My gaze landed on the general; his familiar features weighed down by the depth of sorrow he bore. I could tell, even in the worst of times, that he had no part in this catastrophe. His eyes, weary and saddened, met mine.

"I can't express how deeply sorry I am," he said, the genuine regret evident in his tone. "But staying here isn't safe for you."

Frustration bubbled inside me. "Why wasn't I informed while I was on the field? Who made that call?"

He paused, drawing a breath. "I made that decision myself."

Pondering his words, I found myself thinking that I might've made the same call if I were in his shoes. "What about her parents?" I inquired, concern edging my voice. "Are they safe?"

"They're in hiding, deeply concerned about you," he replied. "And I assure you, I'll ensure their protection. No one will know their whereabouts. Only you will be privy to that information."

His words, though comforting, couldn't mask the pain in his eyes. "I cannot tell you how devastated I am about their demise," the general continued. "I will do everything in my capacity to find those responsible."

I shook my head, my determination unwavering. "No. This is personal. I'll find them, and I'll deal with them my way."

The air grew dense with sorrow and resolve. "Given the life I've led, a life hidden in shadows, I can't even give them a proper burial," I mused. "Most people don't even know I exist, let alone know I'm alive."

The general nodded in understanding. "Her parents have made a request," he began hesitantly. "They wished for both your wife and daughter to be cremated. To remain united eternally in an urn."

Taking a moment to process the sentiment, I whispered, "That's the least I can do now. It's what I'll do."

The general's gaze shifted, his expression stern yet tinged with sympathy. "I regret the circumstances, but for your safety, we're relocating you to a safe house just outside Okinawa, nestled within a quaint town," he informed me.

Upon arriving, the traditional Japanese architecture of the safe house was juxtaposed with a woman waiting inside. She was seated confidently, her eyes analyzing me intently as I stepped in. Our eyes locked, and a moment passed before the general broke the silence.

"This is your new protector," the general began, nodding toward her. "Her name is Sue."

"Protector?" I echoed, confusion evident in my voice.

"Yes," the general confirmed. "She, along with another operative, will be tasked with ensuring your safety."

I glanced warily between the general and Sue. "And how can I be certain she isn't part of the problem?"

Sue rose, her posture exuding both grace and strength. Her voice, laced with a thick Scottish accent, responded, "I'm here to be on your side and yours alone—not the government's, not anyone else's."

Meeting her intense gaze, I replied bitterly, "The only woman who was meant to be on my side, to care for me, is gone."

Her eyes softened slightly. "I know, and I genuinely mourn your loss. But my role here is to ensure your safety and to be here for you in the capacity that's required."

Feeling the walls close in and the weight of the past hours pressing down, I turned to the general. "I need a break and some fresh air."

The general nodded understandingly but with caution. "Until we root out the mole, you can't be on your own."

Sue interjected, "And that means you won't be going anywhere without protection."

Their words, though meant to be reassuring, felt like chains binding me. However, in the recesses of my mind, I recognized the necessity of it all.

I fixed the general with a steely gaze, my voice a simmering pot of anger and resolve. "After all I've done for this country, after all the people I've dispatched for its sake, they should be quaking in their boots right now."

A slight quirk of an eyebrow played on my face as I leaned closer to the general. "Did you inform her of my modus operandi? How do I operate in the shadows? How do I get things done?"

He shifted uncomfortably, meeting my intense gaze. "Yes, she's informed. But there's still a lingering fear, a concern that the mole might recognize you."

A smirk formed on my lips. "Then it's about time they realized what's coming for them. It'll be a pleasure hunting them down, making them regret every decision that led them here."

The general sighed deeply. "You've become an integral part of the United States government, a classified asset. We can't afford to lose you."

In response, I eased back into an old rocking chair by the fireplace, its wooden frame creaking slightly under my weight. Memories, some as clear as day and others obscured by time, played out in front of the flickering flames. The warmth of the fire did little to thaw the cold weight in my heart.

Then, in the dim glow, a familiar face emerged from the shadows. Linda, the general's wife, approached me. With a gentle touch, she laid a comforting hand on my shoulder. I felt her lean in, her soft curls brushing against my neck as she whispered words of solace.

"I can't begin to understand the depth of your pain," she murmured, her voice quivering with emotion. "But I'm here for you, always."

Looking up at her, my voice choked with grief, I replied, "It's comforting to see a familiar face, Linda."

She gave me a sad smile, her eyes reflecting the firelight. "I'm truly sorry for everything you've been through. Remember, I'm here whenever you need me."

I turned to the general with a teasing glint in my eyes. "How did you manage to land such a beautiful wife?"

The general chuckled softly, shrugging his shoulders in mock surrender. "Truth be told, she chose me. I was just the lucky guy who couldn't say no."

Drawing a deep breath, I looked out towards the horizon, the weight of my reality sinking in. "You know I can't remain here for long. They'll find me. I have to be on the move."

The general sighed in agreement, understanding the heavy burden of my situation. "Yeah, you're right about that."

I rose from my seat, stretching my limbs as I moved towards the porch. Another chair beckoned, and the evening air felt cooler and more inviting. I took a moment to absorb the serenity, hoping it could dull the sharp edges of my pain, even if just for a brief while.

The gentle clinking of glasses broke my reverie as the general stepped out, a beer in one hand and a cigar in the other. "Fancy one of these?" he offered, motioning to the cigar.

I shook my head. "No, thanks."

However, as if on cue, his wife emerged right after him, a gleaming bottle of Coca-Cola in her hand. Her voice was playfully chiding as she said, "I bet he'd prefer an ice-cold Coke instead."

Chuckling, I replied, "Absolutely. You've always known how to take care of me. Perhaps you should share some pointers with Sue."

Linda laughed heartily, her eyes shining with mirth. "Oh, trust me, I've been giving her a crash course."

Amused, I teased, "So she's sticking around, huh?"

With a twinkle in her eye, Linda responded, "This is quite the promotion for Sue. Be gentle with her. She's still learning."

Nodding thoughtfully, I met Linda's gaze, my voice firm with resolve. "I'll protect her, Linda. Just as I would've protected my family and just as I'd protect you and the general. Always."

As the evening deepened, the general and Linda retreated inside, leaving me to my thoughts. There, on that porch, the weight of solitude pressed on me, accompanied by the silent song of crickets in the distance. But as I surveyed the surroundings, my trained eyes couldn't help but notice the positions of several snipers. It was a testament to my expertise that I could see what was meant to be hidden. If I could spot them, how many others could? The foes we were up against wouldn't have difficulty picking them out either, and the consequences of such a discovery would be dire.

Feeling a mix of amusement and concern, I called out, "Hey, guys! Anyone up there fancy a drink or something to eat?"

From a distance, one of the snipers responded, the note of surprise evident in his voice. "No thanks, we've already eaten."

I chuckled, appreciating their presence despite their visibility. "Well, thanks for keeping watch. I'll just be out here for a bit longer, lost in thought."

Sighing, I leaned back, allowing the vastness of the sky above to envelop me. An overwhelming ache clawed at my heart, and with a whisper, I sent a prayer skyward. "God, if you'd send Michael or any angel down, I'd be grateful. I don't want to be here, bearing this pain, feeling this emptiness. Please, take me home."

The world blurred as my eyes moistened. Exhausted, both physically and emotionally, I finally retreated indoors. As I settled into the bedroom, sleep was elusive, but eventually, it claimed me, wrapping me in its embrace.

In this fragile state, a dream began to unfold. The vision was clear and vivid. I stood before the grandeur of the Almighty. His voice, deep and resonating, filled the space around him. "You have a purpose on my Earth," God proclaimed. "You've been chosen to protect and heal those wounded by the wickedness that has seeped into my creation. This life, the trials you face, the pain you endure—it's all to prepare you and strengthen you. You must free others from the shadows, driving out the evil that plagues my world."

I awoke to the rays of the morning sun filtering through the curtains. The weight of the dream and its significance rested on my shoulders. This path I tread, perhaps it, was destined. The battle against darkness, both within and outside, had only just begun.

The weight of the divine message resonated deeply within me. My purpose had been reaffirmed, and there was a newfound vigor burning inside. "I put you on this Earth to combat the wickedness Satan has wrought," echoed the voice from my dream. "You are destined to hunt them down and purge them."

The morning sun was high when I stirred from my slumber. Its light filled the room, and I could hear soft murmurs from the other side of the door. As I pushed myself up, I was met with the comforting scent of a hearty breakfast wafting in. Linda and Sue, evidently early risers, had ensured that the day started right for me.

Apologies were in order, and I voiced them, "I'm sorry about my outburst last night. I... it's been tough."

Catching the general's eye, there was an urgency in my voice, "Where's my next assignment?"

His surprise was evident, "You sure you don't want a break first?"

Shaking my head, determination evident in my gaze, I responded, "No. I need to do what I'm best at—eradicating evil."

And so began a journey spanning over three decades. I tracked the vilest of beings, from sinister humans to creatures of lore, across vast terrains and diverse cultures. My skills in tracking, honed to perfection, allowed me to navigate diverse landscapes, from bustling cities to treacherous jungles. With each mission, I connected with locals, absorbing their wisdom and culture while in pursuit of my targets.

But life wasn't all about the hunt. Throughout my journeys, love and passion found their way into my heart, and while brief, each encounter left an indelible mark. I fathered children, many of whom remain unaware of their mysterious patriarch. Yet I watched over them from a distance, a silent guardian, always present for the milestones, swelling with pride at their achievements.

However, amid these fleeting moments of joy, there was an ever-present ache, a void. Memories of Lily and my daughter haunted the recesses of my mind. Despite the years, the pain of their loss was as raw as that fateful day. The quest for vengeance and the yearning to bring their killers to justice fueled my every step, reminding me of the mission that lay at the heart of my existence.

Despite the support network around me, it was a life steeped in isolation. The general was my anchor, a beacon of guidance in the tumultuous storm of my existence. Sue, my tireless advocate for close to four decades, always ensured that logistics were never my concern. And then there was Linda, the general's wife, ever the enabler, arranging supplies and resources even before I knew I needed them.

Yet, not all encounters were as fortuitous. I was reminded of a rather irksome individual who insinuated himself into my life nearly three decades ago. A diminutive figure with an oversized attitude named Max. This man, with his incessant need to challenge everyone around him, was introduced to our team a decade after Sue's arrival. Our initial encounter in Washington, DC, was anything but pleasant. He was the antithesis of my style and demeanor.

The memory was still fresh. The sun was shining brightly over the capital as I stood waiting for a contact when Max's aggressive silhouette approached. The first words out of his mouth were not greetings but criticism. With a disdainful squint, he sneered at me, "Honestly? I've heard so much about you, and I'm not impressed."

Taken aback by his audacity, I retorted, "Who the hell are you to pass judgment? What's your trade?"

His smirk widened, showing a set of yellowed teeth. "That's none of your business. But let's just say I'm here whether you like it or not."

I frowned, trying to control my rising temper. "It's a basic courtesy, Max. You don't shout at strangers, especially when you don't know the first thing about them."

Unfazed by my words, he scoffed, "If you think you're going to be my boss or something, think again. I've got a gut feeling about people, and let's just say it's singing loud and clear around you."

I had half a mind to cut our meeting short, but deep down, I knew that Max, despite his abrasive nature, might be valuable. Only time will tell if our contrasting personalities will find a middle ground.

Max's dark eyes bore into mine with a disturbing intensity. "You need to see a psychologist. There's a program designed for operatives like you before you're deployed back into the field. Honestly, I think there's something profoundly off with you. You're a ticking time bomb, a danger to society and everyone within it," he spat out with utter disdain.

His words incensed me. My nostrils flared as I inhaled sharply, trying to control my burgeoning rage. I rose from my chair and leveled a chilling gaze at him. "You tread on thin ice, Max. Push me too far, and one day I'll end you," I threatened.

Max's smirk, a mere twist of his lips, was full of contempt. "This right here? This is precisely what I'm talking about. You're unhinged! You seriously think of blowing my brains out and then going for a meal?"

My fingers twitched at my side, yearning to wrap around the cold grip of my .38 magnum. "Keep pushing, Max," I murmured, a deadly promise in my voice, "and maybe you'll get to see firsthand."

Max stepped closer, his voice dripping with derision. "You're nothing but trash, and I refuse to let you stain my reputation."

Interrupting our standoff, the general's firm voice echoed through the room, "Enough! Both of you, sit down." Turning to me, he said, "I will handle this. For now, you need to walk away."

I gave Max one final warning look before exiting. The last thing I witnessed was the general attempting to placate an irate Max. As I moved further away, I could see Max, seething in anger, move towards his car. His lips were moving rapidly, and he was muttering to himself, likely cursing both the general and me. He then sat on the hood of his gleaming new vehicle, lost in thought.

Max's glower was unrelenting as he shot both the general and me a venomous look. "I can't fathom how you tolerate this guy, General," he spat out, his voice dripping with disdain. "He's insufferable."

The general, a beacon of patience and understanding, guided Max away from the heated atmosphere, his voice low and calming. They engaged in what appeared to be a lengthy conversation. From where I stood, it was evident that Max was still incensed.

Shaking his head in frustration, Max went over to sit beside Sue, unloading his grievances about me on her. Sue, however, had had enough of the constant bickering. "Enough, Max," she chided, "Just... stop."

I couldn't help but smirk at the exchange, throwing a playful jab at Max. "I'll get my day with you, Max," I teased.

The general then turned his attention to me, his concern evident in his wise eyes. "This hostility needs to end," he implored, his voice filled with urgency. "Both of you need to find common ground for the sake of the mission."

Max seemed to momentarily shed his stubborn exterior, approaching me with a grimace that was likely his version of an apologetic look. "Look, I shouldn't have lost my cool earlier," he admitted, albeit grudgingly. "I may not always get things right, but I'll refrain from speaking to you that way again."

Before I could respond, he added, "Just give me a minute," and started to walk away.

"Perhaps your walk might lead you to a shop where you can purchase some manners," I retorted cheekily. I couldn't resist one more jab. "You know, being a decent human being doesn't come with a price tag. Maybe if you tried, you wouldn't need someone else to teach you basic etiquette. I'd gladly pitch in for that lesson."

Max stopped in his tracks and shot me a penetrating gaze. "Do you even understand who we're up against?" His voice held a rare note of seriousness. "We're dealing with someone who terrifies even the most heartless of criminals, someone who makes them pray for mercy. And we have to face him together."

I locked eyes with him, letting the weight of his words sink in. There was truth in what he said, and for a brief moment, our differences seemed inconsequential.

However, Max's familiar sarcastic tone returned, breaking the heavy atmosphere. He arched an eyebrow, a smirk forming on his lips. "Do we need a written invitation from the president just to have a conversation with you?"

I tilted my head, a sly smile forming on my lips. "Maybe you do," I retorted.

His face softened slightly, the edges of his frustration blurring. "Look, I know I've been difficult. But not everyone has an ironclad temper. We all have off days."

Sighing, I responded, "It's not just about today. I'm constantly on edge, cleaning up the messes others create. It's a lonely job, Max. Most days, it feels like I'm the only one who really gets the gravity of it all."

The general stepped in, trying to defuse the palpable tension. "Let me handle him," he said, nodding toward Max. "Just take a breather. We need you at your best."

I nodded, my thoughts already shifting to the task at hand. "I need to prepare for the next mission. It's quite a drive from here, and I should make a stop at my place to gather some essentials. Especially if I'm going to be away for a few weeks."

Max looked surprised. "You have a place nearby?"

"Not exactly 'nearby,'" I replied, "but it's close enough. I have things there that I'll need."

I took a moment to survey the scene, locking eyes with each member of the team. "I'll see you all later."

Approaching Sue and the general, my voice softened, hinting at regret.

"I hope you can both understand why I acted the way I did today. And I hope you can find it in your hearts to forgive me."

The general stepped forward, his gaze solemn. "There are times when we can halt the course of events," he began. "But what happened today was an exception." His eyes searched mine, conveying the weight of the situation. "I have a pressing matter that requires your immediate attention."

Positioned in front of my truck, he barred my exit momentarily. Looking up at him, determination evident in my eyes, I responded, "If you need my help, I'm there." Nodding, the general stepped aside, granting me access to my vehicle.

Before climbing into my truck, I paused, raising my gaze to the vast expanse of sky overhead. The world seemed so vast, its beauty momentarily taking me away from the urgency of our situation. I took a moment, drawing a deep breath and absorbing the serenity.

Sensing my pensive mood, Sue approached, her soft voice breaking the silence. "Is everything okay?"

Turning toward her, my voice was low and contemplative. "You know, Sue, maybe it's time. Time for us to consider retirement. We've been in the game for so long; perhaps it's a sign that we need to seek out a quieter, more peaceful life."

She regarded me with a gentle smile, her eyes sparkling with a mix of amusement and understanding. "You've dedicated a large part of your life to this cause. Maybe it's time. Perhaps you could find a quaint house somewhere. And who knows? There might even be someone out there waiting to share the rest of your life with you." She playfully winked, her laughter lightening the mood. "There's always someone for everyone."

I sighed, contemplating her words. "Is there truly someone for me out there? After everything I've been through, it's difficult to imagine settling down. When I'm on a mission, it's just me alone. And mingling with people afterward? It always feels like a challenge. It's as if I've lost the ability to connect."

Sue's eyes softened with sympathy. "You might be surprised. The right person has a way of appearing when you least expect it."

Returning her smile, I responded, "That would be the day." Then, with newfound determination, I added, "But for now, I need to get moving. The mission awaits."

Sue looked deep into my eyes as if probing my very soul. "Remember, when it comes to Max," she began with a gentle tone, "forgiveness is the sweetest revenge."

I paused, the weight of her words sinking in. "You're right, Sue. Maybe it's time to let go of the bitterness." With a tender smile, I added, "I'll see you soon."

Having recently been discharged from the hospital, the sensation of freedom was palpable. I climbed into my truck, taking a moment to savor the refreshing breeze that brushed my face from the open window. The world seemed to come alive around me. Trees lining the road passed by in a blur, each more magnificent than the last.

In the front seat beside me, my loyal wolves sniffed the air, their keen senses alert to every nuance. And then there was Rocky, the squirrel, darting about playfully, a curious addition to our little family.

Watching the telephone poles zip by, they resembled a rapid succession of toothpicks. I felt a wave of gratitude wash over me, and I whispered, "Oh, God, thank you. Thank you for being by my side and for placing such incredible people and creatures in my life."

The road to recovery had been far from easy. After that harrowing incident, which sidelined me for over two years, it took every ounce of my strength, both mentally and physically, to claw my way back. Max, despite our differences, sometimes had a point. My mental well-being was as crucial as my physical recovery.

The scars ran deep, not just from the physical injuries but from the memories that haunted me. One such memory was etched in my mind: the day a male Bigfoot, with all its imposing size, approached my mangled, U-shaped truck and gently pressed its gigantic hand to my face. I can still recall the deep sadness reflected in its eyes. A moment of shared pain and understanding.

Shaking off the past, I reminded myself of the long road ahead. The six months in the hospital had been grueling, followed by another year and a half of rehabilitation. But I wasn't alone. My wolves provided unwavering companionship, and the playful antics of 'Rocky' the squirrel brought moments of much-needed levity. Yet, amidst all these blessings, Sue stood out—a beacon of support, understanding, and love.

Those months of recovery had also allowed for quiet mornings and contemplative routines, moments where I could appreciate the little things in life that I had once taken for granted. As the memories of the previous day's blessings replayed in my mind, a new day began to dawn.

As the sun began its ascent, casting a soft orange glow over the horizon, I laced up my shoes, preparing for my morning run. The peaceful chirping of the birds and the cool morning air felt like a gentle embrace, signaling the start of a new day. My feet felt eager to hit the ground and feel the rhythm of the earth beneath them. Yet, just as I was about to embark on my usual route, the roar of an engine echoed down the lane, breaking the serenity of the morning. I looked up, surprised, to see the familiar vehicle of the general pulling up.

Before I could greet him, he stepped out, urgency etched across his face. "We need you," he said breathlessly. "A group of armed men has wreaked havoc across several towns. They're not just robbers. They're cold-blooded murderers. They've left fourteen innocent souls, including children and the elderly, dead in their wake. This time, they've gone too far, taking the sheriff hostage. And she's not just any sheriff. She's one of the few female sheriffs in the region."

Following his gaze, I saw Sue standing on the porch, her face a mix of concern and determination. The general's eyes widened in realization. "I wasn't aware...," he started.

I interrupted, my tone icy, "Of course, you weren't."

The general held up his hands in a placating gesture. "Honestly, I had no idea. But I'm glad to see you've found someone. However, right now, we need your expertise."

From the porch, Sue's voice rang out, unwavering, "Just make sure it's your last mission."

The general nodded somberly, "It'll be mine too, and likely hers." His statement held an unspoken gravity, hinting at the dangers that lay ahead.

"Why not deploy the military?" I questioned, my eyebrows furrowing.

The general's face darkened. "We did. Twice. The first team... they never returned."

I sighed deeply, feeling the weight of responsibility settle on my shoulders. "Alright, assemble the team. But I leave tomorrow."

The general's voice held an edge of desperation. "We don't have that luxury. We leave now."

I cast a longing glance at Sue, the woman who had become my anchor. "She'll be here, doing what she does best," I responded to the general's unspoken question.

"And what's that?" he inquired, genuinely curious.

"Taking care of me," I replied with a soft smile.

Quickly, I gathered my weapons and essentials, loading them into the truck. Turning to Sue, I took her in my arms, the warmth of her embrace offering momentary solace. "When I return, let's talk about the future. About us. Maybe even... marriage?"

Sue looked deep into my eyes, her voice gentle yet firm, "We'll talk when you're back."

And with that, the general and I left for our journey to Montana. The trip was arduous, taking five grueling hours. As we approached our destination, a quaint little town emerged, its serenity marred by the presence of local police, FBI agents, and high-ranking military officials, all gearing up for the impending showdown.

As I surveyed the scene, a particular face caught my eye: Max. Accompanied by two towering individuals who must've been around seven feet tall each, it was evident they were his bodyguards. My disdain for Max was hardly a secret. He carried himself with an arrogance that suggested he had all the answers. Yet, from what I'd observed, he couldn't figure out simple problems, let alone handle the complexities of our mission.

"Look who's here," Max jeered, his voice dripping with sarcasm as he approached me. "Hey, Executioner, see what I've got? Bodyguards that tower over even you."

I shot back, "Well, they don't seem to have much work with you. What do they guard? Half a body?" The room echoed with a few snickers, but I wasn't here for a verbal joust with Max.

As I entered the room where the men were gathered, their gazes turned to me, sizing me up. "All right, gentlemen," I began, feeling their undivided attention, "I'm sure you've received your brief from Max, but let me set a few things straight. First off, where are your guns?"

"We were told not to bring them," one of them replied hesitantly.

I sighed, "You can call me 'sir.' And before any of you get into the 'I only address officers as sir' routine, let me be clear. I carry the rank of a five-star general, so yes, you will call me 'sir.' Is that understood?"

The men shifted uncomfortably, realizing that they might've underestimated the situation.

"Now, listen up. I've been in this field for over 40 years. The things we're going up against aren't just myths or legends. They're real. And they're deadly. Creatures like Bigfoot, Dogman, foul human beings, skinwalkers, and many others. They're all out there, lurking in the shadows, waiting for a chance to strike."

Just as the weight of my words began to sink in, I took out my phone and dialed my supply guy. "Bring the big truck of goodies. We need them now," I ordered.

While waiting for the supply truck, I continued briefing the men. "Once the truck arrives, choose the weapon that best suits you. We set out at dawn. Rest well tonight. It might be your last peaceful sleep for a while."

The weight of the upcoming mission settled in the room, thick like fog. I added, "I'll be heading to the safe house for some supplies I forgot. I'll be back shortly. Be ready." With that, I left, hoping that these men would be as prepared as they needed to be.

# CHAPTER 4

✦✦✦✦✦✦

**T**HE ROAR OF MY TRUCK'S engine pierced the early morning stillness as I set out for one of my discreet safe houses. Tucked away from prying eyes, it held a trove of firearms, ammunition, and other specialized equipment I had meticulously amassed over the years.

The drive was longer than I'd remembered, giving me ample time to think. With each mile marker, memories of past missions flooded back—both triumphant and haunting. These thoughts were occasionally interrupted by the rhythmic hum of the tires against the asphalt and the mesmerizing patterns of trees passing by.

Once I arrived, I immediately went for the steel rods. I had a gut feeling I'd be needing them this time. As the hours wore on, hunger gnawed at me. Grabbing a quick bite from my stash, I decided to rest my eyes for a bit. Fatigue was one enemy I wasn't prepared to face.

Waking up with renewed vigor, I geared up. My Spas-12 shotgun lay at the ready. I took two cases just to be sure. Next, my custom 'BAR' specifically designed for long-range precision. A beast of a weapon, it could nail a target from two miles out, making it indispensable. I secured two cases of ammunition for it.

Nestled next were my dual .44 mag revolvers equipped with armor-piercing rounds. Similarly, I grabbed my .44 mag auto mags and an additional three cases of rounds for them. My .50 caliber handgun revolver—a beast in its own right—was up next, with two ammo cases.

Lastly, my two small sixteen-inch swords, two larger twenty-four-inch swords, a pair of axes, and a flare gun with a stash of flares were secured—each weapon, with its own purpose, ready to face what lay ahead.

Dialing my reliable buddy Jason, I confirmed the delivery of the truck packed with weapons. "Jason, those drops you're handling better be on point," I said, ensuring he had all the arrangements in place for both our journey to the site and our return. These supply drops, which ranged from food to medical supplies and more ammo, were crucial.

I added, "I can't have any fuck-ups like the ones Max gave me. He's shit at handling the logistics, you know?"

Jason's voice was steady, "Don't worry. I've got your back."

A pang of resentment flared up as I thought of Max. He was a constant thorn in my side, and there were countless reasons, many still raw, for my distaste toward him.

The truck's weight shifted noticeably as I loaded it with all my gear, weapons, and additional canisters of gasoline. Glancing at the road ahead, I mentally calculated the journey, noting the darkening skies.

They'd told me the rendezvous point was a two-and-a-half-hour drive away, but with a sense of urgency, I managed to shave that time by half, reaching the destination in just an hour. The fading sunlight painted a dramatic backdrop to the chaotic scene that awaited me.

As I pulled in, the site was already teeming with activity. A sea of blue and black uniforms - local police, state troopers, and even the unmistakable dark suits of the FBI agents. I could feel their hostile gazes on me. The air was thick with tension; every time I showed up, it meant they had a problem too big for them to handle, and they hated admitting that.

Hopping out of the truck, I surveyed the scene. The General was already there, his presence undeniable. Max strutted in close behind, flanked by his hulking bodyguards. And there, to my surprise and relief, was Sue, her concerned eyes scanning the area and finally settling on me.

With a smirk plastered across his face, an arrogant-looking FBI agent approached me. "Need a hand there?" He sneered, his tone dripping with condescension.

Suppressing the urge to retort with venom, I responded, "No thanks. I've got it covered." Always better to kill them with kindness, I reminded myself.

Making my way to the back of my truck, I began arranging my equipment. Just then, Max, in all his infuriating glory, ambled over.

"What the hell do you think you're doing? You don't need all that shit," he barked, glancing disdainfully at my stash.

I squared up to him, my patience fraying. "What would you know, dumbass? We're about to tread on grounds you can't even fathom, facing threats you wouldn't believe even if they stared you in the face."

Max tried to interject, but I cut him off. "Things can turn from bad to absolute fucking chaos in a heartbeat. And guess what? They know we're coming, so the advantage? Not ours. Now back the fuck off and let me work."

His arrogance deflated slightly, but before he could muster a response, Sue stepped in, her voice firm but calm. "Max, just get lost."

Clearly unwilling to argue with Sue, Max shot me a dirty look and stomped off. Sue watched him go, shaking her head. Then, turning to me, her tone softening, she asked, "Anything else you need?"

I took a deep breath, feeling the weight of the situation. "Actually, yes, there's something," I said to Sue, my eyes darting toward the smug-looking FBI agent who'd given me a hard time earlier. "Ask him to come over. I need to chat."

Sue, always the diplomat, approached the agent with a polite demeanor. "Would you mind talking with him for a moment?"

The agent sauntered over, exuding that unmistakable aura of bureaucratic arrogance. "Alright, what the hell do you want?"

I met his gaze, unflinching. "I need specifics. Last sightings? When? How recent? Details, man."

The agent shifted uncomfortably, clearly caught off guard. "Well, I don't have all the particulars. I've heard rumors of supplies going missing, but I'm in the dark as to who, when, or where."

I arched an eyebrow. "What about family connections in the area? Do you think any of them could have local knowledge? Routes out without being spotted?"

The agent shrugged. "Your guess is as good as mine. But I've heard one of them's a survivor of some sort."

I clenched my fist, feeling the frustration boil over. "You should've closed down the park immediately."

"That was done three days ago," a park ranger chimed in, overhearing our conversation. "We believe no one's inside now."

"You 'believe?' You should've been certain before I even got here," I snapped. I took a moment to rein in my temper, then turned back to the FBI agent. "You and your team should be gathering this intel from park staff. If they're out there, we're wasting precious time."

The agent's smugness had faded. He looked taken aback, maybe even a bit humiliated. I continued, "I've been doing this shit for 40 years. Every damn time it's the same story. You guys mess up, and then you call me to clean it up. I handle the cases nobody else can or wants to."

A moment of silence hung in the air. The FBI agent finally responded, his tone markedly different from earlier. "Do you need any assistance? Anything at all?" Respect had replaced arrogance.

I took a deep breath, attempting to keep my raging emotions in check. "Yeah, coordinate with the Rangers. Get a team out there. Check if anyone's stuck, hurt, or in danger," I told the FBI agent, my voice laced with urgency.

Before I could continue, Max, in his characteristic smugness, interrupted. "Are you planning on getting going anytime soon, or just going to keep barking orders?"

My eyes darted to him, fire igniting behind them. But before I could speak, the FBI agent, newfound respect in his voice, cut in, "Thanks for the guidance. We'll handle it from here."

Max sneered, "Seems foolish not to utilize their help."

I shot him a piercing look. "Mind your own business, Max. They can't assist me with what I need to do. Stay out of it."

The General, sensing the escalating tension, approached. His voice was calm, but the concern was evident. "Everything okay here?"

I shook my head, exasperated. "No, it's not. Either you get Max out of here, or I swear I'll do it permanently."

The FBI agent's eyes widened, clearly not expecting such a blunt threat. He took a step back, lifting his hands in a placating gesture. "Hey, I didn't hear anything," with that, he moved off, giving us some space.

From a distance, as the air grew tenser, Max shouted defiantly, "You've lost it! Fucking unhinged! A real madman!" His footsteps echoed his anger as he walked away, glancing back sporadically.

I turned to the General and Sue, my voice raw with frustration. "Keep him away from me, or it won't end well."

I pulled out a map, plotting my initial route. "I'll start here. If all goes according to plan, I should track him down in two to three days. I'll radio in when I'm closing in."

Sue's face was painted with concern. "When you find... the body... the General needs you to retrieve some form of ID. We need proof of the kill."

I nodded, appreciating her professionalism. "Understood."

She looked me in the eyes, sincerity flooding her voice. "Take care out there."

Max's spiteful voice echoed one last time as I began to move toward the dense forest. "Hope the creatures get you, you worthless shit!" He laughed, a bitter sound that faded as I ventured deeper into the wilderness.

The thought swirled in my mind as I trudged further into the woods: I'll fucking kill him one day. The weight of Max's spiteful words and my unresolved feelings bore down on me. But, pushing them aside, I focused on the task at hand.

Although I didn't mind the solitude of the wilderness, it sometimes weighed heavily on me. The quiet, the isolation, the sense of being completely alone with only your thoughts and the whispering wind.

But despite the enveloping solitude, I've always taken solace in its clarity. Each step, each rustle of leaves, each chirping bird - all play a vital role in unraveling the story of the forest. As much as I cherished the silence, the silent woods made me extra vigilant. My senses sharpened, looking out for the tiniest indications, even the faintest signs, that someone had been here before me.

I was making decent headway when I stumbled upon a scene that sent a chill up my spine. Distinct footprints, unmistakably human, but right alongside them were the unmistakable marks of something else - large canine prints. Judging by the spread and pattern, I estimated at least four, no, perhaps seven creatures. A pack. This was going to be much more complicated than I'd anticipated.

Thankfully, there was no sign of blood, meaning either the elusive "dogmen" hadn't caught up to our missing person, or perhaps they weren't hunting him after all. I was deep in thought, plotting my next move when a gunshot ripped through the silence.

My heart raced; no accompanying cries of pain meant the shooter had missed their target. A rookie mistake; now the pack would be on high alert.

The night was falling, and I had to act quickly. I knew I was possibly a day behind whatever was unfolding, but the immediate concern was making camp. An unsettling realization set in: tonight, my worry might not be the dogmen but something far more sinister - a skinwalker. I'd much rather deal with a pack of "dogmen" than encounter that ancient evil.

I hastily gathered wood, igniting a roaring fire. Placing my five steel rods into the flames, I knew they had to be heated until they were glowing red. I kept an eye on my temperature gauge: 70 degrees for now. But if legends were accurate, the presence of a skinwalker would cause an unnatural, rapid drop in temperature.

My instincts screamed that I wouldn't have to wait long. And sure enough, as the forest darkened around me and the night creatures began their serenades, the temperature plummeted. I braced myself, knowing that the night ahead would be a test of every ounce of my training and resolve.

The palpable tension in the air was almost suffocating. I could sense the approach; the dread settling deep in my bones was a telltale sign that something unnatural was drawing near.

Grabbing my gloves, I placed them next to the steel rods, their ends glowing ominously in the fire. Legends spoke of these creatures always traveling in pairs. The waiting game was agonizing, but sleep was out of the question. They'd always get you when your guard was down.

Moments felt like hours, and every rustle or whisper of the wind felt like a portent of doom. My watch read 1:30 am, but time seemed to have slowed. The drop in temperature, now a bone-chilling -12 degrees, confirmed what I already knew. They were here.

The slow shuffle of footsteps from the dark woods mingled with the hushed rustling of falling leaves; the only other sound was the deafening beat of my own heart. And then, a presence directly behind me. Turning slowly, my blood ran cold.

The creature was grotesquely beautiful - slender, almost skeletal limbs supporting a slim frame, covered in alabaster skin that almost glowed in the dimness. Had it stood upright, it would have towered at almost ten feet, but instead, it crept forward, its movements unnervingly graceful.

For a moment, our gazes locked, and it hissed in a voice that sent shivers down my spine, reminiscent of scales sliding on stone, "Are you afraid of me?"

Swallowing hard, I remained silent. Not out of fear but strategy. I needed it to stand, expose its chest, and give me a clear shot.

Almost as if it heard my thoughts, it began to rise. Seizing the moment, I drew my .44 auto mag, loaded with armor-piercing shells. Two shots rang out, echoing in the quiet woods, finding their mark straight in its heart. A guttural scream of pain filled the night.

Without wasting a moment, I pulled out my flare gun, shooting a flare straight into the same wounded spot. Its screams intensified, a haunting melody of pain and fury. Slipping on my thick gloves, I grabbed one of the white-hot steel rods from the fire and, with all the strength I could muster, plunged it directly into its heart, pinning it to the earth.

Rushing back to the fire, adrenaline pumping through my veins, I seized another rod and drove it straight through its head, ensuring it couldn't retaliate. Scrambling, I heaped the dried wood I'd piled earlier onto the creature, dousing it in lighter fluid. Striking a match, I set the pyre ablaze.

Its screams pierced the night, a symphony of agony echoing through the woods until they gradually subsided. The fire roared, consuming the creature, and the hostility that it represented was reduced to mere ashes.

The eerie quiet following the creature's death was soon interrupted by the sensation of being watched. The second skinwalker. It had been lurking in the shadows, waiting for its moment, and I knew I had to act before it chose to strike. My eyes darted around, searching the underbrush and shadows between the trees.

There! A slight rustle. Eyes, glowing a malevolent yellow, peered from the thicket about 15 feet to my right. This one was different. Silent. Deadly. Its very presence seemed to suck the warmth and light from the surroundings. Stepping toward it, I tried to assert dominance, to let it know I wasn't prey. It responded with a grotesque slither, not unlike a snake preparing to strike.

Without hesitation, I drew my .44 auto mag and fired directly at its head. The creature reared up, releasing an agonizing scream that echoed through the forest. Two more shots pierced its heart. And just like its counterpart, the flare gun delivered the final blow to its wounded heart, eliciting another tortured cry.

I immobilized the creature using the steel rods, ensuring it was well and truly dead. Piling dried wood atop the lifeless being, I set it ablaze, the flames devouring the body with a fierce hunger.

However, as I began to relax, another set of eyes emerged from the shadows. Wait, four eyes? These weren't the eyes of a skinwalker. They were something entirely different, something I hadn't encountered before. Their gaze was filled with a cold intelligence that unsettled me. Slowly, they retreated into the forest's depths, their intent unclear.

Grateful for the repelling effects of the fires, I set about the grim task of decapitating the fallen skinwalkers, ensuring their spirits would find no respite in this world. As the flames continued to crackle, I slumped against a tree trunk, fatigue pulling me into a restless slumber.

I was jolted awake by the sound of authoritative voices. Two park rangers stood before me, their expressions stern, their intent clear – they were unhappy about the fires. Their scolding was cut short when I gestured toward the smoldering remains.

"Take a closer look," I rasped, my voice hoarse from the night's events. The rangers paled as they took in the sight. "Those were skinwalkers," I added. "They tried to take me down last night."

Their initial anger transformed into a mix of shock and disbelief. Clearly, they had heard the legends but had never encountered the real thing. Now, faced with the undeniable truth, they were forced to confront the nightmares of their ancestral stories.

One of the park rangers scoffed, his disbelief evident. "You expect us to believe this crap?" He exclaimed, pointing at the smoldering ashes. "You're lying!"

But the other ranger, older and with lines on his face suggesting he'd seen his fair share of mysteries in these woods, shot him a silencing glare. "I've heard the whispers," he said gravely. "Survivors have talked. They mentioned creatures – monsters. I didn't want to believe it, but when the government stepped in, it told us to hush up... I knew something was up." He eyed me warily, "You're the one they sent?"

I shook my head, the weight of my mission pressing down on me. "I'm not here for the skinwalkers. There's another monster I'm tracking, a human monster. But I knew I'd probably run into these creatures, given the territory."

A pause settled between us, the air heavy with the implications of the night's events.

"I need a favor," I continued, pointing to the decimated remains. "Bury them. The heads need to be separated from the bodies. It ensures they won't rise again."

The skeptical ranger muttered curses under his breath, clearly not thrilled about the idea. "Why the fuck should we?" He growled.

But his comrade's voice overpowered his protests. "We owe this man," he said. "He rid us of a terror we didn't even know how to face. We'll do it." Shooting the younger ranger a stern look, he added, "Quit your bitching, get the shovels, and let's get this done."

I nodded in gratitude. "Thanks. You have no idea how crucial this is."

As they set about their task, my attention returned to my original mission. Fresh footprints caught my eye, nearly obscured by the commotion of our encounter. Bare, distinctly human, and scattered haphazardly – as if whoever made them was running, afraid.

I motioned to the rangers, my voice urgent. "I've got to follow these. Once you're done burying the creatures for your safety, leave this area quickly."

The sight before me was gruesome – a visceral reminder of the dangers lurking in these woods. A cluster of footprints from the feral human beings was imprinted around a gruesome scene. The overwhelming number indicated a larger pack than I'd initially assumed. The implications of that discovery sent a shiver down my spine.

I noted the twisted formation of three trees bent into an 'X,' a clear territorial marker. I'd heard stories of Bigfoots doing this, but seeing it firsthand? It was an unnerving sight, almost mocking in its starkness against the dense foliage. It signaled that I was not just walking into Bigfoot territory but also amidst the menacing feral human beings.

A potential alliance between them? The thought was deeply unsettling. My intuition screamed that the two had formed a terrifying union bolstered by the more enigmatic threat of dogmen. It was as if nature itself had conspired to assemble a nightmarish trifecta.

"Shit, this is a fucking mess," I whispered to myself. I could feel the weight of the situation pressing down on me, each possibility more daunting than the last. The idea of turning back did cross my mind. It'd be the safer bet. But every bone in my body told me to press on. It was in my nature to confront such horrors head-on.

I trudged forward, my .38 magnum in hand, the metallic coolness of the gun serving as a minor comfort. Hours seemed to meld together as I continued my grim journey. That was until I stumbled upon the grotesque tableau of one of my quarries.

The carnage was unspeakable. Flesh and bone strewn everywhere, the earth saturated in crimson. Whatever had done this didn't just want to kill; it wanted to send a message. In this morbid jigsaw, I found a solitary finger, surprisingly intact. Slipping on a glove, I gingerly placed it in a zip-lock bag, securing it within my evidence kit. A part of me sighed in relief. One less evil to pursue. But what of the others?

The enormity of what I was about to embark upon began to weigh on me. Staying ahead of the feral human beings would be a trial of both my wits and agility. The woods seemed to pulsate with danger. Every rustle and every creak became suspect. The game was afoot.

I suddenly spotted two feral human beings in a clearing. Their hunched posture and wild eyes were unmistakable. Setting down my backpack and the reassuring weight of my .38 magnum, I stalked closer, every sense on high alert. I was so close I could hear their guttural murmurs and the unsettling grind of teeth.

Moving with the stealth of a panther, I lunged at the nearest one, snapping his neck in one swift move. The other barely had a second to register the danger when my knife found its mark, embedding deep into his throat. Blood spurted, and he collapsed without a sound.

Working quickly, I concealed the bodies with brush and foliage, trying to erase any evidence of the altercation. My instincts urged me to move and move fast. Fortune seemed to be in my favor; I encountered no other threats as I distanced myself from the location of the skirmish.

A vast clearing soon sprawled before me, its landscape dominated by a cliff rising like nature's own fortress. I estimated it to be about two hundred to two hundred and seventy-five feet high. Cliffs and I, we never got along. However, the drama unfolding below seized my attention.

From the vantage point, the spectacle was otherworldly. There were cries of distress, the unmistakable sound of trees splintering, and the cacophonous barks and growls of unknown creatures. A smaller, hairy creature, standing roughly six feet, scrambled for cover behind fallen timber. It was pursued by a more imposing figure - a Bigfoot. Even from a distance, I could see the creature clutching something that glinted menacingly in the dimming light. A tool? A weapon?

I dropped my backpack, feeling the weight of my BAR rifle. Bringing it to bear, I peered through the scope to get a clearer picture. The magnified view provided details I couldn't see with the naked eye. This was no ordinary hunt; it was a dance of predators and prey, and I was about to join the fray.

From my perch on the cliff, my scope revealed a panorama of primal confrontation, tension thrumming in the air. To my surprise, another Bigfoot emerged, staggering under the weight of an enormous tree branch. Blood streamed down its side, painting a poignant picture of its desperate bid for survival. The two original Bigfoots, presumably its kin, were backed up against the tree, cornered, and clearly preparing for what seemed to be their last stand.

A pack of dogmen, fierce and relentless, advanced on the beleaguered Bigfoots. Their lupine features twisted in predatory anticipation while their eyes gleamed with cold, deadly intent. The alpha male Bigfoot squared up, ready to fight until his last breath. The very essence of raw, untamed wilderness played out before me.

"Well, fuck," I muttered under my breath. No creature should have to face such odds, especially not on my watch. I steadied my breath, took aim, and released a shot, finding its mark on the hindmost dogman. The creature crumpled instantly, its skull shattered.

To my amazement, the other dogmen seemed unfazed, their focus singular and intense. I squeezed the trigger again, dispatching the next farthest dogman with a shot to its neck.

The atmosphere grew tense, thick with anticipation. The female Bigfoot's gaze met mine as the two remaining dogmen took in the scene of their fallen comrades. The intelligence and the raw emotion in her eyes struck me deeply. Yet, I couldn't afford distraction. Refocusing, I dispatched the penultimate dogman with two shots – one to the chest and another to his skull, ensuring he wouldn't rise again.

The last dogman stood frozen, a tableau of confusion and fear. For a brief second, we locked eyes through the scope. I hesitated no longer and sent a bullet racing, ending its reign of terror.

The male Bigfoot, wearied from battle, gave me a long, searching look as if trying to communicate gratitude or perhaps just trying to understand the human who had aided them. Then, he sagged to the ground, exhaustion overcoming him.

Suddenly, a rustling from the opposite tree line caught my attention—another dogman lurking, watching. Calculating the distance and adjusting for the wind, I realized this would be one of the most challenging shots I'd ever taken. But there was no turning back. I exhaled, steadied myself, and prepared to fire, hoping against hope that my bullet would find its mark in this high-stakes moment.

The dogman, almost stealthy in his approach, carefully navigated the terrain. For a fleeting moment, as he raised his head over a fallen tree, our worlds converged. Seizing the opportunity, I instantly pulled the trigger, blasting away its head. The dead weight of the creature collapsed onto the tree, lifeless.

Still reeling from the adrenaline, I looked over to the female Bigfoot. Her dark, intelligent eyes were studying me, myriad emotions dancing within them. Astonishingly, a hint of a smile played on her lips. She recognized me. Relief washed over me as I realized these were the same creatures I had saved from the cliff, and now they had a child. Our lives were inexplicably intertwined.

But the reunion was short-lived. A rustling from my left immediately put me on high alert. Another dogman emerged, charging at full tilt. My instincts kicked in, dropping my gear. I drew my shotgun, loading it with armor-piercing shells. In one fluid motion, I took a knee and fired. The creature's head exploded in a shower of gore, its lifeless body crashing into a tree with a sickening crack.

Rushing to the Bigfoots' side, I did my best to tend to their injuries. Realizing the severity of the situation, I decided it was time to call in reinforcements. The General was my best bet.

Before I could even process the next series of events, the ground vibrated with heavy footsteps thumping. Spinning around, my .44 auto mag at the ready, I was met with another rampaging dogman. Without hesitation, I pumped two bullets into its chest and two more into its head. The creature collapsed, its threat neutralized.

The subsequent hours blurred into a chaotic whirlwind. The distant thrum of helicopter blades signaled the arrival of the General, accompanied by a team of medics and an entourage of personnel. Sue was among them, her face a mask of concern. Max, with his imposing new bodyguards, was there too, their stern faces scanning the scene.

The General, taking in the aftermath, locked eyes with me. "This the body count?" He inquired, nodding toward the scattered corpses.

Offering him a defiant middle finger, I replied, "The dogmen got to them first. All that matters is they're dead."

His lips pressed into a thin line. "That's the primary target taken care of then."

Max, ever the opportunist, piped up. "And the bodies of our other guys?"

I locked eyes with him, my voice dripping with disdain. "What about them?"

"Why don't you check their stomachs?" I responded briefly, then pivoted on my heel and headed toward the Bigfoot family. A mysterious man, whom I hadn't noticed before, approached the General.

Their exchange was brief, and then he walked over to converse with the Bigfoots. The way he spoke was odd, full of intonations and incomprehensible sounds, but strangely, the Bigfoot family seemed to understand him perfectly.

Max, ever the instigator, decided to put in his two cents. "What are we even paying you for?" He sneered. "You let these creatures run the show, and you're no better than they are. You're an outcast, a menace. You belong with them. In fact, you should be put down like the rabid animal you are."

My patience, already worn thin, snapped. "No, it's you who should be put down," I spat back. Drawing my .38 mag, I fired four rounds into Max's chest. He crumpled, gasping, blood blossoming from his wounds. Approaching him, I leaned down, ensuring my words were the last he'd hear. "I warned you not to push me," I whispered before delivering the final shot to his head.

The entire clearing went silent. No one flinched. No one cried out. Instead, there was a collective air of indifference as Max's bodyguards moved his lifeless form into one of the helicopters. Their loyalty had been to their paychecks, not the man.

The two men regarded me for a long moment, then turned their attention to the General. "What's the next move?"

Seeing an opportunity, I interjected, "Take over Max's old position."

The General seemed to agree, nodding slowly.

"There's an opening now. Care to step in?" He proposed, his gaze steely.

Both men hesitated momentarily before answering in unison, "Yes, sir. Thank you."

The scene around us bustled as personnel loaded the fallen dogmen onto helicopters. While the Bigfoot family had been tended to, a decision was made to keep them for observation for a while longer. Their mysterious nature, combined with their apparent connection to me, made them invaluable assets.

The male Bigfoot, despite his hulking frame, looked vulnerable. His injuries were deep, showcasing the severity of the fight he'd been in. After the cleanup, we grouped, preparing to head back.

The General approached, seeking my input. "Given what you've seen here, should we keep this park closed?" He inquired.

I didn't hesitate. "I'd recommend it. The hills are alive with beings far beyond our comprehension. If you open this park, you'll be sending unsuspecting people to their deaths."

He took a moment to consider my words. "I'll present this to the higher-ups. We'll see what they decide."

As we boarded the helicopter, I settled next to Sue. Her voice was quiet, filled with concern. "Do you think they'll actually close the park?"

Gazing deep into her eyes, I replied, "No, not until the situation escalates. Not until they send me back in to eliminate every cryptid threat."

She sighed in agreement, her fingers finding mine in a comforting squeeze.

Back at the main camp, the two bodyguards - formerly Max's but now seemingly without a clear direction - approached. Their gratitude was evident. "Thanks for looking out for us back there," one began, "And if you ever need backup, know we're on your side."

Before I could respond, the General took a seat beside me, his tone grave. "We've got another situation. There are a few individuals causing havoc. I need you on this, and I need you now."

I was taken aback. "Another mission so soon?"

He nodded, handing over a file. "They've taken a Sheriff hostage after robbing a bank. We need her back. Alive."

I felt a surge of adrenaline. "A team?"

"You'll have one," he confirmed. "Time's tight, so I'll select them. I assure you, they'll be the best of the best."

Sue stepped in, "Once we're on the ground, I'll handle the local authorities and the press."

Grinning wryly at the two bodyguards, I asked, "Want to see what I do for a living? Up close and personal?"

Their eagerness was palpable. "Count us in."

# CHAPTER 5

✦✦✦

"**W**HEN I ASKED YOU GUYS if you wanted to go with us, you thought I was kidding?" Their initial disbelief had quickly given way to readiness, and we all boarded the next chopper together. As we took off, the machine's rotors slicing through the air, the affirmative "Yes!" still hung between us, binding us in some silent pact.

As we soared over the dense canopy below, the General leaned in closer to make himself heard over the chopper's din, "Your truck has been moved to the base. It'll be there, ready for action, just like you."

I nodded, my mind already elsewhere and my heart heavier than usual. The present mission couldn't help but resurrect memories of the first time I'd ever led a team. That was when Max and I realized how much we fucking hated each other. And now he's gone, leaving a ghost of conflict and unresolved emotions.

Oh, how vividly I remember that day — Four bastards robbing banks, stores, hell, even snatching purses from old ladies. Their cruelty knew no boundaries — no witnesses meant no survivors. They didn't care if you were old or young, male or female. They'd kill you just for looking at them — *funny*. And then, as if playing some twisted game, they'd run into the woods and disappear deep into the mountains for weeks, sometimes months. It's like the mountains swallowed them whole, making a mockery of the ensuing manhunts.

Local police, the fucking FBI, and other government agencies had thrown everything they had at finding these dicks, but they'd always come up empty-handed. That was where I came in. Nobody, I repeat, nobody, gets away from me.

The locals, desperate and without other options, had called for help. The tip led us to a small town in Minnesota. It was quaint, a postcard of American innocence, and yet it was marred by the last horrifying event. When I got there, the General and Sue were already waiting, their faces grim as if the weight of the world rested on their shoulders. And then there was Max, the proverbial thorn in my side.

I remember him sneering at me, his eyes always full of distrust and judgment. "So, you're the big shot they brought in to clean up our mess? Can't wait to see you fuck this up," he'd muttered, oozing disrespect from every pore. How I wished to shut him up permanently right then and there, but duty called. There were lives at stake, and as much as I hated Max, he was, at that time, a necessary evil.

I walked into the town hall meeting room, my boots thudding against the worn wooden floor. The team was already assembled, with their faces having a mix of eagerness and trepidation. They were green, perhaps, but ready to go.

Max, already there, seemed to wear a shit-eating grin. "I've briefed the team," he said, standing there like he'd just split the atom.

"And who the fuck gave you that authority?" I shot back. "I'll be the one to give them the lowdown. These are my guys."

"Don't you think I know what's going on?" Max retorted, his voice tinged with a condescension that made my fists itch.

"No, Max, you don't have a fucking clue what's out there. You have no idea what it's like on the field, what monsters walk among us. Unless you've been in the thick of it with me, don't pretend to know shit," I was getting hot now, each word escaping my mouth like steam from a boiling pot. "You want to go after these guys? Where would you even start? You know, jack shit, so let me do my job and get the hell out of my way."

My eyes met Max's, locking into a glare that neither of us broke. I finally looked away first, dismissing him with a wave of my hand, "Don't say another word. Just go."

That's when I noticed it — no guns, no supplies. "Max, where the fuck are the supplies? The weapons?"

"You won't be needing them," he yelled back as if this was some twisted game.

"Who the fuck is this guy?" I looked at the General, my eyes pleading for some clarity. "Get him away from me. I'll do this on my own."

"When you're going after four or five desperate men, you go in with the understanding that they'll do anything to stay free. That means they're likely not coming out alive, and maybe you won't either," I said, my voice low but charged with the weight of experience.

Turning my back on the General, I pulled out my phone and dialed a number that I knew by heart — a man I've depended on for a long time, a man who was damn good at his job. As I waited for the familiar voice to answer, I felt a slow burn of anger mixed with a growing resolve. Whoever these bastards were, wherever they were hiding, they were about to meet a fate they couldn't even begin to comprehend.

It was time to gear up. And this time, there would be no room for error. No room for Max's bullshit. Just a team united in purpose, equipped to deal with the very worst humanity had to offer.

So, when my guy answered the phone, I got straight to the point, "Pack up everything. We're going hunting, and I need the supplies. No compromises."

The voice on the other end chuckled — a low, knowing sound that sent a chill down my spine, "You know you can always count on me."

I hung up and looked back at the town hall door. They were my responsibility now, and like hell would I let Max, or anyone else, jeopardize that. We had work to do, and we'd be damned if we didn't do it right.

I pushed open the creaking double doors of the town hall meeting room, taking in the rows of uncomfortable folding chairs, the peeling paint on the walls, and the faces of the men before me. They looked as green as the moldy ceiling tiles but also eager. Damn eager.

"I'm the guy in charge," I began, cutting straight through the pleasantries. "You can call me by my first name, but that's the last casual thing you'll get from me. I've been doing this shit for more years than some of you have been alive. I've been to places that don't even fucking exist on maps. Now that we're done blowing smoke up each other's asses let's get to brass tacks."

Their eyes were fixed on me, each man a mixture of awe and uncertainty. Good. Keep 'em on their toes.

"There are three non-negotiable rules in my outfit," I continued, pacing back and forth in front of them, each step a clear punctuation of my words. "Follow these rules at all times, especially out there in the field. If you can't, then get the fuck out now. Understand?"

The room filled with a chorus of "*Yes, Sir.*"

"First rule: There are no 'buts' in my operation. I run the show. Got it?"

"*Yes, Sir,*" they answered in unison.

"Second rule: You shoot when I say shoot. No fucking cowboy antics, you hear me? You shoot only when I give the order. Clear?"

"*Yes, Sir,*" they echoed, their voices tinged with a newfound respect.

"Third rule: Stick together. No lone wolves. If you stray, you're an easy target. That's how they get you — when you're alone. Comprende?"

"*Yes, Sir,*" they shouted with widened eyes, finally grasping the gravity of what was at stake.

"Now, I've heard Max gave you some preliminary info. Forget it. That guy doesn't know dick about the reality on the ground. We're not going on some camping trip; we're stepping into a world of shit, and you better be armed to the teeth. I've got a guy, someone I'd trust with my life, flying in our supplies and weapons."

As I paused, letting the weight of my words sink in, I could feel the room's atmosphere shift from tension to a sort of electric anticipation.

"So, keep your eyes peeled, your noses sharp, and for fuck's sake, listen. Listen to the wind, the wildlife, the eerie quiet — especially listen to me. It might just save your life and the lives of the men beside you."

Pausing for a moment, I scanned their faces, "Anyone here ever hunted humans before?"

A few hands went up. Not everyone's, but enough.

"That's fine," I said, pacing again. "Because the targets we're after aren't just any humans. They're feral human beings, regressions of our species, devolved back about twenty thousand years. They've got nothing to lose, which means we've got everything to lose."

The room was silent, men exchanging glances filled with a combination of disbelief and dawning comprehension.

"Yes, you heard me right. Feral human beings. Can't reason with 'em, can't negotiate. So, if it's them or you, you better make damn sure it's them."

The room was so quiet that you could hear the rusty hands of the clock on the wall ticking away, each second pulling us closer to the mission, to the unknown, to the clash that was inevitable.

"And gentlemen," I added, my voice dropping to almost a whisper, "in this line of work, it's often kill or be killed. So, let's make sure we're the ones left standing."

With a sigh, I leaned against the worn, wooden podium that had seen better days, its splintered edges a metaphor for the unraveling situation. "Gentlemen, we've got another wrinkle in this already fucked-up scenario," I began, locking eyes with each man in the room. "These feral human beings... They're not your typical backwoods sociopaths. They've got some — let's call them 'roommates' — that make this mission even more perilous."

A murmur rippled through the room, eyes narrowing in confusion and curiosity.

"Yeah, you heard me right," I continued, my voice tinged with a seriousness that sliced through the room like a hot knife. "Bigfoots. A whole family of 'em, usually. And let me make this crystal clear: these hulking, fur-covered behemoths are protective as hell over their human compatriots. If they sense us as a threat — which we are — they won't hesitate to rip us apart limb by fucking limb."

The tension in the room tightened like a noose. You could cut the atmosphere with a knife.

"So, listen up. If a Bigfoot charges at you, you aim for the head. Kill shot. At first attempt," I ordered, my gaze sweeping the room, drilling into each man. "Don't worry about preserving the body for some scientific study; this isn't National Geographic. We're here to survive, and that means eliminating the threat by any means necessary."

"Understand, men?"

"*Yes, Sir,*" they chorused, eyes wide as saucers and mouths set in grim lines.

"For humans — feral or otherwise — I personally prefer a .38 mag. But if you can, use a knife. It's quick, it's quiet, and it doesn't send every woodland creature for miles howling the alarm. The last thing we need is to send a signal flare to every fucked-up thing in the forest that we're here and ready for a fight."

"But, gentlemen, let's be pragmatic. Sometimes, you need more firepower. That's why we've got an arsenal coming. A truck is on its way, packed with enough .44 mag revolvers and other implements of destruction to level a small village. You take whatever the fuck you need. This isn't the time to be a choosy bitch."

The room shifted, the aura transforming from one of impending dread to a spark of determination. Finally, they were beginning to grasp the weight, the utter gravitas of what lay ahead.

"As for communication," I added, almost as an afterthought, "Sue's handing out satellite phones. Don't even bother with your cell; where we're headed, it's about as useful as a snow blower in the Sahara."

Sue stepped forward then, distributing sleek, black satellite phones to each man. Their hands closed around the devices as if clinging to lifelines, which, in a sense, they were.

"I appreciate the satellite phone, Sue," I said, taking the sleek, black device from her hands. Then, turning back to the room, I announced, "Alright, men, the truck's here. Gear up with whatever the fuck you think you'll need. We're moving out. And make it fast."

The room jolted to life, men rushing out like hounds released from their leashes, each scrambling to arm himself with an assortment of lethal tools. Meanwhile, I eyed the new guy — some greenhorn who'd said he'd done a bit of tracking.

"New guy," I barked, "you up for taking point?"

He looked at me, swallowed hard, but nodded, "Yes, Sir."

"Good. Move your ass, then. We've got half a mile 'til we hit the prime hunting ground."

As we filed into the dense forest, our boots crunching through the underbrush and snapping twigs; the atmosphere was tense, thick with anticipation and uncertainty. I could feel the mood of the men swing like a pendulum between excitement and fear.

"So," I began, throwing a casual glance over my shoulder at the faces of my ill-fated recruits, "any of you ever hunted Bigfoot, Skinwalkers, Dogmen, or any other cryptids?"

A brief silence followed my question, punctuated only by the occasional rustle of leaves and the distant call of some unseen bird. The men exchanged looks of incredulity and skepticism.

"Listen up," I warned, "if the woods go silent or if the air turns stale and every fiber of your being screams that something's off, trust that feeling. You won't see these fuckers until it's too late, but trust me. They're out there."

My words, heavy with a kind of foreboding that made my own skin crawl, seemed to penetrate their incredulity — at least for a moment.

"You'll feel it. Anxiety creeping up your spine. The hair on the back of your neck standing up like a scared cat. And there's a smell — oh, you'll never forget it. A rank, putrid stench that'll stick to your nostrils long after we're out of this hellhole."

Pausing for effect, I added, "Ever heard of Dogman? How 'bout Grassman?"

That got their attention. They stopped dead in their tracks, eyes widened, jaws slack. One brave soul, perhaps gripped by a cocktail of disbelief and bravado, spoke up, "Are you fucking kidding? Are these creatures real?"

I walked up to him, my gaze piercing into his soul, "Yes, they're as real as the loaded guns you're carrying and twice as deadly."

He swallowed hard, regretting his brief moment of defiance.

"All I want is to get out of this alive," another man mumbled, his voice tinged with the raw edge of impending doom.

"What I'm telling you is not some campfire horror story. It's a bloody field report," I snapped. "If you don't want to be here and if you can't follow orders to the 'T,' leave. Now's your fucking chance."

There was a brief, charged silence. Finally, one guy broke ranks, calling me *'nuts'* as he turned back toward the safety of the town. I watched him go, no part of me willing to stop him.

"Anybody else got cold feet?" I challenged, my voice as icy as the resolve hardening in my veins. "Because once we're deep in that forest, it's too late for second thoughts. If I see any of you running the other way when shit hits the fan, you're a dead man. I'll pull the trigger myself — if the creatures don't get you first."

Their faces were pale, their eyes like saucers, but each man nodded, sealing their fate with that simple gesture.

"*We're staying, and we'll do this. No matter what,*" they said, almost in unison, as if pledging an unholy oath.

I looked at the group, my eyes scanning each of their faces. "You all ready to handle a gun and a knife? 'Cause if you ain't ready to kill with 'em, you're just holding your own death sentence in your hands. That's the law out here."

The air got thick as if my words were something solid, something you could touch. "Get your Bowie knives ready. We're stepping into their world now. And anyone stepping into their world is marked '*Death*.' You also better have two smaller knives at the ready. And let's set the record straight — I want every single one of you to have two guns ready, day or night, .38 mags or .357 mags, and a .44 mag loaded with armor-piercing rounds."

One guy piped up, his voice laced with irritation, "Didn't we already go over this? Do we really need all that firepower?"

I got up in his face, my eyes drilling into his, "You ever come face to face with an eight-foot creature? How about nine feet? Ten feet? You wanna kill it, you better bring some serious fucking firepower."

I took a step back, letting 'em stew in it for a second. "Now, you all still wanna go? Talk it over. I'll be over there," I said, nodding toward a fallen tree trunk. "Don't take too long deciding."

It was less than a minute before they came walking over to me, determination stamped on their faces.

I pulled out my sword, the metal gleaming in the dull light. "Listen up. Everything you got from Max, put it in the black bags. No excuses."

They followed orders, filling up the bags. Once they were done, I pulled out a thermite charge. "This is a burning bomb. We're gonna destroy everything in these bags. Can't let any of that crap sabotage our mission."

I set the charge, sealing the bags. A moment later, the thermite ignited, incinerating the bags and everything inside 'em. "Now, let's get the hell out of here and do what we came to do."

The tension spiked; they started yelling at me. I shot back, "He told y'all you could keep those devices, right? Said they're yours?"

They muttered a collective "*Yes*."

"He also says you could keep 'em as long as you're workin' for him, huh? Don't you get it? Those trackers are so they can keep tabs on you, so they know every move you're making. And trust me, they don't give a shit if you live or die out here. It's all about the money."

I triggered the thermite charge, burning away any trace of their old lives. I moved to the other side of the path on the mountain flank. I thought I heard something. The guys stared at me in disbelief.

"Look, if you're pissed off at me for destroying the stuff, I'll replace it, alright?" I broke the tension, shifting focus.

We started trekking toward the mountain path. Then it hit me — the old ankle pain. The swelling surged up from past injuries. And the heat — oh, the heat. It was reaching into the high 90s.

We had to stop. We were all drained, wrung out like old washcloths. Luckily, the new track guy found us a stream.

"Everybody getting enough water?" I asked, glancing at their faces. Sweat dripped from brows, and eyes were bloodshot. "Let's eat something. Keep it light. And for the love of yourself, keep drinking water."

"*Right, Boss,*" some echoed. The heat was taking its toll; it reminded me of my war days — hot, arid, and merciless.

I knew we had a lot of ground to cover before sunset. "Keep hydrating!" I yelled. But some didn't listen. Their faces turned ashen; I could see they were about to keel over. We had to stop. Again.

I glared at my team, "Listen up, the day's still young. You want to get heatstroke? Fine. But you're more likely to just drop dead. So, drink up!"

And with that, we mustered whatever energy we had left and pushed forward, each step a little heavier than the last, each gulp of water more vital than ever. The oppressive heat, the looming creatures, the haunted past — all of it was now part of this harrowing journey into the unknown.

"Alright, listen up, guys," I said, breaking the stifling silence that had settled over us in the blistering heat. "How much are you fuckers making on this trip? 'Cause I'm making a million, and let me tell you, even that's not enough if you're dead and buried."

Their eyes met each other's, then turned back to me. "Insurance ain't gonna mean shit for you or your families. Money comes and goes, but dying out here? That's permanent, guys. You won't be worth a cent to anyone if you keel over right here, right now."

The tension was palpable, every one of us feeling the sweat dripping down our brows. "We gotta get you back to your families, to your loved ones. Fuck a condolence letter and a shitty check from your superiors. So, keep chugging that water. Your life's worth more than a few sips."

I was pissed off, my emotions boiling over. "Don't trust Max, alright? The guy's a grade-A dick. You really think I've been doing this for thirty-five fucking years 'cause I trust pricks like him? Hell no!"

I slammed a fax paper onto a rock, smoothing it out so they could see. "This is the fucking truth, boys. I'm still kicking because I trust no one but myself. And I need to trust you guys, got it? We all wanna get out of this shithole alive, right?"

You could feel the emotional weight of the moment, like a heavy fog settling over us. "Look out for the guy next to you, and make sure that man does the same for another. That's how we'll get out of this alive, got it? Now, who wants to fucking live? And who wants those million dollars?"

Their eyes met once again, and a moment of silent agreement passed between them. Finally, one of them broke the silence, "Yeah, we want to live. And fuck yeah, we want that money."

"So, let's gear the fuck up," I barked, scanning the faces of my ragtag crew. "Spazz shotguns, you get one if you're the first or last guy in line, and the third one gets it too. Got it? Everyone's got each other's backs."

They nodded, the gravity of the situation sinking in.

"The Gatling gun stays in the middle. If shit hits the fan, we all hit the ground and let that beast do its job. Kill everything in sight. Capiche?"

The guy with the Gatling gun gripped it tighter, nodding solemnly.

"As for handguns, keep 'em ready. Best case, they scare off whatever's out there. Worst case, we're forming a defensive line. Understand?"

A chorus of affirmatives rose from the group.

"So, what's the plan if we're ambushed? What are you doing?" one of them dared to ask.

"Fighting for our damn lives," I snarled. "All I want is loyalty. You cover my ass, I'll cover yours. When the going gets tough — and it will get fucking tough — we're all we've got. We'll make it through. Another five miles and we make camp. After that, you'll get your money, and don't forget the bonus at the end."

The mood lifted slightly, a glint of excitement breaking through the collective fatigue.

"And if you don't make it," I added, "make sure you've picked your next of kin. They'll get your cut."

The smiles wavered, but they got back to work. Six of them were visibly lifted by the promise of reward, busying themselves with scouting our first campsite. Out of the corner of my eye, something shifted. Couldn't make out what the fuck it was, but I knew it was time to be vigilant.

"Keep your eyes and ears open, everyone. I've been saying it for a reason. One slip, and we're all fucked."

Scouring the terrain for footprints turned up nothing. "Anything on your end?" I called out to our lead tracker.

"Not a damn thing. No human prints, no animal prints. Nothing," he responded.

Darkness loomed on the horizon as we trudged along, each step taking us further into uncertainty. Time was running out, and I hadn't anticipated what would happen next. It was camp-making time, no two ways about it. We were all spent, running on fumes.

Without a word, we set up camp. I stoked the fire, inserting metal rods for later — tools we'd desperately need in case we ran into any Skinwalkers.

"You don't wanna be figuring this shit out last minute. Trust me, it'll be a fucking disaster," I cautioned, watching as the men meticulously checked their firearms. The tension was palpable. The last thing anyone needed was a jammed gun when the hell broke loose.

My mind was already racing ahead, strategizing about the next steps of this mission. We had to find those bastards before they razed another innocent town.

"Listen up, guys!" I called out, gathering them around. "Tonight ain't gonna be a regular night in the woods, got it? Not that any of this has been regular."

Their faces twisted into varying degrees of annoyance and fatigue. I could tell they weren't thrilled with what was coming next.

"Look, I get it. We're all fucking tired. But work a bit more, set up, and then try to get some shut-eye. I'll take the first watch."

"You sure about that?" one of them asked, skeptical.

"We work together, we can kill these fuckers. Just do what I say, and nobody gets hurt. You have my word."

"What 'fuckers' are we talking about here?" another one chimed in.

"Skinwalkers," I said, locking eyes with each of them. "Don't worry, I know how to kill 'em."

It was the first time I saw their eyes clouded with genuine fear. Something about the term "*Skinwalkers*" seemed to break through the layers of machismo and adrenaline-fueled bravado.

"We're gonna make this place as uninviting as possible. Break down dead tree branches and gather some brush. We'll douse it in lighter fluid and keep the fire raging all night."

While they busied themselves with fire preparations, I took the metal rods and thrust them into the fire. They would be our last line of defense, searing hot and ready to pierce through flesh and bone.

Just then, one of the guys let out a low whistle. "Hey, come look at this," he called, pointing to the ground near the edge of the clearing. Dog-like footprints, massive ones, marred the earth.

"Over here, everyone!" I yelled. "Looks like we've had visitors tailing us all day."

The men crowded around, staring at the footprints in a mixture of awe and horror.

"We're probably gonna get attacked. Could be tomorrow morning, could be in the afternoon. The point is, it's not a matter of *if* but a matter of *when*. So, stay sharp, and for fuck's sake, stay alive."

The guys asked, "How many do you think?"

"I don't fucking know how many there are, alright? Just stay on your toes," I responded, the weight of leadership settling on my shoulders. "Look, this is why we're packing all this firepower. Tonight, it's probably just a couple of Skinwalkers. They'll keep the Dogmen at bay for now."

"So, it's Skinwalkers tonight and Dogmen tomorrow? What's next?" a guy groaned, wiping the sweat from his brow.

"Yeah, Skinwalkers tonight, Dogmen tomorrow, and who knows what the fuck else later," I confirmed. "Plus, there's something else: I haven't seen any tracks belonging to the guys we're after or the sheriff. Something's off."

One of the trekkers, his face layered with grime and fatigue, piped up, "I haven't seen any tracks from the woman either."

I scanned the faces around me, each etched with a mixture of concern and tension. "Anyone else see anything?" When they all shook their heads, a knot tightened in my stomach, "Damn, I hope she's still alive."

"So, what are we up against? Bigfoot? Dogmen? Some sick humans?" someone asked, nervously clutching his shotgun.

"I heard the FBI guys say they're armed," another guy interjected. "Some shotguns, a long gun they think is a .30-30, and some handguns."

"So, we have to rescue the sheriff before all hell breaks loose. That's our job, gentlemen. Got it?" I reiterated, looking each man in the eye.

They nodded, a sense of resolve settling over the group. "If we see or hear anything, you'll be the first to know."

"Good. Now, try to get some fucking sleep. We've got a long day ahead," I advised.

"And we're watching for... what, again?" a younger recruit asked, his eyes wide and alert.

"*Skinwalkers*," I replied, emphasizing the word as if it could summon the creatures themselves.

The night pressed on, as tense and thick as molasses. Hours ticked away, and yet there was no sign of anything. It was unsettling, this lull before the storm, and I could sense that everyone felt it, too.

"Some of you try to get some sleep," I finally said, though the thought of closing our eyes while unknown threats lurked in the darkness seemed like a tall order. "We're going to need all the energy we can muster for whatever shit show is waiting for us come dawn."

The heat was relentless, almost hitting a hundred degrees as the day wore on. By the time darkness started to settle, a chill crept in, its sharp contrast to the daytime heat almost shocking. We set up camp on the darker side of the tree line, about 300 yards from what I suspected was the main thoroughfare for whatever it was we were gonna end up fighting. I glanced at the falling leaves — those fuckers love the trees.

"Man, is it getting cold, or is it just me?" one of the guys muttered, pulling his jacket tighter around him.

"Yeah, it's getting cold 'cause our friends are about to pay a visit," I shot back. "Skinwalkers. Get your shit together, boys. We're not alone."

I turned to John, a former Army Captain with the Rangers. "I want those metal rods white-hot. Someone, put on those gloves and get ready to grab 'em when I give the word. Got it?"

John nodded, his eyes never leaving the tree line. "There's something else over there. Something's moving."

My senses went into overdrive. "Everybody, get ready to defend yourselves!"

And that's when I saw them — five or six figures, vaguely human, standing on the other side of our camp. They didn't look happy.

"Don't take your eyes off 'em. There could be Bigfoots here too," I cautioned the group. The human figures looked at us, muttered something incomprehensible to each other, and then bolted back into the forest. One stayed behind for a moment longer, glaring at us before disappearing into the dark.

"That spooked 'em, but stay sharp. We've got something else coming," I warned. My eyes darted around until they fell on it — a ten-foot creature emerging from behind us. A fucking *Skinwalker*.

And he looked pissed off.

But what really got me was the look on his face. The left side of it bore an expression so malicious it felt like I was staring down the embodiment of pure, unadulterated hatred. My heart pounded like a drum in my chest, every beat screaming at me that this was it.

"Boys, grab those hot rods! It's showtime," I yelled. "Get ready to face this Skinwalker. And you better not miss."

The air grew even colder, the tension so thick you could cut it with a knife. We were standing on the edge of a blade, and any misstep could mean the difference between life and a gruesome death. This was it: the moment we'd been waiting for, dreading, and now it was here, ugly and terrifying. It was a showdown, and none of us were sure we were ready for what was about to happen.

My eyes were locked onto the creature, my heart racing like a sprinter at the final stretch. "I'm taking the first shot. Nobody else fucking shoot. Someone, put on the gloves — *now!*"

The creature was towering, a disturbing ten feet at the shoulder. Its skin was pale white and stretched taut over its bones, giving it a skeletal appearance. Long, sinewy arms ended in grotesquely elongated fingers tipped with claws sharp enough to gut a man in a single swipe. Drool dripped from its mouth as it sniffed the air, its nostrils flaring, assessing whether we were its next meal.

This was my chance. I raised my .44 Auto Mag and fired two rounds directly into its heart. The creature let out an ear-splitting scream, and its eyes widened in what seemed like disbelief and agony. Before it could recover, I fired my flare gun into its heart. A burst of flame and smoke erupted from its chest as it fell to the ground.

"Now! Rods in its heart — another one in its head!" I yelled.

One of the guys lunged forward, his gloved hands thrusting the white-hot rod into the creature's chest. Another shoved a second rod into its skull. A third guy threw dried wood onto the beast and set it ablaze. Quickly and efficiently, another teammate severed its head with a machete.

Just as I was about to let out a breath of relief, movement in the trees caught my eye, "Hold up, we've got another one!"

My fingers were sweating around the grip of my .44 as the second Skinwalker lurked among the trees, almost as if it was contemplating its odds. It's a good thing I wasn't planning on giving it time to decide.

I aimed for its shoulder, pulling the trigger. It let out a guttural howl and tumbled to the ground. Not wasting a second, I aimed my .44 auto mag again and pumped two rounds into its heart, then another two into its head for good measure. A flare shot from my gun burst into its heart, setting it ablaze.

"Same drill, guys — cut the head off and torch it!"

The team went to work, and soon enough, the second monster was a burning pile of ashes, its head severed and cast aside.

I exhaled deeply, my body trembling from adrenaline and exhaustion. "Is that all of them? Tell me that's all of them."

As if on cue, another rustling sound came from the tree line. I felt my gut sink. Whatever it was, we weren't done here. Not by a long shot.

"Ready up, boys," I muttered, cocking my .44. "This night's not over yet."

My eyes darted to the source of the new movement. "Holy shit," one of the guys exclaimed, his gaze locked on a small hill. There, backlit by the dawning sky, stood two menacing Dogmen. As if summoned by some dark spell, four more emerged from the tree line.

"You've gotta be kidding me," I muttered. But it wasn't over. From another angle, two massive Bigfoots — Sasquatches, if you prefer — appeared, one eight feet tall and the other easily topping ten feet.

"Nobody shoots. Just wait. This feels like fucking Vietnam all over again," I said. My voice was barely a whisper, but it carried the weight of raw tension.

The supernatural menagerie seemed to enter a standoff, Bigfoots and Dogmen eyeing each other, both sets of eyes occasionally flickering in our direction. As the first rays of dawn broke through the night, the creatures appeared to reach an uneasy détente.

"So, what's the consensus? Real or not?" one guy snickered nervously, his words tinged with both awe and fear.

"We can't go uphill. We have these Bigfoots and their canine pals in the way. Our other option is trying our luck with the Dogmen down this path," I weighed the options out loud, my eyes scanning the map in my hands.

"If we have to pick a side, I'm going Bigfoot," John, the former Army Ranger, spoke up. "Those Dogmen look like they're born from the bowels of hell. At least Bigfoots look... somewhat human."

"I'm with John," I said, my finger tracing a potential escape route on the map. "Let's just hope there are more Bigfoots out there. They're gonna need all the help they can get."

We broke camp as swiftly as our adrenaline-pumped bodies would allow. "We're moving straight ahead toward the Dogmen territory. If we're lucky, they'll be too busy dealing with the Bigfoots to notice us," I instructed.

Just as we entered the woods, we came upon more Bigfoots and Dogmen, who seemed too preoccupied with each other to care about us. "Well, that solves one problem, at least for now," I mumbled, feeling a modicum of relief.

"Leave the Skinwalkers to burn," I said, my eyes still on the trees. "We stay close to the tree line. Maybe we can avoid being seen by these things."

We had barely covered a few hundred yards when an unnerving cacophony erupted from the direction we had just left — screams, howls, barks, a dreadful symphony of violence. It was as if the forest itself had become a battlefield for the damned.

"Fuck, they're at it," John murmured. "Doesn't sound good for the Bigfoots, does it?"

"I say we'll be dead meat in a few hours if we don't help the Bigfoots. Who's coming with me?" I looked around, my eyes meeting the steely gazes of my team. "Maybe they'll owe us one, and we'll all get out of this shitshow alive."

To my relief, the men nodded. "Alright, let's go save some fucking Bigfoots."

The consensus was clear; we'd be in an even worse situation if we didn't help the Bigfoots. It was going to be a gunfight either way, and the idea was to choose the lesser evil. "Let's get back there and figure out how to jump those Dogmen from behind the trees."

We had barely moved a few yards when a snarling Dogman burst through the foliage, its eyes glowing like hot coals. Without missing a beat, I aimed my .44 mag and shot it square in the head. Its body thudded to the ground, lifeless.

"Headshots, boys, headshots!" I yelled, the adrenaline coursing through my veins.

Almost as if on cue, another Dogman appeared, a guttural growl reverberating from its throat. One of the guys unleashed a torrent of buckshot from his Spas-12, dropping the creature where it stood.

"We gotta move fast, keep pushing," I hollered. "Tom, keep your eyes on that damn map. We need a quick way out once this craziness is done."

Tom nodded, his eyes darting between the map and the barely lit trail. "Got it, just keep those things off me."

Just as I was about to advance, a massive Bigfoot landed in front of me with a ground-shaking thud. Our eyes locked. For a moment, it was as if time stood still. We were two warriors in an arena of chaos, sizing each other up.

I could've pulled the trigger, but I didn't.

Just as a flicker of what seemed like understanding crossed the Bigfoot's eyes, a feral scream broke the silence. A Dogman leaped from the shadows, launching itself at the Bigfoot from behind.

"Son of a bitch!" I cursed, lifting my gun. The creature's ambush was underhanded, even by the brutal laws of this twisted wilderness. And as much as these woods were a kingdom of kill or be killed, there was something utterly dishonorable about backstabbing in the midst of a battlefield.

I aimed my .44 auto mag squarely at the Dogman's head and pulled the trigger. The creature fell like a sack of bricks, life extinguished in an instant. The Bigfoot, seemingly more intelligent than we'd given it credit for, used its massive hands to shove the Dogman's corpse away. It looked at me, and I felt like it was sizing me up, deciding my intentions. For a long, lingering second, our gazes met, and then the Bigfoot grunted softly and lumbered away into the shadows of the trees.

"Alright, let's get the fuck outta here!" I said, snapping back to reality. "To the clearing, everyone. Let's get our guns hot and ready!"

Everyone started reloading their firearms, their movements mechanical but fast, honed by years of practice and a heightened sense of survival. Within a minute, we were loaded up and ready to move.

"Now or never, boys. Forward march!" I commanded, and we started walking toward the site where we'd heard the battle cries of the mythical creatures.

As we arrived, the sight was something out of a nightmare: toppled trees, scratches on bark that looked like runic symbols from hell, and blood — a lot of it. A wounded young Bigfoot was struggling against a Dogman that was moving in for the kill. Without a second thought, I fired my .44 into the Dogman's head, saving the young Bigfoot, who then hobbled away to its clan.

When the dust finally settled, the Bigfoots had won. They were injured, bleeding from wounds that would have killed lesser creatures, but they were alive. A low rumble of what I guessed was their vocalizations for gratitude filled the air.

"Now, I hope those big furry fuckers will remember that we helped 'em," I muttered, half to myself. "Alright, boys, we need to get to a location for resupply. Tim and John, stay on each side. Eyes open, heads on a fucking swivel."

Tim and John nodded, hands gripping their .44 mags and Bowie knives strapped securely to their belts.

"We're not just worried about Bigfoots or Dogmen. There could be other humans around. So, stay alert," I cautioned. "Stick to the middle of the path, and for fuck's sake, yell out if anything looks even remotely suspicious. Let's move!"

The tension was palpable as we started walking again, our boots barely making a sound on the leaf-covered ground. After about an hour of nerve-wracking silence, we reached a section of the forest that felt unusually still. Too still.

I noticed it first. The forest was utterly silent — no birdsong, no rustling of small creatures in the underbrush, no creaking of trees. It was as if every living thing had decided to hold its breath.

The moment the Dogman charged out of the foliage, its unearthly howl ripping through the silence like a blade, I yelled, "Stay cool!" With practiced ease, my .44 auto mag thundered, and the beast's head exploded in a shower of gore, dropping it like a sack of wet cement.

"Everyone okay?" I hollered, scanning my comrades.

"Shit, no!" Tom screamed. Just as he said it, another Dogman lunged from a tree, soaring through the air like some twisted, feral angel of death. Tom fired three rapid rounds into its chest. The beast let out a blood-curdling shriek and hit the ground. I took aim at the second one and fired twice into its chest. It, too, fell dead.

But then my eyes met another Dogman, sizing me up. He hesitated for just a split second before charging at me like a bat out of hell. I aimed and fired. The bullet grazed the side of its head, throwing it off balance. It screamed — a mix of pain and unbridled rage. Just as it was about to regain its footing, Tom fired another round into its chest, followed by a shot to the head. The beast finally went down as if the forest floor itself had pulled it into a grave.

Behind me, the loud pop of gunfire filled the air. Swiveling around, I saw another Dogman sprawled out on the ground. More gunfire echoed, and before I knew it, Jack had plunged his Bowie knife into yet another beast's chest. I quickly aimed my .44 and fired, putting it down for good.

"Reload, everyone! Prep for another round!" I barked. "Sound off! Is everyone alright? I want names!"

One by one, their voices came through. "John," "Jack," "Tim," "Sam," "Mat." They were all accounted for.

"No one's hurt, boss. That's a good start," Sam affirmed.

I holstered my .44 and pulled out my shotgun. "I don't like the look of this, boys. Bring out the high-powered guns. Round two's gonna be a fucking nightmare if it happens."

We resumed our trek, our eyes scanning every shadow, every rustle of leaves. We were four hours from the drop zone, but those would be the longest four hours of our lives.

"Stay at the top of your game," I cautioned. "We're not out of the woods yet — and yeah, no pun intended."

Mat, his face lined with weariness and something darker, looked at me, "Why are they still hunting us like this?"

I sighed, a heavy feeling settling in my gut, "They're getting even, Mat. They won't rest until they've made us pay for what we did to their kin. This isn't just survival for them; it's fucking retribution."

Out of nowhere, the lady sheriff appeared, a surreal vision among the chaotic tangle of woods and blood. We were all taken aback.

"Who the hell are those 'Fin' people?" she yelled, eyes wide, referring to the group that had attacked her. "They just came at me, screaming in some fucked up language!"

"They're feral human beings," I responded, trying to make sense of her sudden appearance. "Are you saying they're all dead?"

She stared at me incredulously, "Yes, dead. Those creatures killed them. You don't believe me, do you?"

I looked her straight in the eyes, "Are you alright?"

"I don't fucking know what 'alright' is anymore," she snapped, then immediately softened her tone. "What the hell is going on?"

"Sorry, I didn't mean to piss you off. We're fighting for our lives, same as you were with those assholes you escaped from," I told her. "Mat, give her a gun, some water, and a health bar. Now."

"Thanks. So, what now?" she asked, taking the supplies from Mat.

"We're fighting to get out of this shithole alive," I declared, looking her in the eyes. "Do you want to live or die?"

She met my gaze unflinchingly, "I have a young daughter. I want to live."

"And what will you do to ensure that?"

"I can handle myself. Don't think I'm some farmer's daughter," she retorted defiantly.

Mat handed her ten clips. "That's all well and good, but some things out here are pure evil. All of them are now out to get us. You think you could handle these creatures all by yourself?"

She paused, contemplating. "With your level of experience? Maybe, maybe not. But I'll certainly give it a different voice."

"Enough chatter," I cut in. "There are even worse things out here than what we just fought. Let's get moving. The drop zone is still far off."

I gave Mat a sidelong glance and a quick smile, a brief moment of camaraderie amid the hell we were trudging through. We'd been walking for about two and a half hours when I sensed movement about twenty-five yards away. I raised my hand, signaling everyone to stop on the spot.

My eyes were locked on a big tree. Something wasn't right. With a subtle hand signal, I got everyone's weapons up and ready.

"Sam, what's going on?"

"Keep your eyes open," I whispered tensely. "Thought I saw a feral human being by the tree."

Suddenly, on the other side of the path, a Dogman's head popped out, howling something unintelligible but clearly aggressive toward the feral human being. Unbelievably, a Bigfoot emerged, making a protective stance in front of the human, and started yelling at the Dogman. As if summoned by this unearthly cacophony, two more Dogmen and additional Bigfoots arrived. The atmosphere was thick with tension, each creature sizing up the other, feral energies rippling through the air.

An idea flashed in my mind. "If these cryptids go at each other, we might be able to slip by," I muttered to the team.

Just as the words left my mouth, a feral human being lunged at me out of nowhere, and my Bowie knife found its heart in a split second. The bastard fell to the ground, life oozing out.

"Move, fucking move!" I yelled as adrenaline surged through my veins.

Another feral human being lunged at Mat, who reacted instantly, firing his gun. The feral human being dropped dead in its tracks. A third one came at Jack from the opposite side of the path. Jack parried its knife with his own, then shoved his blade into its throat with surgical precision. The human choked and dropped, clutching at its ruined throat.

My eyes darted back to the original standoff between the Dogmen and the Bigfoots, just in time to see chaos erupt. Bigfoots and Dogmen were tearing into each other with savage ferocity. But what shocked me was seeing a couple of feral human beings siding with each Bigfoot. One of them managed to plunge a knife into a Dogman, bringing it down. Not willing to let any more unknown variables fuck up this already complicated equation, I raised my .44 mag and shot the remaining Dogman square in the head. The creature fell backward with a thud, a pool of dark blood quickly forming around its head.

The path ahead was a corridor of chaos, echoing with howls and guttural cries — no way out but to shoot our way through. "Guns out! We're busting our way through this hellhole!" I yelled, my voice laden with urgency.

"Stay two by two and follow me! Let's get the fuck out of here!" I commanded, readying my shotgun. With a squeeze of the trigger, I blew away two feral human beings who were foolish enough to run toward us. The others scattered into the undergrowth, giving us a brief but clear path.

We sprinted like madmen toward the tree line, my heart pounding in my chest like war drums. As we broke into the forest, I collided with a Dogman lurking in the shadows. Without missing a beat, I pumped a round into its chest, then a second one into its skull. It went down like a sack of bricks.

I hastily reloaded the shotgun and double-checked the .44 mag, ensuring it was locked and loaded. But just as I did, a sharp, agonizing pain shot through my side. A feral human being was trying to gut me, his knife digging deep. Mat, swift as ever, fired a shot, and the human's face went slack as he crumbled to the ground. I yanked the knife from my side, grimacing as blood stained my clothes.

The sheriff, her eyes wide with a mix of fear and adrenaline, supported me. "You're gonna be okay," she whispered, her tone not entirely convincing even to herself.

"We need to move. Now. If those Bigfoots realize we've killed their buddies, we're all fucked," I growled. My words hung in the air like a dark omen.

There was an urgency now, a palpable tension that gripped each of us. Our pace was slower, burdened by my injury and the weight of what we had just been through. But the alternative — to remain in this nightmarish landscape — wasn't an option. Every step we took was a step closer to life and a step away from the terrors of this unholy place. Yet, we all sensed it: this ordeal was far from over.

The sheriff's grip on me tightened, lending her strength to my faltering steps. Time was a bleeding wound, and we had to staunch it — fast. The cacophony of the skirmish between the Bigfoots and the Dogmen escalated, a symphony of screams and roars that split the air and shook the very ground beneath us. The tension in the air was so thick that you could carve it with a knife.

"We shoot whatever the fuck gets too close, got it?" I barked as we maneuvered through the maze of battling cryptids. Bigfoot or Dogman, if it threatened us, it got a bullet.

This was a badlands opera set on the edge of madness, and it froze your marrow just being a part of it. Just as we thought we had a window, another feral human being lunged at me. But before he could close the distance, the sheriff blasted him square in the chest. His body crumpled to the ground, and his life was extinguished in an instant.

"Move, move, move!" I yelled, adrenaline surging through my veins as we bolted down a steep, three-hundred-yard hill. At the bottom, I caught a Bigfoot's gaze. Our eyes met, and I sensed understanding — a mutual acknowledgment that we weren't the problem. It seemed to gesture — just go.

Every one of us was a constellation of aches, scrapes, and fatigue, but stopping was a luxury that we couldn't afford. Another human jumped out from my left, a jagged knife glinting menacingly in his hand. But before he could make his move, Sam shot him dead.

Finally, after what felt like an endless gauntlet of dread, we had to pause. We found ourselves in a grotesque tableau — body parts strewn about, the detritus of violence and death.

The sheriff broke the silence. "These are the guys who took me," she muttered, her voice tinged with a mix of relief and horror as she surveyed the campsite.

Just then, another human bolted toward John, weapon in hand. John was unaware, his back turned. My finger tightened on the trigger, but Mike was faster. His shot rang out, dropping the human in his tracks.

We all looked at each other, our faces ashen. The realization sank in — they were following us. And that meant one terrifying truth — this nightmare was far from over.

We were all haggard, running on fumes and pure instinct. My eyes darted back to the campsite, where we'd collected some body parts in bags — gruesome souvenirs to prove the inexplicable horrors we'd faced.

Then it hit us — the shrieks of Bigfoots, slicing through the forest air like sonic knives. I felt a shiver crawl up my spine.

"Circle up," I ordered, my voice laced with urgent severity. "We make our stand in that open field up ahead. Move!"

As we broke into the clearing, I caught sight of the drop zone — our lifeline. Parachuted supplies lay in crates, tantalizingly close yet swathed in peril.

"Sam and John, haul ass and grab those supplies. We'll cover you," I shouted.

Sam and John bolted, their boots pounding the ground in a desperate sprint. My eyes locked onto the tree line where a macabre theater unfolded — four humans lingering in the shadows, transfixed by a Dogman ripping apart one of their own. Steadying my trembling hands, I hoisted my .50 cal and took aim. With a deafening roar, the bullet shot through the air, obliterating the Dogman's head. I stumbled back, weakened from blood loss and sheer exhaustion.

Just then, a colossus emerged. A Bigfoot so massive that its size defied reality. It towered over the trees — easily hitting the eleven-foot mark — and glared down at us. He barked out a series of guttural sounds to the humans, who looked at me with disdain burning in their eyes.

It was a Mexican standoff. Time hung suspended in a cruel limbo. The Bigfoot roared again, seemingly instructing the humans. They hesitated, clearly torn but ultimately submissive to the behemoth. With begrudging steps, they retreated back into the shadowy labyrinth of trees.

Except for one.

His eyes clung to mine, an unspoken vendetta forming in that locked gaze. "I'll be seeing you," the look said, and I nodded subtly, accepting the unvoiced challenge.

"We need to get the fuck out of here," I announced, breaking the spell. "It'll be dark soon, and I'll be damned if we spend another night in this forsaken place. Move!"

We picked up the pace, every muscle screaming in protest as we navigated the treacherous path. The sky dimmed, a dying ember in the encroaching darkness.

As we trudged onward, the atmosphere around us seemed to thicken with every step. That's when Jack's voice sliced through the tension.

"A Bigfoot is following us!" he yelled, his voice tinged with panic.

"Just keep going," I assured him, wheezing through the pain in my side. "He's making sure we're out of their territory."

After what felt like a relentless, three-hour sprint through the wilderness, I spoke to Jack again, "Is it still following us?"

"No," he gasped, "we must've cleared its territory. Can we stop?"

"Yeah, we can make camp here," I conceded, feeling the weight of my injuries crashing down on me like a ton of bricks. "Jack, scout the area, make sure we're not being tailed."

As Jack disappeared into the woods, I collapsed onto a fallen log. The world swayed around me, my vision blurring at the edges. "I don't think I'm going to make it to retirement," I rasped to the sheriff. "Tell Sue that I loved her."

"Cut that shit out," the sheriff retorted, "you can tell her yourself."

"If we follow this path for about an hour, we'll reach the choppers," I instructed, fighting to keep my eyes open. "I can't go much further. Losing too much blood. Just get everyone out of this cursed place. There might still be stragglers on our tail."

They looked at me with eyes filled with a mixture of admiration and despair. "We all leave together, or no one leaves. Got it?"

Just then, something rustled in the foliage to my left. I crouched low, gripping the hilt of my small sword as I listened intently. Footsteps. Soft, calculated, nearing.

And there he was — emerging from the shadows with his makeshift knife — The Feral Human Being. The one who'd locked eyes with me back at the clearing, the one who had defied the Bigfoot's warning. His eyes glinted with a mix of malice and madness, and I could feel his anger radiating, building up like a storm waiting to break.

Time slowed to a crawl. His eyes met mine, and the world condensed to this single moment, this final confrontation. It was him or me, and by God, it wasn't going to be me.

He charged at me like a feral animal, his makeshift knife glinting menacingly in the dying light. Just as I braced myself for the impact, a gargantuan hand shot out of the shadows and gripped the man by the neck. The male Bigfoot lifted him off the ground as if he were a ragdoll, snapping his neck with a casual twist before tossing him aside like garbage.

The Bigfoot's eyes met mine, and, at that precise moment, I swear, an understanding passed between us. His gaze seemed to say, "He had it coming. He didn't listen."

With surprising gentleness, the giant creature grabbed the feral human being's lifeless foot and dragged his body away into the dark underbrush. Then he turned and lumbered away, leaving us in stunned silence.

"Did — did you all see that?" I stammered, my voice shaky.

"Yeah, we did," the sheriff replied, her eyes wide with disbelief. "And I'd say that Bigfoot just saved your life."

We resumed our trek back to the camp, a new sense of urgency driving us. Each step was excruciating, but stopping was not an option. Just then, we saw the unmistakable silhouette of a Dogman peeking from behind a tree. I signaled for quiet, and the sheriff began to stealthily approach the creature. She was about five feet away when it sensed her, lunging at me with frightening speed.

Before it could land on me, I drove my sword through its belly, feeling its guttural snarl vibrate through the blade. But as I turned around, there he was again — the same Bigfoot. He stopped just two feet away, locking eyes with me as if sharing an unspoken truth. Then, without a word, he turned and walked back into the wilderness.

I collapsed, my legs giving way under the accumulated stress and loss of blood. The guys rushed to help me up.

"We need to get back to base," I rasped; each word seemed like a labor. "Thank you all, but you shouldn't have risked your lives for me."

The guys chuckled. "We thought you were a goner for sure," one of them said. "Guess we all made it out, didn't we?"

Back at the base, the tension started to dissipate, replaced by an exhaustion so deep it felt like it had seeped into our bones. "Try to get some sleep," I suggested, though the idea seemed laughable.

And then I noticed it — the chill in the air, from 85 degrees to seeing my own breath in a matter of hours. My gut tightened. I knew something was coming, something far more sinister than what we'd already faced. I couldn't shake the feeling that we were far from safe and that the real nightmare had only just begun.

My gut was twisting tighter with each passing second. I grabbed everyone's attention, "Wake up, everyone! Keep your eyes peeled!"

The sheriff raised an eyebrow, visibly unsettled. "For what?"

"Skinwalkers," I uttered, my voice tinged with a dread that seemed to hang in the air like thick fog. "They know one of us is wounded, and that makes them more dangerous than ever. Get the fire roaring. Make sure those steel rods are in there. We've only got four left, understand?"

I continued, "Whatever you do, don't let it touch you. Its touch is like a lethal frost. You'll freeze from the inside out, and then you'll be one of them."

Everyone's eyes were saucers. Mike, trying to mask his fear with a facade of bravery, looked at me, "So, what the fuck do I do if one shows up?"

I looked him dead in the eye, "You shoot it in the heart, then hit it with a flare gun, and then stuff a burning rod into that same heart. Understand? This might just save your life one day."

Just then, I heard it — an almost inaudible rustling in the trees. "It's here," I whispered, gripping the flare gun tightly.

Slowly, the creature emerged from the darkness. It was an abomination, a grotesque parody of a human form. Emaciated limbs and paper-thin skin stretched over a skeletal frame, revealing the contours of its bones. Its face was the worst part — almost translucent skin, enormous hollow eyes, and a gaping mouth that seemed to mock the very essence of humanity.

The men moved away instinctively, but not Mike. He stood his ground, positioning himself in front of me. His hand trembled slightly, but his aim was true. We waited for the perfect moment. When it was close enough to make your skin crawl but far enough to give you a fighting chance, Mike pulled the trigger.

Boom! Boom! Two .44 magnum rounds pierced the heart of the monstrosity. It let out a blood-curdling scream that echoed through the night like the wail of a banshee. Without missing a beat, Mike aimed the flare gun and fired. A ball of blazing red shot straight into its heart.

Sam, who'd been waiting by the fire, sprang into action. Grabbing my mitts to protect his hands, he pulled a steel rod out of the roaring flames and charged toward the creature. With adrenaline-fueled strength, he drove the glowing rod through its heart. Grabbing another, he did the same to its head. The thing let out one final screech as they threw dried wood onto it, touching the flame to its ghastly form.

It was over. The creature lay there, its body consumed by the flames. The smell of burning flesh mixed with the sweet scent of pine. We stood there in silence, each of us contemplating the hell we had just been through.

"I told you, Mike, this might save your life one day," I finally said, breaking the silence. "And tonight, you just saved ours."

We looked at each other, nodding, our faces illuminated by the dying embers of the fire. I could feel the cold retreating, but in the deepest recesses of my soul, I knew the fight was far from over. Still, for that one brief moment, we allowed ourselves to believe we'd survive this hellish night.

"I'm warning y'all, there might be another one of those Skinwalkers. Cut the head off that burning corpse and bury the parts separately," I instructed, my voice as coarse as sandpaper. "Some of you can sleep now. With any luck, we're going home tomorrow."

As the men followed my instructions, I took a moment to look up at the starry night sky. It should have been a moment of solace, but it wasn't. I felt watched. My eyes darted around, finally settling on two eyes — reflective and strangely protective — hovering about eleven feet above the ground. It was him, the male Bigfoot. He was watching me, almost as if to say thank you for eliminating the Skinwalker. With a nearly imperceptible nod, he vanished into the night, soundless as a shadow.

Somehow comforted, I finally allowed myself to drift off into a restless sleep. When I woke up, I was being carried by the guys. My eyes fluttered open to see Sue's face, contorted in a blend of relief and lingering fear.

"I'm fine," I rasped, "the guys saved me. I'd work with them again in a heartbeat."

As we gathered our belongings, I noticed a pile of stones stacked in the shape of a pyramid. I couldn't help but chuckle.

"What's so funny?" one of the guys asked, scratching his head.

"It's from a friend," I answered, my eyes twinkling with a mix of exhaustion and amusement. "Just leave it."

We packed up and made our way to the pick-up zone, me on a stretcher. I had lost a lot of blood, and each step the guys took seemed to drain them a little more. We finally reached the zone in about twenty minutes. The

General was there, stern and unyielding as ever. And there was Sue, her eyes still shimmering with tears.

The General's wife was also there. "Oh, you got hurt. Did you cry?" she chuckled condescendingly.

Ignoring her, Sue assisted me into the chopper, which whisked us straight to the hospital for some much-needed medical attention. The sheriff came over, her face flushed but relieved.

"Thank you for saving my life," she said, extending her hand.

"We saved each other out there," I replied, my voice tinged with hard-earned wisdom. "We worked great as a team."

"So, are you heading to the hospital?" I asked her.

"No," she sighed, "I'm just tired and hungry. But before you go, make sure to say goodbye, alright?"

"Of course," I nodded, "And if you ever need help, don't hesitate to call. We'll be there."

"Let's get going, then," one of the guys shouted, injecting some much-needed levity into the moment.

As we left the woods behind, a cacophony of emotions washed over me — relief, exhaustion, and a hard-to-place feeling that sat somewhere between triumph and dread. But for now, we were alive, and that's all that mattered.

# CHAPTER 6

U NDER THE CLOAK OF A darkening blue sky in New York City, two college girls, filled with the exuberance of youth, walk home after a night class. They giggle, chatter, and share dreams that stretch as far as the horizon. Suddenly, the summer night is shattered by an earth-shaking explosion.

A massive ball of fire engulfs the entire block, instantly extinguishing the lives of the two girls and fifty-five other souls. The laughter that filled the air just moments before is replaced by the deafening roar of chaos and the anguished cries of the city itself.

At that very moment, I was gingerly stepping out of the hospital, still nursing wounds from my recent mission. Unbeknownst to me, an eruption of disaster was unfolding, which would personally scar me forever.

The New York Police Commissioner's sleep was abruptly interrupted by his night captain.

The ringing phone cuts through the stillness like a knife. "Commissioner, there's been a catastrophic bombing near a college campus in the city. Many are dead. We're in a crisis."

The Commissioner's face turns ashen. "I'll get the FBI, Homeland Security, and ATF involved right away."

"Sir, this is bad—real bad," the night captain reiterates, sweat trickling down his forehead. "Should I call in all available personnel? We need every hand on deck."

"Do it," the Commissioner instructs, his voice tinged with an urgency that the captain had never heard before. "But you should know something that makes this tragedy even more chilling. The Executioner's Daughter has been killed."

The words hang in the air like a dark cloud, their weight palpable. Calls are made to the Secretary of State, who in turn alerts the President of the United States. With a heavy heart, the President gives the nod. The General receives the call that changes the course of everything.

As I was packing my gear for an overseas mission, my phone buzzed with a call that froze my blood. It was from the General.

"Glen," his voice breaks through the static, each word hitting like a sledgehammer, "There's been a change in your mission. Your daughter was killed in the bombing in New York City tonight."

The room spins, my knees buckle, and my world implodes. My weapons, my armor—none of it matters now. All the horrors I've faced pale in comparison to the nightmare that has just unfolded. My baby girl was extinguished in a flash, leaving only ashes and an unfathomable void in my soul.

Now, everything will change. The game, the stakes, the world as I know it—everything.

As this gut-wrenching revelation crashes over me like a tidal wave across the base, Sue receives the same life-shattering call. Her hands tremble as she puts down the phone. Her eyes scan the room frantically.

"Base Commander, find Glen. Now!" Sue's voice, usually steady and confident, quivers with a blend of fear and urgency.

Her eyes lock onto the base sergeant. "Sergeant, have you seen Glen?"

"No, ma'am," the sergeant replies, his eyebrows knitting together, sensing the gravity of the situation.

"Well, get everyone looking for him. Now! It's an emergency."

"I've heard something's gone down in New York City," the sergeant mutters, almost to himself.

"I'm headed to the base airport, going to New York City," Sue's voice cracks as she makes her declaration. She finds me at the airport, her eyes meeting mine, both of us in an unspoken understanding of the world-altering catastrophe we're caught in.

Sue doesn't say a word. She just starts crying and wraps her arms around me tightly. "Glen, I'm going with you," she finally manages to say between sobs.

"Sergeant, tell the General we're heading to New York City NOW!" Sue's voice rises in intensity. "Tell him the Executioner is off the reservation. Code red. Got it? Go!"

"Yes, ma'am. Making haste," the sergeant responds, already turning to execute the orders.

I find myself sitting in the airplane, my head buried in my hands, an abyss of despair threatening to consume me. Sue comes over and gently grabs my arm. "Please, Glen, keep your head on," she implores.

I look up at her, and the fire and hate that blaze in my eyes is almost palpable. "Whoever did this to my family is going to die. Understand me, Sue? If you want out, this is your last chance," I seethe, my voice tinged with almost feral ferocity.

"I'm telling you now. I'm going to find out who is behind this. They will pay, and they will pay dearly," I grit my teeth, my voice laden with an unspeakable rage. "This time, I'm not stopping for anything. By God, I will kill them all!"

My eyes lock onto the horizon, a cold, burning fire lighting them up. Sue knows at that moment, as does anyone who ever doubted it, that absolutely no one can stop me. And that realization instills a fear in the higher echelons of government that is, quite literally, Godly.

The General's voice crackled through Sue's phone. "How far will he go to end this nightmare? Is he there?"

"Yes, General. He's off the reservation. Code red. He's gone," Sue replied, her voice trembling.

Inside the plane, the atmosphere turned thick with tension. No one made a sound other than the drone of the jet engines. Sue moved to the opposite side of the plane, away from me.

"General, you'll need to call the Governor of New York. Tell him it's 'Code Red. He's gone.' We'll need all the help we can get," Sue said.

The General paused before speaking. "I'll do everything in my power, Sue, even if it means going directly to the President. Just try to keep him from completely losing it."

Sue shook her head, her eyes heavy with an emotion that lay somewhere between despair and resignation. "General, it's too late for that."

"Then what about the city's investigators? They won't be enough?" The General asked, sensing the gravity of the situation.

"Right now, General, local interference is the last thing we need. If they give him any trouble..." She left the sentence hanging, a grim prophecy.

The General caught the dark implication. "God help us all."

"I heard that," I chimed in from my seat. "Look, I'll play nice with the New York officers, okay? But I'm not taking any shit from them. I'll share info and work with them until they give me a reason not to."

Sue glanced at me, then relayed my message to the General. He remained silent on the other end of the line. The air inside the plane was charged with terrifying electricity. Everyone knew the world had shifted, and nothing would ever be the same. The look in my eyes was a cold, burning fire fueled by loss and deep-seated hatred. It was a look that put the fear of God into everyone onboard—and far beyond.

As the New York skyline grew nearer, Sue shifted to the seat beside me. I felt a storm of emotions brewing inside me—nervousness shifting into a boiling rage. Sensing my internal upheaval, my hands started to tremble uncontrollably, and Sue gently held them.

"Now I'm on a one-way track, Sue. There's no stopping me. This time, it's all about my family's safety. I've got to end this, once and for all."

The General's voice came through the radio, tinged with somber resignation. "I've informed the President. You're officially off mission duties. Take this to the end, even if it costs me my career or life. This vendetta, whoever it involves, killed his wife and child years ago. Now they've taken his daughter. This has to stop."

I looked at him through the screen. "General, this started years ago in Japan, and now, it ends. No more games. Either they die, or I do. Understand?"

Sue looked at me, concern flooding her eyes. "I understand, Glen. I really do."

"And anyone who gets in my way," I warned, my voice dropping to an almost guttural growl, "Is fucking dead. Got it? Good."

The tension was palpable, each face on that plane wearing a mask of fear. As we approached the New York airport, the billowing smoke from the devastation was clearly visible against the darkening sky.

"Sue," I whispered, my voice tinged with a chilling foreboding, "I'm going to a dark place now. I'm not sure I can find my way back in a place so deep. You sure you want to stick around for that?"

Sue clamped down on my hand, her fingers digging into my skin as if she could transfer some of her strength into me. "Glen, listen to me. I'm with you until the very end, no matter what it takes. Your daughter was like my own, especially after her mother died. I'm all in."

Her voice wavered and broke as she spoke, a clear sign of the emotional storm raging within her. She reached for my arm, rested her head on my shoulder, and let her tears flow freely. I'd never seen Sue like this before. The sight pierced through my armor of fury and touched a vulnerable core I had forgotten I still had.

We landed, and I made a beeline for the garage where my Bugatti was housed. I pulled off the cover, checked the lights worked, ensured it had a full gas tank, and fired up the engine. The car roared to life as if sharing my urgency.

"Sue, call the state and local police," I barked as I accelerated onto the freeway. "Tell them I'm coming in hot. And make sure they fucking understand the gravity of it."

Sue grabbed her phone and dialed the number for the Commissioner's office. "Commissioner, this is Special Agent Sue Thompson. I must inform you that Federal Marshal Glen Michaels is en route to New York City. He'll be coming in hot."

"Who's coming in? What did you just say?" The Commissioner's voice crackled with confusion over the line. He hadn't been informed of my involvement yet, which irritated the hell out of me but wasn't surprising. "Who the hell—or what the hell—is a United States Federal Marshal doing getting involved in this?"

Sue's voice turned icy on the phone. "Commissioner, let me lay it out for you. Glen Michaels isn't just a boss. He's your boss for this investigation. You're going to have to work with him whether you like it or not. So, how do you want to play this? It's your call."

She paused, letting the gravity of her words sink in, before continuing, "He'll conduct his own investigation and share his findings with you and your team. Likewise, you will share everything you find with him. Do I make myself clear? The man lost his daughter tonight. He's barely hanging by a thread, so don't even think about pissing him off."

Her words were punctuated by silence. A silence weighed heavy with the Commissioner's hesitation on the other end of the line. "Do you want me to go above your head to the Secretary of the U.S.? Do you want that, Commissioner?"

Her patience waned, each ticking second amplifying her irritation. "I'm waiting. Do I make the call? Don't test my patience."

Sue's voice dropped to a threatening whisper, "He can make your life a living nightmare if you obstruct him. So, what'll it be?"

Still no answer.

"Fine," Sue spat out, her temper flaring. "I'll let the Governor know you're being uncooperative with higher-ranking government officials. How about that? You can deal directly with the Secretary of State, and trust me, she won't be thrilled."

Her finger hovered over the end call button. "Or maybe you'd prefer I take it up with the President? What's it gonna be, Commissioner? I'm done talking."

The line went dead. Sue redialed, her face flushed with frustration and her voice tinged with finality, "When we arrive, everything better be in place. If it isn't, maybe you'll enjoy early retirement. If there's any trouble, any at all," she raised her voice, her words practically a snarl, "You will play nice, do you hear me? PLAY NICE! NOW GET ON THE BALL!"

As she ended the call, I could feel the atmosphere inside the car thicken.

Sue hung up the phone with a sense of finality and looked over at me, her eyes awash with worry. "Glen, listen. I'm here to back you up, but please, don't go off the deep end. You're needed here, and your daughter needs you wherever she is."

I glanced at her, taking in the sincerity in her eyes. "Let me handle the locals, okay? You focus on her and on your family."

I nodded, the lump in my throat making it hard to speak. "Yes, Sue, thank you. I love you, too."

As we approached the crime scene, the air grew heavier, as if it could sense the gravity of what had happened here. I pulled up to the yellow tape line that marked the boundary of despair, the Bugatti's engine falling silent as if in deference to the solemnity of the moment. Sue stayed in the car, her concerned gaze fixed on me as I stepped out.

I showed my credentials to the officer at the scene. "Yes, sir, we've been expecting you," he said, a tremor of sympathy in his voice. "I'm really sorry about your daughter. They haven't moved her body yet. She's over there where those two officers are standing guard."

My eyes followed the direction he pointed, then met Sue's. I thought to myself, fuck, this is the part I can't stand. The part I wish I didn't have to do.

Sue seemed to understand, as she always did. "But you have to, Glen," she said softly. "You have to claim her for yourself and for your family."

Nodding, I said, "I will. Will you be okay here?"

"I'll head to the command station. If you need me, that's where I'll be," she replied. "Are you sure you're okay to do this?"

"No," I admitted, my voice breaking. "But I have to. Just keep the cops out of your way, and I'll handle this part."

Taking a deep, steeling breath, I walked over to where my daughter lay. I fell to my knees beside her, whispering a tear-choked word, "I'm so sorry, baby. I should have protected you." The cold reality settled over me like a heavy fog.

After what felt like an eternity, I stood up and walked back to Sue. "I'm done taking care of her," I said, the words tasting like ash in my mouth.

Sue looked at me with tear-filled eyes. "You're never done, Glen. And deep down, you know it."

Taking her hand, I clenched it tightly. "I'm heading to the blast zone," I said. "I'll start there and work my way out to the streets. See what I can find."

Sue nodded. "Alright, Glen. I'll see you later. Good luck, and take care of yourself. God knows you're walking a razor's edge."

"Thanks, Sue," I replied as I turned to face the haunting abyss that awaited me. I knew I was about to dive deep into the darkness, but at least I wasn't diving alone. Sue would be there, just as she always was, making the abyss less terrifying.

I began to walk toward the covered bodies, each step pulling me deeper into a dreadful feeling I had come to know all too well. I got about twenty-five feet away and stopped, my eyes blurring as memories of my daughter flooded my thoughts.

How could this be her end? She had so much ahead of her—only two years left before she would have become a lawyer. I had no doubt she would have been brilliant at it.

My heart twisted in pain as I thought about the empty space she would leave beside her mother, who had passed away four years ago from cancer. They were a team, proud of each other in a way that made my heart swell. Now, both were gone, and I was left grasping at words I never had the chance to say to them.

Then I felt Sue's hand slip into mine, her grip firm yet tender. "You okay?" She asked softly.

"No," I said, my voice quivering. "It's like when we first met, remember? I hurt then, but now it's worse. I have to go through it all over again. How many times will I have to do this, Sue?"

Sue looked at me with eyes that carried a depth of understanding. "I'll go ID her body for you."

"No, Sue. She's my daughter, and I need to do this for my little girl. Thank you, though." The words caught in my throat. "I already miss her. I just talked to her a week ago from the hospital."

Taking a deep breath, I began to move toward the area where the bodies lay. Before I could get far, a police officer yelled, "Where the hell do you think you're going?"

Before I could open my mouth to respond, a voice from behind the officer shouted, "It's okay! He's one of us, and he's lost someone too," the voice was filled with solemn respect, the weight of the situation settling around us.

The officer looked back at me, his eyes now softened. "Go find who you need to find, sir. Take your time."

I nodded, unable to conjure any words. A somber cloud seemed to hang over the whole area, thickening the air as if it, too, mourned the loss. Each step felt like a mile as I approached the spot where my daughter lay. I bent down to lift the cover, my hand shaking and my soul bracing for a pain I knew would be unlike any other. But it was a task I had to do—for her, myself, and the endless love that would now have to find a way to survive in a world with one less beautiful soul.

My gaze lingered on my daughter one last time before I reluctantly pulled the sheet back over her, sealing away her face from the harsh world that had so violently taken her away from me. As I continued down the row of bodies, my eyes caught another familiar face: Emily, my daughter's best friend since childhood. Fuck, not her too.

The sight was another brutal blow, a stark reminder that my daughter wasn't the only life cut short; she was just one star in a whole sky that had suddenly gone dark.

Then, I noticed the other mother, her eyes darting nervously behind the police tape as if hoping for a miracle. "Let her in," I ordered the officer.

The officer hesitated before lifting the tape. "Go ahead, ma'am," he said, letting her through.

She hurried over to me, her eyes filled with a mixture of gratitude and despair. "Thank you," she choked out. "I've been waiting to find out but was afraid of what I'd see."

Together, we found Emily. The woman screamed a haunting sound that echoed through the night. She grabbed me, holding on as if I were a lifeline in a sea of sorrow.

Sue arrived, her face etched with concern and fatigue. She helped steady the grieving mother. "I don't have money for a funeral," the woman sobbed, holding onto Sue now, "What am I going to do?"

"Listen," I said, my voice hoarse with emotion, "I'm going to cover the funeral expenses, not just for my daughter, but for Emily and anyone else who needs it."

"No, I can't let you do that," the woman said, attempting to refuse my offer.

Sue and I exchanged a look, an unspoken agreement passing between us. "You don't have to worry about anything," Sue assured her. "We'll take care of it. And for the fuck's sake, don't argue. He's already on edge."

Just then, the police captain approached. "Is everything okay here?" He inquired, his eyes flitting over the somber scene.

"Captain, I want these funerals taken care of. All of them," I declared, making sure there was no room for argument.

He nodded. "I'll make sure of it."

Sue turned to me, her eyes a blend of warmth and steel. "I'm taking this lady to the temporary shelter. The police will let others in to identify their loved ones. Are you headed to the command center?"

"Yes," I said, a lump forming in my throat. "And Sue, make sure she's okay. And tell them to let others find their loved ones, too. No one should go through this alone."

Sue nodded, her face solemn. "I will."

I took a deep breath, steeling myself for the next phase of this nightmare. "I'll see you soon, Sue. We've got work to do."

Sue met my eyes. "Yes, we do," she said softly as if acknowledging that our personal losses were now colliding with our professional duties in the worst possible way.

Sue turned to the captain. "Can you take care of the lady, please?"

"Yes," the captain nodded, his eyes meeting Sue's in silent agreement.

Sue looked back at me, her gaze steady. "I'll handle any issues here. Do what you need to do."

I was met with a sea of skeptical glances when I reached the makeshift command center. Cops, firefighters, first responders—all eyes were on me, but none looked pleased. I thought to myself, "I don't give a flying fuck if they're happy to see me or not. I've got a job to do."

"Is the bomb squad here?" I demanded, cutting through the uneasy silence.

The sergeant on duty eyed me cautiously. "Yes, they're here, but you can't go into that building."

Ignoring him, I brushed past the barricade and headed straight into the crumbling structure, the sergeant's protests echoing behind me. "It's unstable! The building could collapse!"

The devastation inside was gut-wrenching. Twisted steel, shattered glass, and hunks of concrete were strewn about like the building had been shaken by a giant hand. Firefighters and officers navigated carefully through the chaos, their movements cautious, their faces a mask of concentration and urgency.

Another sergeant, different from the first, shouted at me as I moved deeper into the wreckage. "Get out! It's not safe!"

"I need to be here," I snapped, flashing my credentials. His eyes widened, and I could almost see his mind recalibrating. It was that "Oh shit, it's Bigfoot" look I'd seen a hundred times before.

"Do we know what kind of explosive material was used here?" I asked, changing the subject.

"We're waiting for the ATF," he stammered, still caught off guard by my presence.

"Waiting for the ATF?" I scoffed, incredulous. "We don't have time for that bureaucratic bullshit. I can identify the material right now."

I inhaled deeply, tuning out the surrounding chaos to focus on the scent lingering in the air. It was faint but distinctive—a mixture of chemicals and burnt residue.

"Smell that?" I asked, locking eyes with the sergeant. "That's Semtex. High-grade, military-level plastic explosive. And if I'm right, there could be more in this building. We don't have a minute to waste."

"The sergeant looked incredulous. "But Semtex is banned in the United States. Nobody uses it here."

I shot back, "Banned, yes. But some terrorists don't give a shit about bans. We're not dealing with law-abiding citizens here."

The sergeant raised an eyebrow, still skeptical but slowly yielding. "So you're saying this is an international operation? That's a heavy claim. How do we even begin to trace the origins of the explosive?"

I clenched my jaw. "First, I have some deeply personal, gut-wrenching business to attend to. After that, I'm going to England. I've got a few contacts in Scotland Yard and MI6 who owe me a favor or two."

The sergeant was about to respond when I started walking back toward the command center. As I moved, my eyes scanned the crowd of onlookers, desperate faces etched with fear and disbelief. Then, one face caught my eye—a man I knew from my time in England. A vile individual, but one who might have the information I needed.

Turning to a nearby officer, I instructed, "Follow that man discreetly. If he goes into a building, notify me immediately."

The officer nodded and began tailing the man, keeping a safe distance to avoid detection.

Upon returning to the command center, I found the captain clearly agitated. "I hear you're running your own operations now. Who authorized this?"

I was about to launch into a full-blown tirade when Sue stepped in, her timing impeccable as always.

"Captain, I suggest you call the Commissioner," she said, her voice low but razor-sharp. "He'll inform you that all operational decisions are now coming from this man right here," she pointed at me, "And me. Do you understand?"

The captain's face flushed a shade of red I hadn't seen since my last trip to a whiskey bar.

Sue continued, "If there's a problem with that, I can arrange for your immediate relief of duty and the subsequent disciplinary action. Do you want to go down that path, Captain?"

Sue, loud enough for everyone in the room to hear, declared, "We're in charge now. Is that clear? Now, get back to work, and thank you for your time."

An officer approached me, breaking the momentum of Sue's decree. "Sir, the suspect entered a building five blocks from here—further than the blast radius. I have officers stationed at both entrances. He's not getting away."

My jaw tightened. "It's Tom from India. I remember him from my days overseas—a real piece of a shit arms dealer. I bet my bottom dollar he's mixed up in this. I'm going after him."

Sue looked concerned. "If you're going, make sure to bring backup. And keep him alive. We need answers, not another corpse."

"Yeah, I got it," I replied, motioning to a few officers. "I'm going in. You all secure the perimeter. Make sure he can't escape."

Two detectives rolled up as I approached the building, looking eager for action but out of the loop. "Listen up," I quickly briefed them, "We're here for Tom. He's likely in that building. This guy doesn't stay put for long, so we need to move—now."

Spotting an open window on the fourth floor, I wasted no time. Age had slowed me, but it hadn't stopped me. Scaling the side of the building with a vigor that belied my years, I felt like some geriatric Spider-Man. By the time I reached the fourth floor, I was out of breath but full of adrenaline. I peered inside; the apartment seemed empty.

Gingerly, I crawled through the open window and dropped onto the worn carpet inside. The room smelled of stale cigarettes and cheap cologne—a scent I associated with Tom. I pulled my gun from its holster, the cold metal grounding me, and started to move through the apartment. Each step was measured, and each breath was calculated. If Tom was here, I didn't want to give him the drop on me.

As I moved through the dimly lit space, my eyes fell upon a table that looked more like a general's desk in a war room than something you'd find in a typical apartment. Maps with scribbles and markers, burner phones, and a laptop humming with what looked like encrypted software were scattered. My gut clenched; I was standing in an operations center of some dark design.

Just then, I heard a faint shuffling sound from below. I crept downstairs, gun at the ready, and there he was—Tom. His face paled the moment our eyes locked. I lunged forward, grabbing him by the collar.

As I secured my grip, two other men came barreling down the corridor, guns drawn. Reacting instinctively, I pulled out my .38 magnum and fired. One guy clutched his shoulder, screaming in pain. I slammed Tom's head into the wall with a force that dropped him to the ground, unconscious.

I lunged at the second man without wasting another second, sending him crashing through the window. The crunch of metal followed the sound of shattering glass as he landed on a car roof below.

Just when I thought I had a moment's respite, a third guy emerged from another apartment, brandishing a knife. A well-placed punch between his eyes sent him tumbling backward down the stairs to the second floor. I didn't have time to find out whether he was dead or unconscious.

My eyes widened as I noticed wires snaking along the baseboards and leading into various rooms. The building was rigged to blow. Tom, regaining some consciousness, laughed—a sound that oozed malevolence.

"Going to join your daughter, are you?" He sneered.

Something caught my eye. Papers that looked critically important were strewn across a desk. Ignoring Tom's sadistic chuckles, I grabbed the papers and shoved them into my coat.

Adrenaline surged through my veins. I had to get out and fast. An idea flashed through my mind. Hoisting Tom onto my shoulder in a fireman's carry, I bolted toward the opposite window.

As I leaped, I could see a large window on the building across the alley. It was a long shot, but it was our only shot. With a Herculean effort, I hurled us through the air. The window shattered upon impact, and almost on cue, the building we'd just evacuated erupted into a fireball, sending a shockwave that pushed us further into the apartment we'd just invaded.

We crashed onto an old bed, which immediately splintered under the impact, sending us both plummeting through the floor. Wood splinters and tattered upholstery surrounded us as the second floor also gave way, depositing us unceremoniously onto the ground floor.

Groaning, I picked myself up and walked over to Tom, who was struggling to get to his feet. I grabbed him by the collar of his stained shirt and dragged him toward the doorway, my mind a mix of victory and impending questions.

"Police brutality! This man is insane! I want a lawyer!" Tom yelled, his eyes wild as I handed him over to the detectives, snapping cuffs around his wrists.

"You're the one who's fucking nuts," I retorted, my voice tinged with a lethal calm. "If being 'nuts' means bringing down scum like you, then I'll wear the label proudly."

One of the detectives, face flushed with irritation, raised his voice at me. "You know you just destroyed all our evidence with that explosion, right?"

Holding his gaze, I reached into my coat, pulling out the crumpled papers I had seized earlier. "Here's your damn evidence," I said, jamming the papers into his hands.

A wave of dizziness washed over me. My vision blurred. The last thing I heard before blacking out was the detective muttering, "Get this piece of crap off my street. It doesn't look good."

When I woke up, I was in a sterile hospital room with bright lights that hurt my eyes and an IV drip in my arm. After a quick examination by the doctors and some time to regain my composure, I was discharged. Sue picked me up, and we headed straight for the Police Commissioner's office.

Sue excused herself to use the restroom, so I entered the meeting room alone. As the door swung open, I saw the Commissioner, his deputy, the same irate detective from last night, the Captain, and two other reps from the force. A couple of unfamiliar faces were there as well. The atmosphere was thick with tension.

As I stepped in, it was as if I'd tripped a wire. They all started speaking at once, a cacophony of blame and questions. I stood my ground, waiting for someone to take charge.

Finally, the Commissioner raised his hand, and the room fell silent.

"What the hell happened last night?" The Commissioner's eyes bore into me as if trying to dissect my very soul.

Drawing a deep, steadying breath, I started, "My daughter was killed in that bombing last night. I came here to find her body and, in doing so, tried to help others find their loved ones. In the midst of this, I saw Tom. He's an arms dealer from Great Britain who's been on the radar of MI6, the FBI, and Interpol. This guy used to supply bomb-making materials to the IRA, for fuck's sake. One of your officers approached me and offered to help. I asked him to tail Tom."

The Captain, incredulous, blurted out, "Who the hell do you think you are? You have no authority to instruct anyone on my force!"

I locked eyes with him. "I think I'm someone who's trying to prevent more deaths. I asked him nicely, and he agreed. So what's your fucking issue?"

The Captain huffed, "During your cowboy antics blowing up another building, you pulled my officer from his post. I've suspended him for ten days without pay."

My nostrils flared with indignation. Striding over to him, I pointed a firm finger at his chest. "You will reinstate him with pay. Do it now, or you'll find yourself handing out parking tickets at the waterfront for the rest of your miserable career. Don't think he can save you," I jerked my head toward the Commissioner. "Now shut your mouth while I talk, and get the guy back, with pay."

The room was charged with palpable tension, like a powder keg ready to explode. "We're in this together now!" I roared, my voice filling the room. "When I say something, you jump! We're a team, understand?!"

The Commissioner, unfazed, raised an eyebrow. "By whose authority?"

Taking a deep breath, I listed, "By the authority of the President of the United States, the Vice President, the Secretary of State, the Supreme Court, Congress, and the Senate."

You could hear a pin drop. The weight of my words slowly sunk in, changing the atmosphere subtly but definitively. The Commissioner sighed, sinking back into his leather chair.

"Look, I'm fucking tired, and I still have to make funeral arrangements for my daughter," I spat, my voice quivering with a blend of exhaustion and ire. "So she can be laid to rest next to her mother."

The Commissioner, seemingly unmoved, pressed on. "Do you have any written authority for what you're claiming? Anything at all?"

I clenched my fists, my knuckles whitening. "You'll get your precious written authority when the Secretary of State arrives. Happy now?"

Unable to contain my fury any longer, I gripped the edge of the Commissioner's desk and heaved it aside with one arm. "You should ask the Secretary of State all your bureaucratic questions. As for me, I'm heading to England. You've all done a stellar job of pissing me off! As for Tom, where is he?" My eyes darted around the room, narrowing when they landed back on the Commissioner.

The Commissioner hesitated. "We let him go."

My ears started ringing. "What did you say?"

Before he could repeat himself, I walked over to the overturned desk, lifting it once more with one hand and hurling it against the wall. My momentum carried me forward, pinning the Commissioner against the wall.

"Do you have any idea what you've just done? Tom will be alerting his whole fucked-up network that I'm here. And now I have to hunt him down again!" My voice roared like thunder, filling the room.

Just then, Sue rushed in, her eyes wide with concern and horror. She wedged herself between me and the Commissioner, looking me directly in the eyes.

"Go. Take care of your daughter," she implored softly.

"I'm handling this mess right now!" I barked back, my focus unyielding.

"No," Sue insisted, her voice tinged with an urgency that chilled me to the bone. "Your daughter needs you more than ever. You have to go. Right now."

I looked at Sue, my eyes brimming with a pain I couldn't quite articulate. I turned to leave, my boots heavy on the carpet, but I was interrupted. One of the commissioner's staff, a pencil-pusher with a name badge that screamed 'inconsequential,' stepped in front of me.

"You have to put the desk back where it was," he said with the haughty air of a man drunk on a thimbleful of power. "And you owe the boss an apology."

"No," I said, every syllable coated in a thick layer of disdain. "Now, get the fuck out of my way."

The staff member didn't budge. "Not until you apologize."

"Move. Now," I barked, fury building like a storm inside me.

From the corner of my eye, I caught Sue's tense posture. "Don't hurt him," she yelled, her voice tinged with desperation.

Ignoring her, I placed my hand mere inches from the staff member's chest and focused on the energy bubbling up within me. He stood there, a dumbass grin smeared across his face like he was some kind of immovable object. I pushed him, expending little effort, and watched as he flew back like a ragdoll, crashing through the office's glass doors. He hit the floor with a thud, gasping for air as if he'd just surfaced from the depths of my disdain.

I stepped over him just as the Secretary of State made her entrance.

"Well, Glen," she said, casting a swift, judgmental glance over the chaos, "I see you still know how to make friends and influence people."

I said nothing, merely continuing my march down the sterile, government-issue hallway.

"Pick him up," the Secretary of State ordered her bodyguards as I vanished from view.

My next destination was the city morgue, where I had grim obligations to fulfill. When that was done, I met Sue at a hole-in-the-wall pizza joint tucked into a forgotten city corner. We sat down in a booth with worn-out cushions, the scent of tomato sauce and melting cheese serving as a meager comfort.

We ate in weighted silence until Sue finally broke it. She reached across the table and took my hand, her fingers a warm refuge. "I'm so sorry about your daughter," she said, her voice barely above a whisper. "I'll miss her too."

"I appreciate that, Sue. Really makes me feel a bit lighter, all things considered," I said, gratitude cutting through the fog of emotions clouding my mind.

Sue looked at me, her eyes reflecting a blend of compassion and resolve. "After you left, the Secretary of State told the Commissioner to apologize to you. She put him in his place, to put it mildly. The detective and the assistant district attorney tried to chime in, but she told them to sit down and shut the fuck up. Guess what? They've been assigned to us, and we've got the President's full support to get this shit done. You're in charge, no matter where we go."

I leaned back, taking in the implications. "So that means even if we have to step outside U.S. soil?"

"Yes," she emphasized, "Everywhere."

I thought of the task ahead and sighed. "Good. Because we're going to England tomorrow."

Sue tilted her head, puzzled. "Why England?"

"There's someone there who knows about the bombing. A key person, someone who might have answers that even the MI6 or the FBI haven't found yet. We need to talk to him," I explained, my voice firm.

Sue picked up her phone and texted briefly. A moment later, her phone buzzed with replies from the detective and the assistant district attorney.

"They're asking 'why'—and they don't seem too thrilled about it," she said, showing me the text messages laced with annoyance and disbelief.

The first light of dawn barely touched the horizon as we boarded my private plane. I'd had it outfitted with a secure, direct line to Scotland Yard and MI6 so we could get down to business as soon as we touched British soil. It had taken me two solid hours of strenuous negotiations just to secure the right to speak with him—the terrorist with more than three decades of experience in all manners of hell-raising.

I looked over at Sue and the assigned detective and assistant district attorney, who were already taking their seats. "When we land in London, we're going straight to the high-security prison. Sue, you're with me in the interrogation room. You two," I gestured at the detective and ADA, "You're just there to watch and listen."

The detective, his ego clearly bruised, snapped back, "I know how to conduct an interrogation, you know."

I stared into his eyes, letting my gaze turn cold. "This isn't a common criminal we're talking about. This man has spent thirty-five years mastering the arts of bombing, lying, and killing. He has blood on his hands— babies, kids, old people, women. This isn't some run-of-the-mill thief or scam artist. He's a cold-hearted, professional killer, and he and I have a history. So sit your ass down, watch, and maybe learn a thing or two. Take notes if you have to."

The tension in the aircraft was palpable as we landed at a military base just outside of London. Waiting for us were two sleek black cars and a representative from MI6. Standing beside him was a General I'd worked with, now with a fourth star on his epaulets.

He saw me and stepped forward, his face a mix of stern professionalism and genuine concern. "Glen," he extended his hand, "I'm so sorry for your loss."

I shook his hand firmly. "Thanks, General. I see they bumped you up—four stars now?"

"I was on the brink of retirement, so they gave me the fourth as a parting gift," he chuckled, then his eyes shifted to Sue, and he greeted her warmly.

Turning to business, the MI6 representative spoke cautiously, "Do you really want to go through with this, Glen? This individual has a well-known issue with authority."

I smirked, "I'm fully aware of his antics and all the tricks up his sleeve."

The MI6 agent raised an eyebrow, clearly intrigued.

"So I'll appeal to his more 'lovable' side," I said, a hint of sarcasm dripping from my voice, "Or I'll fucking kill him."

The General nodded, understanding the gravity of the situation and my resolve. There was no room for error; too much was at stake. We were not just confronting a killer; we were untangling a web that could hold the safety of entire nations in its snare.

"Very well," said the MI6 agent, "Let's get this over with."

As we made our way to the waiting cars, the morning mist hovered over the ground like a spectral army—fitting because what we were about to engage in was nothing short of a war. And in war, there are no rules. Just the promise of blood and the thin hope for justice

It took an additional three hours to finally reach the prison—a high-security fortress cloaked in an ominous atmosphere. As we entered through a concealed door, it became clear that this place was designed to keep its secrets hidden. We were ushered into a chamber where visibility was deliberately limited; no one would see us come or go.

The first guard met us with a skeptical eye. "Any weapons?" He inquired.

When his gaze fell on me, he softened. "Could you please leave your belongings here?"

"As long as you're the one watching them," I said.

He nodded solemnly. "I promise."

"Thanks," I replied, unstrapping my sidearm and laying it on the table. I noticed the detective's puzzled expression.

"What was that all about?" The detective inquired, clearly thrown off by the exchange.

"They know me and know if you ask nicely, I'll comply. It's called respect," I shot back, irritated by the constant questioning. "Something I didn't get much of back in New York."

Turning back to the guard, I inquired, "Is he in there yet?"

"Yes, sir," the guard responded, "You can enter whenever you're ready."

"Thank you," I said curtly, gesturing for Sue and the others to go in ahead of me.

Sue began speaking as she entered the room. "Mr. Hensley," she started, but the man in question interrupted her impatiently.

"Why am I in this meeting? I have better things to do," Hensley grumbled, barely glancing up.

That's when I walked in. "Still mad about our little tussle, are you?" I smirked, recalling the event that had put Hensley and seven of his men in the hospital for months.

His face turned a shade redder. "You hospitalized me and my men for months, you dick!"

"Fine," I cut him off, "Let's get straight to the point. Do you want to get out of here and go home?"

His eyes narrowed. "You know I do."

"Good," I said. "I've got a deal for you. Want to hear it?"

His eyes met mine, calculating. "This is about my nephew, isn't it?"

I leaned closer, my voice tinged with controlled anger. "No games, Hensley. Yes, it's about your nephew—the one who's been playing with explosives. You know, 'booms.'"

Hensley sneered. "I'm going to kill him, and there's fuck-all you can do about it."

I tightened my grip on the table. "Where is he now?" I demanded, locking eyes with him.

"How the fuck would I know?" Hensley shrugged, an insufferable grin curling the corners of his mouth. "I'm stuck in this hellhole, ain't I?"

I felt my hands clench into fists. "So you want to play games now?"

"No games," Sue interrupted, sensing the rising tension. "Maybe it's time for my associates to step out. We can continue this conversation privately."

Hensley chuckled. "Makes no difference to me. These guards are just a backdrop. They won't let you do shit."

Sue glanced toward the window and tapped on it. The guards promptly exited the adjacent office, leaving us in this pressure-cooker atmosphere. She looked back at Hensley. "We're going to go now. I can't say the same for you. You see, Glen's daughter was killed in the New York bombing. So he's not playing games. And he's got two options for you," Sue continued her voice a blade. "Either you cooperate and benefit from a generous offer, or he beats the living hell out of you—maybe worse. We don't give a shit. You'd just be another dead inmate."

My eyes narrowed as I stared at Hensley. "Like she said, either way, I don't care. I'll unleash every ounce of pent-up rage and sorrow on you right now."

Hensley's eyes flicked between Sue and me, his grin finally fading. "Alright, what's the deal?"

"You give us your nephew's location. In exchange, you get transferred to a facility in Ireland, serving a life sentence on your home turf. But step one foot off that property, and I'll come back here and kill you with my bare hands. Got it?" My words were laced with ice.

Hensley seemed to weigh his options before finally nodding. "Fine. How do I know you'll keep your end of the bargain?"

Sue leaned in, her eyes like steel. "I was there when the deal was struck with the government. It's legit. You walk when we get your nephew."

The detective, who had been silent till now, chimed in, "It's true."

"But I walk when you get him, right? What if he slips away? What if it's your fault?" Hensley's eyes were shrewd, calculating.

"You still go home," I reassured, maintaining eye contact. "Now, where is he?"

Hensley hesitated, then looked at Sue as if expecting betrayal. "He's going to lie," the detective muttered.

"No, I'm not. I want the deal," Hensley finally said. "He's in Florida. Dade County. Somewhere along the waterfront. He has a friend with a boat, so if things go south, he'll flee."

"Thanks, Mr. Hensley. We'll be in touch," Sue said, gathering her things.

"Don't forget about me. We have a deal," Hensley called out as we moved toward the door.

I paused, locking eyes with him one final time. "Yes, we do. Goodbye," I added, the word tinged with relief and a strange sense of foreboding. As the door closed behind us, I couldn't shake the feeling that this was just the beginning of an even darker chapter.

# CHAPTER 7

+ + + + + +

T HE SOUNDS OF THE PRISON slowly faded behind us: the clanging of cell doors, the distant murmur of guarded conversations, and the oppressive weight of the walls surrounding us. The air felt much lighter as we neared the exit. The taste of freedom was something most took for granted, but in places like these, it was a luxury.

Stepping out, the cool London breeze hit our faces, causing me to involuntarily shiver. Dark clouds scudded across the horizon, and the muted colors of the London skyline provided a gloomy backdrop to our departure. It was a sharp contrast to where we were headed—sunny Florida.

Detective Danny, his face lined with suspicion, couldn't contain his doubt. "How can you believe him?" he asked, his voice laced with skepticism.

I met his gaze squarely, a steely determination in my eyes. "He's not going to lie. He knows I'll come back here and kill him. He's staring at a lifetime behind bars, Danny. That's a heavy realization for anyone. His freedom—his life—is in my hands. He knows that."

The city lights began to play on Danny's face, revealing his conflict. As we walked, the soft patter of rain began, melding with the sound of our footsteps on the cobblestones. "So, if he wants to go home, he'll have to go through you, huh?" Danny asked, his tone lighter but still filled with a hint of incredulity.

"That's right," I said, my tone firm. "And don't ever challenge me again. I've been dealing with these kinds of people all my career. I know how they think, how they operate. When it comes down to it, they'll do anything to save their own skin. He'll cooperate with me at all costs."

The rain began to intensify, and I could feel the droplets trickling down my neck, soaking into my collar. But it was Sue's soft voice that pulled me out of my reverie. "Glen," she murmured, touching my arm lightly, concern evident in her eyes. "Let's not get worked up. You got what you wanted. We should all get some rest. Tomorrow is going to be a long day."

I nodded in agreement, feeling the weight of the day's events press down on me. With the intel in hand, we were one step closer to finding the man responsible for the devastation in New York. I was determined; I'd go to any lengths.

As we walked on the streets, a black SUV pulled up in front of us. The window rolled down to reveal a familiar face. "Get in," the driver ordered.

Without hesitation, we clambered into the vehicle. The streets outside were silent, save for the distant hum of city life. The atmosphere inside the SUV was tense. Every second counted, and our destination was clear: the airport.

As we pulled onto the tarmac, a sleek private jet awaited. Its engines purred softly, ready for takeoff. The pilot, a stout man with graying hair, gave us a nod as we boarded, and moments later, we were airborne.

In the plane's dimly lit cabin, the hum of the engines created a monotonous backdrop. A few overhead lights pierced the darkness, their soft glow reflecting off the windows to reveal the vast expanse of the night sky.

Danny shifted uncomfortably in his seat, clearing his throat before speaking. "Look, I'm sorry," he began, genuine regret evident in his eyes. "We all are. Losing your daughter... it's a pain I can't even imagine."

I nodded, taking a deep breath. The raw wound of loss threatened to engulf me again. "Thanks, Danny. It's hard. I appreciate your concern. And I understand the pressure we're all under. But I've been doing this for a long time. I need you to trust my instincts, even if it feels wrong to you at times."

Danny nodded slowly, the weight of my words settling on him. "I trust you. I just... It's not every day you work with someone who's so personally involved, you know? It's a lot to take in. But my sister and I are both with you every step of the way. We'll get these bastards."

"I appreciate that," I said, my voice cracking slightly. "You both have been a rock for me. I can't thank you enough for sticking by my side during this shitstorm."

Sue, her eyes glistening, chimed in, "We're a team, remember? We've got each other's backs."

"We'll be touching down in Florida in about five and a half hours," I announced, trying to steer the conversation to more practical matters. "Sue, can you call Commissioner Howard from Day County and let him know we're en route?"

She nodded. "Already on it. He's expecting us at the airbase."

I sighed, feeling the weight of fatigue pull at my bones. "Once we land, could you also sort out hotel rooms? And maybe some fresh clothes? We've been in these outfits for too long."

Sue smirked. "Always worried about appearances, huh?"

"Just want to feel fresh when we meet Howard. It's been a hell of a few days."

Sue raised an eyebrow, about to make a quip about expenses, when I cut her off. "Yes, whatever you choose is on me. That goes for you too, Sue. You deserve it."

She laughed, her face breaking into a genuine smile. "I'll make sure to pick out something nice then. And thanks, Glen. It means a lot."

I leaned back in my seat, closing my eyes. The gentle vibrations of the plane seemed to lull me. "All of you are the best thing to happen in my life lately. Especially you, Sue. Don't ever forget that."

The plane's ambient hum was occasionally punctuated by the overhead announcements or a burst of conversation. Even with the vast sky outside, the atmosphere inside the cabin was thick with tension. Danny, who had been lost in his own world, turned his attention back to the group, focusing on our discussion about the gear.

"You seriously want me in a suit, Glen?" Danny asked, his brow raised in bemusement.

"No, just some jeans and a shirt for me," I replied, trying to keep the mood light. "And maybe a sweatshirt."

Sue, with a mischievous glint in her eye, interjected, "You heard the man. Three new suits and whatever else he desires."

Danny shot her a wry smile. "I told you, no on the suits."

145

But Sue was relentless. "They're not just any suits. They're bulletproof. We're not taking any chances. You're getting them."

Danny sighed, rubbing his temples. "Alright, alright. Just make sure you get something for Nancy, too."

As we descended, the shimmering lights of Florida greeted us. The airstrip was quiet, save for a few ground crew members and a familiar figure. SIU Commissioner Howard stood, arms crossed, waiting for our arrival. His stern face broke into a slight smile as we approached.

"Glen," Howard began, extending his hand. "It's been a long time."

I nodded, shaking his hand firmly. "Too long, Howard. Been playing hermit up north."

Howard's face darkened as he said, "I heard about the New York bombing. I'm so sorry about your daughter."

Tightening my jaw, I replied, "This is personal, Howard. It was a hit."

The commissioner's eyes widened in realization. "Do you have any idea who's behind this?"

Nodding grimly, I responded, "Shan H. He's elusive. Every time I got close, I was always redirected elsewhere. Not this time, though."

Howard furrowed his brow. "Where do you think he's holed up?"

"We have reason to believe he's at Harbor Pier 23. But we need to tread carefully. Shan's notorious for his love of dynamite."

A shiver ran down Howard's spine. "That bastard. So, what's the plan? And what do you want me to do with the bodies afterward?"

Sue, ever the pragmatist, replied before I could, "Just pile them up. We'll call in some favors and ensure they're taken care of."

I added, "Howard, I need SWAT. We need to secure about a two-mile perimeter around the pier. Knowing Shan, he'll have explosives, and we can't risk any civilians."

Exiting the safehouse, we headed toward a fleet of black vehicles waiting by the curb. The throb of engines started reverberating through the otherwise silent street. I hopped into the lead SUV, glancing over at Howard, who was still on the phone. His face wore a look of intense concentration, reflecting the stakes at hand.

As our convoy made its way through the city, the streets blurred by in a medley of colors and sounds: taxi horns blaring, neon signs of businesses flickering, and the distant hum of nightlife gearing up for another evening in the city that never sleeps.

We crossed the historic Brooklyn Bridge, with its iconic Gothic arches looming overhead and the East River shimmering below. The towering skyscrapers of Manhattan began to give way to the warehouses and cranes of the industrial district. The setting sun cast a golden hue over the city, reflecting off the water and painting the horizon with hues of orange and pink.

And then, Pier 23 came into view.

The sun, now just a sliver on the horizon, cast long shadows on the concrete, making the deserted pier appear eerily extended. The stillness was unnerving; it felt like the calm before a storm. As the SWAT teams quickly disembarked and took their positions, there was palpable tension in the air. They peered toward the dark, looming building at the pier's end, their hands gripping their weapons tightly.

"Listen up," I said, my eyes scanning the faces surrounding me. "I'll lead in first. Do exactly as I say, when I say it. Our priority is to get everyone home safe, understood?"

A chorus of "Yes, sir" filled the crisp afternoon air.

We found ourselves crouched outside the looming, dilapidated structure that hosted God-knows-what horrors inside. A cold breeze whispered across the pier, carrying with it the salty sting of the ocean. Our eyes scanned the exterior, but no surveillance cameras were in sight. That was the first red flag.

With nimble and practiced steps, we tiptoed around the building, checking for any other anomalies. The door yielded easily under my hand—unlocked. "Suspicious," I murmured. The eerie silence that welcomed us seemed to echo the shadows dancing on the grimy walls.

"Alright," I whispered, "No radios, no cell phones from here on out." The room held its breath as I exhaled deeply, pushing the door ajar.

The darkness swallowed us as we tiptoed inside, our senses heightened. About fifty feet in, the deadly realization hit—the building was rigged to blow. My heart pounded against my ribcage, but the resolve in me forged forward like a steely blade.

"Get out. Now," I commanded the SWAT, my voice barely rising above a whisper yet slicing through the ominous silence.

The sergeant, a stoic man with worry lines etched onto his face, was questioned with his eyes reflecting a storm of concern. "And what about you?"

"There's someone I need to find. Go, now! And get everyone clear of the blast radius!" The urgency in my voice hurried them out into the safe embrace of daylight, leaving me with a ticking tomb.

As I navigated through the murky darkness, the figure of my buddy, Tom, emerged. He was in an office with two others. Before I could call out, one of the men spotted me, and bullets began to sing their deadly tune. Tom yelled, the terror apparent in his trembling voice, "Stop, you fuck, you'll kill us all!"

Without missing a beat, I squeezed the trigger of my .38 mag, and the guy dropped, a horrifying stillness replacing his murderous intent. Tom screamed, "Didn't you fucking hear me?"

Ignoring his frantic cries, I scooped Tom onto my shoulder, breaking into a sprint through the crumbling halls towards a back door, hoping it wasn't locked. My heart raced as the bullets followed us, seeking flesh. Behind us, the third guy took the wrong turn—a deadly mistake. A thunderous roar filled the space as the explosives went off, nipping at our heels.

With Tom clutched tightly, I burst through the back door. The world outside seemed to hold its breath for a moment before we plunged into the cold, forgiving ocean below. A deafening explosion rattled the pier; fire and debris mushroomed into the sky, painting a terrifying picture of what could have been our fate.

As the cold water embraced us, buffering us from the hell above, Tom began to scream hysterically, "You're fucking nuts! This is the second time you've done this to me. I hate you!"

Drenched and gasping for breath, I retorted with a smirk, "Well, you're welcome, buddy. Just saved your life. Again."

The waters around us simmered with the fallout of ashes from the burning remnants of Pier 23, as we awaited rescue, the chilling reality of our world sinking deeper into our weary bones.

The ocean's waves, now calmer after the explosive climax, lapped gently at our legs as I dragged Tom to the shore, our clothes dripping with the brine of the sea. The immediate danger had passed, but an air of tension hung thick between us.

"What the fuck are you talking about, Tom?" I growled, water droplets splattering from my lips.

"He's out to kill you too, you moron!" Tom spat out, his voice tinged with a mixture of fear and contempt. "You think Shan H's playing favorites? You're just another name on his hit list."

Before I could respond, the coast guard's boat cut through the waves, moving toward us. They threw us a lifeline, and in moments we were onboard, surrounded by the stark white of the vessel and the pungent smell of gasoline.

"I hate you," Tom hissed, his eyes cold and angry.

I shot him a steely glare. "That's fine, Tom. Now, either you play my game or I might just feed you to Shan H. You decide, live or die."

Tom's defiance faltered. "What do I have to do?"

A smirk played on my lips. "I want Shan H., not you. You help me nail that bastard, and I'll grant you freedom with a little bonus of ten million dollars."

Tom looked hesitant and trapped, but the lure of the reward was evident in his eyes. "What's the catch?"

"Do we have a deal?" I pressed, ignoring his question.

After what felt like an eternity, he nodded. "Yes."

I leaned in close, my voice a threatening whisper. "You pull this off, and you're a free man. No one will hunt you down. But if you double-cross me, Tom, I'll make sure you meet a fate worse than Shan H's hands."

Tom gulped. "How will I contact you?"

"You won't need to," I replied confidently. "I'm everywhere. I'll find you."

We reached the next pier, and I released Tom. With one last wary glance, he disappeared into the busy crowd, and I hoped I hadn't made a grave mistake.

Turning back to the remnants of Pier 23, I noticed figures gathered a couple of blocks away—the response team. Among them was Nancy, the district attorney, whose familiar face contorted with concern. Danny, her brother and my detective partner, stood by her side. Both were assigned to me by the Secretary of State, and their loyalties, while mostly clear, still had moments of murkiness.

Nancy rushed over. "Are you okay?" she panted.

Brushing off her concern with a nod, I said, "Stay here."

Walking towards the assembly point, I locked eyes with Howard, who was busy conversing with about six men, all of whom seemed straight out of a biker gang—mean and ready for a brawl. Their glares weren't casual; they were filled with pure hostility.

I knew right then that I was in for it. Those men looked like trouble, and as they began advancing toward me with fists clenched, it was clear what was about to unfold. "Sue?" I called, my voice an urgent whisper.

"Why?" she shot back, clearly not getting the imminent danger.

The commissioner piped in, "He owes me. Whether they leave this pier temporarily incapacitated or permanently out of the picture, it's all the same to me." It was clear then that Howard had some hand in orchestrating this face-off. The hint of a smirk on his lips was all the confirmation I needed. This was payback for something from our shared past.

I readied myself, feeling the familiar adrenaline surge. Spotting the leader, I acted first. Swiftly, with practiced precision, I swung my left foot into the side of his head, knocking him off balance. In a fluid motion, I lunged at the guy to my far right, delivering a clothesline so brutal that he crumpled instantly. The next adversary on my left met my fist squarely between his eyes, collapsing before he could even react.

The fourth hesitated for a brief moment—a fatal mistake. Seizing the opportunity, I grabbed him, forcefully slamming his head into a nearby telephone pole. The two who were beginning to regain consciousness didn't stand a chance. The leader came charging at me again, but a powerful right hook sent him sprawling back to the ground. Another swift kick ensured he wouldn't be getting up again.

The remaining threat lunged at me from behind, but I was too fast. Gripping him in a chokehold, I locked eyes with Howard. In that split second, a wordless message was conveyed—the culmination of years of rivalry and pent-up aggression. The sickening sound of a neck snapping echoed through the quiet street.

Releasing the lifeless body, I walked toward Howard. The crowd, sensing the finality of the confrontation, parted like the Red Sea. As I passed by Howard, I rasped, "Satisfied?"

Howard smirked, a hint of grudging respect in his eyes. "Yes, but I would have been quicker."

Ignoring the macabre scene around us, my stomach growled audibly. "I'm starving. Let's get some food."

Nancy, shock evident in her eyes, exclaimed, "You're absolutely insane!"

I raised an eyebrow. "Fine, dinner's on me. Happy?"

A hint of a smile tugged at the corners of her lips. "That'll do."

Sue chimed in, "You sort of grow accustomed to his... peculiarities after a while."

As we walked to a nearby eatery, I turned to Howard. "Can you have someone fetch my Bugatti to the restaurant?"

He nodded, still slightly bemused by the earlier display. "Of course."

The night continued relatively uneventfully. We all sat down to dinner, sharing stories and laughing; the earlier confrontation was almost forgotten. As we left, my sleek Bugatti awaited, glistening under the streetlights. Climbing in, I turned to the group and said, "We've got to rest up. We're headed to Florida in the morning."

Danny, intrigued, asked, "Why Florida?"

"I have some ties there," I replied cryptically. "We'll need supplies and intel for what's ahead.

We had barely begun to settle the dust from our ten-hour drive when the faded sign for a quaint cafe came into view, marking the threshold between Florida and Texas. The sun's golden rays basked the earth, lending an amber hue to everything in its path. "Just a little longer till Texas," I remarked, glancing at the rearview mirror. "Let's grab a bite and stretch a bit."

The cafe, framed with worn wood and boasting a rustic charm, promised a much-needed respite from the monotony of the road. The inviting aroma of freshly brewed coffee mingled with that of bacon and eggs, wafting through the air. However, what caught my attention first was the adjacent gun shop. Its display window showcased a myriad of firearms, but one in particular held my gaze—an 1865 45-cal navy revolver, visibly battered by time. Its worn handle and rusted barrel narrated tales of its glorious past. "I've always had an eye for treasures like this," I thought.

Even in its sorry state, I saw its potential. Without much hesitation, I handed over $2,400 for it. I envisioned restoring it, cherishing it, and maybe even sharing its story someday.

Meanwhile, Sue, Danny, and the rest had already claimed a booth in the cafe, the weary travelers they were. The place hummed with activity, locals chattering away, the clinking of cutlery, and soft music playing in the background. But this serene scene was soon interrupted.

The cafe door slammed open, announcing the entrance of a group. They exuded arrogance, their smug grins and swaggering gaits betraying their local notoriety. Time seemed to slow as they made their way through, their presence drawing attention, not all of it amiable.

Sue, ever so radiant, even after hours on the road, was their chosen target. The leader, a tall brute with greasy hair and a scar running down his cheek, sneered, "Hey, sweet thing. How 'bout you come sit with a real man instead of these losers?" His laughter, backed by his gang, filled the cafe.

Danny, always the protective kind, responded, trying to maintain a level tone, "Watch your mouth. She's a lady."

A slap echoed, a harsh reverberation amidst the now-tense atmosphere of the cafe. Danny's face reddened at the sudden blow, his eyes blazing with anger and shock. The surrounding diners gasped, their forks frozen midway between their mouths.

"Weren't you taught not to interrupt adults when they're talking, boy?" The thug sneered. His cold eyes bore into Danny's, challenging him to react. Leaning in closer, his breath stale with the scent of tobacco and whiskey, he whispered venomously, "Stay in your place, shithead."

Danny's fingers curled into fists, knuckles white, but Sue gently touched his arm, her voice calm yet insistent. "Stay put, Danny."

The thug's smirk grew wider. "That's right, boy. Listen to the lady. Sit. Stay. Good dog." He chuckled, entertained by his own sick joke, his cronies joining in. The sickening symphony of their laughter filled the room.

As Sue made a move to head towards the restroom, he swiftly blocked her path, a sinister glint in his eyes. "Where do you think you're going, sweetheart? I didn't give you permission."

Sue, defiant and unyielding, shot back, "If you and your goons don't back off now, the wrath you'll face will be beyond your worst nightmares.

You'll be begging for mercy from a storm that takes no prisoners. You might think you run this place, but that can change. fast."

He laughed with a mocking, deep guffaw. "You think some hero is gonna burst through that door and save you? This ain't a fairy tale, honey."

But what he didn't know was that I had seen it all. Sue was more than a friend; she was family. And no one laid a hand on her when I was around. Noticing the scene from outside the gun shop, I quickly assessed the situation. It seemed like the universe had a way of constantly throwing shit my way. But this time? I'd be the one throwing it back.

With a swift and determined stride, I entered the cafe. My rage was palpable, and I could feel the eyes of the room on me. But my focus was singular: the main antagonist. His smug grin, however, was interrupted as I grabbed his henchman to the right by the collar, slamming his face into the bar counter not once but three times. He crumpled to the ground, unconscious.

As he went down, two more goons, thinking they could take me in a joint attack, approached from my flanks. In one fluid motion, I clasped the skull of the one on the right and used it as a battering ram, smashing it against the left one's head. Over and over, their foreheads collided until both men, dazed and defeated, collapsed to the ground.

The rest of the cafe was dead silent, all eyes on me and the remaining thug, the main guy who had instigated this entire situation. Our stares locked, an electric tension building in the air.

The atmosphere grew more charged with every step I took towards the lead thug on the pool table. The once-cocky demeanor he wore was swiftly replaced by a mask of fear. I noticed another one of his gang members reaching for the ankle holster housing a .38. Before he could even blink, I smashed his face against the bar railing. He was out cold, his body dangling lifelessly.

Keeping my gaze fixed on the lead thug, I taunted, "You think you're tough? You lay your filthy hands on Sue, and you think you'll just walk away?"

From the corner of my eye, I noticed the bartender, a tall brunette with a severe expression, reaching behind the counter. In a split second, she pulled out a shotgun. Simultaneously, one of the thug's buddies tried to ambush me from behind. Reacting instinctively, I snatched the shotgun from the bartender with my left hand, while with the right, I caught the assailant, pushing him forcefully into the bar. The man wheezed, struggling to breathe.

I warned the bartender, "Step back unless you want a taste of your own medicine!" Instead of heeding the warning, she lunged at me. With swift reflexes, I used the butt of the shotgun to knock her out. As she crumpled to the floor, blood seeping from a gash on her forehead, I spun around to confront the lead thug. Our eyes locked, and I could see the malice burning brightly. "You think it's fun, bullying innocent people, terrorizing the whole town?"

Interrupting the face-off, the cafe's doors swung open to reveal two police officers, one of whom was clearly the sheriff. His badge gleamed, and he wore a smirk. "Looks like you've caused quite a mess here," he said. "You're coming with us. That's if you can even walk after this."

However, as the deputy began to distance himself from the sheriff, I caught a glint of silver from the corner of my eye. The bartender, despite the injury, was back on her feet, gun in hand. A shot rang out, narrowly missing me. Without hesitating, I drew my .38 magnum from its holster and fired back, hitting her square in the head. The sheriff, realizing he was outgunned, fumbled to draw his weapon, but I was quicker. Another shot, and he too hit the floor, blood pooling around him. The lead thug, seeing the odds no longer in his favor, made a desperate lunge for the bartender's fallen gun. I didn't give him the chance. One last shot, and he too, lay motionless.

The cafe, which had been filled with commotion and chaos just moments ago, fell into an eerie silence. All eyes were on me, the only one standing amidst the wreckage.

I fixed my unwavering gaze on the deputy, the gun still trained on him. "So, what's it gonna be, officer?"

His response took me by surprise. "Thank you. Those bastards needed to go. But there's more to the story." He cleared his throat, looking uneasy. "The sheriff was the brother of the mayor. The other men you took out? They were his other brother and nephew. You've just taken down half of the town's corrupt power structure. But there's still the mayor to deal with."

I sighed, rubbing my temple. "Fuck, can't a guy just get a meal in peace?" Taking a deep breath, I asked, "Where can I find him?"

"He's probably at the town hall, in his office on the second floor, last door on the right. But be careful," the deputy warned. "He's always got a couple of goons with him. They're armed and dangerous."

"Of course he does," I muttered under my breath. "Lead the way, then."

I looked over at Sue; her eyes were filled with concern. "I'll be back," I assured her.

Danny, ever the loyal friend, piped up, "I'm with you on this one."

I nodded in appreciation. "Thanks, Danny. Let's get this over with."

The town hall was a looming structure, a relic of the past that had seen better days. It had a foreboding aura, hinting at the secrets it held within its walls. With the deputy as our guide, we quickly reached the second floor.

"I'll be in this room here," he said, pointing to an office adjacent to the mayor's. "Second door on the right. I'll cover the exit in case they try to escape."

Danny and I proceeded cautiously down the dimly lit hallway, our footsteps muffled by the aged carpet. As we approached the door, the low murmur of voices could be heard. Without hesitating, we burst in.

The mayor, a portly man with a face reddened by years of indulgence, looked up in shock. Behind him stood two imposing figures, their hands inching towards their holstered weapons. As they reached for their guns, Danny and I acted swiftly, shooting them dead before they could even blink.

The mayor, gasping and trying to recover from the shock of seeing his guards fall, smirked weakly. "I heard you were coming. Thought you could surprise me?"

I leaned against the door frame, a sardonic smile playing on my lips. "People sure love to talk in this town. Oh, and just a little update - your son? He's dead. Your brother and that corrupt sheriff of yours? They're gone too."

"That's a shame…" the mayor responded but was cut off by the sound of a sharp gunshot that pierced through the atmosphere.

I turned in shock to see the mayor slump over, a dark crimson stain spreading rapidly across his chest. My eyes met Danny's cold, unflinching gaze.

"Why, Danny? Why did you shoot him?" I demanded, my voice strained with a mix of surprise and understanding.

His gaze met mine, a hint of frustration evident. "You know as well as I do that he would've wriggled his way out of it. With his connections? He wouldn't have seen a day behind bars. It's this fucking town and its corrupt system."

Nodding, I couldn't disagree with him. As much as I abhorred senseless violence, I knew that sometimes it was the only way to break the chains of corruption. We exited the office, descending the old creaking stairs to find the deputy waiting below.

He looked at us, his face pale. "Is it over?"

I met his gaze. "For now. The mayor and his goons won't be a problem anymore."

A sincere look of relief washed over the deputy's face. "Thank you."

"We're heading back to the cafe," I told him. "There's a meal with my name on it."

But fate had other plans. As Danny and I settled into our seats at the cafe, another deputy burst in, his face contorted in panic. A distressed woman trailed behind him, her tears leaving streaks on her dirt-smudged face.

She took a deep breath, trying to compose herself. "A creature... some kind of cryptid, took my son. It was massive, at least eight feet tall, and walked on two feet. It disappeared into the woods."

My appetite vanished. Sue stood up, pointing at me. "Lady, you're in luck. This here is the best cryptid tracker and hunter around."

All eyes in the cafe turned to me. Sue, always the dramatic one, shouted, "Hey, exterminator! Looks like your dinner's gonna have to wait."

Rolling my eyes, I replied, "Again with the interruptions." But there was no time for humor, especially with a child's life at stake. "Call the general. I need my truck here ASAP. And someone better ensure my meal is packed for the road!"

"We don't have a moment to waste," the mother said, her voice trembling. "Please, you have to help us."

Grabbing my gear, I turned to Sue and Danny, "Let's head to the lady's house. We'll pick up the trail from there."

The thought of a cryptid roaming these parts wasn't comforting, but with a child's life hanging in the balance, we had to act fast. The wild, untamed woods beckoned, promising another adventure and perhaps a hint of danger. But come what may, I was ready for it.

# CHAPTER 8

◆◆◆◆◆

THE SUN WAS SETTING, CASTING a soft orange and pink hue over the yard, dimly lighting up the distressed faces of the townspeople. The warm, moist air carried the scent of fresh earth and distant rain. A nervous energy permeated the atmosphere. Their collective fear was palpable.

Walking through the gathered crowd, I could hear their whispered concerns. Most of their words got lost in the collective murmur, but the sentiment was clear: fear of the unknown.

As we approached the house's entrance, an older woman, likely in her sixties, was fervently praying, clutching a rosary so tightly that her knuckles had turned white. A couple of kids were huddled together, their innocent eyes wide with confusion and fear.

"I get it. Everyone's scared," I began, trying to get their attention. "But a child's life is at stake here."

A burly man, his face rugged and etched with years of manual labor, stepped forward, his voice defiant. "No, we've lived here our entire lives. We've heard the tales, seen the aftermath. Whatever's out there isn't natural. It's pure evil."

Before I could counter, the sharp, determined voice of a young woman broke the tension. "All of you should be ashamed. Hiding while a child's out there, probably terrified."

I turned to see a fiery-eyed girl, probably in her late teens. Her face was resolute, and her grip on her gun showed she wasn't just all talk. "Betty," she introduced herself, a streak of rebelliousness evident in her tone.

Appraising her, I raised an eyebrow. "You've got guts. But you'll need more firepower than that." I motioned toward the 38 special she was holding.

As if on cue, the low rumble of an engine echoed in the distance, growing louder as the truck made its appearance. It was a heavy-duty military-grade vehicle, its intimidating presence a stark contrast to the serene environment. Dust billowed around as it came to a halt in front of us.

I gestured for Betty and Danny to follow me. The truck's back doors swung open, revealing an arsenal of weapons. I grabbed a Spaz twelve shotgun and handed it to her, our fingers brushing momentarily.

"Grab those shells from the side bin," I instructed Danny, pointing at four or five boxes of armor-piercing shells. "Put them into those cloth bags. One for each of us."

While Danny busied himself with that, I picked up a hefty .44 magnum, feeling its reassuring weight in my hand. I handed it, along with several boxes of armor-piercing shells, to Betty.

"Listen," I began, looking intently into her eyes, "if we run into this thing, aim for the head or chest. At least two shots. We're not trying to piss it off; we want it down and out."

Betty chuckled, a hint of mischief in her eyes, "Yeah, the last thing we need is an angry cryptid on our hands. It's gotta be dead, not mad."

My gaze shifted downward, taking in her worn-out shoes. "You'll need new boots, Betty."

She looked down at her battered footwear, then back at me, a hint of embarrassment coloring her cheeks. "I can't really afford new ones, especially not the kind that look as good as these."

With a gentle nudge of my head, I motioned her towards the stacks of boots that were part of our gear. "No one's getting snakebit or wet feet on my watch. And those boots you've got on have seen better days. Grab a pair – hell, take two pairs. They're on the house."

As she moved to pick a pair, I added, "You're brave for stepping up, so you deserve it. Plus, you'll be compensated for guiding us."

I could sense the ripple of envy that coursed through the gathered crowd as they overheard our exchange. Predictably, someone piped up, a tinge of greed evident in his voice, "Hey, what about us? We should get paid too, right?"

I met the indignant gaze of the onlooker with a cold, piercing stare. "You had a chance to step up, but you chose fear. You chose to sit on the sidelines. That's your loss."

The gravel crunched under tires as the new sheriff's vehicle pulled up. He leaned out the window, "The General's back at the café, thought you'd want to know."

Nodding my acknowledgment, I addressed the deputies who had stepped forward, seemingly unshaken by the potential danger that lay ahead. "Get yourselves some new boots and upgrade your firepower. We're not dealing with common thieves in the woods."

They saluted, a crisp acknowledgment, "Yes, sir."

Motioning to the sheriff, I instructed, "Watch over my truck. And let your men know they should change into better boots."

"Sue," I called out, pointing at the amassed gear, "make sure none of these freeloaders get their hands on anything. If they didn't step up, they get zip."

One of the deputies approached and extended his hand, gratitude evident in his eyes. "Thank you," he said, giving my hand a firm shake.

As I nodded, the sound of a car door drew my attention. A young voice piped up, "I'm coming with you."

I eyed the newcomer – a determined kid, probably around eighteen. Next to him stood a woman, her eyes filled with anxiety yet shining with a kind of resolute pride. It didn't take a genius to figure out she was his mother.

The young man, chest heaving with emotion, wrapped an arm around his mom. "I'll bring him back, mom," he vowed. "One way or another, he's coming home."

Introducing himself as Jeff, he wiped away tears. "And I could use some of those new boots," he said, glancing down at his worn-out pair.

I motioned him towards the gear, silently applauding his bravery. Turning to address the assembled crowd, my voice was laced with contempt, "See that? That's courage. It's not about grabbing free gear. It's a fire that comes from within, from the heart, from the soul. And most of you? You've shown you lack it. Just go home."

With that, I dismissed the crowd, the taste of disappointment heavy on my tongue.

159

Sue's voice echoed softly in the dense woods as she relayed our situation to the General. "We might need backup here later on. The crowd's getting rowdy, and this house might be in jeopardy."

The General's gruff voice crackled through the phone. "Stay safe out there. Call me if you need any assistance."

I glanced at my team, a medley of anxious and determined faces. "We might come back with some creatures tailing us. Be on your guard," I warned them.

With a final check of our gear and a nod to each other, we began our trek. The woods seemed to close in around us, the sounds of distant animals and rustling leaves accompanying our steps. Betty confidently led the way, with Jeff occasionally chiming in with his knowledge of the terrain.

After a while, we took a short break. I turned to Betty and Jeff, "Do you two have any idea where these creatures might reside?"

To my surprise, they both nodded in sync. Their eyes darted to each other, sharing a silent communication. "There's more than just one of these... things," Betty murmured. "I've heard talk of maybe up to ten."

Jeff chimed in, "I once followed one to the far side of that mountain," he pointed to our left, "There's a cave there. I know a route that leads right up to the entrance, without getting noticed."

Taking a deep breath, I met their gaze squarely. "Are you both sure about this? We'll be targeting every last one of them. It's not going to be easy."

The determination in their eyes was unmistakable. "We know," they replied almost simultaneously.

Pondering our next move, I sought more information. "How many have you personally witnessed?"

Betty held up three fingers, while Jeff showed four. One of the accompanying officers, John, added, "I've seen about three myself."

The other officer, Sam, scoffed. "I've never seen any such creature. I think this is just a bunch of hogwash."

We all shot skeptical glances at Sam. The dense woods around us seemed to grow eerier by the moment, but his cavalier attitude was truly unsettling.

"Really, Sam?" I asked, exasperation clear in my voice. "You joined this expedition for a laugh? You think this is some kind of twisted comedy?"

Jeff, his face red with anger, snapped, "Listen up, dumbass. These creatures aren't a myth. They're as real as the gun in your hand, and they're vicious. They won't hesitate to rip you apart."

Sighing deeply, I tried to convey the gravity of our situation, "I've seen the aftermath of their attacks. The way they dismember a body... it's grotesque. These creatures stand well over seven feet tall, weighing anywhere from four hundred to a thousand pounds. They're apex predators, and we need to treat them as such."

John's concern was evident. "Look, I didn't realize we were searching for Jake. That boy has been through enough already. We need to find him."

I leveled with the group, emphasizing, "This isn't a damn party. It's a rescue mission, and potentially a fight for our lives. Every moment we waste debating here jeopardizes that boy's chances."

Sam's cocky demeanor faltered a bit. "Alright, alright. So these things are real?"

I nodded, "Very real. I've had the unfortunate duty of dealing with them all over the world, from the chilling forests of Russia to the wild terrains of South America. Governments worldwide call me in when they have a creature problem, and it's never pretty."

Hearing this, Sam seemed to grasp the seriousness of the situation. "Alright, I get it. I'm in. I can't just abandon Jake to these... monsters."

With a renewed sense of purpose, our group continued on. As we neared the suspected den, the atmosphere grew palpably tense. "Alright, team," I commanded, "check your weapons. Ensure every gun is loaded with armor-piercing shells. We need all the firepower we can get."

Sam, looking a bit lost, raised his hand slightly. "I didn't get one of those guns. What do you have?"

A smirk tugged at my lips. "Good thing I carry extras. What do you prefer, a 44mag or a 44auto mag?"

Sam considered for a moment. "The 44mag revolver for me."

Sam examined the weight of the 44mag revolver in his hand, appreciatively eyeing the heft of the weapon. "Alright," he grunted, a hint of begrudging respect in his voice. "I didn't expect a gun selection out here."

Handing him a handful of speed loaders, I reiterated, "Head first, then the heart. And always double-tap to confirm the kill. Assume there are ten, but stay vigilant. These woods could be swarming with them."

Betty gave a curt nod, determination in her eyes. "We get in, find Jake, take down the threats, and get out. No heroics, just the mission."

Sam looked nervous for a moment but then straightened up. "We've got this. They might be monsters, but they bleed. Let's make sure of that."

I scanned the group, ensuring everyone was ready. "Alright, let's split. Jeff, you're with me. We're going in the back, using the natural cover. Betty, take Sam and use the front entrance. John and Jack, you're looping around the back right. We'll be surrounding them, but keep your guard up."

Jack gulped, trying to summon courage. "Yeah, I know the route. But I won't lie, I'm scared shitless."

"We all are," Jeff admitted. "But we've got each other's backs. And we've got a job to do."

Betty took a deep breath, "Once we start, it's going to be chaos. Expect them to scatter. They'll either fight or flee. Either way, we need to be on our game. None of these things can escape. Not one."

With a grim nod, I said, "Betty, give us a ten-minute head start. We'll move into position and signal when ready. Then, set your ambush point. Let's get this done and bring Jake home."

With stealthy movements, we progressed deeper into the thick woods, the smell of damp earth and moss filling the air. The sun barely penetrated through the dense tree canopy above, casting the woods in an eerie semi-darkness that was occasionally pierced by a stray beam of light. It was almost surreal, like walking into a different world.

I could feel the tension in the air, the sort of anxiety that precedes the storm. It wasn't long before Jeff, alert and sharp-eyed, gestured ahead. Hunched over and partially hidden by the foliage was one of the creatures. Its coarse, mottled skin and grotesque features made it look like a relic from a forgotten time.

With whispered urgency, I instructed Jeff to stay silent and hold his position. From my backpack, I carefully retrieved a collapsible bow and swiftly assembled it. The silence of the woods was pierced only by the soft sound of me drawing an arrow from my quiver.

Taking a deep breath, I focused, drawing on years of experience and training. The arrow released, whistling briefly through the air before embedding itself deep into the creature's skull. Before any of us could react, the echo of our encounter drew another of the grotesque beings from the underbrush behind us. Quickly nocking another arrow, I released it, watching as it hit its mark right between the eyes. The creature crumpled, lifeless.

Jeff's astonishment was evident as he murmured, "Fuck, that was... incredible. Are you always this precise?"

Without breaking my focus, I responded, "Precision is essential in our line of work. Aim, breathe, release, and always double-tap." To emphasize my point, I took my silenced .44 mag and dispatched two rounds into the creature's chest. "No chances," I muttered.

Jeff nodded in agreement, clearly impressed. "Got it. Silence is key."

Continuing our ascent, we maneuvered cautiously. Each step we took was calculated, ensuring minimal noise. The path took us around the mountain, and soon, the cave entrance loomed ahead. Its dark mouth seemed to beckon ominously.

From our vantage point, we heard the faint sound of a child's whimper echoing from the depths of the cave. My heart raced. We were close. Very close.

The atmosphere grew tense as we prepared ourselves, adrenaline pumping through our veins. We couldn't have asked for better timing, for just then, Betty and her team emerged from the brush, seamlessly sliding into position.

With every echoing cry from Jake, a chill ran down my spine. Time was of the essence. If these grotesque creatures lost their patience, Jake wouldn't stand a chance. Surveying the surroundings, I spotted a potential advantage. The cave's entrance was a perfect choke point.

Gesturing towards Jeff, I whispered my plan, holding up a smoke grenade. Jeff nodded, understanding instantly. He clutched another grenade, preparing for my signal. The weight of our mission was evident in his eyes, but there was no room for hesitation.

Without a second thought, I tossed the grenade towards the cave's entrance. As the smoke began to bellow out, a guttural, inhuman scream pierced the air. From the thick veil of smoke emerged a towering behemoth, easily ten feet tall, eyes wild with rage. It was a sight straight from the deepest of nightmares.

The creature's roars were deafening, but Betty's aim was unerring. The sharp crack of her rifle rang out, and the creature staggered, a shot having found its mark in its chest. Before we could even react, another of its kind lunged from the smoke. My fingers wrapped tightly around the grip of my .44 auto mag. Time seemed to slow. But as luck would have it, the second creature tripped over its fallen comrade. Jack didn't waste a moment, firing two fatal shots into its head, silencing the monstrosity for good.

Jeff, always the opportunist, quickly dispatched the first creature with his silenced weapon. But the forest wasn't done revealing its horrors. A bone-chilling roar echoed from above. I looked up to see another beast, this one perched menacingly on the cliff above us. But Danny, always a step ahead, had seen it too. The blast from his weapon was near-deafening, but the sight that followed was even more astonishing. The creature's midsection erupted in a macabre display, painting the ground with gore. Before the echoes of Danny's shot could fade, he fired again, decapitating the creature in a gruesome spectacle.

The mighty creature plummeted from the cliff's edge, striking the ground with an ear-splitting crash that echoed through the forest. Three creatures down, I felt a split second of triumph before everything went sideways. I was blindsided as the fourth creature lunged at me from the cliff, its mammoth hands intent on crushing me. Just as I braced for the impending impact, two simultaneous shots rang out. The creature's head exploded in a grotesque shower, and its chest cavity was torn apart.

Looking up, I saw Sam, his face a mask of grim determination, dash into the cave. He emerged moments later with Jake clutched tightly in his arms. The relief of seeing Jake alive was short-lived, as right on Sam's tail was another hulking beast. Jeff and Betty, acting in tandem, blasted it with their shotguns. The beast's demise was swift, and its remains sprayed the vicinity, drenching me in gore.

"Fuck!" I yelled, wiping the viscera from my face. "Are there any more of these bastards?"

"Two more on your right!" Jeff yelled back, his eyes wild and focused.

Reacting quickly, I hurled a grenade in the direction Jeff indicated. As the grenade flew, Jeff opened fire, unleashing a hail of bullets. Not wasting a moment, I pulled the pin from another grenade and tossed it into the fray, effectively cutting off any escape route for the creatures.

Sam descended from the higher ground, Jake safe in his arms, just as another creature burst forth from the cave's entrance. The sheer velocity of the beast caught me off guard, but Sam didn't miss a beat. With a deadly precision that belied his earlier skepticism, he fired his .44 mag, obliterating the creature's head in a gruesome explosion.

"Jeff, cover me," I barked, my voice hoarse with adrenaline. "I need to ensure that cave's clear."

As I moved forward, the pungent stench of blood, gore, and something far more foul hit me, threatening to make me retch. The air was thick with a stench that clung to the back of my throat. I steeled myself, knowing that ensuring the safety of the town depended on our thoroughness now.

Jeff and I proceeded cautiously, every sense heightened, and it wasn't long before our vigilance paid off. There, lying on the ground, was one of the creatures feigning death. With swift precision, I unloaded two .44 mag rounds into its skull, silencing it for good. The cavern's interior was an unsettling sight – a grim mosaic of scattered bones. The remains of countless victims lay strewn about, and a chilling realization dawned upon us: many were human.

I turned to Jeff, my expression grave. "You think there are more of these fuckers lurking around?"

Jeff frowned, clearly on edge. "Why do you ask?"

"Something doesn't sit right with me. Call it a gut feeling," I responded, scanning the shadowy recesses of the cave.

Emerging from the cave's darkness, we were met by the rest of our group, a tangible tension hanging in the air. "How do we get down from this place?" I inquired.

Jeff pointed to a series of ledges. "We can jump from one cliff level to the next until we're back on solid ground."

As we started our descent, a sudden movement caught our eye. A creature burst forth, but before it could advance, Jeff silenced it with two swift shots to its head.

"We need to get Jake to safety," I stated firmly. "He's been through hell. We need to reunite him with his mother and get him some medical attention."

I turned my gaze to Betty, who stood her ground, determination burning in her eyes. "I'm staying with you," she declared.

Though I tried to dissuade her, she remained steadfast. It was comforting to know I wasn't alone. I instructed the others, "Form a protective circle around Jake. Jeff, you carry him. Two of you walk a few steps behind to cover our rear, and one leads the way. Make sure your guns are loaded and be ready for anything. Move quickly and stay alert."

As the group headed out, Betty and I stationed ourselves near the cave entrance, watching vigilantly. Our patience soon paid off as two more creatures emerged. I gestured for Betty to hold her fire, but she was one step ahead, expertly drawing her bow and sending an arrow through the first creature's head, swiftly followed by another to its heart. It crumpled in a heap.

The second creature didn't fare any better. Betty's shotgun barked twice, piercing its heart and head. As it fell lifelessly from the cliff, I felt a swell of admiration for her. "Impressive shots," I complimented.

However, our respite was short-lived. From the cliff above, another creature appeared, wielding a massive boulder. Its intentions were clear as it aimed Betty. Acting instinctively, I pulled her out of harm's way just as the rock crashed down. Not wasting a second, I aimed my .44 auto mag and fired, the bullet finding its mark in the creature's head. With a final, guttural scream, it tumbled down, meeting the same fate as its kin.

There was the sudden sound of gunshots that broke the silence of the creature, plummeting to its death.

Hearing the gunshots, our adrenaline spiked. We sprinted in the direction of the echoing sounds and were met by the sight of the ninth creature, lifeless, with two gunshot wounds puncturing its head. Betty's face was a mixture of disbelief and exhaustion. "How the hell did we miss so many?" she panted.

"They're masters of camouflage," I explained, "masters of their terrain." Even so, I took no chances. Drawing my gun, I shot two rounds into its chest to ensure it wouldn't rise again.

We made our way back to the house, where a crowd had gathered. All eyes were on us, filled with a mixture of anxiety and hope. They had gathered, hoping to see Jake, the rescued boy, and witness whether we had lived up to our promise. To their palpable relief, we had delivered.

As we approached, I pulled the general and the new sheriff aside, briefing them on everything we had encountered. The general's face was graver than I had seen it before. "I'll have to report this," he muttered.

Interrupting him, I said, "Before you do that, promise me one thing. When your guys arrive – especially those Men in Black assholes – they are to leave Betty and Jeff out of it. Those two have been through enough. They don't need to be grilled or intimidated."

The general's brow furrowed, a hint of irritation flashing in his eyes. "You mean the MIBs? Shit, I'm tired of their games too. They always swoop in, acting all high and mighty, causing more harm than good."

"You make sure they understand," I asserted, my voice firm, "this is personal. Betty and Jeff went above and beyond. They didn't owe that kid anything, yet they risked their lives. They deserve respect, not harassment."

The tension could be sliced with a knife as the men in black approached. Their confidence was evident from their gait - heads held high, shoes clicking on the pavement. As they got closer, the other helpers grew restless, darting glances in my direction as if seeking assurance. I locked eyes with Sue, who looked visibly disturbed by their sudden arrival.

Sam, his protective instincts kicking in, approached me. "These the pricks you warned us about?"

"Oh, yeah," I replied, my voice dripping with distaste. "Top-grade assholes. They think their badges give them the right to push anyone around."

I noticed Sue's confrontations with them from the corner of my eye. She was never one to back down, but they seemed intent on asserting dominance, probably to make up for the lack of respect they received from the townsfolk. When one of them shoved her, that was the final straw for me. I strode over, grabbing the offender by the collar and throwing a punch that knocked the wind out of him. He crumpled, hitting the ground like a sack of potatoes.

The cafe's outdoor area was filled with murmurs and gasps as another agent stepped forward, finger-pointing aggressively. "You're under arrest for assaulting a federal agent!"

My reply was swift – another punch that left him sprawled next to his colleague. I towered over them, every ounce of my being emanating threat. "Who's next?" I taunted, glancing at the remaining agents. Their bravado seemed to waver, even though they tried to hide it.

"You'll regret this!" One of them shouted, trying to drag his unconscious colleagues away.

I leaned in closer. "Listen closely. If any of you bastards so much as glance in Sue's direction, you'll wish you hadn't crossed me." I paused, letting my words sink in. "Now get your sorry asses out of here. And if I ever see you again, it won't be a friendly reunion."

"And now you guys get your friends and get the hell out of here. I never want to see you again! And tell your smug friend here, if he so much as lays a finger on Sue, he'll regret it," I warned with icy determination.

The four men exchanged glances and burst into laughter. Their sneering faces filled with mockery. "Oh, what's the big guy going to do?" one of them teased.

Sue, recognizing the dangerous glint in my eyes, tried to intervene. "Just leave it. They're not worth it." But their derisive laughter continued to echo, igniting a fire within me.

"Want to test just how tough I really am?" I challenged, my voice dripping with anger. "Come on, all of you at once."

The situation intensified as Sue filled me in on their earlier altercation. With each word, my rage built until I felt like a pot about to boil over. The agents, seeing my visible fury, doubled down on their mockery.

Their laughter was suddenly interrupted when the General's car pulled up. He assessed the scene quickly, his face slightly paling when he saw the anger in my eyes. "Gentlemen," he warned the agents, "you might want to reconsider."

But it was too late.

I lunged at the nearest one, my fist connecting with his face. The sharp crunch of bone signaled a broken jaw. Another tried to flank me, but I quickly pivoted, landing a solid kick to his knee. The sickening snap was followed by a scream of pain.

Two of them tried to mount a joint attack, but they were no match for my heightened senses and rage-fueled strength. In mere moments, both were sprawled on the ground, one clutching his head and the other gasping for air.

It was then that the General stepped forward. "Enough, Executioner! Stand down!" he shouted, using my codename to snap me out of my battle rage. The last two agents, sensing their impending doom, started to retreat slowly, sheer terror painted on their faces.

Sue, tears streaming down her face, stood in front of me, her hands on my chest. "Please, just stop," she pleaded, her voice trembling. And as I looked into her tear-filled eyes, the fog of anger lifted, and I was once again anchored to reality.

I locked eyes with Sue, the anger that had consumed me a moment ago now replaced with a deep sadness. "They touched you, Sue," I whispered, the weight of those words pulling at my heart.

She smiled gently, soothing my troubled spirit. "It wasn't them," she said, nodding towards the man gasping for air on the ground. "I'm okay."

As I took in the scene, the General approached, gratitude evident in his eyes. "Thank God you can be controlled. We can't have another incident like this. He might not survive next time."

The two other agents exchanged nervous glances, the bravado from earlier gone. One of them mumbled, "Is he like this all the time? Fucking insane."

Hearing his words, I felt that familiar rage begin to bubble up again. But before I could react, Sue's grip on my arm tightened. "Come on," she said, leading me away, "Let's eat something."

The agent wasn't finished. His voice trembling with fear, he called out, "This isn't over!"

I stopped in my tracks, turning to face him. Sue's hand still wrapped around my arm, I whispered coldly, "You've made an enemy today. Remember this face. I will find you."

Sue's gentle voice interrupted my dark promise. "We need to take care of the others," she said. "The ones who helped. We owe them."

I nodded, still seething but realizing she was right. "Thanks, Sue."

As we walked towards the cafe, the emotions of the day caught up with me. Turning to Sue, I was struck by her beauty. It was in this vulnerable moment that I confessed, "You know, Sue, I haven't felt this way since Lily years ago. I think I'm falling in love with you."

She looked into my eyes, her voice firm yet tender. "We can't mix our personal feelings with our professional duties. Not at work."

I took a deep breath, the weight of my emotions pressing against my chest. "Sue, I don't care about the rules anymore. I'm in love with you." Turning to the General, I challenged him, "And what are you going to do about it?"

The General rolled his eyes, a smirk playing on his lips. "Took you long enough, dumbass."

Pushing through the swinging doors of the café, the chatter of the patrons came to an abrupt halt. A resounding applause erupted as we entered. With a wave of my hand and a mock frown, I said, "Shut up, all of you! I'm starving. Let's eat." The room filled with laughter, lightening the heavy atmosphere of the day.

Pausing, I cleared my throat and addressed the group. "You all out there today... You were incredible. You watched each other's backs. You got the job done. Most importantly, we all came back in one piece. That's the biggest win." The murmurs of agreement and nods of appreciation filled the room. "Be proud of yourselves."

As the sheriff walked in with the boy in tow, the crowd surged forward. Those who hadn't seen Jake yet eagerly inquired about his well-being.

"Just a few scratches and some bruises, but he's alive," the sheriff assured them.

Jake's mother, tears of gratitude streaming down her face, spoke up. "Thank you, each and every one of you. God bless."

Catching Betty's eye, I motioned for her to come over. "For you and the rest," I said, handing her an envelope. "A little token of appreciation."

Sam, peeking into the envelope, whistled, "That's quite the reward for a job well done."

Betty, grinning, chimed in, "Sheriff, after today, I'd say hiring me as a deputy might not be a bad idea."

Nodding in agreement, I added, "She's right. Best decision you'll make." Turning back to the group, I grimaced, "But first, I need to get to the hospital. My shoulder's killing me."

# CHAPTER 9

✦✦✦✦✦

FTER BEING DISCHARGED FROM THE hospital, my sore shoulder, cuts, and bruises serving as grim reminders of the recent battle, we headed straight for the hotel. The weight of the day pressed heavily on me, and I desperately needed a bed. But Danny, eyes wide with awe and curiosity, was bursting with questions.

"So, is this the kind of madness you always deal with?" Danny asked his tone a mix of disbelief and admiration.

With a tired sigh, I replied, "Yeah, most of the time these days. These cryptids... they're getting bolder, more aggressive. Sometimes, the military gets called in for the big messes, but for discreet, silent operations, they call me." I leaned in closer, "And the pay? Danny, it's more money than you can imagine."

I sat down on the edge of the bed, feeling every year of my age at that moment. "But truth be told, I'm nearing the end of my run. Growing old, growing tired. I'm thinking it might be time for a new chapter. And I'm wondering if that chapter could include training someone like you to take over."

Danny's eyes widened in surprise. "Me? Oh hell no! I don't have the training, the knowledge... I mean, cryptids? And those other freaky things you chase down? I can't do what you do."

"But what if you could?" I challenged, looking him straight in the eye. "I've been doing this for years. I can teach you."

Danny sat down beside me, rubbing his temples as he considered the proposal. "But who else knows this stuff like you do? What if I run into something I can't handle? And if you're leaving, who's going to back me up?"

I chuckled, "Danny, you're thinking too far ahead. Sure, there's a lot to learn, and no, there isn't some handy manual I can give you that'll answer every question. But I promise I'll be there every step of the way. And the money? It'll ensure that your family's taken care of for generations."

The room fell silent as Danny absorbed the weight of my words.

"Danny, why do you think I've stuck around for so long?" I asked, leaning back in my chair, my face lined with the wear and tear of countless battles and sleepless nights.

He shrugged, "I always figured you had nowhere else to turn to. This life, as chaotic as it is, seemed like your only path."

I let out a soft chuckle, the weight of the years heavy in my laughter. "You know, I used to believe that too. I thought this job was all I had. But Sue... she showed me there's more to life than just chasing shadows."

I sighed, looking down at my weathered hands. "I've got kids, Danny. Over the years, a few women have had my children. And every time I see those kids, it's a brief moment once every few months, if I'm lucky. They need more from me now, not just the occasional visit. Some of their mothers don't want me around, and honestly, can I blame them? They think I'm just a guy who travels a lot for work. They don't really know the dangers I face, the things I've seen."

I paused, taking a deep breath, the weight of regret evident in my eyes. "I saw my little girl in New York, hiding under a blanket, scared and alone. And that... that broke me. While I'm gallivanting around the world, I realize I've failed them in the most fundamental way. I can't be their protector, their constant when I'm always gone."

Danny and Nancy exchanged concerned glances but said nothing.

"You know, sometimes I feel like there's no hope left for me. Like I've let my family down too many times. And now, with someone out there hunting them down, I've never felt so helpless. Instead of ensuring their safety, I'm chasing after cryptids and shadows."

A burning rage flickered in my eyes. "I swear, Danny, I'm going to find whoever's behind this, and I'll take them down. And if that means everyone knows about my dark, dirty job, so be it. I need to save my family. That's what a good father does, right?"

Danny and Nancy just stared at their faces, a mixture of shock and empathy, at a loss for words.

"Danny, Nancy," I started, with a heavy weight in my voice, "Do you believe it's a constant duty to protect one's family?"

The two exchanged a brief glance, their faces riddled with concern.

"It's not about belief," Danny murmured, "It's about instinct. Every bone in your body screams to keep them safe."

I nodded, my eyes distant. "That bastard, Shan. He's messed with the wrong guy. Tapping into my worst fears. Now, he'll understand what it means to be on the receiving end of my full attention."

I took a deep breath, trying to contain the swirling emotions within. "Did you both ever hear that I was in the 'military'? Simultaneously part of it, and not?"

Nancy shook her head, looking perplexed. "No, we hadn't heard about that."

Chuckling, I continued, "The government keeps tabs on every move I make. Yet, in the military framework, I hold a rank that goes beyond the ordinary - Five Star General with a diamond. It means I make the decisions, irrespective of what anyone might think. A mind-bender, isn't it?"

Noticing their surprised expressions, I added, "With such power, I can overturn decisions made even by a state's Supreme Court. If a judgment seems off, I can rectify it. And in my thirty-five-plus years, never once did I misuse this authority. Every asset I possess wasn't accumulated by exploiting my position. Instead, it was by doing right by people. By helping those who were oppressed, abused, and sold into a life they didn't choose. Standing up against bullying, whether it's from police, governments, or any damned agency."

I could feel the passion and anger rising in my voice. "And for all the shit I've done, while some label me 'nuts,' in many places, they call me a hero. I'm the reason many can live freely in their countries without fear. And the irony? My own government has attempted to off me multiple times. And they failed every single time."

Letting out a weary sigh, I finished, "When they tried to take me out, I ensured they felt the weight of their decision. Sent back their operatives piece by piece." A dark smile touched my lips. "Now, if you'll excuse me, it's been a long day, and I need some rest. Good night."

Nancy leaned forward, her curiosity evident. "I don't mean to overstep, but this...this world of yours, it might not necessarily be the same for your brother," she said cautiously.

I sighed, the weight of the day pressing on me. "I know, Nancy. I'm just tired. It grates on my nerves when I'm pulled into missions so abruptly like tonight." I took a deep breath, pushing the irritation aside. "Look, let's get some rest. We're driving to Dallas in the morning. I'll see you then."

By the time the sun painted the horizon with its early morning hues, we were all gathered for breakfast. Sue gently massaged my sore shoulder as I addressed the group. "Take your time eating. I'm going to get my Bugatti ready for our drive to Texas. Then, it's on to LA."

Danny, eyebrows raised, said, "I can understand Texas, but why LA?"

"I've got someone to meet in Dallas," I explained. "A Texas Ranger. And after that, we head to LA."

Danny looked skeptical. "How long is all this going to take?"

I grinned, savoring the surprise I was about to unleash. "You'll see. For now, I'll get my car. Finish up, and I'll pick you all up in style."

Leaving them with a sense of anticipation, I went to the garage where my 2020 Bugatti Chiron - the rare four-door version - had been delivered. As I approached, its sleek design beckoned, every curve and line an epitome of perfection. I filled up the tank and drove to the hotel entrance.

As I pulled up, I couldn't help but chuckle at Danny and Nancy's stunned expressions.

Danny's jaw practically dropped. "What the hell is that?"

"My Bugatti," I replied nonchalantly. "It needs a good run, and a long drive to LA seems just right."

Nancy's eyes sparkled with excitement. "Can I drive it? I've always wanted to get behind the wheel of one of these."

I smirked, feeling the rush of the upcoming journey. "Of course. But let's save your turn for the stretches of the Arizona desert, alright?"

Sue's glance carried a weight of both concern and understanding. "Let's go then," she sighed, motioning for us to follow.

I gave a slight nod, and we set out for Dallas. With my Bugatti roaring beneath us, we made the journey in just an hour and a half. As the imposing facade of the Texas Rangers headquarters loomed ahead, I slowed the car and turned to Nancy. "How about filling up the car and grabbing us something to eat? This might take a bit."

Before I could say another word, she grinned and chirped, "Got it! Be right back!" In a burst of youthful enthusiasm, she revved the Bugatti and zoomed off, leaving a trail of burnt rubber in her wake.

Danny, chuckling at her antics, glanced my way. "Guess it's just us then."

The headquarters felt familiar, yet distant. The receptionist, recognizing me instantly, picked up her phone. "Sir, the Executioner is here, along with a few others," she announced. Moments later, she motioned us forward. "He's waiting for you."

Inside the spacious office, a large desk sat with a grizzled man behind it. His eyes brightened upon seeing me. "Ex! It's been years! How've you been holding up?"

Sighing deeply, I gestured towards Sue and Danny. "It's been... complicated. I need some information. Anything you've got on a few individuals connected to the New York bombing."

His face contorted with a mix of sympathy and anger. "Sorry about your daughter, Ex. That was a nasty business."

I nodded, my voice thick with emotion. "There's a former US military colonel, went off the grid. Heard he's selling humans, and anything else for the right price. There's also this idiot named Tom, another gun runner. Anything you've got on them?"

The Ranger leaned back, lacing his fingers. "They're working for a New Yorker, but the puppet strings trace back to an IRA member from Ireland."

I leaned in, eager for more. "Shan," I breathed out, anger igniting in my veins. "He's most likely the one who took my daughter from me and nearly claimed my son in Florida."

I studied the boss's face for any sign of deceit but found none. "So, do you have any leads?" I pressed.

He rubbed his temples, a weary sigh escaping his lips. "Ex, you never were one to chase small-time thugs, huh?"

"No, Boss. They brought this to my doorstep. I just need names, locations, and any associates they've got."

He looked at me square in the eyes, the weight of understanding evident in his gaze. "I have to ask... after you get this information, what's the next step?"

I met his gaze, unwavering. "I find them, and I kill them all."

He took a moment to absorb the gravity of my words. "I can forward all this to Healy for you," he offered, but there was a hesitant pause. "But considering your... history, do you really think she'd want to get involved?"

"It's not about what she wants," I said tersely. "This involves her too. She has to help, whether she likes it or not. It'll take time, but could you pass it on for me?"

The Boss chuckled, a sad, resigned sound. "Good luck with that, Ex. I've got a feeling she's gonna hit the roof when she finds out."

I grunted, not particularly concerned about Healy's potential outburst. "Just send it to her. Thanks." We left the office, making our way to the main lobby.

Nancy had returned and was waiting with my car. The engine hummed smoothly as we all climbed in. She gripped the wheel, determination in her eyes. "Ready to head to LA?"

About two hours into the drive, the police radio crackled to life. A high-speed chase was underway, with a Lamborghini tearing through Nevada, bound for Arizona. My gut tightened. "I'd bet anything that's Tom," I muttered.

Nancy glanced at me. "What do you want to do?"

"I need to drive," I said firmly. Swapping places with her, I slammed my foot on the gas pedal. The Bugatti roared to life, hurtling us forward with breathtaking speed, as we closed in on our prey.

The roar of the engine combined with the wind outside was intoxicating. As the speedometer climbed, the scenery blurred past, transforming the desert landscape into a kaleidoscope of colors.

Sue quickly dialed the local dispatch. "This is Sue with special agent Ex. We're in pursuit of the Lamborghini. Advise all units ahead to give us a clear path."

The voice on the other end crackled. "We can't keep up with him. Neither can our chopper. He's all yours."

Sue grinned, a glint of mischief in her eyes. "Don't worry. We'll handle it. Tell them not to blink or they might miss us."

Danny's grip on the seat tightened, his knuckles white. "Are you sure about this speed? Isn't it too dangerous?"

"We need to go faster if we're going to catch him," I replied, my voice calm despite the adrenaline pumping through my veins.

As the Bugatti continued to devour the road, Nancy's eyes sparkled with excitement. "This is incredible! I've never experienced speed like this!"

I glanced over at Sue, signaling her to communicate with the police again. "Ask the units ahead to move to the right and give us space. We're closing in."

Nancy pointed ahead. "Look! There's the helicopter! And there... I see the Lamborghini."

The sleek silhouette of the Lamborghini grew larger as we closed the distance. The radio buzzed again. "All units be advised, the Bugatti is gaining on the Lamborghini. Clear the way."

Danny swallowed hard, his eyes wide. "This is insane!"

Keeping a close eye on the road, I could see the Lamborghini's driver glancing frequently in the rearview mirror. A look of realization crossed his face. He must have understood that there was no way he could outrun us.

As if acknowledging the inevitable, the Lamborghini's brake lights flashed, and he began slowing down. I maneuvered the Bugatti, positioning it right in front of him, ensuring he had no avenue of escape.

The deafening sound of sirens filled the air as multiple police vehicles arrived, surrounding the Lamborghini. The chase had ended. The predator had become the prey.

Tom's confused expression was visible through the car window, his eyes darting around as if trying to find a way out of the situation. The woman beside him, an attractive brunette with fear evident in her eyes, whispered anxiously, "Who the hell are they?"

"Just keep quiet," Tom growled back, his knuckles white on the steering wheel. "I'll handle this."

Upon recognizing me, a mixture of disbelief and rage clouded his eyes. "You?!" he spat, glaring in my direction. "Can't you ever leave well enough alone?"

Danny stepped forward, his .44 mag aimed squarely at Tom's chest. "Out of the car, Tom. Hands where we can see 'em."

Reluctantly, Tom and his companion emerged, their hands raised in surrender. Tom, however, wasn't about to go quietly. "Every damn time!" he shouted, a string of expletives following, each more colorful than the last.

Ignoring his tirade, I approached the lead police officer. "I need him held for a few hours. Then release him and the woman."

The officer looked taken aback. "After all this? Are you kidding?"

I met his gaze evenly. "He's working for me now. We've got bigger fish to fry. There's a man causing chaos on the east coast, and Tom here can lead us to him."

"What the hell," the officer sighed, rubbing his temples. "Alright, fine. But if he pulls any shit, I'm holding you responsible."

I nodded, turning back to Tom. "Three, maybe four hours. Then you're free. But you better be ready to work, got it?"

Tom sneered, his eyes full of disdain. "Three hours, and then you and I have some business to settle."

I couldn't help but smirk. "Looking forward to it. Oh, and thanks again."

Tom's angry gaze met mine, his litany of insults rolling off like water on a duck's back. Sometimes, a person's temper reveals more about them than their words ever could. This was Tom, all bluster and fury, with a desperate need to assert dominance. But beneath that bravado? He was just another pawn in the game, and I'd use him as such.

We climbed back into the car, the sleek engine purring as we sped towards LA. I handed the keys to Nancy, figuring it was time for a change. The open road stretched endlessly before us, the monotony broken only by Danny's incessant curiosity.

"Alright, spill it," he said, his eyes glinting with anticipation. "What was that Ranger talking about? You and this mysterious 'she' have some juicy history?"

I took a deep breath, my grip tightening on the steering wheel. "It's personal, Danny."

But the young detective wasn't one to let things go. "Come on, we're in this together. If there's history that could jeopardize the mission, I want to know."

The air in the car grew tense, silence punctuated by the rhythmic thrum of tires against the asphalt. Before I could speak, Nancy chimed in, mischief evident in her voice, "Sounds juicy. What's the story?"

Trying to break the tension, Sue shot me a wry smile. "Maybe you should've let that creature have a bite of him back there." Her laughter was infectious, and I couldn't help but join in.

"Would've been animal cruelty," I quipped.

Danny looked momentarily confused. "Those creatures weren't dumb, you know."

Sue and I exchanged glances, biting back our amusement. "Wasn't talking about the creatures, detective," I retorted, a playful smirk on my lips.

It took a moment for realization to dawn on Danny's face. "Hey, you're talking about me!" His mock outrage was met with peals of laughter from all of us.

"Some detective you are," Sue teased.

"Fine," I began, taking a deep breath, "I won't give you the entire tale, but it involves some children - mine and hers." I hesitated, casting a sidelong glance at Sue, whose eyes bore into mine with an intensity I couldn't decipher. "You see, many years ago, Healy and I... we had a couple of kids. And no, Danny, before you jump to conclusions, those aren't my only kids. I have... more than a handful scattered around. But these particular two, they mean something else."

A mixture of curiosity and confusion etched across Danny's face. "Wait, so Healy doesn't know about them?"

"That's the complicated part," I replied, the weight of past secrets heavy on my shoulders. "I kept them from her. It's... it's messy."

Sue released an exasperated sigh, the kind that says volumes more than words ever could. I winced, knowing full well what was coming. "So, I guess there's more to this than just kids, right?" Danny pressed, unable to resist digging deeper.

Sue shot him a look, her voice tinged with a warning, "It's deeply personal between Glen and Healy. It's best left alone."

"But if I'm gonna be working alongside you, don't I have a right to know?" Danny countered.

"Look," I interjected, my tone weary, "You'll find out soon enough. For now, let's just say there are skeletons in my closet I'd rather not unearth."

As our conversation grew tenser, Sue's phone buzzed. She swiftly answered and, after a brief exchange, looked at me. "The captain says they can hold Tom for another hour. Then they'll release him."

"Good. Thanks, Sue," I replied, trying to keep my tone neutral. But she wasn't having any of it.

"Don't think you're off the hook so easily," Sue retorted, her gaze icy. "We're gonna discuss this – later."

Speeding into LA, the towering buildings of the cityscape greeting us, I braced myself for the storm that awaited at NCIS headquarters. It was here I'd confront a past I'd hoped to leave behind. Pulling up to the entrance, I looked over at Sue. "Coming in?"

Her cold voice responded, "I'll take the car to the safe house. Call when you're done."

Taking a deep breath, I turned to the siblings, "Alright, Danny, Nancy, ready for the next chapter of this saga?"

Danny smirked, "Wouldn't miss it for the world."

Nancy, her eyes glinting with a mix of mischief and curiosity, chimed in, "Hell, after that bombshell, I'm all in. Lead the way."

Stepping out of the car, the weight of impending confrontation heavy in the air, we marched towards the NCIS building. I input the familiar security code, granting us access. The long hallway led us directly to the vestibule where Healy stood, her poised demeanor in stark contrast to the storm raging behind her eyes.

For what felt like an eternity, we just stared at each other, the air thick with tension. Danny, clearly growing uncomfortable with the silence, cleared his throat, "Well? Are either of you going to say anything?"

Before I could gather my thoughts, Healy snapped at him, "Shut it." I couldn't help but smirk, appreciating her fire, even after all these years.

"We need to talk, Healy," I declared, trying to keep my voice steady.

Her team, poised for action, eyed me with a mix of curiosity and suspicion. One particularly brave—or foolish—agent stepped forward. "You'll talk here, in front of all of us."

Giving him a withering glare, I replied coldly, "You really don't want to test me right now. Step back."

Healy, ever the diplomat, intervened, "Everyone, back to your desks. Stand down. That's an order."

But before we could proceed, the door swung open again. Sue. Her unexpected entrance momentarily threw me off, but I refocused on the matter at hand.

"Healy, remember our kids? The ones you decided we'd put up for adoption?"

Her eyes widened in shock, "You did what?"

"I kept them, Healy," I confessed, my voice choked with emotion.

"But... but we agreed, for their sake, to keep them away from this life, from us."

"You decided that, Healy. Alone," I shot back, bitterness evident in my tone. "I returned from the field to an empty home and a letter. It tore me apart. If not for the General, I might've hunted you down then and there."

A heavy silence settled between us, broken only by Sue's firm voice, "Enough of this. No more threats."

Healy's eyes, filled with a mixture of anger and sorrow, met mine, and for a brief moment, the years and the pain melted away. But then, as quickly as it came, the moment was gone.

Healy's eyes darkened, her voice trembling but resolute. "I believed I was doing right, protecting them from all of this. But how could you not tell me?!"

"YOU NEVER GAVE ME A CHANCE!" I roared, my patience spent. "You need to see the life you abandoned. Our son, now a commander of a task force in England, our daughter, a mother of two, including a newborn. Your granddaughter."

She looked stricken, her face ghostly pale. "I... I had no idea."

"Do you want to meet them, Healy?" The question hung in the air, thick and heavy. "Do you want to see the family you left behind?"

Sue intervened her voice a calming presence, "Ex, give her a moment. This is a lot to take in."

Tears welled up in Healy's eyes as she met mine. "I'd heard about Cindy. I used to call her and chat with her. She always mentioned you. I can't believe she's gone." Her voice broke, her sorrow genuine. Pulling me into a tight embrace, she whispered, "I'm so, so sorry."

I gently pulled away, "It's a fucked-up world, Healy. Now, about our kids and grandkids. Do you want to be a part of their lives or not?"

The raw emotion in the room was palpable as she fought to find her voice. "Yes, I do."

Taking a deep breath, I nodded, "It's time to reintroduce you then. But first, you need to be aware of the danger surrounding us. Our enemies aren't just after me; they're targeting anyone related to me."

Healy's analyst, Ms. Jones, arrived just as the weight of the situation seemed to sink in for Healy. Her eyes wide with panic, Healy turned to her assistant, "Ms. Jones, this may sound insane, but everything you're about to hear is God's honest truth."

Hesitantly, I began detailing the threats our family faced. How three of her sisters were already targeted, one of her brothers injured, and how these enemies would go to any lengths, even killing their own, to get to me.

Moments later, Sue entered.

Sue's voice was shaky, the weight of the news evident in her eyes. "Glen, I'm so sorry... your son... he couldn't pull through."

The words hit like a sledgehammer. I turned to Ms. Jones, my voice cracking, "Yes, I'm your father. We had to keep you safe, away from all this shit. I didn't even know Healy hadn't told you. Or the General."

Tears welled up in Ms. Jones' eyes as she struggled to process the information. "So, my brother is dead because of this mole?"

I nodded gravely, trying to maintain my composure. "There's a mole, alright. I think he might be from the war days, but every time I get close, he vanishes. There's a bastard named Shan pulling the strings. But Tom? He's just a pawn, always goes to the highest bidder, selling guns and whatever the hell else."

Healy's gaze shifted between Sue and me. "Shan? I thought Tom was our main problem?"

"No, Healy," I replied tersely, "Tom's just the middleman. It's Shan we need to focus on. Did the Rangers send you anything?"

She shook her head, "I just got back. I'll have to check. But yes, we need to work together to save our family. The stakes are too high now."

I nodded, hoping for unity in these tumultuous times. "Healy, we need to be on the same page to save the rest of our family. Is that understood?"

She looked pained, her voice barely above a whisper. "I need some time to process all of this. Another child is gone because of the choices we made."

Suddenly, anger flashed across her face, and she landed a solid slap on my cheek. "That's for keeping our kids a secret!" she shouted. Without waiting for my response, she struck me again. Pulling me close, she buried her face in my chest, her sobs shaking both of us. "Find them, Glen. Do what you're best at and kill every last one of them."

After a few moments, she pulled back, wiping her tears. Her voice was steely, "About our children, Glen. What's the plan now? They're here with their families. My grandchildren. How do we save them and put an end to this? We need to decide, and fast."

Healy's voice wavered, "Can I see them? Right now?"

I nodded, reaching out to grip her arm reassuringly. "Yes, Healy. I've always been here for you. And I always will be."

A tall, broad-shouldered figure appeared at the end of the hallway. "Mom," he called out gently, hesitantly. "It's me, David."

Healy's eyes widened in disbelief. "My son..." she whispered, taking tentative steps towards him. Their embrace was heartfelt, raw emotion dripping from the scene.

And then, from behind David emerged a young woman holding a baby, with another little one clutching her hand. "Mom," she said with tears in her eyes, "this is Cindy, your granddaughter. And this," she pointed to the toddler, "is Michael."

Healy, overwhelmed, reached out, tears streaming down her face. "I can't believe this," she murmured, holding the baby close to her heart.

A steely determination replaced the tenderness in Healy's eyes as she addressed the room. "Whatever it takes. I'll do whatever it takes to protect this family. We need to find these bastards and end this."

Nancy and Danny entered the room, with Danny stating firmly, "We're in, too. We're a team."

Healy nodded gratefully, then turned her focus back to me. "We have to locate this base Tom operates from. If we can track him, we can get to the root of this nightmare."

Mis. Jones, newly invigorated with purpose, chimed in. "I'll do everything in my power to help. This is my family now, and hell hath no fury like a woman protecting her loved ones."

I couldn't help but smile at her determination. "Thanks, Jones. We received intel that Tom is flying into LA from Dallas today at 6 pm."

She nodded, "We'll tail him from the airport and find out where he's headed. We'll get this information, Ex."

A warmth spread through the room as David, Sue, Cindy, and even the young ones came together, wrapping me in an embrace. This was family, and we'd face this storm together.

Mis Jones' voice echoed with newfound determination, "No one, and I mean no one, is going to hurt my family." Her eyes sparkled with a fierceness that was both surprising and heartwarming. "For the first time, I truly feel what it means to be part of a loving family."

I watched as the team began to strategize, moving pieces on the board and planning their next moves. The weight of responsibility and the lives at stake drove me to seek some solitude. I needed clarity, some moments to process everything, to strategize without distractions.

I found a secluded spot, a little alcove away from the hustle and bustle of the main office. Deep in thought, pondering how to approach this without jeopardizing my newfound family, I was startled by a familiar voice.

Healy.

"You always did have a flair for the dramatic," she remarked dryly.

I glanced up, meeting her gaze. "Wasn't it worth it, Healy? This revelation, this chance for you to have a family, to retire and be free of all this chaos?"

She tilted her head, regarding me with those piercing eyes. "You think after all of this, you can just walk away? Leave us again?"

Before I could react, her hand made contact with my face. A stinging reminder of the emotional tumult our history evoked.

"You're still the same," she muttered bitterly. "Always the hero, always the martyr."

I rubbed my cheek, the sting still fresh. "This isn't about revenge, Healy. It's about ensuring that our family, our children, and our grandchildren can live without looking over their shoulders. But I know the path I've chosen may end with my death."

She stepped closer, her voice softer now. "You always were ready to lay down your life. But do you truly believe that by dying, you're ensuring our safety?"

"I believe," I started, "that if my death ensures the eradication of this threat, ensures a peaceful life for all of you, then it's a price I'm willing to pay. Even if it includes Sue."

Healy sighed deeply, "I know you won't stop until they're all gone. But promise me, Glen, that you won't throw your life away needlessly."

I met her eyes, seeing the depth of pain and love they held. "I promise, Healy. I'll do whatever it takes to keep our family safe."

With a furrowed brow, Healy leaned against the wall, processing everything I had just divulged. "You're saying an official from San Francisco is involved? Along with the commissioner?"

"Yes," I nodded firmly. "The truth runs deep, and he's a pivotal piece in this tangled web. We need to get to him. Find out what he knows."

Healy seemed lost in thought for a moment before responding, "It's always the ones we least suspect, isn't it?"

"Seems that way," I replied. "And there's more. We have another son. I only learned about him from the general yesterday."

A brief smile tugged at the corners of Healy's mouth, amusement dancing in her eyes. "Let me guess, you had no idea about this one?"

Biting back a smirk, I replied, "Exactly. And I have to protect him. He's in grave danger."

Healy's features softened, "Always the protector, Glen. Remember, you've got us. You don't have to do this alone."

Sighing, I said, "I need to do this, Healy. I need to ensure that our family is safe. If anything were to happen to me, I need you to tell them – all of them – that I did this for them."

Healy's eyes shimmered with tears, "That's what makes you unique in this game. Your unwavering loyalty. It's why I fell for you all those years ago."

Swallowing hard, I replied, "There's more evil heading towards them than they can imagine. I have to head it off. Stop it before it reaches them."

Suddenly, urgency seeped into Healy's voice, "Where will you start?"

"Jones. She's keeping an eye on Tom's landing at the airport. I have a hunch he'll head straight to that old abandoned warehouse on the docks. He's always had a fondness for such places."

Healy raised an eyebrow, "And our son?"

"If he's eager to join the big leagues, now's his chance. Send him with Danny and some of your team to the airport. They'll tail Tom," I said.

She smirked, "Always thinking two steps ahead. Now, what about transportation?"

I scoffed, "Come on, Healy. Do you think I'm going to risk a car worth four million dollars? Got something a bit more low-key?"

Rolling her eyes with a playful smirk, Healy replied, "Always the pragmatist. I'll see what I can rustle up for you."

Healy, always quick on her feet, responded, "Alright, alright, I'll get you a car. Just make sure it comes back without a scratch, alright?" There was a playful yet worried undertone in her voice.

Grateful for her unwavering support, I headed straight to the warehouse. Its decaying edifice loomed ominously in front of us. Over the years, it had become a refuge for the desperate: vagrants, addicts, and the lost souls of the city. My gut churned. These innocents couldn't get caught up in our operation. We had to move them out before anything escalated.

Every step we took into the warehouse was calculated. My son, Danny, and I, flanked by a few officers, worked diligently, ensuring that every transient was carefully and quietly ushered to safety.

I whispered into the radio, alerting the team, "Listen up. Do NOT harm Tom. We need him alive. If he bolts, I'm pretty damn sure he's gonna come this way. We capture, we interrogate. We get to the bottom of this shit."

The echo of our footsteps seemed magnified in the cavernous space as we moved forward. Officers were positioned along the sides, their eyes scanning every nook and corner. Suddenly, Tom's figure became visible. He'd spotted us. Panic painted his features, and like a caged animal, he started to run.

Chaos erupted. As we closed in, some of his cronies seized a few unfortunate souls who hadn't yet been evacuated. But one man stood out to me. I knew he held the answers. He was my key to finding Tom.

By the time we managed to corner this particular guy, Tom had vanished. "He hopped into a car," the man muttered nervously. With my heart racing, I quickly relayed a message to Danny. "I need a pick-up. I'm two blocks from the warehouse entrance. We don't have much time."

# CHAPTER 10

T HE CITY STREETS BLURRED BY as we trailed Tom's car. The scent of gasoline and the muted sounds of distant sirens set the backdrop for this high-stakes chase. About five to six miles in, Tom's car slowed to a halt in front of a business building. Despite its worn-down facade, it seemed like a palace for the kind of sleaze Tom embodied.

"Danny, park the car two blocks away," I instructed. The concrete jungle seemed eerily silent around us as we made our approach. Buildings loomed overhead, their aged exteriors speaking of years gone by.

As we neared the building, Danny's eagerness to move forward was palpable. "Wait," I whispered, but he was already moving closer to the entrance.

We walked boldly through the main doors, the lobby's dim lighting casting long, eerie shadows. The desk clerk's eyes locked onto mine; a flash of panic crossed his face as his hand darted for the phone.

"No, no!" I warned, drawing my gun in a swift motion, leveling it at him. The weight of the situation anchored him to his seat, his face pale with fear.

The sudden arrival of backup was a surprise, even to me. I gestured to one of the officers, "Stay with him. He looks like he could use some company."

I needed information and fast. My eyes darted around the room, landing on an elderly gentleman who seemed to be assessing the situation. Noticing my gaze, he crookedly smiled and said, "Fifty bucks, and I'll tell you where your man went."

Not in the mood for games, I quickly handed him the cash, desperate to maintain our lead.

"Sixth floor," he whispered, eyes glinting with mischief. "Two guys followed him up."

Danny was ready to move. "Stairs or elevator?"

"Stairs," I replied, my breath a little more ragged now, feeling the pressure. We made our ascent, taking the steps two at a time. But as we climbed, I heard the familiar ding of the elevator.

"Shit," I muttered, quickening our pace.

We reached the sixth floor just as the elevator doors slid open, revealing none other than Nancy and Sue, looking defiant and ready for action.

"What the fuck are you two doing here?" I exclaimed, panic and frustration evident in my voice.

Before they could answer, Danny chimed in, his voice filled with urgency. "Now what?"

We found ourselves trapped in a maze of dimly lit corridors, each one echoing with the remnants of past confrontations. The game had just begun.

The sixth-floor corridor was eerily silent, with doors lining each side that looked as if they hadn't been opened in decades. The faded paint and cracked plaster told a story of neglect and decay. The atmosphere was thick, a mix of old dust and the fear of the unknown.

Danny whispered, his voice barely cutting through the silence, "It's too quiet. Do you think they've heard us?"

I motioned for silence as a faint, muffled sound reached my ears – the undeniable tone of people arguing.

Handing my .38 mag to Sue, I whispered tersely, "If they come out, and they're not us... shoot."

She nodded firmly, "Understood."

The voice grew clearer as we tiptoed closer, guiding us to a door three down from where we stood. My heart raced as memories of prior confrontations flooded back.

Pausing momentarily to gather ourselves, Danny and I kicked the door open. The sight that met us was chaotic: Five men around a table scattered with maps and weapons. Their expressions changed from surprise to defense within seconds. As one reached for his gun, I reflexively fired my .44 mag twice into his chest, watching as his life was extinguished in an instant.

"Nobody fucking move!" I yelled, my voice echoing through the room.

My gaze settled on a familiar face, a face from my past. A short, stout man, his eyes widening in recognition. "I remember you," I growled. "Japan. You got arrested for some petty shit like speeding. But it was more than that, wasn't it? You were at that house fire..."

He backpedaled, his voice quivering, "I don't know you."

I felt a rush of fury. "Yes, you do. You were there. You killed my family."

I could feel the cold anger coursing through me, my trigger finger itching.

Another man tried his luck, lunging for a weapon, but Danny was quicker. A single shot to the head ensured he would never harm anyone again.

The room was heavy with tension, the remaining men frozen in fear. My eyes never left the fat man. "You did it," I said, my voice dripping with venom. With a sense of finality, I shot him dead.

Breathing heavily, I turned my attention to the rest. "I'll ask once, and only once: Where is Shan? I know he's connected to the colonel."

A trembling voice piped up from the corner, "I don't know about any colonel, but Shan... He mentioned San Francisco. Something about prepping for his next job. That's all I know, I swear."

With a cold fury burning in my eyes, I told him, "You're a lying sack of shit most times, but I believe you this time." Without waiting for a reaction, I pulled the trigger, sending a bullet straight through his head. The room echoed with the deafening blast, and the tang of gunpowder mingled with the metallic stench of blood.

The other man in the corner, already paralyzed with fear, met the same fate.

Danny looked at me, his face a mask of disbelief and horror. "Why?"

I exhaled, steadying my emotions. "They were part of the team that took everything from me. I told you, every last one of them is going down."

Tom was on his knees, his face pale and his eyes wide with terror. "Thought you'd save your own skin, huh?"

I crouched down to his level, staring into his eyes. "Here's how this is gonna play out, Tom. We're going to play 'Let's Make a Deal.' You spill everything you know, and maybe, just maybe, I let you walk out of here breathing."

Tom stammered, "We... we had a deal. There's a guy... he deals in explosives, new-age weapons. I think... I think he was expecting you. He's got about five, maybe six, guys with him, waiting for you."

I smirked. "No, Tom. They're not here for me. They're here to ensure we don't leave. He's planning to bring this whole building down, burying all of us in rubble. But that's not going to happen, is it?"

Fear shone in Tom's eyes. "How do you even know all this? How did you know about my family?"

I leaned in closer, my voice a low growl. "I've been watching you for years. I saw you in Taiwan. You're not as under-the-radar as you think."

Taking a step back, I readied my weapon. "I'll take the lead. Tom, you're in the middle. Danny, you cover our six. And if Tom tries anything... don't hesitate to put him down."

With caution, we approached the stairwell. A quick glance down revealed two guards, chatting without a care. Without hesitation, I leaped, grabbing one by the throat and sending a swift kick to the other's head. As one went down, a gunshot sounded, and Danny took care of the other, shooting him cleanly in the neck.

The tension grew as figures emerged from various doors. Danny, ever alert, caught another one emerging from a doorway further down the hall. Without hesitation, he shot him three times in quick succession.

Tom, gasping for air, managed a shaky, "Three down, two to go, right?"

I closed the distance between us, pressing the barrel of my gun to his temple. "What are you talking about, Tom?" My voice was low, dangerous.

Tom's eyes darted left and right, panic evident. "There are snipers on all surrounding buildings. Whichever way we go, we're fucked. And if the sniper doesn't get us, he'll just blow this entire place to smithereens."

I tightened my grip on him, my anger boiling over. "On principle alone, I should blow your brains out right here, you worthless piece of shit."

He whimpered, "He threatened my family! That's why you should keep us alive. I had no choice!"

Drawing a deep breath, I hissed, "Be a man, Tom. Own up to your choices. If you have anything that can help us get out of this shitstorm, now's the time."

Taking a shaky breath, Tom said, "Well, Shan had ordered for a car bomb to be planted on your vehicle when you arrived."

I stared deep into his eyes, the fury evident. "Is that all?"

With a voice on the edge of breaking, Tom confirmed, "Yes, that's all, I swear!"

Danny, now regaining his composure, intervened, "The immediate issue is, how the fuck do we get out of here?"

Suddenly, Sue and Nancy appeared, their faces flushed with a mix of concern and adrenaline. Seeing them, I remarked to Danny, "Relax."

The women, catching their breath, asked, "What's happening?"

"Remember when I told both of you to stay put in the lobby? You should've listened," I chastised gently. "Right now, we need to find a way out of this deathtrap."

Nancy's eyes darted around, taking in the scene, while Sue interjected, "Let's get to a safer spot, and I'll call the front desk. We'll get everyone to gather at the front entrance. It might give us a chance."

As we descended the stairs, making our way to the fourth floor, Sue's warning cut through the tension, "There's a guy coming out of a room on the other side of the hall!"

In a split-second decision, I aimed and shot the emerging figure in the chest. He crumpled, falling heavily to the floor. My actions were swift and in the process, I had to shove Nancy aside to get a clear shot at the threat.

"Sorry," I apologized hastily, checking her over, "You okay, Nancy?"

She nodded, her face pale but determined. "Yes. Let's keep moving. Only three floors left, right?"

"Right," I affirmed.

Carefully, I opened a door on the third floor that wasn't locked, revealing a dimly lit room. Moving cautiously, I approached the window to assess the situation outside. The vantage point was clear, and I could distinctly make out two snipers – one positioned on the left and the other on the right of the adjacent building. *These are going to be tricky shots,* I thought, gripping my .44 auto mag.

Taking a deep breath, I aimed at the sniper on the right and pulled the trigger. He went down instantly.

"Sue," I called out, trying to suppress the adrenaline pumping through my veins. "Call the front desk and check if my BAR has arrived. If it's here, ask someone to bring it up. And tell them to hurry!"

A short while later, a police officer, his face masked with uncertainty, handed the BAR over to me. I nodded in gratitude, knowing that the weapon was going to be crucial for our escape.

With the BAR in my grasp, I carefully aimed at the sniper on the left. Three shots later, he was down. But the other sniper had been alerted by now and was trying to locate me. *I need a new angle,* I thought.

Silently, I made my way to the back of the room. Sticking to the shadows, I hugged the wall as I inched closer to another window. A quick glance forward, then to the right, and finally to the left revealed him scanning the street below. He was distracted, giving me the advantage. Carefully, I took aim and dispatched two bullets. They found their mark, and he fell sideways, lifeless.

*Not too shabby,* I mentally complimented myself.

But Sue, who had been observing the entire scene, looked at me with mixed emotions. "Are you proud of yourself now, Glen?" She questioned, her voice dripping with disdain.

I met her gaze, unapologetic. "Yes, I am. We need to move."

*I hate when she questions me like that;* I couldn't help but think, the frustration gnawing at me.

"Danny, you see anybody else up there on the roof?" I asked, glancing upwards.

"No, I don't. Now let's just fucking go!" Danny replied, his voice tinged with impatience.

The chaos in the lobby was intense as we reached it. People were in a frenzy, their voices raised in fear, shouting about the shots they'd heard. "Quiet! Everyone, just be quiet!" I commanded, trying to regain some semblance of control.

After a moment of hesitancy, I continued, "I was the one doing the shooting. Now, everyone stay calm." Turning to Danny, I said, "Check outside for anything out of the ordinary. And look up—check those windows where those bastards could be."

He shot me a wary look. "And why the fuck should I?"

"Well, unless you want to end up with a bullet in your head, you might want to give it a shot," I snapped back, my patience thinning.

Sighing in exasperation, we went outside, veering toward the back of the building. A quick scan showed another sniper positioned on the corner of the top of another building. *Shit, no clear shot from here,* I thought, my heart pounding.

Returning to the front entrance, Danny, looking increasingly anxious, asked, "What's the plan now?"

"I'm going to the other building to take out those snipers. But first, I'll check from the fifth floor of this one. Might get a clearer shot."

I mused, my mind racing. Heading up, the fifth floor proved fruitless. *Damn, I bet those bastards have a backup plan.*

While the realization settled in, Danny interjected, "Look, I can handle myself. Let's just get those assholes and get the hell out."

Suddenly, the familiar voice of Sue broke through, holding up my BAR. "You forgot this—your fifty-caliber long gun."

I smirked. "This is one time I needed to be fast and silent, but that might just do the trick."

Tom, having heard our conversation, stepped forward, a determined look in his eyes. "I'm coming with you. Those dicks threatened my family. Made me work for them. But now? I work for you. They won't lay a finger on my family. So, let's go."

Danny's gaze narrowed, skepticism evident. "How do we know you won't bail on us the moment shit gets real? Or worse, turn on us?"

Tom's voice was laced with desperation. "They'll kill me regardless, but I have to save my family. I'm the only one they have left."

I studied Tom for a long moment, searching for any hint of deception. His eyes held nothing but raw determination and fear. With a sigh, I responded, "Listen, if shit goes south for me, you better ensure our deal stands for your family. They're counting on you. You got that?"

Tom nodded fervently. "I promise."

"So, you're in?" I asked, needing to be certain.

Tom squared his shoulders, resolution clear in his eyes. "Oh, by the way, I do want to save your family, Tom. We're all in this together, fighting the same fight."

I couldn't help but smirk at his resolve. "Alright then. By the way, need a .44 mag? It's good to have some real firepower."

Tom's face broke into a smile, albeit a grim one. "It'll be nice to hold a real gun for once."

Taking a deep breath, I addressed the group, "Listen up. I'm leading the way. Danny, you've got rear security. Make damn sure those doors lock behind us. Tom and I will stick close to the walls and move fast. We need to get to the other building's corner before they spot us."

With a final scan of the area above, I searched for any movement— *nothing so far*, I thought, a bit relieved. Taking the lead, I broke into a run. The sudden echoing of gunshots shattered the silence, bullets striking the ground perilously close to my heels. I darted forward, the rush of adrenaline making everything seem surreal. Reaching the designated spot, my heart raced as I realized both Tom and, surprisingly, Danny had made it too. The stakes were higher than ever.

I cast a quick glance at the pair, a hint of exasperation evident in my gaze. "Let's get inside," I muttered, pushing through the entrance. As the large, ornate doors swung open, another unexpected sight greeted us: The lobby was buzzing with unsuspecting civilians. "Shit, why are there so many people here?"

Before I could fully assess the situation, movement at the periphery of my vision caught my attention. A man, gun raised, eyes gleaming with malicious intent. Without missing a beat, Tom, Danny, and I drew our weapons, firing in unison. The assailant crumpled to the ground, a lifeless heap.

"Fucking hostages," I spat, the realization dawning on me. "We've got to clear this place out."

From the crowd, a trembling voice piped up, "Sir, there were two of them. You've taken one out. Only one more to deal with."

Rubbing his temple, Tom added, "There might be more reinforcements. Expect at least four more. With you as the prize, they won't hold back."

I raised an eyebrow, taken aback. "Why? Am I such a catch?"

Tom smirked, "Well, a two-million-dollar bounty on your head might be enticing to some. Plus, a growing faction wouldn't shed a tear if you disappeared."

I couldn't help but roll my eyes. "Wonderful. So, the bastard's stingy, and I've made a lot of enemies. Anything else?"

Tom let out a dry chuckle. "People seem to have a nasty habit of dying when you're around. It's like you bring a plague of death wherever you go."

Danny, never one to hold back, added with a sardonic grin, "And sometimes that shit's contagious."

I shot them a wry smile, "Not *everyone* drops dead around me, you know."

Danny winked, "Rule number one: Never argue with a crazy person or a corpse."

"Alright, enough chit-chat," I urged, my tone becoming serious again. "We need to secure this building. Anyone volunteering to stay behind and safeguard these folks?"

A burly officer stepped forward, determination clear in his eyes. "I'll stay. But when you give the signal, I'll ensure everyone's evacuated."

Nodding in gratitude, I replied, "Good man. Let's head up, guys. We have a job to finish."

We began our ascent toward the second floor with a collective sense of purpose.

Danny's gaze zeroed in on a shadowed figure down the hall, and with remarkable precision, he fired. The man jolted but didn't go down immediately. Gasping for breath, blood oozing from his side, he sneered at us, "Go to hell."

Tom aimed and fired a single shot without hesitation, piercing the man's heart. His body slumped lifelessly to the ground. I glanced at Tom, raising an eyebrow. "Now that," I remarked dryly, "Is a definitive case of death."

Our momentary reprieve was shattered when another man boldly stepped around the corner, weapon in hand. We locked eyes, a silent standoff. I tried reasoning with him, "Drop the gun. All your backup's down. Don't be stupid."

But whether out of blind loyalty, desperation, or sheer madness, he lunged at us. Both Danny and Tom reacted swiftly, their bullets finding their mark. The man's body twitched with the force of the shots, then lay still.

Tom, panting slightly, asked, "Do you think there's more of them?"

"If there are," I replied, "They're holed up higher in this building, probably the snipers."

"We need to evacuate these people. Now," I said with urgency. Dialing back to the ground floor, I barked out, "Get everyone out! I've got a gut feeling there's one or two more of these bastards lurking. I'm going to clear the rest of the building."

Without waiting for a response, Tom and Danny bolted for the stairs, leaving me alone to continue my ascent. I methodically worked my way up, each floor eerily silent. The third and fourth floors yielded nothing.

As I reached the fifth, I could faintly hear the muffled cries and hurried footsteps of people evacuating below. But what drew my attention was a slightly ajar door on the sixth floor. *This isn't right,* I thought, my instincts on high alert.

Moving stealthily, I approached the door. An unsettling thought flashed across my mind: *He's on the other side of this door.* As if to confirm my suspicion, I spotted him at the end of a walkway. My fingers tightened around my gun's grip.

Suddenly, a bullet whizzed past, grazing my left shoulder. I winced from the sting but retaliated immediately. My shot found its target, the bullet striking him in the head. He staggered, a look of sheer disbelief in his eyes as he crashed backward through the door he had emerged from.

I stumbled toward the fallen assailant, quickly spotting a foreboding glint of metal strapped to his chest – explosives. *Fuck! He's rigged!* Without a second thought, I sprinted toward the building's exit, every muscle in my body pushing for maximum speed.

I had just reached the lobby when a roaring explosion consumed the space. The violent symphony of shattering glass, choking smoke, and a cascade of debris overwhelmed me. I felt sharp, biting pains as fragments struck my back, head, and shoulders. As I collapsed to the cold marble floor, a singular thought echoed through my mind: *This is it. I'm dead.*

But as my consciousness began to fade, strong hands gripped me, dragging me away from the chaos. Tom and Danny hauled me across the street, using their bodies as shields against the flying debris. The acrid smell of burnt concrete filled my nostrils, mingling with the smoke that clouded the air.

Coughing, Tom looked at me, eyes filled with concern. "Was there another guy?"

I nodded weakly, my voice barely audible above the ringing in my ears. "He's the reason the building went up."

"We need to get you to a hospital," Danny said urgently.

Before I could protest, Sue stormed up, her face a mixture of fury and relief. She slapped me – hard – her voice shaking with anger. "Don't you ever do that again."

Attempting a joke, I quipped, "Better get me to the hospital before she finishes me off, huh?" Tom and Danny chuckled, but Sue's glare was icy. I'd clearly crossed a line.

"Our men took down two trying to flee the scene. One got away," Tom reported, looking grim.

Pushing through the pain, I tried to rise, "We need to—"

But Sue wasn't having it. She forcefully pushed me back down, her voice thundering. "You're going to the hospital. NOW."

I'd never seen such fiery determination in her eyes before.

Healy, who'd witnessed the entire event, approached, her eyes filled with a mix of sympathy and disappointment. "I'll ride with him," she told Sue. "You take Nancy, Danny, and Tom and meet us there. I need to have a word with this *dickhead*."

Once inside the ambulance, Healy turned to me, her gaze cold and piercing. "That girl loves you," she said tersely. Before I could interject, she snapped, "Shut up. You pull these reckless stunts, not thinking of those who care about you. Sue, your family... They all love you. Stop being a dumbass. I'm sick of it."

"But Healy—"

"*Shut up*," her voice cracked with emotion. "You need to consider retirement. You're not invincible. You need to slow down. What about next time? What if there isn't a next time?"

"Can I say something?" I ventured, trying to gauge her mood.

Healy just stared coldly back, her patience wearing thin. "Shut up. Again."

"I'm tired, Healy," I started, voice shaking with emotion. "I don't want this life anymore. I want Sue... my kids... even you." Before she could retaliate, I quickly added, "And I mean it, Healy. But first, those bastards who took my family from me? They need to *pay*. And they will. Nothing and no one will deter me from that."

Her expression softened for the briefest moment. "After it's all said and done, you're walking away from this life? Truly done?"

"Yes." My voice was firm. "I promise. I'll retire. Not in a permanent, 'six feet under' sort of way. But to genuinely spend time with all of you. The people I care about."

I had known Healy for over forty-five years, and during all that time, I'd never seen her eyes shimmer with tears the way they did now. "Healy... I love you too."

She exhaled sharply, brushing away the emotion. "Oh, just shut up." But she couldn't hide the tear tracks that marked her cheeks.

With a smirk, I whispered, "Our little secret, alright?"

Healy gave me a tender look I hadn't seen in ages. "You've changed. And for the better. I never thought you'd bare your soul like this." She clasped my hand tightly. "I love you too, Glen."

We reached the hospital, the frantic pace of the medical staff palpable. They wheeled me into a prep room. "Everyone out!" I commanded. Even the doctor looked taken aback. Healy quickly escorted him out, leaving me alone with Sue. "We need to talk," I rasped.

Sue's expression was wary yet hopeful. "I love you, Sue," I confessed, causing her eyes to widen in shock. "Once this mess is sorted, I'm retiring. I want us... for the rest of our lives. What do you say?"

She blinked, processing. "You spring this on me now? But... yes. Yes, I'll marry you. And for the record? Glad you had to think about it."

Chuckling, I replied, "I love you too, Sue." But our tender moment was interrupted by the doctor's return.

"Let's get you patched up, shall we?" He said, a note of exasperation in his voice.

Healy cornered him, her face inches from his. "You get in there and ensure he's alright. Do your job, or you'll answer to me."

Hours later, post-surgery, the doctor approached my bedside. "That little woman of yours... quite the force, isn't she?"

I smirked, wincing from the pain. *"You have no idea what that woman is capable of."*

The surgery was grueling, lasting four hours. But thanks to the skilled hands of the medical team - and perhaps a little bit of Healy's intimidation - I was on the mend.

# CHAPTER 11

◆◆◆◆◆

THE STERILE CLINICAL LIGHTS IN the hospital room did little to illuminate the weight in the atmosphere. As I slowly blinked away the remnants of anesthesia from my vision, I recognized the worried faces of my friends and allies gathered around my bed. Despite the severity of the situation, there was a mix of relief and mirth in their expressions. It was as if they couldn't decide whether to scold or joke about my predicament.

Sue, her eyes glittering with a peculiar happiness, grinned down at me. Beside her, Heady maintained her usual stoic demeanor, though I could swear there was a hint of relief in those eyes of hers. *Have I really made them that worried?*

Chuckling weakly, I asked, "When can I get out of this place?"

Heady replied her tone firm, "Two weeks, at the very least. And while you're healing up, we have some work to do. Some people fled before the blast, and we need to track them down. Sue, keep an eye on him. Make sure he doesn't try any of his typical stunts."

Sue nodded, her smile softening as she squeezed my hand. Heady then motioned to Tom, indicating that she wanted a private word. The two exited the room, leaving Sue and me alone.

At NCIS headquarters, the atmosphere was tense. Heady, ever the determined agent, pressed Tom for more information. "I think there might be someone you used to work for, someone who escaped prison. Rumor has it he's hiding near the Salton Sea by Brawley."

Tom's eyes widened, his voice hushed with fear. "I won't go there. You've heard the stories, right? People vanish in broad daylight. Sometimes, all that's left behind is a shoe or maybe a backpack. But most times, it's just silence. The wilderness there... it's filled with things that will hunt you down. I've seen them – creatures as tall as eight or nine feet. Monsters, Heady. I'd rather face a bullet than step foot in those woods."

Heady observed Tom's tangible fear, then remarked, "So it seems like a job for the Executioner once he's up and running. All we need to do is figure out how to keep your old boss there."

Tom vehemently shook his head. "I won't go. I don't care about any of it. You can kill me right here and now, but I won't step foot in that cursed place."

Heady's gaze sharpened, and she leaned in closer. "Well, that won't be necessary. But if what you say is true, we'll need to be extra careful. If there's anyone who can handle those woods and whatever lurks within, it's him. All we have to do is get him ready and make sure he stays focused on the mission."

Heady's steely gaze fixed firmly on Tom. "All I'm asking is for directions, Tom. I'm not dragging you up there."

The tension in the room thickened, underscored by the ticking of the wall clock.

Tom's voice wavered as he answered, "Alright, alright. I'll tell you how to get there. But I've made myself clear: I won't set foot in that damned place."

Heady leaned in, her patience thinning. "You've made that abundantly clear, and if you repeat it one more time, I'll fucking shoot you in the face. Understood?"

A bead of sweat trickled down Tom's temple; his lips pressed in a thin line. "Understood."

One of the agents in the room, a tall man with a buzz cut and sharp features, cleared his throat. "Do you think he's up there right now, Tom?"

Tom, or 'Rick' as he was sometimes known, hesitated for a moment before responding. "Rick never strays far from his cabin. He might remain there for weeks at a time, hiding. The man's paranoid, and with good reason. He's a wanted man, and he trusts absolutely no one."

Pausing, he swallowed hard. "Except for one. A man known only as 'The Colonel'. I've never met him, seen his face, or heard his voice. But everyone jumps when he commands. No questions asked. If you want Rick, you'll likely have to deal with The Colonel as well."

Heady's jaw tightened. "Our Executioner will handle him when the time comes. He'll make sure he's silenced for good."

The same agent from earlier piped up again, a spark of hope in his eyes. "We have resources, Heady. We can mount an assault, get this Rick out of his hidey-hole."

Tom shook his head, an almost pitying look on his face. "No. You don't understand. Rick's hideout is practically a fortress. I'd wager that your Executioner is probably the only person who can infiltrate it successfully. Besides, Rick won't welcome any of us. And he doesn't need to venture out. He's got supplies to last months, and I heard he's just been restocked this week."

The head agent turned his intense gaze to Tom, his voice a deep baritone. "Has he done it before, Tom? Successfully stayed hidden like this?"

Tom gulped audibly, the weight of the situation pressing down on him. "Yeah. The guy's a ghost when he wants to be. Paranoid, really. Afraid of everyone he doesn't personally know."

I listened to the exchange and turned to Sue, Nancy, Danny, and Heady. "He's spot on, both about Rick's behavior and those damn creatures around the lake. They're not just legends, they're real, and they're vicious."

Sue's face paled slightly, a mix of concern and determination.

After a moment, I continued, laying out the plan. "So here's the play: Once I'm out of this bed, we first target the house in Belair. There's intel suggesting the man there knows where the Colonel is. We go in hard and fast, alright, Heady?"

Heady nodded, her mind already ticking over logistics.

"As for Rick," I said, "Have some of your team stake out the cabin. But it's isolated, near the darkest part of the lake. The mountain begins about fifty feet from his back porch. When they approach, make sure they're in unmarked SUVs. Camouflage them if necessary. We don't want to be easily spotted but need visibility from all angles."

I paused, the memory of the creatures sending a chill down my spine. "Those creatures, they're territorial as hell. Keep your guys at least one hundred and fifty feet down the road from the cabin. At least one person has to be awake, watching, at all times. Got it?"

Heady rolled her eyes. "This isn't our first rodeo, you know. Remember the shitshow years ago? Turned out to be a damn gunfight. Don't you think we've learned from that?"

I stared hard at Heady. "That's my point. We can't afford any fuck-ups. Especially not now." Turning to Nick, a relatively newer member of the team, I said, "Nick, if you mess this up, you'll be answering to me, the Executioner. Trust me, that's not a conversation you want to have."

Nick gulped, his face pale but resolute. "Understood, sir."

By the time I was discharged from the hospital, I was itching to act. We needed a plan to infiltrate the house. A stealthy approach seemed logical, but the best approach is sometimes the most direct one. I decided to rely on my trusty, fortified truck. All ten tons of it, a behemoth, more tank than a truck.

They all took their positions, waiting for my signal. I revved the engine, took a deep breath, and muttered, *"Here we fucking go."*

As I gunned it, Heady could only shake her head and mutter, "Not again." With sheer force, the truck, my "tank," blasted through the gate as if it was made of paper.

The dust from the obliterated gate swirled around as the truck came to a halt at the steps of the mansion. Heady, always one for wit even in tense situations, gasped sarcastically, "Well, *that* was subtle."

"Dumbass," she muttered, her eyes rolling. "Everyone, move! We need to be inside when he makes his entrance."

As I descended from the truck, guards poured from the house, guns blazing. Bullets pinged off the reinforced exterior of the vehicle, creating a chaotic symphony. The rest of the team quickly fanned out across the yard, guns at the ready. I returned fire, sending shots toward the guards. Soon, Danny, Tom, and the other agents joined in, and the front yard erupted into a full-fledged firefight.

It was over almost as soon as it began. The guards, outnumbered and outgunned, fell one by one. The acrid smell of gunpowder hung in the air, but there was no time to catch a breath.

"Danny," I shouted, reloading my weapon, "Don't just stand there! We need to clear the house."

But just as I was about to enter the opulent mansion, two more guards emerged. I raised my gun but opted for words instead. "Drop your weapons," I demanded coolly.

Surprisingly, they complied.

"I'm looking for a particular individual," I continued, "The man who runs the whole West Coast operation for 'Shans.'"

The guards exchanged nervous glances before one of them gestured toward a door down the hallway. "He's dining," he whispered, the fear evident in his eyes.

Without hesitation, our team stormed down the hall, guns at the ready. We arrived at a lavish dining room where a man sat, seemingly unperturbed by our entrance. Beside him, a young woman looked up, her eyes wide with fright.

He gave me a smirk, wiping his mouth with a napkin. "You could've knocked, you know."

I met his gaze, unfazed. "Knocking isn't really my style. By the way, you might want to invest in a new front gate. The current one is a bit... damaged."

Recognition flashed in his eyes. "I know you. You used to smuggle guns in and out of Japan in the late seventies and early eighties. Branching out to other countries too, if I'm not mistaken."

Heady interjected, her voice tense, "Everyone, out. Now."

Ignoring her, the man, Bob, beckoned toward the food. "There's enough for everyone. Why not join me?"

His audacity was almost amusing. I nodded at the terrified girl, motioning for her to leave. Tom swiftly escorted her out.

"We need him alive, Glen," Heady reminded me, her voice low.

Bob chuckled, the sound grating on my nerves. "Yes, you certainly do need me alive."

Heady shot him a glare. "Dumbass," she growled, "I wouldn't provoke him if I were you."

A moment of silence followed.

Sue's voice pierced the tense silence, "Where is he at on the lake?"

Bob glared at her, then at me, "Yes, he is. But please, keep this savage away from me."

Taking a menacing step closer, I hissed, "Do I even need you alive anymore? I could end your operation here and now, once and for all." The weight of old memories pressed on me. "You played a part in the murder of my family back in Japan, didn't you?"

Bob's mocking laughter resonated in the room. "Oh, I did. It's a damn shame you weren't there with them. Killing you would have been the cherry on top."

I felt my blood boiling. "You should've just taken me. Let them go." I was breathing hard, each word punctuated with fury. "And now, I'm going to enjoy watching the life fade from your eyes."

Heady's steely voice intervened. "Everyone, out. Now. These two need a moment."

Before the room emptied, Heady, with a fire in her eyes, pointedly asked, "Was it you? The hit in the Far East? My children?"

Bob smirked, almost gleefully. "Yes, that was me. Got your kids. Would've made quite the amount off of them. Especially the girl."

Without another word, Heady's gun was up, and a shot rang out. Bob's mocking expression froze as his lifeless form collapsed onto the lavish carpet.

Staring at the corpse, I muttered, "Heady, we needed him alive."

She met my gaze, her expression unrepentant. "Fuck him. He was trash. It's time for the Executioner to take matters into his own hands."

Exiting the room, we were met by Sue, Tom, Danny, and Nancy. Their expressions ranged from shock to horror. Nancy's anguished scream echoed in the corridor.

"We went through all this for what?" Sue demanded, her voice shaking. "All of this, and we're back at square one?"

Trying to find words, I replied, "He had a hand in the death of my family. He had to pay. And it wasn't me who pulled the trigger." I glanced at Heady, who stared back unapologetically.

More screams, more shouts, more accusations flew. The cacophony was overwhelming. But amidst it all, one fact remained - Heady had ended him.

His lifeless body on the ground was a testament to our mission's brutality and the lengths we'd go to seek justice.

The brisk mountain air sent a shiver down my spine as I swung the door open. "We're heading to the mountains now," I announced, scanning the faces of my comrades.

Heady and Tom exchanged a quick glance. Their silent communication wasn't lost on me. "Not me," Heady voiced firmly, raising a brow in challenge.

Tom simply stared at me, his jaw set in defiance. "Have you forgotten our last ordeal? If it's all the same to you, just shoot me in the head now because I'm not — and I mean it — going through that again." He sank heavily into the nearest chair, a weight of memories burdening him.

I surveyed the room, taking in their expressions, some concerned, others utterly baffled. "Is anyone else famished, or is it just me?" I asked nonchalantly.

They stared back, stunned. *What's wrong with them?* I mused. "Look, I don't care about your collective shock. I'm hungry. We're stopping by Monster Lake for some grub. After that, we're fetching that piece of trash — hopefully in one piece."

Our journey resumed, and the surroundings became increasingly ominous as we approached the cabin. Roughly two miles away, I halted the truck. "Wait here," I ordered the group.

Danny's eyebrows knitted in confusion. "Two miles? You plan to trek the rest of the way?"

"Yes," I replied, "This territory is theirs, not ours. You'll be safer here."

He exchanged a glance with Nancy.

"Whose territory? Bigfoot's?" Danny's tone dripped with disbelief.

I nodded solemnly. "And they aren't exactly friendly. Encounters with them in the past haven't gone well, and let me tell you, they remember a face. I'll take my BAR and my Spas-12 shotgun with armor-piercing shells. If push comes to shove, I'll drop one or two of them, rescue Rick, and get the hell out of there."

Nancy gulped, her eyes darting to the dense woods. "If more show up, it won't be just another day out. It'll be a massacre."

I made my way to the truck's back and flung open the compartment, revealing an arsenal that would make any military enthusiast green with envy.

Danny whistled lowly, turning to Nancy. "Shit, Glen's packing more firepower than the entire U.S. Army." The admiration in his voice was evident, but so was the underlying worry.

The weight of the arsenal in my hands felt comforting. With my Spas-12 shotgun loaded with a dozen rounds, I marveled at the cool, familiar touch of the steel against my palm. Then, sliding my .44 mag and .44 auto mag into their holsters, I held up my most treasured weapon. "The BAR," I murmured affectionately, its custom modifications making it more deadly than the standard issue.

I glanced over at Danny, noting the unease in his eyes. "Nothing survives a hit from these babies, especially not from my Spas or BAR. Which do you reckon I should kick things off with? With the BAR, I can nail something two miles off, and with a silencer, they won't know what hit 'em or where it's coming from." I couldn't help the smirk forming at the corner of my mouth.

My focus shifted back to the crew. "Now, I need about three or four hours tops. Why don't y'all head to town, grab a bite to eat, and take your sweet time? This is my play — I've got it."

Danny's voice quivered slightly, "Are there really... you know, monsters up there?"

Nancy echoed the sentiment with a hint of incredulity, "You're not seriously suggesting there's a Bigfoot lurking around?"

"Yes," I replied firmly, my gaze unwavering. "But I've got a man to snatch, and he's vital. I can only hope those creatures aren't guarding him. Once I have him, it's just one more — Shan — and then all this can be put behind me. I can retire. Finally." My voice grew steelier, "And let me make this clear: No oversized gorilla is going to stand in my way. So, get going. Either meet me back here or in town."

With that, I ventured into the thick woods, veering off the trail. *Bigfoots have a knack for shadowing about ten to fifteen feet from the trail.* My instinct was on point. It wasn't long before I encountered one. The massive, hairy creature was observing a herd of deer — presumably considering its dinner options. It shifted its gaze to me, nostrils flaring as it sampled the air. The creature looked strangely familiar, and when it offered a tentative smile, it clicked. This was the Bigfoot I'd saved from that cliff, the one involved with the dogman!

A wave of relief washed over me, and I returned its smile. It turned away slowly, but I called out, "Hey, can you point me to the cabin? I need to find someone. It's crucial he's alive. Can you help?"

The massive creature locked eyes with me just as a female Bigfoot emerged from the underbrush. The moment her gaze settled on me, recognition flashed in her eyes. The two exchanged rapid, guttural sounds that seemed like their version of conversation.

"I need the cabin by the lake," I interrupted, desperate to stay on mission. "Can you help?"

Her lips curled into a slight grin as she pointed Westward. But her male counterpart seemed less than thrilled about aiding me. Their conversation grew heated, culminating with her delivering a resounding smack to the back of his head. His irritation was palpable, but in the end, he begrudgingly led the way, with her following suit.

The terrain was dense, but with the Bigfoots guiding me, we reached our destination much quicker than I anticipated. Along the way, we stumbled upon a small herd of deer grazing. Feeling a need to reciprocate their assistance, I took aim and shot one down, offering them the fresh kill. With grateful nods, they moved to claim their prize, leaving me to continue on.

As the cabin came into sight about half a mile away, a new problem arose — three towering Bigfoots, their aggressive posture evident, were attacking the cabin. *Fuck, not what I needed right now.*

Time was of the essence, and I wasn't keen on any further delays. Gathering my resolve, I stepped out into the open, drawing their attention. Two of them remained fixated on assaulting the cabin, while one, muscles rippling, began approaching me with a threatening stance. Without hesitation, I raised my Spas-12 shotgun. Two blasts tore into its chest, and a third shot to its head sent it sprawling to the earth.

The echo of the shots barely faded before the other two creatures let out thunderous roars. Swiftly, I targeted the one closest, replicating my earlier move. Chest, then head. It dropped instantly. The third, sensing the tide of the battle had shifted, started to flee. I couldn't let him — he'd only return with reinforcements.

Ditching the Spas, I swiftly armed myself with the BAR and fired. Two rounds pierced the back of its skull, and a third ruptured its spine, passing through to its heart. He crumpled in a heap of matted fur.

*Five Bigfoots down,* I thought grimly. *I'll have to contact the General soon, get these bodies out of here.*

Stepping onto the cabin porch, I raised my voice, "Rick! Come out now. If I have to go in there, you're not gonna like the outcome. How about a coffee instead?"

The door creaked open slowly, revealing a man with wild eyes. "Old buddy," I remarked dryly, my gaze unwavering, "I just took out your 'friends.' Time for you to step out before more show up with a vengeance."

The dead Bigfoots strewn around were a grim reminder that their kin might soon arrive, hungry for vengeance. "Those dead friends of yours? Their buddies might come to see my handiwork," I warned, "And they won't be too pleased. So, who'd you prefer to deal with, Rick? Me or them?"

The cabin's door creaked open, pausing midway as if contemplating its options, and then snapped shut with a resounding thud. "Look, Rick, I'm not in the mood to stand around waiting for a Bigfoot reunion. You've got a choice: Walk out of here with me or wait for them to come knocking. So, what'll it be?"

Silence. And then, a muffled response, "What the hell do you want from me?"

"Answers," I replied tersely. "But first, we need to get moving."

The door finally opened fully, revealing a disheveled Rick, clearly unnerved by the situation. "Listen, there's a way out where they won't detect us," he began, but I was out of patience.

Grabbing the door, I forcefully nudged him out into the open yard. "Well, speak of the devil," I muttered, spotting a particularly irate-looking Bigfoot emerging from the tree line. "Your welcoming committee's arrived. I'd start running if I were you."

Before giving him a chance to respond, I frisked him for weapons. Finding none, I gave him a rough shove to set him in motion. "On your feet, Rick! Move!"

Rick huffed, annoyance evident in his tone. "You might want to treat me with a bit more respect. After all, you need me."

"Oh, I can always leave you here," I quipped, my voice dripping with sarcasm, "To discuss dinner plans with your new friends. Maybe you'll even be the main course."

He glanced back at me, desperation creeping into his eyes. "Listen, I know who's behind your family's death. I can help you get to them."

I paused, torn between the urge to keep moving and the information he dangled before me. A single Bigfoot might be around, and one was more than enough trouble. But Rick's revelation was enticing.

As we made our way through the dense woods, Rick continued, attempting to gain my favor, "People have been so unfair to me. I returned the money. I didn't harm anyone else when I escaped."

"You left a cop dead in your wake," I snapped, my voice cold. "Or did that minor detail slip your mind?"

Rick's voice quivered, "I'm trying to help you. Can't you see that?"

I grabbed his collar, pulling him close. "You mentioned 'Shan'. Where is he?"

Rick gulped, his eyes darting around. "Last I heard, he was heading to San Francisco for a job."

My grip tightened. "Spill it, Rick. What's he planning in San Francisco? Or do I leave you here for your forest pals to find?"

The Bigfoot creatures closed in, their every footstep shaking the forest floor and sending shivers up our spines. Dark eyes focused intently on Rick and me, but particularly on the former. They stood a mere thirty feet away, their towering forms casting eerie shadows in the dimming light.

Rick's bravado crumbled in seconds. He began to sob, his eyes wide with terror. "Oh shit," he cried, his voice trembling. "Please, I don't want to be their dinner! I'll go straight to jail, no resistance. I swear on my life. Just... just don't let them eat me!"

I watched him, a mix of disgust and pity in my eyes. *What a baby*, I thought. But his words stirred something in me. Maybe, just maybe, he had the information I needed.

"And Shan in San Francisco?" I pressed. "What's he up to?"

Rick hiccuped through his sobs, "He's gathering information. About you."

I frowned. "About me? Why?"

Rick wiped his nose with the back of his hand. "Someone's feeding him stories, trying to squeeze money out of him."

"Spit it out, Rick. Who's behind this?"

He hesitated for a split second before blurting out, "You've got a son!

A professor in a college. And that Colonel, the one from Vietnam? He wants your son, his friends, his whole damn family dead. You took out his drug operation back when he was just a captain. And in that chaos, at the Cambodia border, you inadvertently killed his son and wife."

My heart skipped a beat. "I... I had no idea I took out his family."

Rick's eyes glistened with a mix of sadness and relief, "Now you see the bigger picture. Shan's just a pawn, but he's tasked with wiping out whatever family you have left."

Staring deep into Rick's eyes, I saw the raw fear in them. "Given what you've told me, Rick, I've no need for you anymore."

Rick's face turned as white as a sheet. "You... you can't be serious! You won't leave me with them, will you?"

Laughing lightly, I retorted, "Relax. Those Bigfoot creatures are my friends. But don't worry, I won't feed you to them. I wouldn't want them getting food poisoning from the likes of you."

"That's... that's not funny," Rick stammered, panic evident in his voice.

Chuckling, I warned, "Keep moving. They'll trail us until we reach my truck. And if you think of bolting, trust me, they're not the kindest when they play with their food. But I won't let them touch you. Now get moving."

We ambled along the winding forest trail, the towering trees on either side enveloping us in their cool embrace. Birds chirped overhead, a stark contrast to the undercurrent of tension that lingered between Rick and me. I dialed Sue, trying to maintain an air of casualness.

"Sue, can you pick up some pies, fruits, and nuts for us? We'll be there soon."

From the corner of my eye, I saw Rick raise an eyebrow before chiming in, "And while you're at it, how about a double cheeseburger, fries, and a Coke for me?"

I shot him an incredulous look. "Really?"

"Did you get that, Sue?" I said, rolling my eyes. "Alright, thanks. Love you."

Rick smirked. "You know, she's on Shan's hit list too. Oh, and your other daughter."

I halted mid-step, my heart pounding. "What other daughter?" I spat out, rage and confusion swirling within me.

Rick smiled, clearly enjoying having an upper hand. "You didn't know? Guess I arrived just in time, then. Looks like you owe me one."

My clenched fists ached to land a punch on that smug face. *Where is she?* I thought, my mind racing.

"I'll give you the details once I get my food," he sang mockingly. "Funny how things turn out. Here I am, free as a bird, getting away from Bigfoot, Shan, the colonel... life really throws you diamonds when you least expect it."

My glare was icy. "The only thing standing between you and those Bigfoot creatures is me, so let's drop the act. Now move. We don't want to be caught out here after dark."

Before long, we reached the rendezvous. Danny and Tom stood waiting, their expressions grim. On my nod, they cuffed Rick, who erupted in anger.

"Hey! We never agreed to this shit!"

"Rick, you clearly didn't understand the deal. So for now, shut up."

Pulling Sue aside, I tried to keep my voice steady. "Why didn't you tell me about our daughter?"

She looked taken aback, her face paling. "You...you know?"

"They know where she is," I pressed, urgency in my tone. "She's on their list. Is she in London?"

She opened her mouth to reply, but before she could, my phone rang. The caller ID read 'John – MI6.'

"John," I began urgently, "I need a favor. I've just found out I have a daughter in London. She's in grave danger. Can you help me find her?"

Sue's voice broke through my spiraling thoughts. "She's at Cambridge University."

I snapped to attention, my heart racing. "John, did you hear that? Can you get her? I've been informed she's been marked."

There was a brief silence, and then John's steady voice returned. "I'll personally see to her safety. I'll call you when she's with me."

Gratitude welled up in me. "Thanks, John. I owe you one."

He chuckled softly. "After all you've done for me over the years? No, I still owe you. We'll be in touch."

My gaze shifted to Sue, concern evident in my eyes. *The fewer people who know, the safer she'll be,* I thought.

Sue seemed to read my mind. "I was trying to protect her. With the enemies from your past, they would've targeted her. They would've killed her."

I stared at her, disbelief clouding my features. "Because of me? There's a mole in our company, Sue. You should've told me. Now she's out there, vulnerable."

Sue's voice trembled. "I've prepared her. Over the years, I told her about who you are, what you do, and how to stay safe if danger ever approached."

"You mean you told her her father is a government assassin?"

"No," Sue retorted, eyes flashing. "I told her you were in the military."

I exhaled slowly. "Close enough, I suppose. But she has a right to know her father. And now, I can't even trust you."

As our confrontation continued, a loud, mocking voice interrupted us. "Thought we had a deal! You get me food, I spill everything, and you let me go."

Rick's smug expression infuriated me. "Never promised any such thing," I shot back. "You're here for a reason. Payback. And you owe someone big time."

I turned to Danny, the steely resolve evident in my tone. "Take him to San Francisco. Lock him up and ensure there's a guard on him at all times. No fuck-ups. We can't afford him escaping."

Danny gave me a firm nod, his eyes determined. "I'll get him there, don't worry."

"Just wait for me," I instructed, glancing at the ever-darkening horizon. "This won't take long. There's someone I need to see. I'll be in San Francisco before you know it."

With that, we parted ways. I picked up the General, who had crucial information about my newfound son. As we drove, the weight of the revelation hung in the air.

"In the late seventies," the General began, his voice gravelly with age and experience, "You had a one-night stand with an aspiring professor. She fell pregnant and had a son. Her then-husband never knew about you until their divorce. Funny enough, for the past decade, without even realizing it, you've been funding the boy's architectural digs."

I took a sharp breath. "So, did she ever tell him about me?"

The General snorted, "I don't know. To be frank, I've no desire to speak with her again. She's too smart for her own good, always a step ahead."

I groaned internally—*great, that's another complication.* "Let's just hope she didn't keep him in the dark. This is going to be a mess."

Night had fully descended when we arrived in San Francisco, pulling up to a pristine, newly constructed house. *This is where my son lives,* I mused, my emotions a tumultuous mix of anticipation and dread.

Gathering my courage, I walked to the door and knocked. A young woman, her features soft under the porch light, opened the door.

"Hi, I'm looking for Larry. Is he here?" My voice was surprisingly steady.

She eyed me warily. "Yes, he's my husband. Can I help you?"

Taking a deep breath, I stammered, "I believe I'm his biological father. Can I speak with him?"

Her eyes widened, echoing the disbelief and surprise I'd encountered so many times recently. "You can't be serious. Larry has a father."

"Please, can I come in and explain? It's a long story."

She hesitated, then finally beckoned me inside. "Larry!" She called out. "There's someone here who wants to speak with you."

A tall man, resembling a younger version of myself, walked into the room. "Can I help you?" His gaze was inquisitive.

Taking a deep breath, I started, "Larry, I'm Glen. I hope you'll hear me out. This might be difficult to process."

His eyebrows furrowed, a hint of irritation in his eyes. "Better be good."

"Firstly, have you spoken to your mother recently?" I ventured.

Larry shot me a puzzled look. *Damn, these surprised expressions are becoming a norm,* I thought wryly. "Why? I haven't, but my best friend communicates with her more than I do."

Nodding, I tried to choose my words carefully. "I understand. But I have some news. It might leave you shocked or perhaps even joyful. You see, I just discovered that I'm your biological father."

Larry's face drained of color. "No, you're not."

"I'm genuinely sorry," I began, my voice faltering slightly. The atmosphere in the room was thick with tension, and the emotions swirling within me made my throat tighten. "This revelation doesn't undermine the bond you have with the man who raised you. He's an incredible person. In fact, he's been a friend of mine for twenty-five years. Neither of us foresaw this complicated mess."

I paused, recalling the memories. "Your mother and I had a fleeting affair, a one-night stand. I was completely in the dark about her marital status. She chose not to divulge anything about it, and later, when she got pregnant, she never breathed a word to me. It baffles me. Over the past quarter-century, despite crossing paths now and then, she never hinted at your existence, let alone that I was your biological father."

Gazing intently at Larry, I continued, "With their ongoing divorce, your father requested the court for a blood test for all the kids. Once the results were in, the court-mandated your mother to break the news to both of us. But she stubbornly kept silent. She was supposed to tell you, but she didn't."

Larry's eyes blazed with a mix of disbelief and anger. "I can't believe a fucking word you're saying."

I nodded, the weight of his skepticism pressing on my chest. "I understand why you'd feel that way. But every agonizing word I've spoken is the truth."

Larry's hands clenched into fists. "I think you're lying. I want you out. Now."

Before I could respond, the door opened, and a couple stepped in — Larry's close friend, Hank, and his wife. "Oh, I'm sorry," Hank began, taking in the scene. "Didn't mean to interrupt."

Larry's wife, her face a shade paler, whispered, "Maybe we should call your mom."

"No!" Larry's voice rose. "I want him out of here. If any of this shit is true, I don't want anything to do with any of you ever again."

Hank, clearly taken aback, asked, "What's going on?"

Larry, his voice dripping with incredulity, said, "This guy claims he's my real father. Claims my mother lived a lie, deceiving all of us."

Hank's wife, concern etching her features, turned to her husband. "Hank, maybe he should just stay. Larry, just call her, okay?"

But Hank seemed to have another plan. "Charles Livingston, don't let him leave!" He ordered, raising his voice in urgency.

I held Hank's gaze, a rush of memories threatening to flood the room. "Did your mother happen to be named Janet?" I inquired.

Hank's eyes widened a fraction, but he nodded. "Yes. How do you know that?"

Larry, his patience fraying, reiterated, "I asked you to leave."

Undeterred, I continued, my focus still locked onto Hank. "I was close friends with your father for over twenty-five years."

Before I could further delve into the past, the entrance opened again, admitting an East Indian man and his elderly father. My eyes instantly recognized the older figure, and a rush of nostalgia hit me. "Doc? Is that really you? What brings you here?"

Doc, his face creasing into a familiar smile, responded, "Glen! It's been a while. Still getting into trouble, I see. A bit roughed up, but still standing."

Larry's impatience was palpable. "I told you to leave. Why are you still here?"

The Doc's son interjected, looking at me with a mix of curiosity and respect. "You know this man, father?"

Doc chuckled, "Of course! Glen, here is the reason we're living so comfortably now. Whenever he or his partner were in town and got into some mishap, they'd call me. Day or night, no matter where. I patched him up more times than I can count."

Larry's voice raised in annoyance. "Enough! I've told you multiple times to leave!"

As I began to comply, making my way to the exit, another figure entered the fray. I instantly recognized him, "Jim? Aren't you from just north of Dallas?"

Jim's face brightened with recognition. "Mr. Tomas? It's been ages! Mom still reminisces about how you saved my life."

Larry's exasperation reached a fever pitch, "Would you just leave already?"

I nodded, weary of the confrontation. "Alright, I'm leaving." As I exited, the door slammed shut behind me with a resounding thud. However, just moments after my exit, a shout emanated from within the house.

Hank's voice cracked with emotion, a mixture of anger and pain. "Larry, that man knew my father! I could have finally understood why he abandoned Mom and me. I can't believe you chased him away. I never want to see you again!" Without another word, he dashed out of the house, desperate to catch up with me.

# CHAPTER 12

❖❖❖❖

T HE ECHO OF THE DOOR slamming jolted the atmosphere as Hank sprinted after me. His shoes beat a rapid tempo against the pavement, matching the rhythm of his racing heart. The streetlights cast shadows that seemed to dance along with his frantic pace. "Wait!" He heard a voice call out from behind. Glancing over his shoulder, he saw his wife, her face flushed from the surprise of the night's revelations, motioning for him to slow down.

"Wait for me!" She called again, her voice tinged with worry.

## Larry's P.O.V

Still standing in the doorway, I watched my brother Hank's receding back, guilt and anger wrestling within me. My wife, her gaze a blend of exasperation and worry, reproached me, "Look at what you've done, Larry! Hank might've finally found answers about his father. Answers that he's searched for all his life. What the fuck is wrong with you?"

The Doctor, leaning casually yet with an air of authority against the wall, quizzed, "Why'd you throw Glen out?"

Defensively, I snapped back, "He was spinning tales about my family!"

The Doctor's gaze was steady, almost piercing. "When Glen speaks, believe him. I've known the man for twenty-five years. He doesn't make things up. Why would he come to your home and lie? If you want the truth, speak to your mother."

I felt a lump in my throat, realizing the gravity of my impulsiveness.

216

"Alright," I whispered, my voice unsteady, "I'll talk to her. I need the truth." Without another word, I retreated, each step echoing my turmoil, until I reached my office. The resounding slam of the door was a clear plea for privacy.

From a corner of the room, Sal, a longtime friend of mine and Hank's, looked quizzically at Jim. "Who's this Glen?" He asked.

Jim paused, a distant look in his eyes. "He... he saved my life," he began. His voice was soft, laced with gratitude. "I was just a kid. Mom had taken me to a store, and I'd wandered to the comics section. I was so lost in a comic that I stepped onto the road without realizing. I didn't see the speeding car, but Glen did. He rushed forward, yanking me back just in time. If not for him..." He left the sentence unfinished, but the implication hung heavy.

Smiling faintly, Jim continued, "He had this calm about him. Even when my mom was furious, Glen just... diffused it. But he made sure I learned my lesson. Warned me about reading while walking. To this day, I heed that advice."

The doctor's son, listening intently, mused aloud, "This is surreal. Glen seems connected to all of us in some way. How?"

The Doctor, adjusting his glasses, responded, "Glen's traveled extensively. I wouldn't be surprised if he's been everywhere. Regarding your father's occupation..." His gaze shifted pointedly to me. "That's something you'll have to discover yourself. But he was deeply involved with the government. Those who went against him rarely lived to tell the tale. Consider yourself lucky Glen's on your side. He's a loyal ally but a fearsome foe."

Taking a breath, the Doctor said, "It's time for me to go. This has been... enlightening."

From my office, I had overheard. Stepping out, pale and fraught with confusion, I managed, "He's... my biological father? I threw my own dad out? Shit, what do I do now?"

My wife, always my rock, took my hand. "Step by step, Larry. First, we reconcile with Harry. We've wronged him tonight. After that, we find Glen."

Resolved, I nodded. "Right. Let's start with Harry." We headed out together, the group joining in solidarity. As we navigated the city streets, destiny seemed to steer our path. We met Harry, arm in arm with his wife.

Taking a deep breath, I approached him. "Harry, I'm truly sorry. I'll make it right."

Harry merely nodded. "We were going to look for Glen. Thought he might be at the downtown hotel. I owe him an apology."

Hope flared in me. "Then let's find him together. Whether he listens or not, I need to try."

Their unified determination evident, the group echoed, "Yes, let's do this together." The city's heartbeat accompanied their journey. But as they turned a corner, a gang of hostile-looking men blocked their way, including my wife's ex. The tension was palpable.

One man, his voice dripping with disdain, sneered, "Look who it is. The prodigal sons."

Striving for calm, I replied, "Whatever issues we had in school, let's keep the past behind us."

But the man persisted, "Oh, the tables have turned. No heroes today." His gaze rested maliciously on the women.

Firmly, I countered, "This is between us men."

Yet, when all seemed grim, the rev of an engine sliced the air. A car, its aura commanding, skidded to a halt. From it emerged Glen, my father, and the atmosphere grew electric.

## Glen's P.O.V

The cold, raw energy of the scene stung my senses, and as I watched the group of hooligans surround my son, a ferocious and primal instinct took hold of me. I swiftly closed the distance between us, the grumbling of the car's engine fading behind me.

Without hesitation, I lunged at the biggest of the lot, landing a solid punch square in his jaw. He crumbled like a bag of bricks, taken aback by the sheer force. The second, a lanky, twitchy fellow, tried to sneak up on me, but I caught his right wrist with my left hand, swinging him to my side. Then, channeling every ounce of force I possessed, I drove my knee into his face. The sickening crunch was almost satisfying, and he collapsed, his consciousness ebbing away.

The third made the mistake of telegraphing his moves; with a snarl, he charged at me. Reacting quickly, I thrust my head forward, breaking his nose with the sheer force of the impact. Blood sprayed, and as he stumbled backward, clutching his face, I seized him by the scruff of his neck and clotheslined him to the ground.

Out of the corner of my eye, I caught the first man, who'd regained his wits, trying to come at me. I didn't give him a chance. *Predictable.* With a swift, calculated motion, I delivered a kick to his right knee cap, causing an audible snap.

He let out a pitiful scream. Seizing the moment, I grabbed him by the back of his head and, using his momentum against him, threw him into my upthrust knee. The impact knocked the wind out of him, sending him careening into a telephone pole. He slumped, motionless.

Another thought he'd seize the moment and lunged, but I pivoted on my heel, sending my left foot crashing into his chin. The force was enough to send him crashing through a nearby glass window.

One terrified man, seeing the destruction unfolding before him, scrambled up a nearby telephone pole like a scared squirrel, hoping I wouldn't pursue. But it was the fifth who caught my attention next.

He brandished a knife, waving it with a false bravado. "What now, big guy? Huh?"

My gaze locked onto his weapon. "Is that supposed to intimidate me?"

He sneered. "It's a knife."

I couldn't help but smirk. "No, son, *this* is a knife." From my side, I pulled out a blade I had been gifted during my time with the Special Forces in India. It was larger, fiercer, and compared to his, it looked like a true weapon of warfare.

To prove my point, I hurled it past his head, embedding it deep into the telephone pole. He followed its path with wide eyes, momentarily stunned. Using this momentary lapse in his judgment, I seized his knife-wielding hand and drove it into his own leg. He crumpled, screaming in anguish.

The first one, despite his broken leg, tried to crawl away. *He's resilient, I'll give him that.* He begged, "Please, stop!" In an act that was half mercy, half warning to any others who dared threaten my family, I hoisted him up and, with a single, focused heart punch, sent him crashing into a large store window. His body went limp; lifeless.

Finally, I turned my attention to the man cowering up the telephone pole. "You planned to harm my family," I called out to him. "Did you think there'd be no consequences?"

His voice trembled, "You're going to kill me, aren't you?"

I looked him dead in the eyes. "You brought this upon yourself. Now come down."

As the weight of his situation pressed down on him, the realization was clear: In trying to intimidate Larry and the group, they had unknowingly poked the bear. And the bear had responded.

Larry's wife, her face contorted with fear and a strange familiarity, rushed toward me. Her breaths were heavy as she pleaded, "Please, don't hurt him. He's my ex."

I glanced from the man on the telephone to her, disbelief evident in my voice. "Are you seriously asking me not to harm this guy?"

She nodded, her eyes filled with desperation. "Yes, and so does Larry."

My gaze settled on Larry, who was approaching with a determined look in his eyes.

The man on the telephone pole hesitated. "You promise you won't hurt me?"

I sighed, my temper cooling a bit, "No, I won't hurt you," I gestured for him to descend. "Now, get your ass down here."

After the man cautiously descended from the pole, I yanked my knife from its embedded position. The cool metal felt reassuring in my grip.

"Alright, alright," he muttered, trying to calm himself.

Larry, now beside Harry, looked at me, guilt and understanding battling in his eyes. "Glen, I'm so sorry. Everything was so confusing. As always, my mom was the root of it all. Can you forgive me?"

The weight of the moment pressed on my shoulders. "Larry, finding out who I was, that I had another son... it was all so overwhelming for both of us. If your parents hadn't separated, we might've never known about each other." I clasped his shoulder, my voice earnest. "Your father did an amazing job raising you. You're a fine young man. I'm proud of your accomplishments. You're intelligent, married to a wonderful woman, and starting a family..."

Larry's eyes widened in surprise, "Dad, we're not planning on having kids yet."

His wife shot him a glance, a playful smirk on her lips, "Actually, we are."

Larry blinked, the news sinking in. "Shit... what a night. I'm going to be a dad?"

Harry stepped forward, trying to ease the tension. "We have a lot to discuss, Mr. Glen."

"Just Glen," I interjected with a slight smile. "And I have something from your father. He loved you deeply. Because of our work, he had to maintain his distance, but he did manage to attend some of your events. We'd stand in the back, watching you. He always tried to be there, in his own way. I'll bring it to your house later."

The sirens drew nearer, and soon enough, the flashing red and blue lights filled the scene. The police officers looked less than pleased as they surveyed the chaos.

One of them, upon recognizing me, stiffened. "Sir, you're a federal agent, aren't you?" I nodded. He pulled out his radio.

"I'll call the General for assistance with this."

The officer, seemingly aware of his obligations, nodded in respect. "Thanks for the understanding, sir."

"What's going to happen with these guys?" He asked, gesturing toward the injured and winded group strewn across the scene.

I rubbed my temples, feeling the weight of my decisions. "It depends on them. If they choose to just walk away, I'll cover their hospital bills. But if they make a fuss, they can expect a lengthy stay in prison, maybe twenty years or so. So, what's it gonna be?"

The men exchanged nervous glances amongst themselves. "We just want to forget this ever happened and go home," one of them mumbled.

I exhaled in relief, "Get them to the hospital then. And let them go."

The officer hesitated, glancing at the lifeless body. "What about him?"

"Check if anyone claims that piece of shit. If not, he goes to the city morgue."

"And if no one claims him there?"

"City burial," I replied curtly.

Larry's voice sliced through our conversation. "Dad, what exactly do you do?"

I met his gaze, the weight of my past evident in my eyes. "Larry, meet me at Harry's. Bring everyone who wants answers. But till then, you're under police protection. For your safety."

They started moving toward Harry's residence, but I raised my hand. "Police protection starts now. No arguments. This officer will ensure you're safe."

The officer nodded, "I'll send a SWAT team to sweep every corner of the house. You have my word, they won't miss a thing."

"Ensure no one gets in or out of that house until I arrive," I instructed. As they departed, a dark thought crept in. *I had to test his loyalty to see if he was truly on my side.*

Later, I found myself outside the officer's residence. I managed to converse with his wife, and the revelations were troubling. He'd been receiving money, buying extravagant items like a new car, and seldom being home. My heart sank. *Shun. He's gotten to him.*

The name "Shun" evoked fear in most. He was a sinister figure who had claimed the lives of some of my own. And now, I had to confront him. His wife, seemingly detached, spoke of her husband's physical and mental abuse. There were no children, thankfully.

"Do what you must," she whispered as I left.

Arriving at Harry's place, I noticed an eerie absence of police. Tension gripped my chest. Moving to the backyard, I peered in, and the scene inside had my blood boiling. *Shun got to him.*

I decided to make my move. Silently, I eased open the back door and crept inside. The officer, caught off guard, whirled around, finding me standing in the doorway. His face drained of color.

"What the fuck are you doing, officer?" I growled.

His eyes were wide with fear, beads of sweat forming on his brow. "I had no choice! They have my family," he pleaded.

I took a step closer, my voice icy and stern. "So, you're going to tell me the truth now? Or am I going to have to get pissed and handle this? Because, trust me, neither outcome will be pleasant for you."

The officer smirked, his arrogance shining through his fear. "Or what, big man? You think you have the upper hand here? I hold all the cards."

He sneered at me, trying to get under my skin.

Before he could utter another word, I shot him right between the eyes. *Nobody threatens my family.* He fell lifelessly, blood pooling around him. The room echoed with the silence left behind by the gunshot.

"You don't ever mess with my family," I growled, staring at the lifeless body. "They always come first."

"S-sir," my son stammered, his eyes wide with shock. "Are you okay?"

I nodded. "When you've been in my line of work for as long as I have, you just... know."

The front door opened abruptly, and Sue stepped inside. Her face paled upon seeing the corpse. "What the hell happened here?"

I exhaled slowly, feeling the weight of the night on my shoulders. "Had to take care of some of Shun's business. Sit down, Sue. It's going to be a long story."

A couple of my trusted men entered, and I pointed to the officer's body. "Get this out of here. And someone, call the police. Tell them it's a Code Red situation."

They nodded, efficiently wrapping the body and hauling it away. The room once again filled with tense silence until the faint sound of sirens approached.

"Alright, listen up," I began, trying to find the right words. "I've worked for the U.S. government, and occasionally, other countries that needed... 'special attention.' Things they didn't want to or couldn't handle, they'd pass on to me. They wanted tasks done discreetly and efficiently. And that's where Harry and I came in."

Sue's eyes grew wide, realization dawning on her face. "So, you're like... covert operatives?"

I nodded, "Exactly. But here's the catch: We never actually worked for any government on record. We were off the books, freelancers of sorts. But we got paid handsomely under the table with a no-tax clause. It was dangerous, incredibly so. If either of us were killed in action, the government would disavow any knowledge of us."

A chill seemed to settle in the room.

"Just like when your dad, Harry, was murdered," I continued, swallowing hard. "A mole got to him, just like how Shun got to my daughter—your sister—and wife in Japan."

The weight of the past pressed down on me, every word a struggle. But they had a right to know.

Sue's voice quivered, the weight of uncertainty evident in her eyes. "How did my dad die?"

Pausing to collect my thoughts, I met her gaze. "Like a hero," I began.

"We were tasked with rescuing a diplomat and his family in Lebanon. They gave us a tight window – just four hours to infiltrate and extract. But it wasn't a straightforward mission. It felt off from the get-go. An uneasy feeling settled in the pit of my stomach."

*Why do these memories always hurt the most?*

"The intelligence was shoddy. When we reached our target, it became apparent we were set up. They were waiting for us. The entire area was a warzone, a twelve-block radius where every building became a potential death trap. We were in the center of it all."

The room's ambiance grew thick with tension, my words painting a vivid picture. Sue's eyes bore into mine, eager and anxious for every detail.

"Despite my gut feeling that something was off, I made backup plans. I had arranged for a chopper to extract us, just in case. Thank fuck I did. We got to our destination around ten PM. But instead of finding our targets, we discovered we'd been betrayed. The safe house wasn't safe. It was a trap."

*Fuck, that was a close call.*

"We fought through, house by house. In one of them, we found a family, innocent civilians, forced into a hellish situation. They were on the brink of selling their children to human traffickers. We couldn't stand by. Not after witnessing such atrocity. We took them with us, vowing to protect them."

Sue's hands clenched into fists, her face a canvas of anger and sadness.

"Six blocks to the extraction point. Every step was a battle. Thankfully, a contact of mine had hidden weapons and ammunition along our path, foreseeing we might need it. We were three blocks away when the fighting intensified."

*I can still hear the bullets, the screams.*

"The extraction house was in sight. As we approached, we spotted our chopper. But in a twist of betrayal, it turned away, leaving us stranded. My heart sank, but then," I smiled ruefully, "I saw our actual rescue chopper coming in hot, just as planned."

"We fought our way to the roof. Our salvation, the chopper, came into view, rockets blazing to clear our path. As we boarded, thinking we were safe, a gunman burst onto the roof. Before we could react, he fired a barrage of bullets."

*I'll never forget that moment.*

"Your dad, without hesitating, pulled his .44 auto mag and fired back, taking the bastard down. But not before one of the bullets found its mark. It tore through his heart and grazed my shoulder. As the chaos raged around us, he leaned in, his voice weak but determined. 'Make sure my son gets everything of mine,' were his final words."

The room fell silent.

Gazing down at him, my voice was barely above a whisper, "he died in my arms. I chose Israel as his resting place, a land of warriors, of resilience." Pulling out a well-crafted wooden box, I handed it over. "Everything of his is right here. I wish things could have been different, Harry."

I watched as his fingers hesitated over the latch. *This moment. Closure, yet so many new beginnings.*

"I'm so sorry for your loss," I continued, my eyes clouded with memories. "There was nothing more I could've done. Everything your father left behind is right there in that box. And if you need any assistance navigating through any of this, don't hesitate to call me." I handed him a card and added, "This number is top secret. No one but you gets it."

Nodding, Harry's fingers finally lifted the lid. Inside lay a collection of papers, bank statements, and photographs of a younger version of his father. His hands trembled slightly as he held a picture, the semblance of tears forming in his eyes.

"I've never seen these bank names before," he murmured, glancing at one of the statements.

"They're Swiss banks," I explained. "That account alone holds about eight billion dollars. And there's more spread across various accounts and assets. You're a very wealthy man now. Use it wisely and make your dad proud."

Turning to Larry, I let out a sigh. "There are things about this job I can't reveal right now. I've taken out countless people and... other things.

Cryptids, creatures that aren't supposed to exist. Many chose their fate, and I was the instrument. I served in the Vietnam War, crisscrossing the globe, undertaking assignments most don't even know exist."

*I am no hero. But I stand by my choices.*

"If you can't handle what I've revealed, tell me now, and I'll disappear from your life." Taking a deep breath, I added, "There's more. You have other siblings. Once I finish my current task, I'll connect you all."

Pausing, I posed a question. "You've seen the bombings in New York and Florida, right, Larry?"

He nodded grimly. "We lost family. Who's behind this?"

A bitter taste rose in my mouth. "There's a mole in our ranks. That's how our family is being targeted. I lost a daughter, your sister, in New York. Your brother was injured severely in Miami. They even tried to take me out in Louisiana. This ends now."

Larry's eyes darkened. "We worked under a Colonel through our job, Colonel Rex. Wasn't he with you in Vietnam?"

The realization hit hard and fast. *It's all connecting.* "It's making sense now," I whispered.

Larry's voice was shaky yet determined. "What are you going to do about him?"

Our gazes locked, the intensity palpable. "I'm going to kill him," I said without hesitation. "It's the only way. He's a threat to our family, to our friends. This has to stop. Now."

# CHAPTER 13

S o, I started to hunt for Colonel Rex's whereabouts. *Should I call Healy?* She was connected and had her ear to the ground—military or otherwise. Without hesitation, I reached out.

Healy's voice came through the line, crisp and efficient. "I haven't come across any Colonel Rex, but I'm on it. If he's as shadowy as you say, he's probably tied to some covert ops outfit."

Her confidence was reassuring. *I'm damn lucky she's got a soft spot for me... I think.*

True to her word, within the hour, she rang back. "Got him. He's stationed two hours from you at a clandestine facility. He won't even see you coming."

With a grim chuckle, I replied, "Bad news for him then."

The journey began after assuring Sue I'd be careful and promising a return to her side. It took only an hour to approach the outskirts of the hidden base—a testament to the urgency fueling me. I found a small clearing off the road, the perfect place to begin my approach on foot.

The final mile traversed in silence. I assessed the guards' routines with a practiced eye. At the back gate, a guard eyed me with a mix of recognition and fear.

"You're the Executioner?" He whispered, barely audible.

"Yes." My response was terse, brooking no argument.

He nodded, leading me in through the secret door of the base. "You have half an hour before the guard change. He's three levels underground. Don't worry about cleanup. We'll handle the bodies. Make it quick, make it silent."

So, this is what it boiled down to—being summoned like a trained dog to do their dirty work. *Funny how they need me now. Kill a man, and suddenly, I'm not such a monster, huh?* The irony of it all was a bitter pill, one that I swallowed down with a sense of fatalistic resolve.

The plan was clear: Get in, end the threat, and get out. All the while, my thoughts lingered on Sue's words, the silent promise of a life beyond this darkness. But first, Colonel Rex would learn that his treachery had a steep price—one that I was all too willing to collect.

The guard pointed me in the direction of the elevator, but I chose the stairs instead. "Three floors, not that bad," I muttered to myself, taking them two at a time.

Reaching his floor, the silence was eerie; it was like a tomb, save for the distant hum of electronics. No guards in sight. Odd, I thought, that they would leave the floor so unguarded. Perhaps they believed the depth of their underground lair was defense enough.

Of the five doors on this level, the first two were securely locked. At the third, I encountered a secretary. Her eyes flicked up to mine, recognition and something else — was it hope? — flashing in her gaze.

"Are you looking for Colonel Rex?" She inquired.

"Yes," I confirmed curtly, my mind already mapping the room beyond her.

"It's the last office on the right. Are you going to kill the bastard?" Her voice had a raw edge, a mix of bitterness and desperation.

I didn't answer; such questions were needless. Her lips curled into a wry smile as she continued, "Tell him I'm going home now."

"And is there anyone with him?" I prodded, ensuring no detail was left unchecked.

"Always has two goons glued to him. One sits outside, by the door, the other's always in the room."

Coward.

As if reading my thoughts, she quipped, "Coward, isn't he?"

Then, with a sudden shift in her demeanor, her voice dropped to a whisper, "Will I still have a job tomorrow?"

"I'll make sure of that, with better pay," I assured her, knowing well the value of loyalty in these treacherous depths.

She stood, shrugging on her coat with a sense of finality. As she was having trouble with her coat, I reached over and helped her, my fingers deftly assisting in fastening the buttons. Then, she asked, "Can I ask you something?" There was a tremble in her voice now, vulnerability peeking through her professional facade.

"Go ahead."

"My ex... he's threatening me. Says he'll kill me if I try to leave him. Beats me when he's drunk with his buddies. Can you help?"

"Call this number," I said, scribbling down Sue's contact. "Tell her what's going on, where to find this piece of shit. I'll handle it once I'm done here. Most likely tonight."

Her eyes filled with tears, relief flooding her features. "Thank you. Be careful, okay?"

With a nod, I watched her depart before turning my attention back to the task at hand. It was time to finish this, one way or another.

With a practiced ease, I drew my .38 magnum, its silencer affixing a hush to the violence I was about to unfold. The door to the last room on the right barely creaked as I pushed it open. The guard inside hadn't time to register the threat; a single, muted shot to the head, and he slumped forward, lifeless.

The door to the next room was thin, the voices behind it clear and distinct. I didn't hesitate. Bursting through, I caught them off guard — the Colonel with that shocked, deer-in-headlights expression, his crony too slow on the uptake. My bullet found its mark before he could fully rise, leaving just the two of us.

The room was suddenly thick with tension, a standoff that had been years in the making. *This is it. The moment I've been waiting for.*

The Colonel scuttled back, his back hitting the wall, with nowhere else to run. "Don't do this," he pleaded, "It makes you as bad as me."

"That's where you're wrong," I retorted, my voice cold as steel. "I'm here to end you. Your time stops now."

He began to bargain, desperation seeping into his voice. "If you let me live, I'll tell you about everyone involved in the New York blast."

"I already know," I cut him off sharply.

"The cops," he continued, gasping, "The ones who helped us get the supplies in..."

"Dead. And Rick's in jail, squealing for a deal," I stated flatly, the facts laid bare before him.

There was no room for mercy, not for this man. Not for the architect of so much pain.

"For my wife, for my daughter," I hissed, leveling the gun at his knees. Two shots rang out, and his screams filled the room.

I watched him for a moment, writhing in agony, then drew my knife. His eyes widened as I showed it to him, a cruel prelude to his end. With deliberate slowness, I plunged it into his stomach, twisting, savoring the justice in his howls.

He fell to the ground, clutching his stomach, a pathetic attempt to hold his life inside. But I wasn't done. Gripping his hair, I twisted his head sharply. A sickening crack echoed, his head lolling to an unnatural angle, boiling with anger, I ripped his head right off. I let his lifeless body drop the floor with a thud.

And just like that, it was over. The Colonel's reign of terror had come to an abrupt end by my hands. A silence enveloped the room, thick and heavy, the weight of justice served — and the cost of it — settling in my bones. I threw his head beside his body as I walked out.

Leaving the base behind, I climbed the steps, the quietude unsettling. The cool night air brushed against my face as I stepped outside, the silence a stark contrast to the chaos I'd just left underground. No one was around to witness my exit. As I made my way back to the truck, that prickling sensation of being watched crept over me. Scanning my surroundings, I spotted a pair of eyes glinting from the woods about fifty feet away. *Keep it cool. Just walk.* I continued without altering my pace; whatever it was, it didn't pursue—*got to stay focused. There's still work to do tonight.*

Reaching my truck, I quickly started to change my clothes, the urgency of the situation weighing on me. My "to-go bag" was a lifesaver, providing a fresh set of clothes to replace the blood-stained ones. I stuffed the soiled garments into a plastic bag, then tossed it into the back of the truck.

With the evidence hidden away, I finally settled into the driver's seat, the engine humming to life. As I dialed Sue's number, my heart raced with anticipation. "Did the lady call?" I asked.

"Yes, she did," Sue's voice was crisp on the line.

"And? Where is he?"

"He's at a bar named 'Up Your Cup,'" she replied, a chuckle breaking through.

"Get a grip, Sue. Where's it at?"

Her laughter bubbled over the phone. "About sixty-five minutes out. You'll make it in less than an hour."

"What's so funny, Sue?"

"Just something Healy said," she gasped out between laughs.

Great, I'm the punchline again. "I'm heading to 'Up Your Cup' now."

Her laughter intensified. Sometimes, it felt like everyone's in on a joke but me. The hour drive was quiet, giving me time to steady my nerves for what was to come. When I arrived, I parked and rang Healy. "Any trouble back at the base?"

"No trouble. He's dead," I said bluntly.

"Yeah, heard you detached his head from his shoulders. You left quite the mess in the office," she retorted.

"The General's cleaning up. He can come here next. It's not going to be pretty."

She chuckled. "At the bar now? 'Up Your Cup?'"

"Yes, and cut the laughter. I've got to go. This shit is never simple."

Before entering, I peered through the window, scouting the scene and spotting my targets. *Showtime.* I pushed the door open, the noise of the bar spilling out into the night. The patrons were absorbed in their own worlds, but one man's gaze latched onto me. *That's him. No doubt.*

I stepped into the fray, the door closing behind me with the faintest click, my presence unnoticed by all but the one who mattered. It was time to get to work.

The sheriff reached for his gun, but my reflexes were quicker. My .38 was already drawn, the sound suppressed, but the outcome was deadly. The bullet found its target, and the sheriff's head snapped back as he crumbled. He fell into the deputy, them both to the ground amidst chaos and confusion. The sheriff's life ebbed away beneath him.

I moved toward the motionless body, stripped the star from his shirt, and fastened it onto the dazed deputy who was struggling to his feet. "You're the new sheriff now," I said, locking eyes with him. "Do things right around here. Protect those who can't defend themselves."

"Sheriff, do the right thing," I urged him, my voice firm. "Be fair, be kind, learn from what just happened. Protect the people, and you'll do good."

After placing the new sheriff's badge on the deputy, I turned my attention to the center of the room. There, amidst a crowd of onlookers, I spotted him. The crowd parted as I walked through, my gaze locked onto my target.

"So you like to hurt women?" I asked, my voice cold and devoid of emotion as I moved closer to him, never breaking eye contact.

Suddenly, a large man lunged in front of me. Reacting instinctively, I brought my elbow up with force, connecting with his face. The sound of a breaking nose filled the air as he crumpled to the ground, unconscious. I stepped over his body without a second glance and grabbed the man responsible for so much pain.

"What are you going to do, call the cops?" he sneered, a smirk playing on his lips.

"No," I replied coolly. In one fluid motion, I spun him around, locking his neck in the crook of my elbow. His eyes widened in terror as I applied pressure, the cracking sound echoing in the silent room. He slumped to the ground, lifeless.

The general walked in at that moment, surveying the aftermath. His eyes met mine, a mix of awe and horror in his expression. "You are a walking death machine," he said, shaking his head. "Everywhere you go, people end up dead. You're worse than the black death."

I ignored his comment, stepping outside to where Sue and Nancy were waiting, their faces etched with worry.

"OK, are we going to San Francisco now? To the docks to get Danny to bring that piece of trash there?" Sue asked and paused for a moment, gathering her thoughts. "Yeah, by the way, there's a problem," she continued, her voice tense. "In Paris, France, they've taken the commissioner's ex-wife, his daughter, and his grandchildren as hostages, just in case you get too close."

"Fuck!" My mind raced. *Alright, think.* "General, call and get my plane ready. Also, call the French government. I'm coming in to get them. If they want to help, that's great, but they wait for my lead. I know where they're holding them. Call Healy and see if she can pull strings to get them back into the US. I'll be back soon."

"What about Rick?" She asked, worry creasing her forehead.

"Just hold him!" I snapped.

"Nancy said we only can for seventy-two hours," Sue replied, her voice strained with the stress of the situation.

"What the hell is wrong with you? He's a terrorist. Just hold him!" I was losing my patience. "He doesn't have rights—he's an illegal alien, a gunrunner, a drug smuggler, a murderer. He's part of the problem, part of the bombing. You keep him at all costs, or I will make sure you lose your job. Got it?"

Sue nodded, her face hardening with determination.

By the time we reached the military airport, my plane was ready and waiting. Sue was by my side, steadfast as always. "I will stay here and wait for you to come back and watch Rick," she said.

"No, you're coming too. You'll go to England first and get our daughter. We're going to bring them all home safe," I commanded.

"What about Rick?" She pressed.

"His bad luck," I replied with a cold finality. "He has to deal with Healy."

"Let's go?" The urgency was clear in my voice as we took off for London. The flight spanned six seemingly endless hours, each minute stretching on as I ran through strategies in my mind. Upon landing, I dropped Sue off with a terse nod, and then I was off to France. The situation there was dire, and time was not a luxury we could afford.

The French government had indeed assembled their forces, waiting with the resources I had insisted upon. "They're being held at a farm outside of Paris, about twenty-five miles away," I briefed the commissioner of police, the SWAT team, and the secret government agents. To my surprise, they deferred to my command—*they're putting a lot of trust in me.*

We stopped two miles from the target. From there, I proceeded on foot, the weight of the operation pressing down on me with every step through the dense woods.

"Kill all," I instructed tersely. "No one lives but the hostages. No one."

My pace quickened, driven by adrenaline, and soon enough, I encountered resistance. A pair of guards stood unaware of their impending doom. One fell silently to my knife, the other to the subdued cough of my .38 magnum. *Just like that, two more breaths snuffed out.*

233

I left their bodies where they fell, an unnerving calm settling over me. Half a mile more to the farmhouse, I spotted it and two more guards milling by the barn. I had to change my approach and move from a different direction. My legs ached, my lungs burned, but I pushed on, skirting the treeline until I found a blind spot.

But then, an error—two more guards appeared abruptly. No time for stealth now. My silenced .38 magnum spoke twice, and two more bodies were hastily dragged into the underbrush.

And then, a twist of fate—a cop signaling me. *He's one of the good ones.* An undercover agent, and he quickly dispatched another guard.

"The rest are coming from the west," I informed him after a brief exchange. His knowledge was invaluable; he knew the inside count, the layout. Together, we approached the second-story window—the first floor was a death trap, rigged to blow.

He nodded at me as I asked about the hostages' safety, his eyes steely with resolve. "Don't worry about them. They're okay for now."

"Okay, let's go," I said, with a shared understanding that every second we delayed increased the danger for those we were sworn to protect. We needed to move fast, move smart, and end this nightmare. The hostages needed us, and we were not going to let them down.

Fortune seemed to be a fickle ally, yet it favored us as we stumbled upon a ladder propped against the side of the house, left by roofers who had no idea it would become instrumental in a rescue operation. With hushed urgency, we positioned the ladder, ascending to an open window, only to find the room beyond occupied.

*Shit, we can't go in there.*

The cop, eyes sharp and alert, spotted another opportunity—a blessedly unobstructed window next to the chimney. He slipped through first, with me right on his heels. We found ourselves in a large, barren room, and without hesitation, we made for the door.

He cracked it open with painstaking care, peering out to scan the area. The vantage point was perfect—we could survey the entire lower level: Living room, kitchen, dining area. He gestured to the left, and I nodded, moving right.

From my position, I could see our backup through the window. I made sure to be seen, signaling subtly, letting them know my location and intended exit point.

Suddenly, I glimpsed the cop, taking down another guard outside. My own confrontation was swift. A guard was surprised and silenced before she could react. The house seemed to bristle with tension as we approached the stairs—two paths, we split without a word.

Chaos erupted then; shots fired, shouts, the unmistakable sounds of a firefight. The cop caught a bullet in his right shoulder but managed to drop two of the assailants. I dealt with three more in a rapid, brutal dance of violence. The remaining enemy combatants, sensing defeat, fled through the front door, abandoning the wired hostages in their haste.

Hearing gunfire from the woods and the opposite side of the house, I knew our teams were engaging, cleaning up. Our luck held—perhaps the terrorists were too rushed or too inept, but the explosives were inert, a lack of a timer or detonator their folly.

The wounded cop descended, blood seeping through his uniform from the shoulder wound. I grabbed a towel from a nearby bathroom, pressing it against the bleeding in an effort to staunch the flow.

With no time to lose, I freed the hostages from their explosive harnesses, one by one, their eyes wide with fear and relief.

Just as the situation seemed to come under control, the other agents burst in, their weapons raised and aimed at the cop who had aided me. "Stop! He helped me!" I shouted, stepping between them and the bleeding man.

The commissioner was skeptical. "He's one of them?" He accused, voice laced with suspicion.

I faced the cop, seeking the truth behind his actions. "Why did you help me then?" I demanded.

His answer came, weighted with sorrow. "They killed my parents who lived here," he confessed, his voice breaking ever so slightly. "And they took my kids, the hostages with kids, little kids... I don't give a fuck what you do, you just don't hurt my kids."

I turned to the commissioner, my gaze steely. We needed to talk away from the others. "Is he wanted for anything?" The weight of the question hung in the air, a pivotal moment that would decide the fate of the man who had stood by my side through the chaos.

"No, nothing too bad," the commissioner finally responded a hint of relief in his voice. "Okay then, get him to the hospital. And then... what do you think? Three years of house arrest and five years probation?"

I looked at the head of the SWAT team, who nodded in agreement. "That is good."

"And you," he said, turning to me with the weight of command in his voice, "Are going to clean up this mess. That's up to you. Do you need me, or can you handle it? Should I assist with this or go and take the people home? What do you want me to do?"

I turned to the Sergeant of the SWAT team, who exchanged a knowing look with the commissioner before answering. "Just go. We can handle it."

Then, the guy, still shaken and disoriented, asked me, "How do I make money? I need to pay taxes and buy food. How do I live?"

"Don't worry about that," I assured him, my mind already formulating a plan. "I'll put enough money in an account for you to retire on. You're good. Work with the local police."

"Okay, let's get these people to the hospital to be checked out," I said, steering the group toward the exit.

They all muttered their thanks. Voices tinged with the trauma they had just survived. Then we heard more shots—the commander confirming that was the last of the hostiles.

I turned to the tall girl in the group. "Your father is the commissioner in San Francisco?"

"Yes, he is. Is he alright?" Her eyes were wide with a mix of fear and hope.

"Yes, he's fine. I'm going to take you home, and the others too. Where do you want to go after the hospital?"

"Home" was the unanimous response.

"Good. Let's go. I have a plane waiting for us."

After everyone was cleared at the hospital, we departed from Paris Airport and jetted to London to pick up Sue and my daughter, Kim.

Her embrace was tight, filled with relief and the bond of family. "It's great to meet you, Dad. I've heard so much about you. I love you and Mom. Thank you for coming to get me."

Sue smiled at me, that same warm smile that always seemed to make everything alright. "Okay, let's go. When this is over, you can return to finish your schooling."

I thanked John, our protector, and Kim chimed in with her own gratitude. "Thanks, John."

"Did you get scared?" I asked her.

"No," she replied confidently, "John took good care of me and did a good job."

"And how many years have you been in school now?"

"Two and a half," she beamed. "I'm really smart—I jumped ahead of all my classmates."

I just looked at Sue, a smirk playing on my lips. "Why am I not surprised? All my kids are smartasses."

Sue laughed. "For you, yes. Me, I'm not so sure."

The flight back to San Francisco was uneventful, a much-needed respite from the chaos we'd left behind. A family reunion was looming on the horizon, and I couldn't help but think, *Great, I'll be the dumb one in a family of smart-asses.*

Once we landed, Healy's call came through. Sue answered and relayed the good news. "They are all safe. We're coming home now."

# CHAPTER 14

✦✦✦✦✦

**W**E ARRIVED IN SAN FRANCISCO swiftly, the city's skyline looming over us as a constant reminder of the stakes at hand. Heady had followed my instructions to a tee, bringing Rick to the designated dock next to the SIU, with the added security of the warehouse provided by the commissioner.

The commissioner looked visibly stressed, his demeanor betraying the weight of the situation. I approached him, a calming presence in the midst of chaos. "Everything's under control," I assured him. "I've brought your family here. They're safe, and they're with me at the meeting place, along with Rick."

The sight of Rick, with a bag over his head, being led into the warehouse was almost cathartic. The moment we entered the dock area, the tension was tangible, the air thick with unspoken questions and anxieties.

"Why am I here?" the commissioner demanded, his voice strained. "I've got a family crisis to handle right now."

I met his gaze steadily. "It's already solved," I replied. I nodded to Heady, who understood the cue perfectly.

As she ushered the commissioner's family into the warehouse, the transformation in his demeanor was immediate. Relief washed over his face, replacing the stress and worry that had been etched there only moments before. The sight of his grandchildren, whom he was meeting for the first time, seemed to breathe new life into him.

"How? When?" he stammered, his eyes flickering between me and his reunited family.

"I found out where they were being held this morning," I explained, keeping my tone even. "Sir, I do things that often can't be easily explained. I just get them done."

As the reality of the situation settled in, his eyes hardened when they landed on Rick, who was now being revealed with the removal of the bag from his head. The look of shock on Rick's face was almost comical, a stark contrast to the seriousness of the situation.

"Well, well, Rick," the commissioner said with a mixture of disbelief and disdain. "We've been looking for you."

I stepped back, allowing the commissioner to take the lead. "Commissioner, he's all yours," I declared, turning to walk away. My part here was done, and the rest was in their hands.

"When they raped your family, the little girl liked it!" Rick yelled with a sick grin as I was walking away. "They told me she asked for more. I heard she wanted more!" He laughed maniacally.

Sue turned white as a sheet. She grabbed our daughter and the kids, yelling "Get out of here, now!"

I saw red. That monster threatened my family for the last time. I turned and strode toward Rick, fury rising in my veins.

The commissioner stepped forward, saying, "He's not worth it."

I fixed him with a cold stare. "Get out of my way, or else. So help me God."

Heady pulled the commissioner back. She told him, "This goes deeper than you know. Leave them be."

The other officers shuffled back, giving us space. I told the one near Rick, "Uncuff him and go. Now."

Rick looked at me as the cuffs dropped. "So big man, whatcha gonna do huh? There are witnesses." He sneered. "What, the great Executioner can't take me?"

I walked up calmly and smashed my fist into his jaw with crushing force. Bone cracked under my knuckles. Rick staggered back, shock and pain on his face.

I grabbed his shirt and yanked him close, my voice low and dangerous. "You think you can threaten my little girl like that, you piece of shit?"

My grip on him tightened, the fury in my eyes unyielding. With my right hand, I delivered another powerful blow, one that dislocated his neck with a sickening snap. He crumpled to the ground, but I wasn't done, not by a long shot.

"You're going to wish you were dead," I seethed, my voice low and menacing.

Rick, in his agony, made a feeble attempt to grab me with his right hand. I caught it effortlessly, twisting it until the cracking of his bones echoed through the room. His screams filled the air, a sound of pure, unadulterated pain.

He struggled to rise, but I was relentless. My right leg swung around, striking his left knee with such force that it shattered. His cries grew louder, but they were music to my ears compared to the vile words he had spewed earlier.

"Is that all you got?" Rick managed to spit out between screams.

I leaned in close, my voice dripping with venom. "Oh, no. You see this pin?" I showed him a small, sharp object. "I'm going to drive this into your neck. It will stop the blood from reaching your head. Then, I'll pull it out. The blood will pour from your mouth, ears, eyes, nose. And just before you pass out, I'll pull the pin out. You'll bleed out slowly, but before you die, I'm going to rip your fucking head off your body."

My words were met with an overwhelming sense of fear from everyone still present. Some left in disgust or shock, others vomited at the sheer brutality of the scene.

With a twisted sense of satisfaction, I watched as Rick, now whimpering and broken, tried to hit me with his left arm. In one swift motion, I grabbed and twisted it until it broke with a loud, gruesome crack that resonated even outside the warehouse.

Through his tears and agony, Rick whimpered a pathetic apology.

"Go to hell," I spat back at him, my voice cold and devoid of any mercy. The time for apologies had long passed. This was retribution, and I was its unforgiving deliverer.

I put the pin in his neck and let it stay there for a bit. Then I yanked it out and, as fast as I could, grabbed his head and twisted it off his shoulders with a sickening crack. His severed head dropped to the ground.

Just then the general walked in. "Fuck! You're crazy!" he exclaimed.

The commissioner just shook his head. "This piece of crap had it coming. He did what we all wanted to do." He called to the others, "Get some guys in here to clean this mess up."

I stood there, covered in blood.

As the others started dragging the body away, she looked at me with fear in her eyes. "Are you alright, Glen?"

I met her gaze coldly. "No. I'm not."

As everyone else walk toward the SIU, I left and walked toward the setting sun at the pier. I sat down on the bench and looked at the vast sea in front of me.

I remained seated on the bench at the end of the pier, lost in my thoughts. The weight of what I had just done was like a heavy cloak around my shoulders. Heady sat beside me, her presence both comforting and unnerving.

"You let your emotions run wild," Heady said softly, her voice tinged with a fear I hadn't seen in her before. "What I saw in there... Glen, it scared me."

I nodded, gazing out at the water. "He had it coming, Heady. But you're right, that part of my life... it's over now."

She hesitated, her eyes searching mine. "Is it really over, though? You still have one more to confront, don't you?"

The general had mentioned it, the final piece of this bloody puzzle. "Yes," I admitted, "one more. And then I'm done."

Heady's fear seemed to grow. "I saw something in you, Glen. A darkness. It's frightening."

"Don't worry about me," I reassured her, though I wasn't sure if I believed my own words. "I'm almost done."

Then, Heady dropped a bombshell. "It's his secretary. She's the mole. She was in Vietnam with the colonel, married to him for thirty years. How did you find this out?"

"It was Tom," I explained. "He's met her several times. She's been leaking secrets all along. I set a trap, and she fell right into it."

Heady looked at me, her eyes wide. "So, what now?"

"The person who owes me one is taking care of it right now," I said, feeling a mixture of relief and emptiness. "They're dealing with her as we speak. And as for Shun, his end is near."

I stood up, feeling the cool breeze off the water. The blood, the violence, the vengeance - it was all coming to a close. One way or another, this chapter of my life was ending. And maybe, just maybe, I could find some semblance of peace after all the chaos.

"So, Heady, what do you want me to do now? After Shun is dead, where do I go from here?" I asked, my voice tinged with weariness. The thought of retirement lingered in my mind, an elusive dream I had longed for but never dared to grasp.

Heady's eyes met mine, a blend of understanding and fatigue mirroring my own. "Do you like the idea of retirement? Is that the best thing for you? Or do you have to stay? I want to see my grandchildren, be a grandma, have fun and not worry about all this," she said, her voice trailing off into a whisper.

I nodded slowly, contemplating her words. "Yes, Heady, and I think we will have someone else too." The words felt foreign on my tongue, yet right.

"Who?" Heady asked, her eyebrows arching in surprise.

"Sue, I think we are engaged," I spoke the words, feeling a mix of anxiety and hope.

Her shock quickly turned to delight as she patted my hand and embraced me warmly. "You two... I knew it would happen sooner or later! That's great! I'm throwing a party for you and all of us. It's going to be amazing. So much fun!" Her enthusiasm was contagious, lighting up her tired features.

I couldn't help but smile, yet the shadow of my final task loomed over me. "Heady, I still have one more to get, and I have a feeling he won't be too happy to find out about his situation in life now."

"I don't care, he's as good as dead now," Heady declared with a steely resolve, a hint of bitterness in her tone. "I have things to do."

"Heady, stop. You can't say anything about anybody until we are done," I cautioned her, feeling the weight of responsibility on my shoulders.

She sighed, her expression softening. "Okay then, let's go wild and get done once and for all."

As we spoke, the commissioner approached me, accompanied by the general. They handed me a piece of paper. "This is for you," the commissioner said, his voice low.

I unfolded the note, a sense of dread filling me. "Thanks," I muttered, scanning the contents. It was a location of Shun—somewhere in the mountains of Utah. "Great, now I have to track him down in the mountains."

Heady chuckled dryly. "Maybe one of the creatures will get him first."

"I hope so, Heady. But call the Canadian government just in case, and tell them what's going on. He might try to get into their country. I'm not stopping until I get him, no matter what," I affirmed, my resolve as strong as ever.

"O, he will be dead that you can take to the bank. How or who will do it... well, that is another story, and I hope it's me," Heady declared with a fierce glint in her eyes.

As I started to walk away, the commissioner turned to Heady, his voice laced with confusion and concern. "Is he nuts or insane?"

Heady shook her head, a small smile playing on her lips. "No, he's the best of the best. He will get Shun before he gets to the border." Her confidence in me was unwavering, a beacon in the tumultuous storm that was my life.

The commissioner, skepticism etched on his face, asked, "I bet the guy gets into Canada before he gets caught, huh?"

Heady, with a spark in her eyes, quickly retorted, "I'll take that bet. A thousand dollars. And I'll give you ten to one odds. He'll get him in two weeks. Dead," she laughed, a hint of morbid glee in her voice.

Then, turning to Danny and Tom, I announced with a sense of finality, "Alright, off we go to the great outdoors. We're headed to the Utah mountains. He's trying to make a run for Canada. Now, if you guys want out, this is your chance. Once I start, I won't stop until his blood is on my hands. So go if you want, or stay. I won't hold it against you. This isn't your fight."

"Yes, we're all in this together," they agreed unanimously. "We have to stop him. If he gets up there, it'll take years to find him! What I want to do is start from the Canadian border and work our way down. We'll push him into a corner he won't want to go, but I've been there many times. Very few make it through."

Danny, a mix of curiosity and apprehension in his voice, asked, "How do you know what's up there is so unbelievable?"

"Well," I began, a solemn tone in my voice, "you've got Dogman, skinwalkers, Bigfoots, and the worst of them all – feral human beings. Danny, not even big bears or wolves dare go there."

"What the hell is a feral human being?" Tom interjected, his face a mask of confusion and fear.

"They are monsters," I explained, my voice dropping to a whisper. "They hunt in packs, like wolves. They eat humans alive. Their mindset regresses over ten thousand years of mental health. If you wander into their territory, they will hunt you down. And that's if you survive the Dogman first. Then there are the skinwalkers. You know they're around when the temperature drops fast, even in winter. And they're the only creatures that come out at night. We're going to push him right into their midst."

Pausing, I looked at each of them. "Now, if you don't want to go, speak up now because once we hit Utah, we go straight to the border, and we don't stop until we get him or find a piece of him. So, are you all in or what?"

They exchanged glances, a silent communication passing between them before asking, "Can we have a quick talk?"

"Sure, you can talk," I said, my voice tinged with a hint of sarcasm. "I'll just walk to my truck and let the girls have their little girl talk."

As I walked to my truck, my thoughts were a whirlwind of strategy and anticipation. *This is it, the final showdown,* I thought to myself. Reaching the truck, I dialed my contact, the one who'd get me to the border and ensure my weapons were ready.

"Yes, I will see you there," my guy responded on the phone before hanging up.

As I ventured into the wilderness, the realization that I was once again on my own in this treacherous journey struck me hard. *So, this is it – the point of no return,* I thought, my resolve hardening with each step. To my surprise, as I reached the designated rendezvous point, I found Tom and Danny waiting for me, their faces a mixture of determination and apprehension.

"Glad to see you two," I said, masking my surprise with a wry smile.

"We're here to help you," they replied in unison, their voices firm despite the evident tension in the air.

"This trip will be a bad one, and we might not make it back either," I warned them, the gravity of our mission weighing heavily on my mind.

I quickly got to work, distributing SPAS-12 shotguns, each loaded with armor-piercing rounds, to Danny. Tom received a .44 Magnum revolver, also with armor-piercing shells, and I handed them four boxes each. For myself, I chose a .50 caliber handgun, a formidable weapon for what lay ahead.

We were stocked with supplies for two weeks – I made sure of that. At the last second, I instructed the pilot, "Head to Utah. We're going to catch him out in the open." We landed about two miles away from the tree line in a clear site, hoping to spook our target into a panic.

Once we were on the ground, we wasted no time and started walking fast towards the tree line. It took us half an hour to reach it, and we immediately found a path. "We'll use this path," I instructed Tom and Danny. "Stay about three steps into the woods, off the path. He's alone – I don't see any other footprints."

We followed the path, staying ten feet off to the side, confident we would catch up to him. "Let's go get him," I urged, a sense of urgency in my voice. "We don't want his body to be alone."

As we trekked deeper into the woods, it wasn't long before I spotted Dogman footprints – and they were big, the biggest I had ever seen. My heart raced, adrenaline pumping through my veins. The danger was real. But so was our determination.

We halted abruptly, the ominous signs before us sending a chill down my spine. I pointed out the tracks to Tom and Danny, my voice low and steady. "We've got company, and they're not the friendly kind." The prints were massive, unmistakably belonging to a Dogman, but not just any Dogman. By the looks of these tracks, it was the biggest one I had ever seen or heard of, easily twelve to fifteen feet tall.

I swiftly pulled out my .50 caliber rifle, loading it with armor-piercing shells. The air was thick with tension. "I won't lie to you. We're going to encounter this monster, so be ready. Headshots only. No screaming, no yelling. If you shoot at this beast, make every bullet count. Aim for the head and the heart."

As if on cue, the creature appeared. It didn't see us at first, allowing me a moment to take aim. Dropping to one knee, I fired at its head, unloading round after round until it collapsed. Tom, with a grim determination in his eyes, drew his .44 Magnum and fired four shots straight into its heart and two more into its chest.

"Are we good?" I asked, eyeing the fallen behemoth.

"No," Tom said, his voice firm, and he cut its head off. "Now I'm good."

With the beast decapitated, a silent agreement passed between us. "Stay together. Let's move," I commanded, and we resumed our trek.

As darkness enveloped us, the heat intensified, a sure sign of impending danger. *Skinwalkers,* I thought, my instincts on high alert. I knew they often came in pairs, one from the west and one from the east. I decided to stay up, keeping watch while the others tried to catch some restless sleep.

Right around two in the morning, they arrived. I whispered to the guys, "Stay alert. Listen for the slightest sounds – a leaf falling, twigs snapping. Be ready for anything."

And then it appeared. A white, long, thin body creeping along the treetops. Its movements were silent but deadly, a predator in its prime. The skinwalker's presence filled the night with an eerie, bone-chilling sense of dread.

In the eerie stillness of the forest, I readied my flare gun, my senses razor-sharp. I was just inside the treeline on the left side, moving in sync with the skinwalker as it descended to the ground. Anticipating its next move, I was just a step ahead when I pulled out my .44 Magnum, loaded with armor-piercing rounds. Two shots to its heart, followed by a flare directly into its chest, brought the creature down.

Beforehand, I had prepared five steel spikes, now white-hot from the fire. Tom, with heavy gloves on, drove a spike into the creature's heart and another into its skull. We covered it with dead branches, and Danny set it ablaze. The skinwalker writhed, its cries piercing the night, but it was dying, and soon it lay dead. We then severed its head, ensuring it would not rise again.

The temperature plummeted, a sure sign that another skinwalker was near. The subtle signs were there - leaves falling slowly, sounds emanating from the south. As I watched it emerge, a shocking turn of events unfolded. The massive Dogman leaped out, engaging in a ferocious battle with the skinwalker. In a brutal display of power, the Dogman tore off the skinwalker's head and hurled it into our campfire, letting out a triumphant howl.

Reacting instinctively, I drew my .44 Magnum, but Tom and Danny were quicker. They shot the Dogman in the head and chest, killing it instantly. I looked at them, a mixture of surprise and respect in my eyes. "Burn the skinwalker's body," they told me. *Give them an inch. They take a mile*, I thought, but I couldn't help feeling proud of how quickly they were learning.

I called base camp to inform them of our situation and provided coordinates for the Dogman's body retrieval. Exhausted but vigilant, we decided to start our next leg of the journey in the morning. Despite some sleep, the looming threat of rain was not a welcome sight. However, I pointed out to the guys, "It's good. We can track him more easily. He will leave footprints, making him easier to follow."

We trudged for eight relentless hours, the silence around us deafening. No birds, no life – a telltale sign of a dogman nearby. As the second day came to a close and darkness crept in, we found a strategic location for camp. Surrounded on three sides with a clear view and our backs against a rock cliff, we finally had some semblance of safety. The night was upon us, and with it, the unknown terrors that lay hidden in the vast wilderness of the Utah mountains.

In the dim light of the early morning, our camp was a fortress against the unknown. "This will help us fend off any 'friends' if they decide to come in hard," I muttered, checking my weapon.

We had spotted Shun, our target, about sixty-five feet to our right, near a large fallen tree by the clearing. Throughout the night, we took turns keeping an eye on him. Sleep came in short bursts, but by morning, Shun had vanished.

I scoured the surrounding area, circling the campsite for a few hundred yards in every direction. It didn't take long to find Shun's footprints. "Either we get to him first, or Shun is a dead man. I want that honor," I declared firmly, feeling a surge of adrenaline. However, the discovery of fresh human footprints near the treeline complicated matters.

With no other choice, we began our ascent up the side of the cliff, a potential ambush looming over us. It took us about half an hour to reach the top, and there it was – a Bigfoot staring at us in surprise. It seemed shocked that we had managed to climb the cliff but eventually walked off in another direction. *It's only temporary; he'll be back,* I thought.

"Now we've got to find out what lives up here and locate Shun," I said to Tom and Danny. "And wonder if he realizes how much trouble he's in. For that matter, us too."

I halted, turning to my companions. "Get ready for anything. All guns ready, eyes and ears open. Listen for anything unusual, and keep moving. We lost all the tracks from down there. We need to find him fast."

Following the general direction of the tracks we had been following, we walked two miles before picking up fresh ones. Among them were Shun's bootprints and some bare human footprints. "Feral human beings are around here. Stay sharp, guys," I warned.

Suddenly, we heard screaming, yelling, and gunfire. "I think we've found them. Let's go," I urged.

Rushing towards the commotion, we found Shun bleeding profusely from his shoulder and right leg. "They're all around here," he gasped. "They run in, stab you, and run away. Then, when you're fixing the problem, they hit you again."

As he spoke, Tom spotted one of the attackers charging at Shun. With a precise shot to the chest, Tom took it down. Then, chaos erupted around us. Screaming and yelling echoed from every direction.

I commanded firmly, "Don't shoot until you see them."

Shun, panicked, insisted, "No, just shoot everywhere!"

I held my ground. "No. Shoot on sight only."

One frenzied attacker charged at me. With a swift maneuver, I flipped him over my right shoulder. He scrambled to his feet, but I was quicker. Drawing my knife, I plunged it into his chest. He staggered back and collapsed, lifeless.

The chaotic scene was abruptly interrupted by a Bigfoot's thunderous yell. Danny, without hesitation, put a round into its head. The creature fell like a massive tree, dead before it hit the ground. The remaining human attackers, witnessing this display of firepower, fled into the shadows.

We quickly attended to Shun, patching up his wounds as best as we could, and then made a hasty retreat. The danger was far from over. As we moved, Tom and Danny, wielding their SPAS-12 shotguns, took down two more Bigfoots that crossed our path. We couldn't afford to stop, knowing more threats lurked nearby.

After about an hour, we paused briefly, only to be confronted by another Bigfoot. Tom instinctively reached for his gun, but I stopped him. "No, this one is different. He means us no harm," I said, observing the creature's cautious demeanor. "He would've attacked by now if he wanted to. Let's leave him be and keep moving."

As we reached the base of the mountain, the Bigfoot still shadowed us from a distance. Suddenly, a Dogman appeared, and the two behemoths faced off. They roared, signaling a brutal confrontation. We watched, transfixed, as the Dogman struck the Bigfoot with a rock, knocking him to the ground. Seizing the moment, I fired my .50 caliber, ending the Dogman's life. The Bigfoot, seemingly acknowledging our intervention, rose and disappeared into the wilderness.

Shun, bewildered, asked, "Why did you do that? You should've shot him too,"

I replied, " I just made a friend we might need later. He was protecting us from that Dogman. I wasn't going to let him die after that."

We continued our journey, walking until darkness enveloped us. Setting up camp, we tied up Shun for the night. I told the guys, "I'll take the first watch. Try to get some sleep. Tomorrow's going to be another long day."

Tom, still on edge, questioned, "What about the skinwalkers?"

"I really don't think they'll visit us tonight," I assured him, keeping my senses alert for any danger. "Get some rest."

The night passed without incident, but as dawn broke, I sensed we were not alone. A pack of Dogmen was trailing us. "Let's move out and fast," I urged, knowing that every moment counted in this relentless pursuit.

# CHAPTER 15

＊◆＊◆＊◆＊

**T**RANQUILITY WAS SHORT-LIVED. OUT OF nowhere, a rock the size of a football came hurtling towards us, striking Shun in the ribs with a sickening crunch. His screams of agony echoed through the air as three of his ribs broke.

"Fuck!" Shun yelled, pain contorting his features.

Another rock flew in our direction, narrowly missing us. But the damage was done – Shun was in worse shape now. "We need to get to a clearing, fast!" I ordered. "We have to see them coming and know what we're up against."

It was a grueling two-hour trek to the nearest clearing. Once we reached there, we positioned Shun in the middle, forming a protective circle around him. Our eyes scanned the surroundings, ready for any sign of movement.

It wasn't long before Tom's voice cut through the tension. "Here comes one now – a Dogman!"

"Remember, yelling won't help," I reminded them. "Headshots only. We can't afford to waste shots."

Tom fired first, taking down the approaching Dogman. Moments later, two more emerged from the underbrush, running as fast as they could at top speed.

They were Dogmen, and they were met with a hail of bullets, killing them. Danny and I opened fire, swiftly ending their charge.

There was a lull, a deceptive calm before the storm. Then, they attacked again, this time in a coordinated formation – five, no, seven Dogmen. I instructed my team, "Get ready. Here they come. Frontal attack."

I positioned myself on one knee in the middle, Tom to my right and Danny to my left. I inserted earplugs, bracing for the imminent onslaught. This was it – our last stand.

As the Dogmen charged, adrenaline surged through my veins. Time seemed to slow as I aimed and fired with deadly precision. Each shot was a lifeline, a desperate bid for survival in the face of overwhelming odds. We were a trio against a pack, but we had determination and years of experience on our side.

In the clearing, amidst the chaos of gunfire and the ferocious snarls of the Dogmen, we stood our ground. This was more than a fight for survival; it was our resilience, our unyielding spirit in the face of unimaginable danger.

The distant sound of the chopper's rotors was like music in the midst of chaos, a couple of miles away but closing in. We knew we had to hold out until it arrived. "We're really in it now," I muttered, bracing for the onslaught.

As the chopper neared, it could see the frenetic battlefield below. Its gunfire joined ours in a symphony of survival. The Dogmen, now charging on all fours, were met with a relentless barrage of bullets. Our ground fire, in unison with the chopper's .30 caliber, created a storm of lead. The fight was brutal but brief. In just two minutes, nine Dogmen lay dead.

But the battle wasn't over yet. An eight-foot Dogman managed to evade the initial firefight. It darted through the trees, but the chopper, hovering overhead, unleashed a volley from its .30 caliber, obliterating the creature. The remaining Dogmen, realizing the tide had turned, retreated into the depths of the forest.

"This was the biggest pack I had ever encountered," I said, catching my breath. The intensity of the battle still echoed in my ears. Another chopper, larger than the support gunship, descended and landed. It was time to leave this hellish battleground.

We gathered Shun's lifeless body, a sobering reminder of the day's grim reality. The military, keen on the Dogmen bodies, instructed us to load everyone onto the chopper. Exhausted, we complied.

As we boarded, I caught a glimpse of a Bigfoot in the trees. It was the one I had spared earlier, blood still staining its face. It had witnessed the entire ordeal, a silent guardian of the forest. The chopper lifted off, and the landscape below became a distant memory.

The two-hour journey to the base was a blur. We were spent, physically and emotionally. Hunger gnawed at us, but it was the exhaustion that weighed heaviest. We had survived, but the cost was etched in our minds and on our weary bodies. The base was a welcome sight, a haven from the wilds we had just endured.

When we finally touched down at the base, a sense of relief washed over me, despite the weariness that clung to every bone in my body. The General, Sue, and Heady were waiting for us, their faces imprinted with a mix of concern and relief. Stepping off the chopper, I immediately wrapped Sue in a tight embrace, the contact a balm to the turmoil within.

I turned to the General, my voice firm with a decision long overdue. "I am finished. As of now, I am retiring. Me, Sue, and Heady too." The words felt surreal, a future I had barely dared to imagine now becoming reality.

The General, a stoic figure throughout our ordeal, revealed his own plans. "Me too. My wife wants me to retire as well. Let's all go at the same time." His words were evidence to the bond we shared, comrades in arms now leaving the battlefield together.

"Let's get cleaned up and go home," Heady chimed in, her usual tough demeanor softened by a hint of excitement. "I have to see the commissioner – he owes me ten Gs, and I want it!" Her assertiveness brought a faint smile to my face. It was good to see her spirits high.

As we walked away from the chopper, my thoughts turned to the future. "So now I am done. We will find a place for me and the kids, and grandchildren. I am finally done. After fifty-plus years, I am done with it all. We are going home, finally."

The weight of those words hung in the air. Fifty years of service, of battles, of survival – it was all coming to an end. A new chapter was beginning, one filled with the promise of peace, family, and a life free from the shadows of conflict as we made our way to get cleaned up. The base, once a symbol of a never-ending duty, now represented the gateway to freedom and a well-earned rest.

However, the General had a different look in his eyes, one that I knew all too well. "I'm sorry, but you're not done yet," he said solemnly. "There's a dangerous assignment, a cryptid in Ohio. It's serious, and they need you."

I felt a surge of frustration. "What's so important that you need me now? Use the military. I'm out of this game."

"You're a United States Federal Marshall," the General replied. "Your job is to help those who can't help themselves. And you're the only one who can handle this."

"What is it?" I inquired, a sense of duty creeping back into my weary bones.

"It's... different. It killed a grassman, ate half of it. The grassman was nine feet tall, and this thing... it's almost invisible."

"Invisible?" I echoed, disbelief coloring my tone.

"You can only see it from certain angles, in the right light," he explained. "We don't know how many there are, but people are missing, grassmen are found dead, half-eaten. This needs to be stopped now."

I stood there, processing the information. Just when I thought I was out... I was pulled back in. The world, it seemed, still needed me. The call to action, to protect those in need, was a siren song I couldn't ignore, even in my yearning for peace.

With a resigned nod, I turned to Sue and Heady. "Looks like I've got one last job to do."

Seeing the emerging tears in her eyes, I reassured her, "I will be fine and back in a week." I looked into her eyes, "I love you, I thought, and I am coming home to you."

She smiled, a mix of fear and faith in her eyes. "Yes, you are. Or I will find you, and trust me, you don't want that."

I couldn't help but laugh at her remark. I got into the truck where Tom and Danny were already waiting. "Let's head to the military airport," I said as we prepared to embark on yet another perilous mission.

As we drove off, I couldn't help but think to myself, Okay, I have a team now. Wow. It was a strange, almost surreal thought. My job was to find something that supposedly didn't exist, to confront and eliminate it. And we would, no matter what it took. This was the reality of my life – a continuous battle against the shadows and evils that lurked in unseen places. The journey ahead was unclear, but one thing was certain – we would face it head-on.

Arriving at the military base in Ohio, I was immediately confronted by a Colonel who clearly wasn't thrilled to see me. His disdain was deep, but I didn't give a damn. I shot him a look of contempt. "Get out of my way and shut your mouth," I told him bluntly. "I'm in charge here."

The Colonel, taken aback by my assertiveness, protested. "By what authority?" he demanded.

Without missing a beat, I pointed to the five stars on my shoulders. "This authority. Now, attention. And salute a higher-ranking officer. Do I make myself clear, or does the Major need to spell it out for you?" I watched him closely, my tone leaving no room for argument.

He looked at me, disbelief mixed with anger. "I am a Colonel in the United States Army, sir!" he retorted, his voice a mix of indignation and shock.

"Your insubordination just demoted you to Major," I stated flatly. "And you will accompany me on this mission if you want any chance of getting your rank back."

The newly demoted Major turned to the General, seeking some sort of reprieve. "He can't do this, can he?"

The General, unmoved by the Major's plight, confirmed my authority. "Yes, he can, and he will. Now get your gear ready."

The base, once a hub of strict military order, was now under my command. The urgency of the mission at hand allowed no room for dissent or dispute. We were here for one purpose – to hunt down and eliminate the unseen threat that lurked in the shadows of Ohio. And nothing, not even military rank or protocol, would stand in our way.

I strode away from the scene, intent on finding a vehicle for our mission. Tom and Danny were already on the hunt for supplies, scouring the base for everything we might need.

Behind me, the disgruntled Colonel muttered under his breath, clearly displeased. "This is not what I signed up for."

Unfazed by the Colonel's complaint, the General closed in on him, his tone menacing. "Move it, or lose your rank and this cushy job. Your choice."

A sergeant, overhearing the altercation, stepped forward. "Sir, I will take his place, sir!" he offered, eager to be involved.

I spun around, fixing the sergeant with a stern gaze. "Do you really want to go with us?" I asked, my patience wearing thin.

The Sergeant hesitated, then replied, "No, sir. I'll take the place for my colonel."

I could feel my frustration boiling over. "Does anybody around here know how to salute a higher ranking officer or address a superior properly?" I yelled, my voice echoing across the base. "I want everyone to salute now. Everyone! Now!"

Finally, they complied, performing the salute as they should have from the beginning. "That's how you treat a higher-ranking officer!" I bellowed, ensuring my message was loud and clear. The chorus of "Yes, Sir" rang out in response.

Turning to the General, Tom, and Danny, I signaled that it was time to leave. The General gave me an acknowledging smile and walked away.

I then addressed the Colonel and the Sergeant. "Let's go, gentlemen. All four of you are coming with me."

The Colonel, still reeling from his demotion, tried to argue. "One more or less won't help you."

I cut him off sharply. "You're wrong. And you will run beside the truck to our destination. Got it? Stop crying. When you see what we're dealing with, maybe, just maybe, you'll become a better person, Colonel."

The gravity of the situation was clear. We were heading into unknown territory, against a foe unlike any other. The team I had, whether they liked it or not, would have to rise to the occasion. We were in this together, and there was no room for dissent or weakness. The fight, as it turned out, was just beginning.

As I looked at the Colonel and Sergeant, I couldn't help but think that they were ill-prepared for what lay ahead. "I'm not a miracle worker, but you two will have to adapt on this mission. And if you run, I will personally take you down," I warned them sternly, my gaze stanch. "Now, load up the truck. I have to get some more things we'll need."

Turning to the sergeant, I instructed, "Come with me. We have a quick errand to run."

As we drove off, the sergeant, now behind the wheel, asked, "What do you need, sir?"

"We need six steel rods," I replied. We found what we needed, packed them into a leather bag, and threw it into the back of the truck. "Let's head back," I said as we got on our way.

After about an hour of driving through the rugged terrain, I told the sergeant to pull over. "Stop here," I commanded. He complied without question, bringing the truck to a halt.

"Now that this is much clearer," I started, addressing the colonel and sergeant, "on this mission, you two are of the same rank. Why? Because the only rank that matters here is mine. Understood?"

"Yes, sir!" they responded in unison, a hint of newfound respect in their voices.

"Good," I nodded, satisfied with their response. "Now, let me tell you about what we're going after.

This mission was unlike anything they had faced before, and they knew it. We were venturing into the unknown, facing a creature of legends, and survival was far from guaranteed.

# CHAPTER 16

I PROCEEDED TO BRIEF THEM ON the elusive, nearly invisible creature we were tasked with hunting. The gravity of the situation was not lost on them as they listened intently, understanding dawning in their eyes.

"I'm heading to my place to pack up some more gear," I said, the weight of the upcoming journey pressing heavily on my thoughts. "The drive alone will take about three days to reach the foothills."

"Look for anything that looks out of place. All, everywhere we go. Just stay loose, and we'll be okay, but remember this is a great danger to us all! And I mean great danger. Life-threatening out here. Got it, boys?"

"Yes, sir," they answered in unison, their faces a mix of determination and apprehension.

"Okay, from here on out, we call each other by our first names until this mission is over, or we're dead," I instructed, emphasizing the need for a different approach. "Sergeant, what's your name?"

"Tom, sir," he replied.

"And you, Colonel, what do we call you?"

"Paul," he said, a hint of reluctance in his voice.

"Me, I'm Glen," I said.

"Don't forget me," Danny added, ensuring his presence was acknowledged.

"Alright then, let's head to where the Grassman's body was found," I said, setting the course of action.

"Glen, what if it's a skinwalker? It won't leave its meal for anything," Tom interjected, his concern evident.

"To be honest, this is new to me as well," I admitted. "I don't know anything about this creature. We will learn together."

"Okay, Glen, what if it's a skinwalker? It won't leave its meal for anything," Danny inquired, his voice edged with a hint of apprehension.

"Well, to be honest, this is new, so I don't know anything about this creature. We'll learn together," Glen replied, the weight of uncertainty heavy in his voice.

So, we're off, two hours driving.

The rest of the drive was silent, each man lost in his own thoughts. This creature... what could it be? I mused, staring out the window at the landscape blurring past. The Ohio countryside was a mix of lush green fields and dense forests, a beautiful backdrop masking the potential dangers lurking within.

"We should be careful," Tom finally broke the silence. "These cryptids, they're unpredictable. Could be dangerous, could be harmless. We won't know until we find it."

I nodded, my mind racing with the possibilities. Invisible at certain angles... could be a trick of the light or something more supernatural.

Paul's voice cut through my thoughts. "Remember, our priority is to gather intel. We need to understand what we're dealing with before making any moves."

The truck eventually slowed, pulling off onto a dirt road that wound through the dense forest. The air was thick with the scent of wet earth and pine, the atmosphere almost creepy in its intensity.

"We're close," Glen announced, his eyes scanning the surroundings.

We stepped out of the truck, the crunch of gravel underfoot breaking the eerie silence. The forest seemed to close in around us, the trees towering like silent sentinels. Every rustle of leaves, every snap of a twig, sent a jolt of adrenaline through my veins.

"We need to move quietly," I whispered, my senses heightened to their fullest. "Stay alert. Watch for any movement, any sign of the creature."

As we moved deeper into the forest, the light dimmed, the canopy above dense and foreboding. The silence was unnerving, with only our footsteps and the distant call of a bird breaking it.

An hour had passed since we entered the forest when Danny suddenly shouted, 'Over there,' pointing to a spot where the underbrush looked disturbed. We crept closer, our hearts pounding in our chests. The body of a grassman lay on the ground. A chill ran down my spine as I surveyed the scene. It looked like a great struggle had taken place, with the earth scarred from a fierce battle.

"This is it," Glen said quietly. "This is where we start."

We spread out, each man taking a section of the clearing. The tension increased, every shadow a potential threat, every whisper of wind a possible sign.

I crouched down, examining the ground. There were tracks, unlike any I had ever seen. They were faint, almost invisible, but definitely there. This is no ordinary creature, I thought, a mix of fear and excitement coursing through me.

"We need to be careful," I called out to the others. "Whatever this thing is, it's unlike anything we've ever encountered."

The forest seemed to echo my words, a sense of foreboding settling over us. We were in unfamiliar territory, facing an unknown and potentially deadly adversary.

But we were ready. We had to be.

A few minutes passed; we came up on two boys who were running alongside the road. "Tom, get ahead of them and stop!" I ordered urgently. The boys were visibly excited, tears streaming down their faces, fear etched in every line of their expressions. Something had happened to them, something terrifying. We had to tackle them both to get them to stop. Tom, taking charge, shouted, "Stop!" but the one boy was in such hysterics we couldn't make head or tail of what he was saying.

Then the other boy came running at us too, followed by a dog. "Whose dog?!" I yelled, trying to make sense of the chaotic scene. The boy grabbed his dog and started to cry, clutching the animal tightly. "It didn't get you, girl, thank God," he sobbed, relief and fear mingling in his voice.

"He's terrified," I thought, observing the scene with growing concern. "Hey, guys, get them some water and towels," I instructed the team. We needed to calm them down if we were going to get any coherent information.

Through tears and gasps for breath, the boys began to share their story. "There's something wrong out there. We couldn't see it until it moved toward us. You can't see it until it's too late!" The fear in their voices was apparent, and it sent a chill down my spine.

"We never saw it, I swear, we never saw it!" The second boy's statement hung in the air, evidence to the terror they had faced.

"Ok, guys, we believe you. Paul, call the local authorities now. Get the boys to the hospital, and don't let them separate the boys from their dog, got it?" I instructed firmly. The urgency in my voice was clear.

"Yes, Glen," Paul responded promptly, already reaching for his phone.

"Tom, we are going to start here," I said, turning my attention back to the task at hand. The woods loomed before us, an ominous wall of trees and shadows.

"Yes, guys, if I stand still—" I began, but then I stopped talking and just stared at the woods. There was something unsettling about the way the shadows played between the trees, something that didn't sit right with me.

Tom, noticing my sudden silence, asked, "What is it? What's wrong?"

"Don't move. I'm looking at something. Don't talk to me, don't touch me, and don't yell at me. Just leave me alone, got it?" My tone was sharp, my focus intense. I needed complete concentration.

"Yes, sir," Tom replied, understanding the gravity of the situation. He began to get the supplies out, moving quietly and efficiently.

I started to walk over to look at the tree line, my senses on high alert. There's something off here, I thought, feeling a prickle of apprehension at the back of my neck. The forest seemed to hold its breath, the usual sounds of nature eerily absent.

As I approached the trees, every step felt heavier, like I was walking into something far more dangerous than I had anticipated. The boys' words echoed in my mind: *You can't see it until it's too late.*

I scanned the tree line, searching for any sign of movement, any hint of the creature we were hunting. The shadows seemed to shift and sway, playing tricks on my eyes. Is it there? Watching us? The thought sent a shiver down my spine.

"Guys, be ready for anything," I called back to my team, keeping my eyes fixed on the forest. "This thing... it's like nothing we've ever faced."

Just when I turned my eyes toward the treeline, I saw it, just sitting there, looking at me. We both were just staring at each other. I could hear it say something in a snake-like voice, "Are yoou afraid of meee?" It hissed, the sibilant echoes lingering ominously. I felt a shiver run down my spine.

It knew where I was from, which scared me. But I thought to myself, "I'm not from here, but I'm going to kill you." I glared at the creature with a burning intensity, a silent vow of retribution. It seemed to sense the lethal intent in my gaze, for it recoiled swiftly, disappearing into the shadowy embrace of the forest. I returned to my crew, my mind still replaying the encounter.

As the police arrived, Paul hastily explained the situation, his words tumbling out in a rush. The officers were initially skeptical, their disbelief evident in their dismissive glances. However, the moment I turned to face the sheriff, the atmosphere shifted. His face drained of color, his expression morphing into one of shock and recognition. "Oh my God, it's you!" he exclaimed. His voice, tinged with a mix of awe and fear, hung heavy in the air.

"Yes," I replied, an undertone of weariness in my voice.

His next question caught me off guard, "And how is your dad?" I glanced at Paul and Tom, their expressions a mix of confusion and concern, reflecting the complexity of emotions swirling within me.

"I saved him from a dogman attack a few years ago," I explained, providing context to our unexpected reunion.

The sheriff's eyes held a tinge of sadness as he disclosed, "My dad passed away years ago. But the help you gave him, and to me, was a godsend. Thank you." His gratitude was heartfelt, and in response, I stepped forward and embraced him, offering condolences for his loss.

The ambulance came for the kids. They didn't want to take the dog. I told them, "Take the dog with them."

He said, "No!"

I grabbed him and rammed him into the side of the ambulance as hard as I could. "Take the dog now to the hospital with the boys," I demanded.

The sheriff grabbed my arm. "I'll take care of the boys and the dog together," he assured.

I looked at the driver with a *you don't tell me what is what* look. "I'll take you out there into the woods, and you'll see what almost got them. Now, get them to the hospital. Now!"

I looked back at the tree line and saw some small leaves falling. It's back, that's good. We don't have to find him, I thought, a sense of foreboding creeping in. I hope there are not two of them. That would make things much harder.

I turned to Tom. "Just look at the tree line. Keep looking until you see something small or unusual."

"What am I looking for?" Tom asked, squinting towards the trees.

"Just keep looking, and you tell me!" I replied firmly. "You too, Danny."

So, they kept looking. Then Paul, with a tone of disbelief, asked, "What the hell is that thing?"

I looked at him, my expression stern. "That is what we are here to kill. Get your stuff. We are going in."

We got ready, and it was still there. We started to walk down the road for a while, then began venturing into the woods.

"Before we do this, if you want out, it's now or never. Never? Paul?" I asked, giving them a last chance.

Paul hesitated, then said, "Well, I wouldn't mind much to stay here and watch the truck."

I looked at Tom, and he looked back at me, his expression unreadable.

"Well, if you want to, but there might be two of them. So, good luck with that!" I replied, a hint of sarcasm in my voice.

It was a weird feeling, an uncanny quietness hanging in the air. "Keep your eyes up into the treetops. They like to be high. Walk slowly and as quietly as possible. Remember, we are a team." I said.

We trekked through the dense foliage for about an hour, the silence around us almost suffocating. Then, breaking the stillness, I suggested, "Someone, anyone, start a fire?"

Nobody seemed eager to take on the task, so I turned to Paul with a firm directive, "Paul, do that now, here." There was a sense of urgency in my voice but also a hint of leadership, guiding the team through unfamiliar territory. "Everyone, keep an eye out for leaves falling and stay alert for the sounds of tree branches being bent or broken. Also, immediately let me know if you feel a sudden chill."

I then addressed Tom, my tone a mix of surprise and reminder. "Tom, why do you have steel rods in your backpack? Did you forget already? You need to put them through its heart and brain. Also, find the gloves. We're going to be out here for the night."

Turning to the rest of the group, I added, "Sargent, when we make camp, I need to talk to you and Colonel Dumass." The words were straightforward, indicating a need for a strategic discussion.

As I was looking up, Tom's voice cut through the stillness of the night. "There! I see it!" he yelled out.

I looked up, and there it was. It wasn't looking at us but was focused on something else. We all stopped in our tracks. I walked over to get a closer look, and what I saw was a Bigfoot. The creature was huge, about eight feet tall, casting a towering shadow in the dim light of the forest. It was an imposing sight, its massive frame silhouetted against the trees.

"Okay, guys, here's the plan," I began, trying to instill a sense of clarity and purpose in our group. "We need to keep a watchful eye on the Bigfoot. We'll stay in camp until those two confront each other, or we get a chance to take down the Skinwalker. Is the fire big enough? If the Skinwalker comes our way, we need those rods to be very hot to kill it."

I could see the tension in their faces, the uncertainty of what was to come. "If it goes after the Bigfoot, we'll jump on the Skinwalker right before it attacks. That's our moment to strike."

Paul, looking skeptical, interjected, "But why don't we just let them fight it out?"

I replied with a sense of urgency, "Because the Bigfoot can't see the Skinwalker and the Skinwalker is fixated on the Bigfoot. The Skinwalker will definitely see us, and so will the Bigfoot. You know, Bigfoots are curious about humans, which means it'll likely bring the Skinwalker right to us. We have to be ready for that."

I turned my gaze back to Paul, emphasizing the next point, "Paul, I also need you to keep an eye out for a second Skinwalker. They often come in pairs. This one seems different, so it might be alone. I sure hope there's only one. But just to be safe, keep scanning the treetops. That's probably where it'd be hiding." My voice was firm, trying to convey the seriousness of our situation while also giving clear instructions to ensure everyone's safety.

"Let's start the campfire so the Bigfoot comes to see what we're doing. I'm going to keep my eyes on the Skinwalker and Bigfoot. Paul, keep a watch out for another one. Someone, get the fire bigger now! If I'm right, they'll be here soon," I directed, my voice laced with authority.

The Bigfoot was hunting for grubs, seemingly oblivious to our presence. The Skinwalker, however, was watching it very closely, yet it hadn't noticed us making camp. But the Bigfoot did, though it was still focused on eating the grubs. I thought it wouldn't be long before it came over here, and it'd bring our friend with it.

So, we got ready for anything. I took out my bow and flare gun, lighter fluid at hand. It would not be to our advantage to scare the Bigfoot off. If that happens, we'll have to keep up and run after it, and that's a lot of running we don't want to do.

We ate nothing, staying alert. Then, I saw the Skinwalker in the trees - a different one. I turned to Paul, frustration building up. "Paul, you were supposed to keep track of the Skinwalker."

"Yes," he replied, confused.

"Then why is it trying to creep up on us now?" I demanded. "It's over there in the trees, and the Bigfoot is gone? You're a moron."

"Ok, Tom, just keep doing what you're doing," I said, trying to maintain control of the situation. "I'm putting the extra rods in the fire and get a lot of dried wood in a pile. And get the starter fluid, too."

"Now, Tom, try to put on the gloves slowly. I don't want to scare it. Just act like we're enjoying the night," I suggested, trying to calm the atmosphere. "Want a beer?"

"Oh yes," Tom replied, trying to maintain normalcy.

"Paul, will you shut up with some of your adventures? I'm trying to keep its attention on the Skinwalker," I said, pulling out my .44 auto mag with armor-piercing shells.

"All I heard was that it is illegal," Paul muttered, but I paid him no mind, focusing on my target.

Ignoring Paul's distraction, I remained intensely focused, waiting for the right moment to take my shot. The tension was palpable, every second stretching out as I prepared for the critical moment.

Suddenly, I turned to Paul, urgency in my voice, "Paul, is there another one?"

All I got in response was a confused "What?" from him, which only heightened my frustration. I couldn't help but think, "Dumass, you've messed up again."

I quickly scanned the surroundings, my instincts on high alert. Sure enough, as I looked up, there it was - another one. My heart raced, a mix of adrenaline and annoyance pulsing through me.

"How did he get to be a Colonel in the first place?" I mumbled under my breath, my frustration with Paul's incompetence growing.

Tom, overhearing my comment, chimed in. "He's an ass-kisser, sir."

"Great!" I exclaimed sarcastically. Now, we had to focus on which Skinwalker would make its first move. The one we saw on the road began to creep toward the Bigfoot, who had returned to investigate our camp.

Tom, confused, asked, "How does that thing not see it?"

"It can't see it, remember? It can only be seen at an angle, and he has no angle," I explained, trying to keep an eye on the unfolding situation. I saw leaves falling, a sign that the Skinwalker was moving. I prepared my .44 auto mag, waiting for the right moment. The Bigfoot, oblivious to the imminent danger, continued its investigation.

As the Skinwalker made its move towards the Bigfoot, my instincts kicked in. I swiftly pulled out my gun and fired twice, aiming straight for its heart. Not stopping there, I quickly grabbed my flare gun and shot it again in the heart, ensuring no chance for it to recover.

The creature collapsed next to the Bigfoot, which reacted with a mix of shock, surprise, and fear. In the chaos, Tom sprang into action, plunging a white-hot rod into the creature's heart and another into its head, following our grim but necessary plan.

I quickly turned to see another Skinwalker attempting to attack the Bigfoot. Time seemed to slow down as I realized I had only a split second to react. I took aim and fired, hitting it in the head. The creature reared up, letting out a piercing scream, and in that brief window, I found my opportunity. I shot twice directly into its heart, watching as it staggered backward.

Not wasting a moment, I fired the flare gun, aiming for its heart, and followed up with two more shots to its head. The urgency of the situation was palpable, and every move critical.

"Tom, put two rods in its heart and head," I instructed, my voice steady despite the adrenaline. He swiftly complied, ensuring the creature would not rise again.

Then, turning to Paul, I commanded, "Paul, it's time. Throw the wood on it and set it on fire." As he did so, three fires blazed simultaneously, illuminating the dark forest with their eerie glow. The rules were clear - we had to decapitate them. We watched as the Bigfoot, still in shock, began to bury the creature's head away from its body cautiously.

Still in shock, the Bigfoot looked at us with grateful eyes. The realization dawned on him over what had been stalking him, and it seemed to startle and scare him. He just walked off into the forest, disappearing into the night.

It was all over, and miraculously, we hadn't gotten hurt.

Finally, it was time to go home in the morning. The morning wasn't far away. It dawned beautifully, with the sky clear and a warm breeze blowing from the south.

And now, I got to go home to my Sue. I finally got to go home, a place I had never been but had always dreamed about. Home! With my love. It's just a great day to be alive.

The camp was quiet as we packed up, each of us lost in our own thoughts, reflecting on the night's events. We had faced something extraordinary and survived. The sun's rays broke through the trees, casting a new light on the forest that had been a battleground just hours before. It was a new day, a day for going home, a day for appreciation and reflection—a day to be alive.

Printed in the United States
by Baker & Taylor Publisher Services